KU-573-019

OLD COUNTRY

MATT QUERY & HARRISON QUERY

HODDER

First published in Great Britain in 2022 by Hodder & Stoughton
An Hachette UK company

This paperback edition published in 2023

1

Copyright © Fort Mazie, Inc. and Columbine Mountain, Inc. 2022

The right of Fort Mazie, Inc. and Columbine Mountain, Inc. to be
identified as the Author of the Work has been asserted by them in
accordance with the Copyright, Designs and Patents Act 1988.

All rights reserved. No part of this publication may be reproduced, stored
in a retrieval system, or transmitted, in any form or by any means without
the prior written permission of the publisher, nor be otherwise circulated
in any form of binding or cover other than that in which it is published and
without a similar condition being imposed on the subsequent purchaser.

All characters in this publication are fictitious and any resemblance
to real persons, living or dead, is purely coincidental.

A CIP catalogue record for this title is available from the British Library

Paperback ISBN 978 1 5293 7545 9

Printed and bound in Great Britain by Clays Ltd, Elcograf S.p.A.

Hodder & Stoughton policy is to use papers that are natural, renewable
and recyclable products and made from wood grown in sustainable
forests. The logging and manufacturing processes are expected to
conform to the environmental regulations of the country of origin.

Hodder & Stoughton Ltd
Carmelite House
50 Victoria Embankment
London EC4Y 0DZ

www.hodder.co.uk

This book is dedicated to Sonya, to Clark, to good neighbors, and to Thibodaux – along with all other dogs keeping watch around the world.

PART I

HEADING
OUT WEST

1

HARRY

WELL, THE FIRST time I killed a person, I actually killed two people. Pretty much at the same time, or back-to-back, within a couple seconds of one another."

In the spirit of radical honesty, my left leg was falling asleep as I spoke these words. I didn't want to shift my weight or do anything to suggest discomfort or angst while talking about this. I figured that's the kind of thing I was here to be scrutinized for. Getting squirmy in a moment of candor, some kind of physical betrayal of emotion.

"It was in Afghanistan, 2010, right at the beginning of Op Moshtarak, the battle for Marjah. My fire team was holding it down up on a berm that ran along a road. The berm was just a little rise, mostly covered in tires and trash and shit, set up six or seven feet higher than the road. We were just holding security waiting for orders. I was with my buddy Mike—we were set about twenty yards ahead of the rest of the guys in our fire team. The rest of our platoon was behind us too, other side of this trash berm, out of view. Most of the company was nearby, actually, but we were just staging, waiting to coordinate the next part of this push."

Goddamn that city smelled like ass. Burning trash, goat shit, sweat, and ass.

"All of a sudden we see these two dudes to our left running down the road, heading toward this little intersection in front of us where another road headed directly away from us." I used my hands to make the shape of this T-intersection.

"The dude in front had an AK and the other one was on a radio and had a big like...hockey bag, a rucksack over his shoulder, fulla spent RPG tubes. They both looked like they were in their late twenties, early thirties maybe—older than me.

"At first, I couldn't believe it, seeing those dudes. There was a big firefight going on to our east, the direction they were running from, and I don't know why, but I guess I figured any Taliban we'd bump into would be running *toward* the scrap. I actually nudged Mike and whispered somethin' like 'Are those fuckin' Tali, bro?' He was as surprised as I was. I mean, in our gut we knew they were bad guys as soon as we saw 'em, but just couldn't believe it. We'd been in-country for the better part of a year before Marjah kicked off and hadn't ever just watched armed militants slowly jogging along a road in the wide open less than two hundred yards away. That's a *rare* thing to see over there. Up until that point, all our encounters with these fuckers were when they were a long-ass way off, taking potshots at our patrol or something. This was like...real clear fuckin' contact, you know? It was just a total trip."

I forced a surprised smile and nodded as I finished my sentence.

"When they got to the road in front of us—the road we were looking down from our spot on the little trash berm, the one that jutted off to their left, away from us—they ducked over and crouched behind this busted old sedan, probably about a hundred, *maybe* a hundred and ten yards away. They had cover from the direction they had been running from, blocking the view of themselves from our left, the direction of the big firefight I figured they were boogeying away from, but they were *completely* exposed to us. I mean, I just had a full view of both of 'em, barely had to move a muscle to keep 'em on scope. Mike and I, we were so shocked we just sat there like complete dipshits, just glassing them, speechless, for what must've been a solid three-Mississippi count. Then, I'm not really sure what it was that got me to act—I *think* it was the closest one looking up at me or in my direction—and so I just...shot 'em both. The one who was holding the rifle first, then the dude behind him with the radio and big bag of RPG tubes. Every shot I took was on target too; they were just... *right fuckin' there.* A hundred yards is really not that far of a range. They were just filling my optic, so it was pretty damn easy."

I left in an intentional pause and looked him in the eye. *Remember to nod sincerely*, I told myself. "They both died right then and there."

I remembered how I'd shot the first guy right below the nape of his neck, and how he'd just dumped forward onto his face. Didn't even move a muscle in an effort to stop himself or anything, didn't let go of his rifle, he'd just straight-up face-planted into the street. Probably would've knocked himself out if he weren't already dead. Figured I'd shot through his spine. The second guy looked down at his buddy after I'd shot him, all surprised like *Tha hell you doin', dude?*, and that's when I'd shot *him* in the chest. As soon as the bullet hit him, he'd dropped the radio he was holding and popped both hands out behind him, reflexively planting his palms onto the road to try to catch himself from falling backward. Looked like he was sitting on a beach towel. He'd looked so confused right before I shot him again. My mind went to another man I'd killed a couple weeks later, the older man, the grizzled warrior. I saw his face a lot in my mind, more than any of the others. It was a face that casually but solemnly assured violence.

I looked up at Dr. Peters, who was nodding almost imperceptibly, looking me in the eye. "Harry, what do you feel as you share that memory with me?"

"Well..." I looked down at the floor for a second, trying to put on my best sincere-consideration face, then looked back up at him. "I don't really feel anything noteworthy just from *telling* that story to someone. I guess the first thing that comes to mind is my buddy Mike who was with me. I haven't talked to him in a couple years...I hope he's doing well."

Peters nodded. "Have you ever noticed that memory, that experience, as one that's intrusive into your thoughts or dreams? Does it ever come back to you in a way or at a time that's surprising or bothersome?"

I made sure to give that one a couple seconds of forced consideration as well. "No, no, not really."

Peters was nodding, waiting for me to say more. Lots of shrinks press with a *Can you tell me more about that?* but Peters just left it open, made me feel like my answer was unfinished. Guess it worked too, because I went on.

"I can't think of that memory coming up in a way that's like… *surprising* to me, or bothersome. It's just like any other memory. I don't feel *guilt* about it, if that's what you're asking. Those dudes would've shot me if the situation were reversed. I really don't mind sharing that story or talking about the other people I've killed. If people ask me about experiences like that, I'm happy to share them. I just don't, you know… bring that kinda shit up on my own without being asked about it."

Peters nodded. His expression suggested I'd gotten the right answer. Or, at least, that he wasn't going to lean into this.

"Well, Harry, we're *way* past our time."

Yeah, no shit, Doc. I've been well aware *of us being past our time for all of the twenty-two and a half minutes since we went over.* I still looked down at my watch anyway and feigned surprise. "Ah, shit, guess I should get goin'."

Peters stood up and walked over to his desk. He grabbed a manila folder, then held it out to me.

"Harry, I've put together some information for you on the VA resources in Idaho. We've got clinics and hospitals in Pocatello, Twin Falls, and obviously Boise. I know this VA runaround can be frustrating, but I really hope you stay committed to this therapy process, and that you work to find someone out there with whom you can develop a healthy trust. It's really important. Even though you and I just started meeting a month ago, I want to make sure you know that I'm always available to talk, whether it's over the phone or video chat. I'll always find a way to make time. Don't ever hesitate to reach out."

I stood up, took the folder from him, and nodded. "I will, Dr. Peters. I really do appreciate your time. You're an easy guy to talk to." He gave me a tight-lipped smile as we shook hands.

"I think it's great what you and your wife are doing, Harry. I'm so happy you and Sasha found a way to go build yourselves the life you've dreamed about. I'm jealous, I really mean that. Not many people get the opportunity to pursue a passion like this. I know this is your and Sasha's dream, and I wish you nothing but happiness and success in pursuing it. I have no doubt you two will thrive out there in that lifestyle."

I gave him a smile. "Denver's getting way too crowded anyway, and if the mountain life isn't for us, well, we can always come back."

"Take care of yourself, Harry."

He held his smile in return as he opened the door for me, but there was certainly some concern in his face as well, some doubt maybe. I wondered if it was intentional.

2

SASHA

No matter how many times I drive the stretch of I-80 through southern Wyoming, I never get bored. Pronghorn, sagebrush, refinery in the distance, weather-beaten rock formation, billboard with a quote from Revelations, more sagebrush, more pronghorn...It's monotonous but harsh and beautiful country. Harry and I'd done at least a dozen backpacking trips in Oregon, Idaho, and the Wind River Range over the previous decade, and had visited friends in Jackson during the last few ski seasons, so I'd made this drive what felt like a hundred times. Pretty sure I can even mentally distinguish the interiors of gas stations in Laramie, Sinclair, Rock Springs, and Evanston.

The voice of my audiobook's narrator was interrupted by a ringtone and Harry's face filling the screen of my phone.

"Hey, babe, you good if we fill up in Green River? It'll be like another hour."

"I'm good, love, keep driving safe!"

I was in our 4Runner, following behind Harry, who was driving the awkwardly large U-Haul we'd packed our entire life into over the last several days.

"How's Dash doin'?"

I looked into the back seat, where our golden retriever, Dash, was curled up.

"He's fine. Ready to stretch his legs, but we're all good back here."

"All right, love, keep driving safe."

Ever since we'd crossed from Colorado into Wyoming on 287, it had started to really set in that—holy shit—we were actually, *finally* doing this. Harry and I had been talking about it since we met in college over a decade ago. On one of our first dates, I'd asked Harry some generic question about his "hopes and dreams" or maybe some even cheesier bullshit like "Where do you see yourself in twenty years?" I don't remember *precisely* how he started his answer to my question, but I'll always remember one part of it, because it enchanted me right away. Might even be the reason I fell in love with him.

He'd said: "I want to find some land in the mountains, somewhere where I can sit on my porch, look out, and the only man-made structures that I can see are my own home, barn, and workshop."

He'd said it with such sincerity and this hopeful longing in his eyes. Although, at the time, I wasn't sure if he was just another dude trying on different personalities and making whimsical bullshit proclamations in an effort to get me to fuck him. Maybe that *was* *actually* part of what he was doing, but either way, it worked. Also, he's certainly maintained his passion for doing exactly that ever since that date, and he's made me fall in love with the prospect as well.

I didn't need too much prodding, though. In fact, I'm actually more familiar and experienced with the prospect of life in the rural Rocky Mountain West than Harry was. Growing up in a wood-burning-stove-heated home in a small mountain town in southwest Colorado with two lifelong ski bum parents certainly greased my axles for it. That's also probably why I was immediately attracted to Harry's "dream," and why, ever since that first date, I have associated it with a deep, warm feeling of *home*.

I'd been bringing up that old quote of his to tease him since we began this process about a year ago—the process of seriously looking into buying land somewhere in the mountains. That process was initiated by reaching out to real estate agents in Bozeman, Missoula, Helena, Bend, and Coeur d'Alene, and even just that experience and having ongoing email correspondence with them, by itself, made it all start to feel real and exciting. Then, when I pitched the creation of a unique position that I could do remotely to my COO and CEO, and then *actually* started working with them to create the position, it got *very* real.

There have certainly been moments when I've felt apprehensive and anxious about doing this. I'm going to miss the hell out of my friends, random happy hours, live music, and being a day trip away from my parents and hometown. That being said, I've been paying attention to the ever-increasing anxiety and gut feeling that we needed to really give this lifestyle a try and commit to it now, or we just never would.

I'd also paid close attention to whether I was doing this just to make Harry happy, and was continuously surprised to find it really was something I wanted for myself as well.

Harry's thirty-five, I'm thirty. Most of our college friends were having kids while getting even busier with work. As for ourselves, we'd begun to feel we were at a junction between either buying a hilariously overpriced little house in Boulder or Denver and working even harder, or giving this lifestyle a try. Arriving at that junction made me realize how badly I wanted to at least attempt the homesteader life, and how fond I'd grown of the idea of making a home with Harry somewhere quiet, beautiful, and wild.

There was a distinct moment when we began taking this dream seriously. We were on I-70 a little over a year ago, heading up to go skiing, and the traffic was so bad it took us *six fucking hours* to get over Vail Pass. Harry and I had been in bad traffic on I-70 countless times before, but I'll never forget the look on his face about four hours into that particular drive. I remember so clearly watching him from where I was reclined in the passenger seat. Watching him stare around at the stop-and-go traffic with a look of resignation and anguish on his face. He finally looked over at me and said, "Babe, we need to get the fuck out of this state."

We'd quickly realized that Bozeman and Bend were dead ends. Land around there was too expensive, and we wanted to find somewhere in the "real West," and Harry—and I, to a certain extent—didn't really feel as though Colorado qualified for categorization as the "real West" anymore. We'd been living in Denver for the last seven years, and it had started to feel like LA or Phoenix. Growing and sprawling, eating the plains more and more by the day.

Our Realtor in Coeur d'Alene introduced us to a colleague of hers who works out of Jackson but manages listings all around the Tetons. Jackson was laughably out of our price range, but this Realtor, Nataly, sent us some amazing listings on the Idaho side of the Tetons that—at least to me—appeared to be bigger, nicer, and a fraction of the price. Harry had taken our dog out to Driggs, Idaho, on a fishing and grouse-hunting trip with a college friend a few years earlier and was immediately, adorably enthusiastic about this part of the country.

I remember sitting on the couch as he showed me a satellite map of the area and pictures he'd taken while he was there. "It's *amazing* country. I can't believe I hadn't considered this area right from the beginning. It's just trout-filled rivers, aspen forests, public land *everywhere*. It's an hour-and-a-half drive from Jackson, around four hours from Boise, and like three and a half from Salt Lake. Babe, trust me, it's fucking awesome."

That past September, we'd driven out to Jackson for a friend's wedding and spent a few days afterward in Idaho meeting with Nataly, looking at places around Teton and Fremont Counties. Harry was right—it was amazing—and the trip certainly got me psyched about the Idaho side of the Tetons, as well. We didn't see anything we *loved* in our price range, but I was absolutely floored by how beautiful the area was and knew right away that Harry was right. This was where we needed to move.

A few months later, our Realtor reached out about a little ranch in a quiet valley outside Ashton and Judkins. Nataly was all hot and bothered about this property too, said it was an amazing deal.

It was a little thousand-square-foot house on fifty-five cattle-fenced acres. New roof, new water heater, it had a separate garage/work-shop, a couple little sheds, a porch that ran along the entire front of the house and wrapped around the side into a big patio off the kitchen, a chain-link-fenced acre around the house that looked nicely landscaped. On top of that, the neighbor to the north and east was a national forest several times the size of Rhode Island.

Nataly explained how the property had been purchased almost a decade earlier by some big ranch-land real estate investment firm for the purpose of being incorporated into some kind of land and ease-ment exchange deal with the Forest Service. That deal with the federal agency had either fallen through or moved forward without the use of this property, so the real estate firm fixed up the little house and the land a bit so it could be approved for financing and was now just trying to get it off their books. She said it would "definitely sell" within a day.

Harry spent almost that entire night on GIS maps, tearing through the property documents he could find on the county's website, reading about the hunting unit the land was in and the seasons, doing water rights searches; he pulled the damn soil classification maps—you name it, he read about it. That next morning, he gave me a full-on *why we should make an offer right now* pitch. I've got to hand it to him too; it was a good pitch.

With the VA mortgage plan Harry qualified for, and having already convinced ourselves both that we loved the area and that it was a sound investment, we were pretty much set, even though we'd never actually been on the property. Besides, it was still cheaper than what our friends were spending on houses in Boulder, Denver, Portland, and San Fran. So, we said fuck it, let's just do this, and we called Nataly and told her to put in an offer. The next morning, we got an email from her saying they'd accepted our lowball offer without any counter. We were officially under contract. A few weeks later we got the inspection and title report, no red flags, so that next Friday we officially closed on our first home.

When it came to actually *affording* a house on fifty-five acres, well...you could say we looked good on paper, but we were mostly just piss and vinegar. That is to say, we both had good credit scores and Harry qualified for a kickass financing option through the VA, even though our savings account was quite modest.

On top of that, because Harry qualified for the "Combat-Related Special Compensation" program, he didn't face many work restrictions *and* we got a nontaxable check every month from the government that could cover a significant portion of our mortgage. As Harry likes to say, way too often these days, "This mortgage and the GI Bill are the only pleasant pieces of baggage that come from six years in the infantry." I know Harry doesn't include the monthly check in that list because it makes him feel guilty. Makes him feel weak.

I've done what I can to convince him not to feel that way, *because he fucking shouldn't*. The number of times we've argued about it and I've heard him use the same old line—"Sasha, the government paid for my degree, I've healed from my injuries, I can work full-time, *we don't need this fucking handout*"—is equal to the number of times I've told him *"The hell we don't."*

I'd be a liar if I said it wasn't *very nice* getting a text every month notifying me that Uncle Sam had just made another deposit into our account, but why shouldn't that be nice to see? Harry deserves every penny of that, and more.

I started dating Harry not that long after he'd learned to physically function again after getting literally blown up and torn apart. I fell in love with him as he learned how to function socially again. I watched his eyes as he'd struggle and fight to act calm and happy around me in a crowded bar or at a concert. I see his scars every night when we get in bed and watch him wince and limp every morning as he gets out of bed. I rub his back to wake him up from nightmares. I see the pain in his eyes late at night as he looks into a fire. I hear the distance and sorrow in his voice when he has a bad day.

There are still places Harry won't go with me. Things that happened overseas. Things he did, things he saw. I think he believes he's protecting me, but it's so much harder having this silence between us. There's this unspoken chapter of his life filled with seismic events he's been a part of and that are a part of him. I could spend all day cataloguing the ways in which the VA is a hopelessly flawed institution, but I was always glad that at least they gave him someone to talk to. If not me, at least there was *someone*. I feel some anxiety knowing that he won't have those regular therapy sessions going forward, at least for a while. He *needs* someone to talk to, and while I've never put the pressure on too hard about it, I just wish he would make that someone *me*. At the same time, I realize I'm probably not the best person for that kind of therapeutic back-and-forth. I don't have the institutional knowledge, and I don't really care to develop it.

I'm sorry, but *fuck* the United States Marine Corps conventional infantry. I might've walked down the aisle with a marine in dress blues, but I have absolutely no fondness for that destructive, maniacal, abusive institution. Thirty-two hundred dollars a month does not even *fucking begin* to adequately compensate my husband for the things they had him do and the sacrifices they demanded, and for what? Our freedom? I've yet to hear someone make a substantive, logical argument connecting *my freedom* to my husband getting blown up on the other side of the planet ten years into a losing war against a *fucking idea*. Having watched the Taliban take full control of Afghanistan within minutes of the United States' withdrawal last summer, it seems no such argument could possibly hold water now, if it ever even could.

So, yeah, we'll be taking that goddamn check.

I saw the U-Haul's blinker flick on when we got to the second exit for Green River, Wyoming, and followed Harry into the gas station, pulling up to the pump behind him.

Dash woke up in the back seat and sat up, alert, leaning forward to look out the front window as Harry got out of the U-Haul and walked back toward me.

I got out of the car and stretched, immediately feeling the cold bite of the Wyoming prairie's dry March air. Harry smiled at me as he walked up. "How you feeling, babe?"

"I'm good! What are we lookin' at, about five more hours or so?"

Harry nodded as he plugged the pump into the 4Runner. "Yeah, seems about right. I'm gonna take Dash to do his business." I watched Harry as he opened the back door of the 4Runner and clipped Dash's leash. "Let's go take a piss, buddy."

"Watch for goatheads and glass, Har; I think rural Wyoming gas station parking lots are designed to fuck dogs' feet up."

He smiled back at me. Dash trotted along at his side, his dark red tail plume waving in the air, looking up at Harry as if he were a god.

3

HARRY

By the time we'd passed through Ashton, Idaho, and were about five minutes out from our new place, I was feeling a giddiness I hadn't felt in a long, long time. I was anxious as well. We'd bought a fucking ranch we'd never actually, *physically* been to, and while Sasha was committed and equally involved in the process of finding this place, I still felt like I was really the one who pushed it, so the pressure was on.

When we got to the turn onto the county road that leads to our place, I rolled down the window and leaned out to give Sasha a big, stupid smile. I could see her laugh and start slapping the steering wheel in excitement, Dash's head out the window behind her.

Our property is about a mile down the road, and the last private property before the road leads into national forest and dead-ends at a parking lot for a trailhead. Most of the private land along the county road, and our neighbor to the west, is part of a 1,400-acre ranch owned by a couple whose names I'd seen on the GIS maps, Dan and Lucy Steiner. I couldn't find much about them online other than the fact that they were always up to date on their property taxes. The property itself was well managed, and quite beautiful with the western reach of the Tetons looming in the background.

I'd talked to Nataly about an hour earlier, and she'd said she'd meet us there. I could see she'd tied some balloons to the gatepost at the end of our driveway. I knew in that very moment that, as long I live, I'd never forget reaching our driveway and laying eyes on our land for the first time.

It was absolutely breathtaking. I was in awe as we took a left onto our long driveway that spurs north from the elbow of the road where it turns south and leads up to the national forest. The driveway is long, and it leads to where the house and garage sit on a little rise, surrounded by meadow and aspen trees. There are several *huge* cottonwoods in the yard looming over the house, and a few poplars along the driveway. There was still quite a bit of snow in the mountains in March, but you could tell that spring was on the verge of getting itself into full torque. The first leaves popping through were tree-frog green, the earliest of the wildflowers were peeking out, birds everywhere; the land felt like it was just humming with vibrance.

The house is *much* smaller than what we were originally looking for—smaller than the place we'd spent the last several years in the Highlands neighborhood in Denver. However, it did have a big-ass porch, a landscaped, fenced-in yard around the house, a separate garage/shop in decent shape, and a couple storage sheds. What stood out more than anything else was that anywhere you looked—in *any* direction— was unbelievably beautiful. The landscape, I knew without a doubt, was what would make us both fall in love with it immediately.

Outside the fenced-in yard there are about forty acres of meadow and pastureland, with a pond nestled below the house, a creek running in and out of it, and around fifteen acres of pine forest that sit above the house along the north end of the property.

We pulled up to the big gravel turnaround between the house and the garage, where Nataly was parked in a pearl Escalade.

The next hour was a blur. Nataly showed us around the house and garage. *Here's the circuit breaker, there's the water line controls, here's the flip for the well pump*, that kinda shit. When she left, Sasha and I just stood in the yard in front of the house, barely capable of speaking, just laughing and playing with Dash. Sasha got out a bottle of champagne that we drank straight from the bottle, passing it back and forth, sitting on the steps that lead from the yard to the patio behind the kitchen.

We both loved it, but Sasha was literally skipping around with a smile glued to her face, just adorably giddy and beside herself with excitement.

I don't have much in the way of family, so Sasha is my entire world. I count her family as mine as well, but her parents are pretty uninvolved, and based on what Sasha's described, their proudest moment as parents was when she moved out. They turned her childhood bedroom into an indoor weed grow operation within a week of her moving. They didn't save a penny to help her pay for school and visited her *maybe* one time in her entire four years of college. They weren't *terrible*, they weren't mean or abusive, they just didn't really give a fuck. By the time Sasha turned fourteen, they'd regularly drive down to Arizona to go on monthlong LSD benders and leave Sasha completely alone, but by that point, she'd normalized lying to teachers and friends' parents about where her parents were.

It was mind-boggling to me, how Sasha ended up such an amazing, brilliant, independent woman capable of such strong friendships, given how she was raised. She's a sociological phenomenon. I have no doubt her coming into my world was, very literally, a lifesaving event.

When I got out of the marines, I pretty much moved straight into the freshman dorms at the University of Colorado, Boulder.

Getting scraped off the road, stitched together, sent directly from a combat zone to a hospital, then to another hospital, then to a stateside duty station, then straight into a massive state university as a maladjusted twenty-four-year-old was pretty fucking stupid—an ill-advised call on my part.

It was a nightmare of emotional isolation and volcanic social anxiety. I quickly, and *enthusiastically*, fell into a violent whiskey-and-uppers-fueled spiral of self-destruction. I was using my entire spending stipend on blow, pretty much gave up on going to class entirely, and spent the majority of that first semester trout fishing, elk hunting, and partying.

I'd grown up in Albuquerque until I was about ten, when Dad drank himself to death, so Mom and I moved to Pueblo, Colorado, to be closer to her brothers. My uncles didn't talk much or dig around to learn about who I was or how I felt. Can't remember having more than a one-minute conversation with either of the grumpy bastards, but they did what they could to play a role in my life, in their own way. For the next eight years, they took me along trout fishing on the weekends, and elk and deer hunting for a couple weeks every fall. That's a long way of saying that flogging a river looking for big browns and walking around the mountains looking for elk was an escape for me as a boy, so the same escape mechanisms came naturally to me as a man.

The CU administration put me on academic probation right about when I'd started ripping an eight ball a night up my nose. I remember justifying my behavior by telling myself: *It's just blow, it's not heroin or pills, it's like a step up from weed, right? You're just an uppers guy, bro. You've earned this.*

I wasn't "suicidal" in the sense that I actively thought about wanting to die or different methods to kill myself, but I sure as shit didn't care about living much longer.

Then, two notable things happened. First, I fell in with a group of guys who were *not* veterans, and *not* toxic machismo pussy-hound frat types either. They were just normal dudes who liked to ski, fish, get stoned, and go to class. While being around them showed me a healthy lifestyle I thought I might be capable of living, it just as often put into focus how far gone I was. I could see who I wanted to be but wasn't sure if I was too far gone to get there. Then I met Sasha. I met her in a bar on the Hill, a part of Boulder that's been effectively relegated to CU students in an effort to corral the complete debauchery that student body is capable of.

I'm not gonna say I fell in love with Sasha at first sight, but I'd never been that blindsided by a woman's *character* before. She was, and remains, the most beautiful woman I've ever known, but—as my stoner buddies put it—it was *her vibe, man*. It's clichéd as hell, but I sincerely mean it when I say that she just immediately made me feel like a better person, *capable* of being a better person, and that hasn't changed to this day. So my downward spiral was stymied by falling in love. As soon as she agreed to go on a second and third date, I had a reason to keep my shit together. As soon as I heard her introduce me as her boyfriend for the first time, I had a reason to quit drinking on weeknights and avoid getting expelled. It just went up from there, with Sasha as the primary motivating factor for self-improvement.

Meeting Sasha brought me back, and I have no doubt her smile—her happiness, her laugh—is quite literally the only reason I'm still alive, and I've thought about that every day for the last decade.

So seeing her smile on that back porch as she looked up at the mountains, watching her react to the first view of the property with that much excitement and happiness, that was all I needed. That's all I'll ever need.

That first night we didn't bother with much of the unpacking and moving in. We ate pasta off our camping stove, sitting on camping chairs on the porch, and slept on our mattress, plopped down in the corner of the living room.

That first morning, we woke up and walked the entire fence line of the property. Even though it wasn't quite warm out yet, we ate lunch by the pond on a picnic blanket, followed the creek from where it came into our property to where it flowed out, and rucked around every little patch of trees and span of meadow on the entire property. I think it might've been the best day of my life up until that point.

We were electric with excitement and made one fantastic and entirely unrealistic plan after another for the property. Pretty sure, within that first three hours on the property, we committed to constructing a terrain park and a set of ski jumps, a ten-challenge archery course, a "tiny home village" for guests, and *several* wine-drinking patios along the creek.

Dash was just about the happiest dog I'd ever seen as well. I'd trained the little dude to hunt upland birds and waterfowl, and we hunted a decent amount, so he certainly had experienced his fair share of adventure and lived a fun life, but he'd still been a city dog for virtually all of his five years, with a tiny little yard to call his own. Now he had an entire fenced-in acre around the house, and a fucking *kingdom* beyond.

The next two weeks of moving and settling in, hanging art, building raised beds, and planting some early stuff in the gardens screamed by. Sasha wore a look of wonder, excitement, and just plain peace every minute of those first few weeks here. Dash, like Sasha and I, was in absolute heaven.

Sasha had planned ahead to get the telecom crew scheduled so we could get internet up and running that first week, and we turned the guest room into her home office, where she'd started taking calls and video meetings, getting into the swing of working remotely. Other than the dudes who came to set up the internet and the car delivery guy we'd paid to drive Sasha's Subaru out from Denver, the only people we saw were the folks passing by on the county road, to and from the trailhead up past our place in the national forest.

The national forest is our neighbor to the north and east and even a bit to the south as well, and the Steiner Ranch is the only private property adjacent to ours, immediately to the west, and to the south across the county road. There's another ranch that's technically "in" our little valley as well, a big 6,500-acre property called Berry Creek Ranch, to the south of the Steiners, but their main driveway is off the state highway. Down the valley and across the road there are quite a few family homes and little ranches on smaller parcels, but on our side of the highway, for the entire length of the county road, there are only three property owners. So, when it comes to the actual county road, Sasha and I and the Steiners are really the only people up here.

That fact—having *only one* neighbor, whose actual house is more than a mile away—by God, that might be my favorite part of this whole place.

It was quiet. It was beautiful. It felt like home.

4

SASHA

At the beginning of our third week in the place, I felt like I was getting into the swing of working remotely. I worked in advertising, so while lots of my colleagues are used to working with project managers like myself who aren't in the same city, I wasn't used to being the one who actually did that. It felt all right, though, and my team had my back. They knew how badly I wanted this.

Also, Harry and I mutually agreed that we were fast approaching the rudeness threshold of not going to introduce ourselves to the neighbors.

That Saturday morning, we made a couple pies, hopped in the 4Runner, and headed over to meet the Steiners. Their driveway ran about a quarter mile from their gate—through their pastures, which were pocked with clusters of ponderosa, aspens, and fat cows—and ended at their house. It was a nice place. Absolutely stellar view of the mountains. Big gardens that were well taken care of. It looked lived in. Good vibes all around.

The house was nestled between a couple massive barns, a tractor garage, and a big workshop. As we approached, I saw an older-looking fella in the driveway turn to face us, then raise a hand in greeting and slowly walk over to where we parked.

"Dan Steiner, and y'all must be our new neighbors!" Dan had a warm smile that invited one in return.

Harry reached out a hand. "Yessir, I'm Harry Blakemore, and this is Sasha."

I smiled and took his hand after Harry. "Hi, Dan, it's a pleasure to meet you."

Dan looked to be in his early seventies but still quite spry. He had a calculation and strength to his movements suggesting he had as many good years left as someone in their forties. His hands were like buffalo leather, and his features looked carved out of wood.

An older woman came out from one of the barns right then as well. She looked about the same age, and just as strong. Her face looked wise, like there wasn't much left behind door number three that could really knock her socks off. She introduced herself as Lucy, and we all went about exchanging the normal pleasantries.

They told us how they'd owned their ranch since the 1970s. They also told us how they'd been close with the family that lived in our place from 1996 to 2011, who were the last family to actually *live* on the property, as it got purchased by the ranch-land investment firm after they'd moved. According to Lucy, since that last family moved, guys from the real estate company popped by once or twice a year, but mostly just to hunt, so Dan and Lucy made it clear how excited they were to actually have full-time neighbors again.

They were very grateful for the pies. Harry expressed a sincere "Please call or stop by if you need anything at all," which they offered right back.

Right as it felt like an appropriate time to drop an *until next time*, Dan pointed up at Harry with a little smirk. "You infantry?"

Harry held his hands out, looking down at himself as he responded. "Is it that obvious?"

Dan chuckled and slapped his knee. "Ha, I can spot it a mile away! Army or marines?"

"I was in the Marine Corps sir, 0311."

"A grunt! But wait, did you say 'was'? I thought the only way out of the corps was dead in a pine box?"

Harry smiled and nodded. "Yeah, I guess 'once a marine, always a marine,' so it's said. But they told me you fine taxpayers would float the bill for my college tuition, so I jumped ship and never looked back." Harry uses that line all the time, always makes old folks laugh. Dan and Lucy were no exception.

"Very good. I was navy enlisted, a mechanic, did my four in Coronado."

Harry nodded in acknowledgment. "Well, I can tell you, having experienced a different military profession, I think you made a far better MOS choice than I did."

Dan chuckled at that. "You make it over to Afghanistan or Iraq?"

Harry nodded once. "Spent some time in Afghanistan."

Dan responded with a grin, but it seemed forced, almost apologetic. "I've heard that was one hell of a place to find yourself as a marine rifleman."

"It was certainly a colorful experience, sir."

"I have no doubt." Dan's smile was replaced with an inquisitive look. "Hey, you know, for the last, well...better part of a decade, the company that owned your land paid Luce and me and some of our seasonal ranch staff to take care of the place. Mostly just keeping the trees and shrubs in order, grazing down the grass before fire season, checking on the well and septic now and again, and Lord knows I've spent lots of time there over the last decades riding and hunting. We know that land as well as anyone alive. We'd really like to share a few things with you, a few pointers when it comes to managing that land that we think are very important. Maybe we can swing by soon and spend an hour or two walking around with you?"

This was time for me to chime in, as I often am required to, *ever so promptly*, whenever Harry is given an opening to put off nonessential social calls. "That would be hugely appreciated! We'd love to pick your brains about the land! Does tomorrow evening work for you guys?"

I looked up at Harry and squeezed his arm, hoping he could feel the message I was trying to send: *Don't be a dickhead, sweetie.*

Harry's response suggested he'd picked up what I was putting down. "Sure, tomorrow evening works great on my end—that work for you two?" *That's my boy.*

Lucy smiled in response. "Sure thing! We'll swing by around five or so. Thanks again for stopping by. I hope you two make a habit of it!"

With that, we hopped in the truck and headed home.

I looked over at Harry. "Don't even start whining about me making that plan, babe. They seem so sweet. That knowledge will be hugely helpful, okay?"

"I know, I know, you're right, I'll enjoy it. They seem like solid neighbors."

I watched his face closely. Interacting with other veterans is hit-or-miss for Harry. Sometimes he feels like they're the only other people in the world he can identify with, the only other people who understand him. Other times, they're the only people in the world Harry never wants to see or talk to again. He's never really done a thorough job of explaining why that is, but he doesn't really need to. I guess I can just feel why it makes sense.

There are these moments when I look at him, when I can see how hard he's working emotionally, and I get this unexplainable rage at Harry's parents. A desire to scream at them for failing to keep their shit together long enough to see the man he's become, despite their neglect. I never met his dad, but I knew his mom and at least got to spend a few weekends with her before she died, but she was just an empty shell of a person. She had a heart attack a few months after our wedding.

My parents weren't winning any awards either, but they gave me a relatively safe childhood, or at least a quiet house for me to grow up in within a safe town. My parents and I grew up in Pagosa Springs; my mom worked at restaurants and grew weed, and my dad has worked at Wolf Creek Ski Area since before I was born. Still works there, skis 150 days a year. They didn't give me a penny for school or a hint of motivation to even *go* to college and haven't given half a shit about any of my achievements since I left home, but they at least *act* like parents... sometimes, to a certain extent.

I wonder, though, sometimes, what Harry would be like if he hadn't gone through what he had before we met. I wonder if he'd be the same. Truth be told, I've caught myself feeling *glad* Harry had gone through so much before meeting me, on the grounds that he'd never have fallen so deeply in love with me if he hadn't.

Whatever the little nature-versus-nurture formula was that resulted in this man I was staring at with the sun on his face, driving me up our driveway through our little ranch in the mountains, thank God for it.

PART II

SPRINGTIME

5

HARRY

In the first two weeks at our place, we'd made several trips into the town of Rexburg to pick up some fencing to make a bunch of raised garden beds, some new tools, and a few dozen T-posts at the farm and ranch store.

Rexburg, a bustling metropolis of around 25,000 people about fifty miles to our southwest, was the biggest town within an hour of our place. Sasha and I had stared silently out the windows of the car as we drove through town the first time. We were both in a sort of quiet reflection on how this town was now the urban nucleus of our lives. There were small grocery stores and some other shopping options in the little town of Ashton, to our northwest, or Driggs, to our south, but Rexburg was "the city," though it didn't even have a Target.

We woke up that Sunday after meeting Dan and Lucy and decided the day would be best spent doing fencing work in the pastures and getting the gardens finished. We'd started looking into getting some sheep in the coming weeks to graze down the grass ahead of fire season, and several lengths of pasture fencing needed some serious TLC. It was a great day, just us and the dog out on the land. One of those spring days when you can just smell how close the long days and warm nights of summer are, like it's in the air.

We'd gone to pick up those new T-posts to replace any that were busted, rusty, or bent out of shape—and there were certainly some of those. It's hard work. Took Sash and I about two hours to replace about ten of them—a rate of ranching work we did not miss an opportunity to make fun of ourselves for.

I was hammering the last post into place, the strong *clang* of the driver slamming into the post carrying through the meadow and echoing off the trees. I caught Sasha looking at me and smiling, so I stopped, leaving the driver over the post, and shook some blood into my numb hands, smiling back at her. "I know I'm not a rancher yet, babe, all right?"

She laughed and shook her head. *She is so goddamn beautiful.* "Oh, Harry, you're doing it, you're actually doing it! You're mending fence on your ranch!" She held her arms out and gestured around at the property, spinning around while Dash looked up at her, prancing around her feet.

She came up and grabbed me around the waist and looked into my eyes. "Are you happy we did this, Harry? Is this what you wanted?"

I kissed her. "I just want you. But yeah…Yeah, this is definitely what I wanted. Are you happy?"

She smiled at me and started to nod. "I sure as hell am. Besides, you're the one who's gotta work this property full-time. I only have to do this hard stuff on the weekends. I'm the breadwinner, you're the land manager."

"Well…I suppose that is the case, isn't it?"

She smiled and kissed me again. "Let's call it for the day. Dan and Lucy are coming over soon." She bent down to pick up a shovel, then pointed with it up the length of the fence line we'd been working on, giving me a mischievous grin. "But I want you out here first thing tomorrow to finish this shit up, big guy."

We'd just finished cleaning up when I saw Dan and Lucy coming up the driveway in their big old F-250, so we went out to greet them. As we welcomed them into the yard with some small talk, they both scanned the landscape knowingly. I noticed Dan smack the trunk of one of the big cottonwoods, then make some comment to Lucy about how the old tree had made it after all. They knew our property well.

We spent the next hour walking around the property with them as they pointed things out and made suggestions, Dash at our heels. They had a whole lot to tell us about the well, the pump, the aquifer, irrigating the pastures at different times of the year. They recommended how to care for some of the fruit trees in the yard during different seasons. They showed us where the elk usually mess up the fences when they start to migrate down in the winter, chased by the snow line. They pointed out where the best mushrooms grow, pointed out some trees they reckoned would die within the next year or two, showed us where the creek floods in bad runoff years. That kinda shit. The kinda shit you can only learn through working on a piece of land and learning to read it, learning to anticipate it.

It struck me several different times during this little walkabout: These two had spent *a lot* of time getting to know the land in this valley. It was impressive, and humbling, seeing folks with this much connection to the natural systems around them. Seeing these people who'd lived here for so long, seeing how intentionally they lived their lives every day. Their knowledge was very humbling, and I wanted that. I wanted it bad.

I'd also noticed Lucy glancing at Dan on several occasions. It was brief, but she would bite the inside of her cheek, lines creased on her forehead. He would meet her eyes for a moment, then look away or continue on with some explanation.

As we walked back up toward the house, Lucy asked Sasha if she could show her where some wild asparagus grows in the pasture. Before they left us in the yard, I briefly saw Lucy give Dan another of those apprehensive looks, which disappeared as quickly as it had appeared. Lucy linked her arm through Sasha's, and I watched them as they walked off, laughing about something I couldn't hear.

Dan asked if we could talk on the porch for a moment, so I asked if he wanted a beer and grabbed a couple before we sat down.

That first sip of cold beer really hit the spot. Dan took a long slug as well, then placed his beer down and moved his chair to face me more directly. As he settled back in, he put his elbows on his knees, linked his fingers, leaned toward me, and looked me right in the eye. I held his gaze for a long moment until I noticed I'd begun to shift my weight a bit in my chair. I was about to break what was becoming an awkward moment when Dan stared down as though fishing for the right words, then looked up into my eyes with a fierce intensity.

"Son, while all the things we just went over will come in handy while managing this land over the years, there are a few other very important things I need to tell you about. A few things that're hard to explain, but you must pay *damn* close attention to. I cannot stress that enough; these things are important, do you understand?"

I couldn't help but smirk—an anxious reaction I have in response to awkwardly timed sincerity. But I admired Dan, so I put my beer down, met his gaze, nodded.

"Sure, Dan. I'm all ears."

"What I'm about to tell you will sound…strange, all right? Maybe even frightening. But you need to take me serious, son. What I'm about to tell you can, and likely will, save your life. You need to listen like I'm an NCO who's been in-country for a year, and you're a green-assed fresh boot who just stepped off the plane."

I usually find military-themed analogies like that cheesy as shit, but I could almost *taste* how serious this guy was, so I just nodded and held his gaze. "I hear you, sir." Dan nodded, then pulled some folded papers out of his jacket and held them up in front of me before placing them on the side table between us. I glanced down and could see *Springtime* written in large letters at the top of the first page. Dan pulled my attention back to his face when he began speaking.

"Back in the winter of '96 when the Seymour family bought this ranch, Lucy and I came over here and had this exact same conversation with them. And that was the last time we've had this conversation with anyone. When we moved here, the old Jacobsons were still here at your place, the Henrys were up the road on the old land grant that Joe bought and is now part of the Berry Creek Ranch, and lastly there was Joe and his family. Now the only three landowners in this valley other'n the feds are Joe, Luce and I, and you two. Ol Joe's family has bought up everything else in the valley."

I nodded. "I've seen the Berry Creek Ranch, quite a large piece of land. You friends with the fella Joe who owns it? I'd like to meet him."

Dan nodded. "Sure. Joe's family at this point. He's Shoshone and Bannock, so while his family's owned land in this valley longer than anyone, they've *lived* in this country since the Roman Empire was still around. Joe's the one who told Lucy and I what we're about to tell you right now."

I nodded and looked away. After a bit I looked back toward Dan, who gave me a side-eyed glance and continued. "I know we just met, but you need ta hear me right now, son. This'll sound batshit crazy— *believe me*, I know—and it's unlikely you'll even believe it at first, but you gotta just hear me out and trust that I ain't pullin' your chain."

He let the words hang. I was kind of speechless. A bit creeped out too, but mostly by the fact that my cool old mountain-man neighbor who'd seemed so grounded and wise just moments earlier was about to rattle on about something he himself was preemptively branding as ridiculous. I sat forward and leaned out, trying to catch a glimpse of Sasha and Lucy, but they were out of view. Dan sensed my anxiety and followed my gaze.

Dan gestured almost impatiently with his thick hand. "They're fine, boy, sittin' down there by the pond." I leaned forward a bit more and saw Sasha sitting with Lucy on a log facing the house, with Dash playing around in the creek behind them. Dan's voice pulled me back to the moment. "Lucy is going over this same stuff with Sasha. I need you to listen clear, all right?"

I nodded. "Sure, Dan, I'll hear you out."

Dan stared at me for a moment, then picked up the folded papers he'd set on the table between us and held them in front of him. "I've written down what I'm about to tell you, because you and Sasha need to memorize these things. It needs to be second nature, son. There are several copies here. Lucy is giving a copy to Sasha right now as well and going over these same things. *Do not* lose them. Copy 'em. Hand-write 'em. Carve them into a goddamn plank and hang it in your bedroom. Whatever it takes."

He slapped the notes back down on the small table between us, folded his hands, then looked back up at me.

"Now, no questions until the end."

6

SASHA

W E STOOD ON the porch and watched in silence as Dan and Lucy turned from our driveway onto the dirt road heading back toward their place.

"Harry...what the *hell* was that?"

He just shook his head slowly as he watched their truck, shrinking as it worked its way down the road. "I have no fuckin' idea."

Once their truck finally disappeared from view and all that was left was a fading haze of dust where they'd driven, Harry and I walked down to the other side of the house, sat on the patio off the kitchen, and began trying to make sense of what had just happened.

I was a bit put off by Harry's conduct at first. Whatever had happened between him and Dan had set him off, and he'd essentially just kicked them off our property. It didn't get violent or overly contentious, but he'd just made a snap decision that they had to leave. So I lit into Harry a bit about how rude it was for him to just kick them out, and how *excruciatingly fucking awkward* it was going to be every time we saw them now.

At the same time, I didn't have a rebuttal to Harry's point about that awkwardness existing regardless of whether we'd have kicked them out or not. "They're either trying to fuck with us, or they're fuckin' crazy, Sash, period. Those two realities are absolutely mutually exclusive. It's really one or the other."

I kind of had to agree with him on that, but I also couldn't help but defend Lucy a bit. She seemed so wonderful, everything about her, and we had this *connection* I felt immediately. It was so hard to believe they'd just go from being these fantastic, well-spoken stewards of this land to...whatever the hell this meant they were.

Harry shook his head and began to openly laugh as he spoke. "*Seasonal mountain spirits*, huh? You do kinda have to give it to 'em, right? I mean, it's a pretty creative story, and *fuck me*, their passion and theatrics, their *delivery*." Harry clenched his fists in front of him to emphasize the last word. "They really were putting everything they have into it. They're either phenomenal thespians or they really do believe in this 'cursed valley' nonsense. Was Lucy as emotional and serious as Dan?"

I couldn't help but giggle along with Harry now. I shrugged in response. "Yeah, I mean, she was certainly doing her best to make me believe what she was saying; she definitely wanted me to take her seriously. And at the end, when she and I had come back up to the yard and you were asking them to leave, the way she grabbed your hands and looked into your eyes, basically begging you to follow their little 'spirit warding' rules."

Thinking back on Lucy's sincerity in that moment sent a chill down my spine. She and I had only been sitting at the pond for about ten minutes when Harry yelled down from the porch and asked us to come back up to the house, right as Lucy was beginning to explain the circumstances of some inane situation she called "the bear chase."

The moment Harry called for us I knew that something strange was going on. Lucy betrayed some recognition of the same in that moment as well. She didn't look back toward Harry, yet her shoulders slumped and she looked down between her feet, then gave me a tight-lipped smile as we stood. She seemed to understand she was being asked to leave before I even knew what was happening. If Harry hadn't cut their visit short, I'd have certainly let her finish the bizarre little briefing out of courtesy, despite how creepy it was.

"Sasha." Harry's voice cut through my recollection of Lucy, and I looked up at him to find his eyebrows raised over an amused smile. His expression shot a bolt of annoyance through me.

"Sash, you don't actually believe anything that those two—"

I knew where he was going and held my hand out to cut him off, forcing some levity into my voice.

"*Harold*—I'm not going to be your debate opponent here. I'm as weirded out as you are, and before you even go there, *no*, I don't believe any of what they just told us. Although, we don't even know they told us the same things."

Harry crossed his arms, then gestured with his head toward the little stack of notes Dan and Lucy had left behind for us on the coffee table on the back porch. "Gist of what Dan told me was that there's some kind of spirit that lives in the valley, and that it takes a new form every season or some shit. It does one thing in the spring, then another in the summer, so on, so forth."

Harry waved at his words as though they were someone else's cigarette smoke. "Also, there are little quirks or tricks or rituals or something you can do to keep it at bay, which are also specific to the season. Did Lucy say the same?"

I nodded, looking past where Harry was standing, out into the meadow. "Essentially, yeah. She only told me about the spring, something about how we need to start a fire if we see a light in the pond. She'd started telling me about the summertime manifestation right when you nixed the conversation."

Harry rolled his eyes and turned to follow my gaze, leaning his elbows on the porch railing. "Yeah, Dan said the same, more or less."

After a moment he turned back to face me with a tired look, then broke into a laugh. "That was just some really, *really* weird shit. They seemed so damn *normal* too, right?"

I laughed as well, then crossed the porch and put my arms under his and my hands on his back, looking up at him. "Well . . . what in the hell are we going to do when we run into them next? You could've been a bit more polite, Harry. Maybe they aren't just trying to scare us, and they actually believe that, like it's some kind of delusion. You didn't need to be so cranky about it." I kissed him as he let out an exasperated sigh.

"I guess...I mean, I wasn't that rude, I just told Dan I really didn't have the bandwidth to entertain something so fuckin' ridiculous right now, regardless of whether it's something he really believes or some fiction they'd contrived just to fuck with us."

I cocked my head as I stepped away from him. "You definitely seemed pissed off, Har, like their creepy story was actually offensive to you or something. They're our neighbors now. Neighbors are important out here. We can't just permanently burn that bridge."

Harry looked down at the decking of our porch, then back up at me. "Well, when I glanced over from where Dan and I were sitting and saw you and Lucy near the pond, you looked scared. I don't like when you look scared. When you feel scared, I feel violent." Harry shrugged. "Always been that way."

I'd heard him say that before. I'd seen it before, too. Harry's not overbearing or necessarily overprotective, but when he can actually see that something's making me uncomfortable, his instinct is to get between me and the source of discomfort and become a wall of aggression. Sometimes it can be a bit over-the-top.

One evening in college, when we'd been dating for a year or so, I was meeting Harry outside my apartment to go to a pub near campus for a burger. I'd broken my ankle skiing a few months earlier and was off crutches but still in a boot. I locked my door, and turned to start down the outdoor stairs to the street when I was shocked so bad I screamed—this massive raccoon that was directly in my path several steps below hissed and snarled up at me. Before I'd even taken a step back from the animal or pulled my hand from my chest, Harry surged out of the darkness and charged up the stairs, grabbed the raccoon by its back legs, and hurled it behind him, sending the creature spinning out into the darkness over the street. I remember the crunch and grunted exhalation when the animal slammed into the asphalt. Before I could even process what had happened, Harry was gently holding me by the elbow, looking me up and down with genuine concern, asking me if I was all right—if I'd been bitten by it or something. I saw the raccoon in the gutter the next morning on my way to class. It was twisted unnaturally with a broken spine from how it had landed, eyes open, fur wet, legs sticking out from its body in rigor mortis.

I forced the memory aside and looked back at Harry. "Yeah, well...as you said, they're either just messing with us or they're actually delusional. Whichever it is, there was no reason for you to be overly aggressive with them while kicking them out. They weren't being threatening, and they're an endless trove of knowledge when it comes to taking care of this place. So, we'll be inviting them back here again soon for a do-over, when you can apologize for sending them off the way you did, *whether you like it or not.*"

Harry pushed his fists into his lower back and stretched his chest out, looking away from me out to the east, toward the mountains, grinning a bit and letting out a relieved sigh as he responded. "Yeaaah, whatever you say, lady."

I laughed as I darted my hand toward his ribs to try to land a tickle, which made him hunch forward defensively and step to the side. I chased after him until we were wrapped in each other's arms again, laughing and kissing. We left Dash on the back porch, went inside, and made love in the living room. *Our* living room in *our* house.

Later that evening we opened a bottle of wine, turned on some music, and Harry started prepping dinner. I pulled up a stool across the kitchen island and sat down with one of the several stapled packets of notes on the "mountain spirit" that Dan and Lucy had left behind for us.

Harry looked up from the veggies he was chopping at the notes in my hand. "Oh, good." He set the knife down, reached into a drawer, and pulled out a lighter, which he slid across the island toward me with a mischievous grin. "The electric starter on the grill is dead; you can use that paper to get it fired up for us."

I giggled and clutched the notes to my chest as I shook my head. "Not a chance, dude. This is pure gold. I can't wait to scan this stuff to send to my friends. No one is gonna believe it." Harry smiled and rolled his eyes as he went back to cooking.

There was a cover page that gave a broad overview of how this *spirit* that haunts this valley manifests differently for each of the four seasons, and what followed was a detailed write-up on what the springtime will bring. I mentioned that to Harry. "I guess they want to keep us in suspense, keep us on our toes as we await more detailed instructions on how to navigate for the summer, fall, and winter!"

Harry didn't look up at me, just offered some noise that came from the back of his throat as a response. The following couple pages contained a detailed description of the bizarre springtime spirit season, and the strange rules we needed to follow to stay safe. I read through this *springtime* description silently, confirming that it was essentially the same as what Lucy had told me. At the end they had added a note indicating that they would share a more thorough description of the next seasons after we made it through this first *springtime iteration*.

I looked up at Harry. "Did Dan tell you that there was a little rule to follow or ritual we had to perform that would offset the danger caused by this spring season's...spirit *thing*, manifestation, the little light in the pond or whatever?"

Harry didn't turn around to respond. "Somethin' like that."

I prodded him a bit. "Harry, come on, what'd he tell you? I'm just trying to see if the explanations they gave us in person even match up with what they wrote down. What'd he say about how we're supposed to offset or undermine the danger of the springtime 'light in the pond'?"

Harry set the knife down, held his hands out to the sides, glanced back at me with a tired smile, and shook his head. "I don't fuckin' know, Sash. What'd Lucy tell you?"

"She said that during the springtime, if we see a ball of light in the pond after sunset, then we need to start a fire in the fireplace right away, and then once the fire is lit, the light will disappear."

Harry tossed a thumbs-up to the side of his body, focused again on cutting board. "That sounds about right. What super-spooky-scary stuff did Lucy say would happen if we didn't actually start a fire when we saw the light like we're supposed to?"

"She said we'd hear something like drumming start to come from the mountains to the east, and that if we heard that, we'd need to cover all the windows as fast as we can and not let anything into the house at all costs..."

Harry walked around me to grab a saucepan from the shelf on my side of the kitchen island. He leaned down beside me as he passed by and gave me a wide-eyed look. "The mighty Tetons, *from whence the springtime devil's drums cometh whilst the hearth lies cold.*"

He managed to get a good chuckle out of me. I flipped over to the summertime page and pointed to a spot for him to see. I spoke through excited laughter.

"You've *gotta* read about the summertime 'spirit manifestation.'" I couldn't help but add air quotes with my fingers. "It's just...so crazy. They only give a vague explanation of what happens, but I guess it all starts when—"

Harry spun back toward me before he'd reached the stove, held his palm out toward me, and cut me off. "Sash, please, can we not? This hoopla is literally the only thing we've talked about all day; I'm just over it. I'm sorry, I'm just maxed out on this bullshit."

I let Dan and Lucy's notes slump in my hand as I looked toward the light fixture above the kitchen island, shaking my head and speaking through a sigh. "Fine, *party pooper*. If it's too scary for you, we can read through it when it's light out and it's not so spooky."

Harry rolled his eyes as he turned back to his cooking. "Thank you."

He set the saucepan down, then snapped his shoulders and headed toward the entryway from the kitchen to the living room.

"What is it?"

Harry squinted, pointed in the direction of the front door, staring at it as though there were something written in small letters he was trying to discern. After a moment he looked at me with surprise. "I totally forgot. Those crazy old bastards left something else for us near the front door, remember?"

He was already striding toward the living room when I remembered what he was referring to. Dan and Lucy had, indeed, left something for us bundled up on the porch. I remember Dan saying something like *Just in case y'all don't have any split yet when the light comes.* We'd only gone in and out of the kitchen door since Dan and Lucy left that afternoon and hadn't used the front door at all, so I'd completely forgotten about it.

I followed Dash as he jogged through the kitchen on Harry's heels and then followed him out the door. I went out onto the porch after them and Harry was kneeling by a large canvas sheet with rope handles, wrapped around a bundle of neatly split firewood. It had been left in the center of our empty firewood rack, which Harry had set up below the living room windows to the left of the front door. Harry pulled the canvas carrying sack open to reveal a box of big matches on top of the stack of wood, with a little note. Harry read the note, shook his head once, then passed it up to me as Dash sniffed at it as though it were a treat.

> *When you see a light in the pond after sunset, use this to start a fire in the fireplace right away.* ~ L.

I was surprised to find that my first emotion upon reading the note was gratitude, as though it were a sweet gesture, like Lucy had left us flowers or a tray of cupcakes. Harry stood up and wiped the back of his hand across his forehead.

I put my arm around his waist. "*Awww*, you've gotta admit it's actually kinda sweet, Har."

I giggled at him as he shook his head and walked back inside. "More like kinda fuckin' crazy."

I grabbed the box of matches and waved Dash back inside, shut the door, then placed the matches in a little basket I'd set on the shelf above the wood-burning-stove in the living room.

We ate dinner at the counter, then finished our bottle of wine on the back porch. The stars here were unbelievable. I'd only ever seen so many so clearly on backpacking trips way up in the southern Rockies near where I'd grown up. I promised myself that night that I'd never let myself get used to it—I'd never take their beauty for granted.

We cleaned up the kitchen, got in bed, and turned on a Netflix show. Harry fell asleep about halfway through, so I shut the laptop, set it on the nightstand, then sat up to shut the blinds across the window over the bed. I stayed there with my elbows propped on the windowsill for several minutes, staring down at the pond, before I finally closed them.

7

HARRY

HUNTING DOGS REALLY hate spring turkey season.

Over the last five and a half years I'd trained Dash to retrieve waterfowl as well as flush upland birds in Colorado. They're very different kinds of hunting, and despite hailing from a long line of duck dogs, he'd become a really solid little upland flushing dog, so we'd spend most of our time chasing grouse up in the mountains and pheasant out in the plains. We still duck hunt a fair amount each season, but Dash and I both get pretty squirrely just sitting quietly in a blind waiting for birds to come to us. So, we trend toward the kind of hunting where you go find the birds. At least forty mornings a year between early September and late January, Dash and I would wake up before sunrise, load up the car, and blast out of Denver up into the mountains to look for grouse, or east to look for pheasant and quail. Nothing in the world makes Dash happier than flushing and retrieving birds. This dog certainly likes hunting more than I do. It's his favorite thing in the world. Without him, I probably wouldn't bird hunt at all.

However, when the strangely timed spring turkey season comes along, Dash gets *really* pissed. You aren't allowed to use dogs to hunt turkeys in the springtime, but Dash obviously doesn't read the state Fish & Game regulations, so he doesn't know it's turkey season.

All the hunting dog knows is that I'm waking up before sunrise, getting the shotgun out, making coffee, and microwaving burritos—all he knows is that we're engaging in our early-morning ritual that precedes his favorite thing in the world. He's so stoked he snakes between my legs, shaking with excitement and anticipation, and frolics around the house.

Then comes the moment I must leave, when I put my pack on, throw the shotgun over my shoulder, and open the door. The moment of great betrayal. I have to block the door with my leg, preventing Dash from escaping out into the yard to bound with glee toward the car in the pre-sunrise darkness, just as he has before on hundreds of autumn mornings during upland bird-hunting seasons past.

The *fucking look* he gives me as I scoot out the door, as I'm apologizing and promising him I'll be back in a few hours. I had no idea canines were capable of mustering such exquisite expressions of betrayal and heartbreak. His eyebrows really do convey: *You're a goddamned traitor, Harold. How fucking dare you.* It's unreal.

I'd gone through this agonizing springtime turkey season ritual—the heart-wrenching ordeal of betraying a hunting dog's trust and love—a few hours earlier when I'd left the house to head up to a spot to try to find a turkey. It was opening morning of the season, my first solo outing, my first adventure outside the house on my own in my new home. I felt good.

I'm not a world-class turkey hunter, but I've been able to get into some nice toms before. The trick is getting out early and settling into a good spot near the trees they roost in at night. I'd seen a big group of turkeys on some public land a week or so earlier when Sasha and I were taking a drive about twenty minutes from the house, the day after Dan and Lucy had come over to regale us with their bizarre warning about the *mountain spirit*. So, with opening morning of the season here, I figured I'd try to sneak in there and call in a nice tom turkey.

I enjoy hunting because I like being awake before everything else around me. I love being settled into a beautiful spot in the wild to watch the animals wake up, watch the natural world stretch and shake off the aches of a cold night. I especially love being out in time to listen to the first birds start to sing.

It's certainly a lot better than doing blow all night and staying up so late that you hear the birds as you're all strung out, finally trying to go to bed. Lord knows I suffered through enough of those agonizing moments of regret and self-loathing. Maybe *that's* actually why I enjoy getting out to hunt before sunrise so much, because it's done of my own volition, instead of as a result of my own mistakes. Or maybe it's because so many early mornings in the marines were so hellish, and these early mornings are ones I have control over.

Whatever it is, sitting out in that mountain meadow, nestled into a rock outcropping, thermos of hot coffee in the rocks next to me, listening to the first larks and robins start to sing, it's therapeutic for me. Almost religious. Using my binoculars to watch the first pikes and curls of sun creep through the granite cuts and crags in the Tetons, watching coyotes and deer trot through the gullies and draws below the ridge where I'd sat. I guess you could say *that* is why I like hunting.

Still, as had been the case ever since Dan and Lucy had come by with their glowing hogwash about the valley being haunted by some malevolent earth spirit, I was having trouble relaxing. I didn't believe a word of what they'd told us, but I couldn't figure out what their motive was in coming at us with all that ridiculous bullshit.

I knew Sasha had been thinking about it regularly as well, and that it had creeped her out more than she'd let on. Sasha's a bit of a hippie. I'd teasingly described her as *earthy*, or perhaps she's just easily taken with the *energies* in places and things. It suits her too. It's one of the things I love about her. She's not some goddamn Wiccan priestess or something, but she's certainly always been fascinated by powers and forces that can't be seen or easily measured.

I wouldn't say she believes in magic or the supernatural, so to speak, but she's certainly one who appreciates the assignment of a special significance or power to certain places or things. I, on the other hand, am a stubborn skeptic to my core.

If someone gets up in front of me and espouses a deep belief in something and holds themselves out as a representative of whatever that something is—be it a religion or a political party—and suggests there is some importance to that something being accepted and embraced by the world, I usually dislike them, and their something, *immediately*. It really doesn't matter what the political affiliation or theological flavor at issue happens to be. Whenever I'm in the proximity of impassioned people discussing politics or religion, I just have this beacon in my brain that starts broadcasting, *This person is full of shit, this person is full of shit*, and I can't help but completely disregard what they have to say without giving it proper, independent consideration. It's not because I'm incapable of discussing abstract issues; I consider myself a fairly smart person, at least compared to people I grew up or was in the marines with. I just find *people* who are deeply committed to an idea repulsive, even though I know it's unreasonable.

Either way, over the past week, with respect to the whole spirit-haunted-valley stuff, it had become fairly clear that Sasha was going to be playing the *maybe some of what they said could be true* side of the board. For myself, I was not only confident that these neighbors were fucking with us and completely full of it, but I intended to ridicule even the hypothetical exercise of entertaining validity in what they'd told us. It wasn't something we spoke about much; Sasha and I just know each other very well. We knew these were going to be our positions on the issue without even having to delineate the roles.

Neither of us could figure out what their *motive* was, and it was their fucking motive that was on my mind on this beautiful morning in this mountain meadow, interrupting my peace. I sat out there actively trying to zone out and disregard any concerns that were not in front of me. Trying to *meditate*, I guess. I'd done some meditation classes in the VA and in the hospital after Afghanistan. All those classes were held inside. Never thought of meditation as something that made much sense to do inside.

The guilt I still harbored after seeing the look of disbelieving betrayal on my dog's face earlier that morning was almost surprisingly hard to shake. I mean, I love that creature, but he's still just a fuckin' dog.

I have this memory from my childhood that is so vivid I can recall almost every detail. For some reason it's always the memory that comes to me when I'm either anxious or relaxed. Stressed out in a public space or feeling calm by myself, it comes to me. It's like a sun spot in my eye.

The memory is of an experience I went through countless times as a boy. When the memory comes to me, it's accompanied by a physical sensation that's shockingly detailed and nostalgic. I can remember exactly how it sounded, how it smelled, what I'd do with my hands, the dust in the air, my dirty shoelaces. All of it is still so clear.

In elementary school, the spot where I'd get picked up by the school bus was off a main road a few blocks from my house. To get there, I'd have to walk by a junkyard that filled up a square block between my neighborhood and the main road. This junkyard had the most stereotypical guard dog you can imagine, a fast, angry, slightly underfed pit mix.

For one reason or another, the dog was never out in the mornings, but on any afternoon of the year, you could bet your ass that dog would be patrolling the fence line, or lurking somewhere among the rusty old boats, trucks, and dryers, close enough to sense if someone was near the fence. As soon as I'd get within view or earshot of the dog, it would charge up to the fence, raging and furious, barking and chomping at the air so hard I could hear the snap of its teeth echo off the wooden fence that ran along the backyard of the house across the street. I can still remember the pattern of the sprinkler stains on that old fence.

At first, I was so terrified of the dog that I'd walk on the other side of the road, along the sprinkler-stained fence. Although that wasn't much better, because that was Kelly Stears's house. Kelly was a couple years older than me, and probably the first girl I ever had a crush on. She intimidated the shit out of me. I'd have been paralyzed with fear if she ever talked to me. Eventually, the prospect of running into her was actually more stressful than being near the furious dog, so I reluctantly went back to the beast's side of the street.

After enough of these encounters, it became clear that the fencing was sound, and that the beast wasn't aware of any method to actually escape the confines of the junkyard, so my confidence started to grow. By third grade, it became an enjoyable challenge for me to walk the length of the fence line despite the dog's anger at my proximity.

I can remember *exactly* how I felt as I'd walk along that chain-link fence, staring down in fascinated terror at the furious, snarling dog as it would rage alongside me in a frenzied storm of kicked-up dust, frothy drool, and noise every time I'd pass by—knowing the fence was the only thing keeping the beast from ripping and tearing into my nine-year-old body.

I can still see the dust in the afternoon light. I can still see the wake of grasshoppers evacuating the strip of dead, unmowed grass along the fence as the beast would charge down its length. I can still feel the pressure and warmth of the dog's barks on my little legs. I can still feel the same physical sensation, the coiled wet knots of tension in my muscles as I worked to keep a steady stride while also preparing to explode into a sprint at the first sign of the fence giving way.

It became a ritual for me, to see how calmly I could walk down that block, to see how little attention I could give the furious animal. I remember hoping people would drive by as I walked past the junk-yard, hoping someone could behold my poise and be so impressed by my bravery that they'd actually tell someone else about it later that evening. I remember when that ritual of walking along the junkyard fence was an actual, sincere motivation to make a real friend who actually wanted to come to my house after school so I could share the experience with someone. I remember spending *hours* fantasizing about Kelly Stears watching me walk by the dog, being so smitten with my confidence she'd fall in love with me.

One day in third grade, on my walk home from the bus stop, I got to the junkyard stretch and saw three police cars, an ambulance, cops, and other neighbors all over the place. I slowed my pace and looked toward the junkyard, confused as to why the beast wasn't losing its damn mind at the crowd and all the bustle nearby. As I got closer, I could see where a corner of the fence had become detached from one of the aluminum fence posts and pushed outward. The dog had escaped. A shock of dread hit me, wondering where it was. I actually thought about running up to tell the police to be careful and look out for the violent guard dog, but I just turned around and went the long way home. I saw Animal Control patrolling the neighborhood for the rest of the night, looking for the beast.

The next day at school, I heard about what had happened. Kelly Stears and some friends had been taunting the dog, seeing how close someone could get to the fence, then running away across the street into her backyard. Somehow, the dog made a lucky lunge that busted the fence open. He chased one of the tormenting kids into Kelly's backyard. Whether that was Kelly or not, I don't know, but when it got into the backyard, it was Kelly who got mauled.

She'd had most of her face torn apart, losing one eye entirely, and had her jaw ripped almost entirely free from her skull. I joined a throng of fascinated children on the playground, surrounding one of the older girls who had been in Kelly's yard the day before. She was reveling in the attention, regaling the group with all the gruesome details. She explained what it looked like seeing Kelly trying to crawl away from the dog as her father was fighting to pull it off her, the dog violently shaking one of her legs back and forth as she shrieked and wept through a destroyed face. She explained how Kelly's jaw and chin dangled aloft and dragged along the ground to the side of Kelly's face, only holding on by a few shreds of her destroyed left cheek.

I saw Kelly about a year later when she came back to school. They'd reattached her jaw, but the grafted skin, the scarring on her face, and her missing eye left her terribly and quite noticeably deformed. Her leg had been badly hurt as well, and she was still using a cane—a pink, sparkly little child-size cane.

Never did hear about what happened to the dog. I know they searched for it awhile, obviously to put it down after an attack like that. However, our neighborhood was on the outskirts of town, adjacent to rocky, arid grasslands that stretched out for miles, all the way to the mountains.

I like to think that dog made it out there, made it out into the wild. I like to imagine he held his own among the bears, cougars, and wolves. I like to think he lived long enough for his face to gray and his eyes to start clouding, and that he had a belly full of squirrel as he chose a quiet, peaceful place to lie down for the last time to die. Maybe under a big tree, or in a nice glade next to a stream.

Anyway, those hot afternoons, the dust, the fence, the noise, that dog's rage. The whole scene. Even after all these years, after all the noise, dust, blood, and rage since...Even sitting here in this mountain meadow, I still remembered it like it happened yesterday.

I heard some toms gobble a long way off over the next hour, but it didn't seem like it would be a fruitful turkey hunt unless I sat there all day, which I wasn't very interested in doing. I had my morning peace and reflection. It was already a successful hunt. Around 9 a.m. I started working my way down the ridge toward where I'd left the car on the forest access road and drove home.

★ ★ ★

I passed Dan on the road one afternoon later that week, first time seeing him since I'd kicked him out of our house under pretty awkward circumstances. I wasn't sure how that next interaction was going to go, so I just gave him a kind wave and a smile, which he returned. I didn't slow down, but I could see in my mirror that he'd hit the brakes on his big dually truck, presumably expecting me to stop and chat with him. I felt bad for a second, but it faded just as quickly. Wasn't ready for that anyway.

That next weekend we had a couple friends from Denver come and stay with us. They'd been in Jackson and crossed over Teton Pass to come check out our place. Zach and Sarah. They'd gotten married the year before. I'd met Zach in college. Hunted, fished, and partied with him over the years since. It was really nice hosting our first guests. It was nice seeing the amazement on their faces at the view of the Tetons from our porch and the stars at night, having them comment on the amazing view from the office where we'd set up a bed for them. It was validating. We considered telling them about the mountain spirit theory our crazy neighbors had shared, but we didn't. Not entirely sure why. Sasha loves cooking for people, so we spent the weekend eating, drinking, and also did a fun hike on the upper Fall River, fished a bit. It was a great time.

They left that Sunday morning and called us about nine hours later to let us know they'd made it home safely, and to thank us again for hosting them. It felt like only a couple hours had gone by since they'd left, which felt good for some reason—made us feel a bit *less* removed from the world we'd left behind.

It was really starting to feel like home here.

8

SASHA

❧

AFTER DINNER WE engaged in what had become a bit of a ritual of having a glass of wine on the back porch and watching the moon rise. I'd brought out one of the packets of notes Dan and Lucy had left for us, earning an eye roll from Harry when he saw what I was holding. We hadn't talked about Dan and Lucy's "haunted valley" issue since our friends left, which was actually a pretty nice reprieve.

I'd read through these "Springtime spirit" notes several times over the last week and was increasingly, deep down, a bit frightened by what Lucy had told me, and even more by what was written down in the notes. Not because I'd seen or heard anything to substantiate the insane story we'd been fed, but because there was something about Lucy that I inherently and immediately trusted. Which meant I wasn't as convinced as Harry was that this was all just a ruse to mess with us. I felt it had to be something she believed, at least to a certain extent.

I looked up from the vague description of the autumn spirit visit on the first page of the spirit notes to find Harry leaning on the railing of the porch, staring at me. Harry could read me, and he could read me well. I wasn't saying anything that could be openly interpreted as giving credence to what was written on the page in my hand, but he could still tell I wasn't as convinced as he was that this was all just a work of fiction, contrived in an attempt to scare us. He could read that in me. He went after it.

"Sash, you don't believe a scintilla of that ridiculous bullshit, right?"

He made the comment gently, and was laughing when he said it—he wasn't trying to "win" some argument—but it was still annoying as hell to me. His preemptive posture of challenge pressed a deep button.

I rolled my eyes at him. "Harry, stop. I'm not going to sit here and try to defend the legitimacy of anything we were told or anything in these notes. What I am going to say is—"

Harry looked down at the weathered decking of the porch between his feet, putting on one of his classic *ohhh here we go* smirks. I could see him getting ready to interrupt me, so I held my hand up.

"Stop, Harry, stop. Let me finish." It's actually pretty nice how well that works to get his attention when I can see he's formulating a retort instead of *actually listening* to me. I try not to overuse it. He crossed his arms, nodded, and looked me in the eye.

"What I *am* going to say," I continued, "is that I don't think Dan and Lucy are evil. Lucy in particular. I don't think she came here to feed me some fabricated bullshit story for some sinister purpose. She seems grounded and socially aware, and so I have a hard time believing she's just…"

I drew a blank. Couldn't think of what to say without invalidating my previous point. *Shit*.

"…I have a hard time believing she just came over here to try to scare me with some *entirely* fictional bullshit. I'm not saying what they told us is real, but I am telling you that I think *they* believe it. I don't think they're trying to scare us or fuck with us somehow. I think *they* believe this, or at least that Lucy believes what she told me."

Harry nodded. He held the quiet for a while before responding.

"I hear you. That makes sense, and you could be right. But seriously, Sash, the likelihood of them believing or not believing this shit, does it even matter? I can't help but treat them like they're in some cult or bizarre religion."

I shook my head. "Harry, honestly, do they seem like they're just full-on psychos? Do they seem mentally disturbed? Why on earth would they come over and tell us all of that and *knowingly* establish themselves permanently in our minds as nut jobs as soon as they met their new neighbors if they didn't feel it was important to do that?"

"Sasha, come on, *I don't know*—maybe they don't want neighbors here and are trying to scare us off."

I crossed my arms and leaned into my words. "Harry, that's exactly my point; they seem like *really* normal people, like *surprisingly normal* people. Even you said that last week, and our Realtor said she likes them and described them as highly respected in the community, and that dude at the county clerk's office even said he knows Dan *and* spoke highly of him!"

That was true. Harry had gone into St. Anthony to stop by the clerk's office and talk with the surveyor's office about some old property records, and one of the guys who'd helped Harry knew Dan and said he was a great guy.

"If Dan was a psycho cultist, it would be quite surprising for someone like a county official to sing his praises. Furthermore, at the end of the day, I know you like Dan and Lucy too, and Harry, I know how rare it is for you to like someone after just meeting them once."

Harry cocked his head in *touché* acknowledgment. He turned and rested his elbows on the railing before responding over his shoulder.

"I dunno, Sash, I mean...*fuck*. I guess we just wait to see this battery-powered LED light Dan's gonna throw into the pond while we're out."

We both laughed and let the matter rest, silently agreeing to leave it. It's not like we were going to up and move, and so long as Dan and Lucy weren't dangerous, who cared if we had crazy neighbors?

Before going to bed, I caught a glance of Harry while he was in the office, standing at the window above my desk, staring down at the pond.

The next morning, I had an early meeting, and Harry went into town to meet a guy he'd met online who was looking to either sell some sheep or lease some pasture, and to go pick up a greenhouse kit we'd ordered. I was excited to get the greenhouse set up so we could get some vegetable starts going, as it was still quite cold at night. The land still had that glaze of spring frost in the mornings.

I watched him that afternoon as he started to put the greenhouse together. I was proud of Harry, happy for him. He really was working to turn this place into a working piece of land we could largely live off.

That night, and in the afternoons and evenings for the rest of the week, after my last meeting of the day, we focused on hanging the last of our art and really finishing the move-in. It was still strange to wake up and look out our bedroom window onto a pasture in a mountain valley. The smells and noises were still foreign and unfamiliar, but less so.

That next weekend we took a few hikes from the national forest trailhead at the end of the county road. It had a well-maintained parking area with spaces for horse trailers, but we only saw one or two people a day drive past our driveway and up the road to the trailhead. Harry commented on how we'd see increased traffic once the real spring thaw and snowmelt started in earnest and the routes opened up, as the trails were still quite covered in snow even just a mile or so up from the parking lot.

On our walk down the road from the trailhead, Dash trotting ahead of us, stopping occasionally to investigate a smell here or there, I noticed Harry staring out over the pastures to the left, to the west, the big ranch property.

"Did Dan mention Joe, the owner of that place? What's it called again, Berry Canyon or something?" I asked Harry.

He nodded without looking back toward me. "Berry Creek Ranch. And yeah, he did. He said Joe's the Shoshone guy who taught him about 'the spirit' and 'the rituals' to keep it away." He added air quotes with his fingers for emphasis.

"Yeah, Lucy told me the same thing."

It was a beautiful property, a *massive* property. "It's so big...I can't imagine being in charge of sixty-five hundred acres. I'm intimidated by keeping our fifty-five in decent shape. Is that like, one of the bigger ranches in the area, or the state even?"

Harry shook his head. "Nah, sixty-five hundred acres is certainly a big ranch, but there are several ranches over here on the Idaho side of the Tetons that are twenty thousand, even thirty thousand acres. And,

I mean, there are ranches in Texas, Montana, and eastern Oregon that are hundreds of thousands of acres."

"Dear God…can't imagine what running places like that is like."

"Yeah, no shit, right? Definitely a big job," Harry agreed. "But with a real working ranching operation of that size, you've got a full staff."

Harry picked up a stick from the side of the road as we passed under a big ponderosa. Dash bounded back up to us with his red plume of a tail standing at attention, whipping back and forth, knowing a fetch opportunity was imminent. Harry threw the stick ahead of us down the road and Dash tore after it.

This part of the road was on a hill above our property, so you could only see a little part of our meadow on the other side of the pond from our house. But you could look back up behind us to the east and see the massive granite mountains looming above their curtains of rolling, forested foothills.

To the west, looking down the county road, you had a view all the way to the state highway, all across Dan and Lucy's ranch and a significant portion of Joe's property. It was an amazing vantage point. You could really see how well defined our valley was, how clear the crests of the ridges were and what neat little granite and pine-tree boundaries they formed. Our private sanctuary, nestled between the highway and the beginning of the national forest where the mountains really get started.

Harry stopped and looked out over the view, seeming to already know what I was thinking. He smiled at me and took my hand, then looked back toward the landscape that rolled out away from us. "There are so many of these little drainages on the west side of the Tetons, how fuckin' cool is it that there are only three property owners in this one? We got so lucky."

I squeezed his hand. "We sure did, babe. Didn't Nataly say that guy Joe or the Berry Creek Ranch LLC or something had been buying up most of the private property left in this little valley?"

Harry had actually worked for the City of Denver for the past six years in the surveying office, which resulted in him becoming a *total* map and property record nerd, on top of his already being a history junkie, particularly tribal and American western history. Thus, naturally, he'd sleuthed the hell out of all the neighboring properties before we even left Denver. Point being, I know he gets all jazzed up and excited when I ask him these land history questions, which is *adorable*. I enjoy hearing his answers too. Most of the time, at least.

Harry nodded. "Yeah, I found a lot of the old property records. Joe's family got some kind of government-issued title to a part of their property in 1867, maybe '69, but his great-grandfather and several other family members got the first big contiguous chunk of their land, a thousand acres or so, through the General Allotment Act. There's a lot to say about that law, about how it was used to kill many tribal identities, but functionally it was an effort by the legislature to move away from the reservation model, allowing the feds to issue land to tribal members on an individual basis rather than to tribes or groups. So that's how Joe's family started building the larger base of what the ranch is today. This is Shoshone and Bannock country, so that Berry Creek Ranch family's been here a hell of a lot longer than the United States has existed. Back when they got that thousand-acre parcel under the Allotment Act, the only other family in the valley was the Jacobson family."

Dash dropped the stick at Harry's feet and anxiously waited for him to relaunch it. Harry threw the stick and pointed down the road toward our property.

"The Jacobsons had a federal land grant in the 1870s for six hundred forty acres that covered our place, and their old property boundary ran up into what is now the national forest and up to about where we are now. The Jacobsons partitioned the property out over the years, selling chunks here and there, especially the last generation of Jacobsons, who sold most of their property to the Forest Service, and who were actually the ones to tear down the old house and build ours in the 1960s. When the last Jacobson died in the 1990s—some ol' girl, can't remember her name—it stayed in trust for a while until the Seymours bought it from their estate sale in January of 1996. The Seymours lived in our house until they moved out the spring after we first met and no one's lived here since...real estate firm bought it from the Seymours in 2012, and it sat empty till now."

I had forgotten about the name Seymour until now, and hearing it reminded me.

"Didn't Dan and Lucy say that when the Seymours moved in, in the winter of 1996, they came over and had that same conversation with them, gave them the same spiel about the spirit and whatnot, and that was the last time they'd had to tell a new owner in the valley about it?"

Harry shrugged and shook his head. "Yeah, I guess Dan mentioned that."

"I almost want to like...call them, probe about Dan and Lucy a bit, see what they made of the whole 'spirit' story."

Harry didn't respond. After a moment he pointed back up the road from where we'd come, up the hill, directing the subject back to his little property-record geek-out. "There were actually seven other individual private properties up here, between our place and the end of the road where the national forest trailhead parking lot is. They were all hundred-and-sixty or three-hundred-twenty-acre parcels, which was the size of the land grants given out to settlers under the Homestead Act of 1862."

How in the hell did he remember all this shit?

He pointed down the hill to Dan and Lucy's ranch, along the road below our property, which was obscured by the forest that hugged the west side of the road. "There were actually three other hundred-and-sixty-acre parcels down there too, all of which were bought and consolidated into one ranch by the folks who used to own Dan and Lucy's property. Which is actually pretty crazy..."

He looked at me with his adorable, nerdy excitement. "It's crazy because up until the 1920s or '30s, there were *thirteen different* families on this road. It would've almost felt fuckin' crowded! Even if it is because Joe and the Berry Creek Ranch have been buying people out, while all the cities we've ever been to are getting more crowded, the opposite is happening here...It's pretty awesome."

I smiled in return and nodded. I did feel a surprising flash of regret, or something *like* regret, at the thought that this valley was once filled with thirteen different families. I would've enjoyed that, I think, a bit more community. I loved that we found such solitude, especially near the Tetons. I appreciated the opportunity we fell into, but I still had this dull longing for a slightly larger social world nearby, more neighbors, more people to get to know.

I blocked the setting sun with my hand and looked back over Joe's ranch. "I want to meet Joe. Not just because he's our neighbor, but I can't really imagine another person other than Dan and Lucy being on board with their whole *spirit* narrative. But what if that's what happens, though? What if he's like, 'Yeah, guys, it's real, make sure to start the fire when the light starts before the spirit gets ya.' What would we even say?"

Harry took his hat off and shook his head, then stretched his arms out slowly as he shrugged his shoulders. "I mean...I don't fuckin' know, babe. It's certainly entirely unclear to me how anyone could take such egregiously ridiculous bullshit as that seriously. I was unsure how to respond to that nonsense when Dan fed it to me, can't imagine that being different with anyone else."

It really was frustrating him. I could see it. To me, Lucy and Dan were nice folks who just had a kooky old wives' tale they liked to share with neighbors. Harry, on the other hand, seemed personally offended by it. Like it was an insult, or an attempt to intentionally scare us into moving.

I walked over to him and put my arms around his waist. "Don't worry, baby, I won't let the scary lights or the naked man or the bear or the scarecrows get you. They won't get through me; I'll protect my *big strong marine*." He rolled his eyes and kissed me.

I snuggled into Harry's chest and looked back up to the mountains. "You can really *feel* the warmer days coming...almost like it's in the air, in the light."

I could feel him nodding in agreement and looked up at him. "It's still kinda chilly, not quite full spring yet up here in the mountains. Let's go home and make a fire and get warm, eh?"

Harry kissed me. "Nothing in the world I'd rather do."

9

HARRY

That was great, but I feel like I'm fifteen pounds heavier." I looked up to Sasha. We'd just finished dinner. We'd gotten a new grill a few days earlier, and had just christened it with steaks, baked potatoes, and asparagus. It was a heavy meal, enough to keep us sprawled out on the porch swing, and then the floor of the porch itself, digesting since well after sunset.

"Well…" Sasha stood up and stretched. She held out her arms and leaned down, putting her face in front of mine with a smile. "We should *probably just open another bottle of wine, right?*"

"Yeah, sounds good. I'm gonna finish with this and be right in."

I was sitting on the porch, pulling burrs out of Dash's tail and belly. Before dinner, we'd gone on a hike up the creek, following it from where it crossed into our property from the national forest to a mile or so into the firs and ponderosas up the ridge. It was a beautiful little stream, and it really did feel like the first *nice* day of spring. However, there was an assload of burrs growing along certain parts of the creek, and Dash must've picked up half of the things in the entire valley in his tail and coat. Little bastards were a real hassle to get out of his fur, especially when trying to do it in a way that didn't hurt him.

I was on one of the last ones, which was snugged in tight, right along the skin of his chest. I tried to pull it free, and it wouldn't give. Dash, irritated, tried to roll off his back to escape from where I had him between my legs. "Easy, buddy, easy, last one, I promise." I separated a few more locks of hair from the burr, and it came out.

I held it out in front of his nose for him to see. "All done, buddy boy, all done!" He sniffed it, then I scooted my ass back and he jumped up and gave a full-body dry-off shake.

I lifted my glass to finish my last sip of wine, and something caught my eye from the meadow, reflecting through the liquid in the glass, making it look like blood.

A yellowish ball of light. In the pond. About three feet under the water.

I'd be a lying son of a bitch if I tried to deny that my heart fluttered, and my adrenaline started to surge.

I stood up and walked over to the porch railing. Dash looked at me, followed my gaze, and shot up to join me in staring out over the meadow.

Fuck me. There it was. I thought about taking a picture and sending it to Sasha inside, but I didn't want to tweak her out. For some reason, I didn't even want to mention it at all.

My mind started racing. It was almost completely dark, but I strained my eyes looking down the driveway, expecting to see Dan sneaking away, immediately thinking he'd been nearby, having just finished rigging up some kind of yard light in the pond to fuck with me.

Then I thought about trying to shoot it. I had my 30-06 hunting rifle with a new scope freshly dialed, right inside in the coat closet. It wasn't more than 120 yards away, easy shot. Maybe I blast the fuckin' thing, see what happens?

Then I felt something. Something I hadn't felt in a long time.

I felt like I was being watched—being watched by someone, or something, that I needed to locate before it made a move. Not sure why, but my instincts made me look up at the tree line to the northeast. It seemed that Dash felt it too. I looked down at him as he lowered his head, and saw his hackles go up, and I could hear him let out a low growl. I looked back at the light.

It had *fucking moved*. It was at least fifteen feet from where I'd seen it the first time. I stood on my porch staring down at the light in the pond in complete disbelief.

I was looking for reasons that could explain it. More like, I was frantically ginning up explanations as to how this could be a hoax or some kind of ruse. Some kind of battery-powered light, or solar? Those considerations were drowned out by what Dan had said on the porch the day I'd kicked him out, streaming through my mind like those stock tickers at the bottom of a news broadcast.

You don't need to freak out. Just cease what you're doing and get a fire started—a little fire good enough to heat up some water—when you see the light for the first time, start a fire and call us—if you don't start the fire after seeing the light, and you hear drums, cover the windows and don't let anyone or anything get inside.

Dash was still looking up at the tree line with his hackles raised, letting out low growls with each exhale.

What had him worked up? Wolf, bear, cougar? Coyotes, maybe? Bears were coming out of hibernation around now, and they'd be hungry. Although, he usually just barked at mammals bigger than him; he didn't growl or act like this, even when we ran into bears on hikes. Furthermore, even though there was only a bit of gray light left in the western sky, I could clearly see there weren't any animals in the meadow between us and the forest.

Failing to find the source of the dog's discomfort, I let out an audible sigh. I was embarrassed even hearing it. My heart rate was ramping up; I could hear it in my ears like I'd just taken a run. I realized I had subconsciously started talking to the dog, trying to chill him out a bit. "It's okay, buddy, it's okay, there's nothing up there."

You don't need to freak out. Just cease what you're doing and get a fire started . . .

I looked back and forth between the area my dog was fixated on and the light in the pond. The light was now changing positions every time I returned to it. Darkness was just playing tricks on my eyes, right?

I've spent enough time on night patrols in combat zones and enough evenings archery hunting to know how easily that shit happens, *especially* when your heart rate is up and you're actively looking for something you've been envisioning all day. Your mind starts to lead you on. That's *definitely* what this was.

After a few seconds, the light appeared to be relocating to different spots within the pond at least thirty feet apart.

I rubbed my eyes, took a deep breath, and looked at the pond—saw the light, took note of where it was, looked up at the ridge, blinked my vision clear, looked back at the pond—*boom*, fuckin' thing was in an entirely new spot every time.

I could feel tendrils of panic start to flick at the edges of my mind. My hands were going numb, which only happens when my adrenaline is starting to really course.

I actually forced myself to chuckle out loud, the act of which immediately made me realize how anxious I was—the panicky *sound* of my own voice making me even more jumpy. I realized everything in my body and mind was working to expeditiously rebel against treating any of this as real, and how starting the fire would represent my acquiescence, my surrender to fear.

One internal voice would ask: *What would it hurt to just start the damn fire, dude?*

The louder, more belligerent voice would respond: *Fuck that, this is your land, your slice of the planet, your goddamn terms. This little western folklore narrative can go fuck itself.*

That's when I heard Dash let out a whimper.

I looked down at him where he was standing on the porch, and he was looking right up at me.

"Dash, it's okay, buddy. It's okay!" His ears were back, tail between his legs, and he started doing a slow backpedal as he looked toward the tree line. Then he turned around and booked it, sprinting toward the kitchen door that opened to the porch.

I whipped my head around to look at the area on the tree line that had him so tweaked out, then back at the light in the pond—new spot, fuck me—then back at the tree line. I could feel my hands and shoulders shaking now.

I've had a significant amount of time to practice getting a grip in high-stress situations. When bullets are flying and grown men you've looked up to and admired are panicking, screaming, or bleeding to death, you've got to know how to keep a level head, or at least how to avoid shitting yourself and falling apart.

It had been a very long time, but I forced myself to go through the internal mantra I'd developed and relied on so many times before: *Deep breath, it'll happen or it won't, if it does you won't feel it, you're more dangerous than them, you need to move, deep breath, it'll happen or it won't, if it does you won't feel it, you're more dangerous than them, you need to move, deep breath…*

Dash started yelping and clawing at the door to get inside, something I can't remember ever seeing him do. It shocked me as much as the light did. I felt the pressure change in the air around me. I felt my mouth begin to salivate like I was about to puke.

It hit me right then. Maybe it was the dog's behavior, maybe it was knowing Sasha would've heard Dash clawing at the door and would be coming outside to see what the noise was. It had only been about ninety seconds since I first noticed the light in the pond, but the desire to get a fire going hit me for the first time like a ton of bricks.

My desire for that fire felt primal, felt like it came from my damn soul. It felt like my unborn children and grandchildren depended on it to survive.

Right as I heard the kitchen door open, I wheeled around and started sprinting down the porch to the stack of firewood.

As I passed by the back door, I could see Dash tear past Sasha's legs into the kitchen. Her look of confusion at the dog amplified as our eyes locked.

"Lock that door now. I'm coming in the front door."

I was at the firewood stack a few yards down the porch in what felt like two steps. I grabbed the hatchet and a clutch of the smallest logs in the stack, then bounded inside, slamming the door and locking the dead bolt behind me.

Sasha was already in the living room. "What the fuck, Harry?!"

All I could get out was "The light" as I ran past her into the kitchen. I grabbed some junk mail off the counter, spun around, and jogged back toward the fireplace in the living room, where I dumped the logs, grabbed a couple fire-starter matches, cranked open the flue, and took a knee.

Sasha had gone into her office, which was off the living room, where big windows looked to the south out over the pasture and pond. I could hear her reaction. *"Holy shit, holy shit."*

She paced back into the living room and we locked eyes again. There was a look of real, true fear on her face. "Harry, *holy shit.*"

Dash was pacing around between the two of us, whining and shaking like we'd just finished a morning of winter duck hunting.

Sasha crouched down next to me. "Harry, *holy shit.*" It seemed that was all she could think to say, which was more than I could say myself. I didn't even want to look at her, feeling too embarrassed as I frantically worked on getting a fire going.

I had several envelopes' worth of papers crumpled under a stack of kindling and some of the smallest logs when I heard Dash. Sasha and I both looked back at him over our shoulders, through the living room and into the kitchen. He was standing, barking at the kitchen door to the porch.

That is *not* something he does unless whatever has gotten him all worked up is *right* outside the damn door. My body was screaming at me to grab a rifle and go tearing out into the yard when my mind won over. *Focus, motherfucker.*

"Harry, start the fire, *start the fire right now.*" I could hear Sasha's voice shaking.

I turned back and struck one of the thick fire-starter matches and set it under the papers. Then lit another one, then a third, then a fourth.

As I was watching the flame of one sizzle with ignition as it burned into the resin-soaked pulp body of the match, I realized I was pleading internally not to hear drumming from outside. I grabbed the hatchet and started hacking off smaller strips from one of the pieces of fire-wood, adding them between the paper and logs as I worked.

"Harry...Harry." Dash's barking took on a certain snarl that made it hard to hear her. "I feel...I don't know, I feel something."

I could feel it too, even if I didn't know what the fuck it was. The pressure in my ears, my mouth watering, my heartbeat pounding in my head.

Eventually, I noticed the kindling and one of the logs catching and dropped the hatchet to blow on the flames a bit. Within a few seconds, the fire was going on its own. I added the rest of the logs into the now-crackling fire and took a deep breath.

Dash was next to us, looking between me, Sasha, and the fire, wagging his tail as though he approved of the work.

I looked Sasha in the eyes for the first time since seeing the light.

"Harry...*what the fuck*," she said.

I remembered something else Dan had said during his little "ritual briefing" several weeks earlier. As soon as it came into my head, Sasha said it out loud, almost word for word.

"'When you see the light for the first time, start a fire and call us.'" Sasha went to the fridge to where Dan and Lucy's number was, moved the magnet obscuring the last few digits, and started punching it into her phone.

"Sasha, fucking wait a second."

I went to the closet. With black bears and grizzlies waking up from hibernation in the coming weeks and starting to prowl around looking for chow, a week ago I'd put one of my 12-gauge shotguns in there, a pump-action tube-mag loaded up with five solid steel slugs. I racked one into the chamber.

"Harry... we should call them."

I stopped myself from responding too harshly. "Just, wait a second, okay? Let's just breathe and think for a minute." My body and instincts were still screaming at me to get a headlamp on, grab one of my ARs, and go secure the area.

But I did, undeniably, feel more at ease. I could feel the panic leaving me. I couldn't remember if Dan had said anything about going outside after starting the fire. As though she was reading my mind, Sasha went to the letter desk where she'd stashed the written versions of Dan and Lucy's warnings or rules or whatever the fuck they were, pulled one out, unfolded it, scanned down to where I saw the underlined heading *Springtime*, and began to read through it aloud.

> *Once the fire is going on its own, the light should go out. Go to a window on the south side of the house and look to see if it's still there. If it is, add more wood to the fire. If the light is gone, the spirit is gone, you will definitely feel it, and you can let the fire die out and go about your business as though nothing had happened.*

Yeah, fucking right, Dan. Here I am, engaged in this ritualistic pageantry in an attempt to ward off some evil spirit for the first time in my life, and I'm gonna just pivot back to going about my fucking business *as though nothing had happened*.

That sentence enraged me, or maybe it just rekindled the shame-laden anger I had at being frightened of something this fucking preposterous. In fact, my hands were shaking, I was so angry. Sasha put her hand on my back.

I looked up at her.

"Harry, let's just go look."

We slowly walked toward the office. I kept my eyes down as I approached the window, leaned the shotgun against the wall, and put my hands on the sill. "Harry, it's gone," I heard Sasha say.

She was right. But I did not have much time to let it sink in, because at that exact moment, I, and presumably Sasha as well, experienced what was easily the most profound moment of the entire experience so far.

In the small amount of time that had passed, every part of my mind was engaged in a gestapo-tier suppression campaign against the notion that this "spirit" bullshit was *in any way* real. Despite that great effort, an exquisite relief washed over me the second I saw that the light had disappeared, a sensation of release I didn't know a human could experience without drugs. Sasha gripped my forearm. She was about to speak when she stopped herself.

It was an emotional release, coupled with a fantastic physical relief that felt like I simultaneously took an amazing piss, walked into an air-conditioned building on a hot day, *and* realized I'd lost fifteen pounds, all in the same second.

I shuddered, then smiled and almost laughed.

"Harry, did you *feel that*?!"

"Yeah…what the fuck was…? yeah…"

The dog was completely back to normal as well, standing next to the front door wagging his tail, waiting to be let outside.

Sasha and I looked from Dash back into each other's eyes, completely speechless.

10

SASHA

Harry, we're fucking *calling them*," I said.

It was unfathomable to me why he would be resisting this. He felt the panic and dread when the light was in the pond, and he felt that physical sensation of relief the second it was gone. Even so, the stubborn bastard had been standing in the kitchen arguing with me for five straight minutes, insisting that we not call the Steiners. His reasons had changed five times too, from "They can't do anything to help us, even if this is real" to "It was probably them who put the fuckin' light in the pond."

"Sasha, just stop for a second. Let's slow down and think about this." I could see Harry was panicking. Maybe not *panicking*, but he was angry, angry at what was happening, angry at his inability to explain it.

He'd always gone to great lengths to avoid being angry around me, no matter what the circumstance was; even if I'd done something stupid or said something nasty during a drunken argument, he'd choke down anger to keep me from seeing it, take a few deep breaths, and change the subject or walk away.

"Harry, why, why?! Look at me, Harry. Articulate it for me, in clear words, why we shouldn't call them right now. It even says in their fucking letter that *we would feel it when the light was gone*. They wrote that in their letter. What'd they do, plant a light in the pond and then *drug us through our vents*?!"

To my surprise, Harry did not have any rebuttal. He stared at the floor for a solid ten seconds, then looked up at me, put his hands up. "Okay...okay, Sash," he said. "Let's call them."

I was taken aback. Seeing him cave made this more real than anything else had.

He held his hand out for my phone. "I'll call them. I'll put it on speaker."

I handed Harry the phone, and he punched in their home number. After a few rings, I heard Dan's voice. There was a slight wheeze and strain in it that suggested he was just sitting up. "Well, hey, Harry! How are you guys? How's the move-in going? Y'all getting settled in?"

"Yeah, it's all going fine. Hey, I apologize about calling at this hour."

"Oh, not to worry, we don't hit the sack until around ten this time of the year. What can I do for ya? You guys all right?"

"Yeah, we're fine. I'm actually calling because, well..."

Harry looked up at me and took a deep breath.

"It just so happens, a little bit ago, we saw the light in the pond..."

Dan's firmly toned response came *maybe* a half second after Harry had finished the sentence. "Did you start a fire? Do you have a fire going right now, Harry?"

Harry tried to keep some levity and humor in his tone. "Yeah, yeah, we started a fire right when we saw it, just as I promised I would! The light is gone, so your miracle cure seemed to work. No drumming either!"

I could hear Lucy in the background let out a muffled "Oh thank God" before Dan responded.

"Well, we are both very glad to hear that, Harold. We know how, well...unnerving it can feel, and we just want to make sure you two are all right. Can we come stop by? We won't stay long."

I could see he was about to protest, so I reached for Harry's hand and nodded. Harry shook his head in response.

"We're all right, Dan. No need to come over. I'm sure we'll have an opportunity to catch up about it in person soon."

I gave Harry a challenging look, but I certainly couldn't deny how strange it would be for them to come over right now, to talk about...this, whatever *this* was.

I felt like a nervous middle schooler all of a sudden as I prepared to ask the next question. "Hey, Dan, this is Sasha, real quick...So, it's all right for us to go outside now, right? You said as soon as the light's gone, it's fine to—"

"Oh sure, once the light's gone, it's all clear. You can usually feel when the light is gone, just as well as you can see it's gone, which I'm guessing you noticed!"

My eyes went wide, and I glared at Harry with as much challenge in my eyes as I could summon. He saw it and looked back down at the phone. "We'll talk to y'all soon."

I stepped toward him after he'd hung up the phone. "Harold, look at me. How on earth could they have made us *feel* that if this wasn't real? Harry, seriously..."

He glanced at me briefly, then out the window with a distant look on his face. I can tell when he's working up some kind of plan in his head just from his body language. He turned quickly and headed for the front door.

"Babe, what are you doing?"

He looked back at me. "I'm settling this bullshit. I'll be back in five minutes. Please don't leave the house, Sash, please." Harry opened the door and blocked the opening outside to prevent Dash from following him out into the darkness, prompting Dash to look up at him and whine with frustration.

I shrugged, annoyed, and shook my head. "Okay, be safe."

Harry ran out the front gate and into the garage and emerged with one of his rifles, a headlamp on, and two of his game cameras—those weatherproof, motion-activated, night-vision cameras that he straps onto trees to track animals before hunting seasons start. He jogged back through the front gate, shut it behind him, then ran across the yard to the gate that led through the fence around the yard and into the pasture.

I moved into the office so I could see Harry as he made his way from the back gate, down through the pasture toward the pond. It was always strange to me, watching him carry one of those AR-15-type rifles he had. I didn't see him use them often, only on a few occasions when he'd talked me into going to the shooting range. But it was like it was a part of him, the way he ran through the pasture with the rifle shouldered, the light attached to the rifle illuminating a cone in the dark world before him. It was so natural for him. It was so...predatory.

There was a cluster of small aspen trees next to the pond. Harry went straight for them. Through the light of his headlamp, I could see him let go of the rifle so that it swung down on the sling, and then start to strap the game cameras around two of the smaller trees. I watched him flip open the built-in digital monitors on the cameras and kneel down to, I assumed, get an idea of the angle of the cameras to make sure they were set up correctly. After a little while of messing with the cameras, he turned and jogged back up to the yard. I went out the kitchen door onto the back porch to meet him.

"What're you doing with those cameras?"

Harry unslung his rifle, squeezed my hand and gave me a grin, and started answering me as he headed into the kitchen.

"I figured if those old crazies really had snuck into the meadow to put something in the pond to make that light, they'd be fixin' to sneak it out before morning to keep the ruse alive. Game cams will catch anything going near the pond." He sounded pleased with himself.

I felt like it was unlikely Dan and Lucy were messing with us after talking to them and hearing the fear in their voices when we told them we'd seen the light in the pond. And after feeling whatever it was that I felt while the light was in the pond, and then feeling whatever it was when it went out, I very much doubted this was some ruse that a couple of senior citizens were capable of pulling off. But I wasn't sure I was ready to openly, vocally express doubt that this *was not* some kind of trickery.

I followed Harry into the living room, watching him stash his rifle in the closet and set his headlamp on the runner table next to the front door, unsure what to say.

Harry and I went out onto the porch to split a beer and digest what had just happened. I looked down at the stack of firewood and thought about moving some inside for next time. The idea of that becoming casual splashed some gas on the embers of my earlier anxiety and dread.

As we sat out there, Harry and I went through everything that had happened from start to finish at least three times. It wasn't long until I was doing most of the talking, so I let the subject die and we watched a show and went to bed.

Harry's ability to fall asleep on command has always astounded me. I often need at least an hour of rolling around before I can crash. After going over everything in my head for what must've been the fifteenth time that night, I sat up and leaned over the headboard, putting my elbows on the windowsill above our bed, and looked out into the dark pasture toward the pond.

There was a slight reflection of the moon, but otherwise it was as dark as ink. I wondered, looking down there, whether I'd ever see that light again. My heart rate picked up speed as I considered how likely it was that I would.

11

HARRY

I'D SET MY alarm for 6:15 the morning after the whole light fiasco.

Within minutes of the alarm going off, I was in my fishing waders, crunching through the frost-crusted meadow toward the pond with a shovel, a heavy garden rake, and my rifle.

I suspected Dan and Lucy had either planted some kind of light in our pond themselves or had someone else creep onto our property to do it. I figured they'd creep back onto our place to remove it before sunrise, and thereby get caught fucking around on my game cameras.

If there was nothing picked up on the cameras, then I was going to grid that entire pond, inch by fucking inch, to dredge up whatever the hell it was that had been planted to make that light and move it around. The pond itself only got to about five feet at its deepest spot, so I'd spend all day out there to check every inch if I had to.

I got to the little stand of aspens on the bank of the pond and set all my stuff down, took a knee, and flipped open the monitor on the first of the two game cameras. The monitor shows how many pictures and video clips were taken and allows you to scroll through them. I'd set the cameras apart with different fields of view, this one covering most of the south bank of the pond. It had taken four still photos, and they showed a cottontail rabbit working its way up the bank. I flipped it closed and scooted over to the second camera, which was covering most of the surface of the pond itself. I flipped open its monitor and saw it had taken eight photos. The first four pictures were of a cottontail rabbit, probably the same little fucker the other camera had picked up. The next four were of a skunk that had waddled up to take a drink from the pond.

Well, *shit*. The light and whatever had it moving all over the pond were still in there. Dredging operation it was, then.

Over the next two hours, I trudged around that entire goddamn pond several times over. I'd leave a stick in the muddy bank on one side and walk in as straight a line as I could to the other side, using the garden rake to pull up anything bigger than a twig I encountered in my path. I saved the deepest part for last, knowing I'd likely have to get wet. I got a bit more pissed off with every line I'd walked to find nothing that could've been responsible for the light. By the time the deepest area in the center of the pond was the only unchecked area left, I didn't even care about the frigid water spilling over the line of my waders, sending an icy shock through my legs and chest.

Nothing. Not a damn thing was in that pond other than rocks, twigs, and silt. I grabbed my rifle and trudged up to the house, soaking wet, freezing, and furious.

Sasha had gotten up and came out from the kitchen with Dash and some coffee as I was stripping off my swampy clothes. Dash came trotting up to me with his tail wagging, looking for some affection.

"Jesus, Harry, you're soaked. You must be *freezing*."

"Yeah." I was intentionally trying to avoid eye contact with Sasha. Just from our conversation the night before, I could tell that she was starting to buy into this spirit bullshit. It was monumentally frustrating.

"So…did you find anything in the pond that could've made the light?"

"Nope."

I knew my brevity and unconcealed butthurt were getting a bit ridiculous, but I was pissed. Furious, even, though I wasn't sure at whom or what.

I don't do well with shit I can't explain. I can't really buy into any religion, and never have gotten a kick out of any other kind of lore or fantasy-type stuff. I used to believe in God, even prayed to him, or *it*. That belief was extinguished as soon as I watched a good man—a man I looked up to—die. Sergeant Nichols. He had a positive energy and fearlessness that uplifted everyone around him, officer or enlisted. His presence alone would give an almost amphetamine-type boost to whatever clutch of exhausted, terrified marines he'd crack a joke for. He would completely change a battle space just by being there. He was invincible to me, until he wasn't. I watched, helpless, as this man bled to death in a state of considerable pain and dread. He didn't just die. He writhed and wept in the mud until his lights finally went out.

For me, with the terminal permanence of Sergeant Nichols went the sanctity of the Almighty. Since that day, I've been one to trend toward the concrete, the explainable, and the expected. On top of that, I've always been pretty good at keeping my shit together while I'm feeling threatened.

Unfortunately, my familiarity with feeling threatened and confronting threatening shit was entirely limited to situations where *I actually knew what was threatening my well-being*—which, up to this point, had always been another man, or myself. Both were quite simple to understand.

Sasha had gone inside, leaving the door open behind her, and came back out with a towel she handed over as she sat down next to me, just outside the boundary of stinky pond water steaming in the morning light.

She put her hand on my shoulder as I was drying my head, and I looked over at her as she started talking.

"Babe, there's nothing you can do about this. Sometimes there are things in this world that just can't be explained by—"

My frustration boiled over. "Like what, Sasha?! Like what? Name one fucking thing you've *ever experienced* that is even remotely like this. Name one *supernatural* thing that can't be explained by reason. I saw that fucking light and felt something fucking change. It was in the air. It was in my head. Dash even freaked out too. Name one other thing you know of that you *didn't* learn about on the internet that you can even remotely compare to this."

"Babe, come on, stop, you don't need to get angry at me, I'm just trying to—"

"Trying to what?!" I stood and walked down the porch steps, then turned back to face her.

"What are you trying to do, Sasha? Make me feel good about some horror-story bullshit like this? Trying to make this into something *exciting* and *heady* and *groovy*? Should we have a séance, burn some fuckin' sage, and lay out some protective crystals? Sash, if this shit is for real, you think this is gonna be all exciting and mysterious?"

I knew I'd gone overboard before even finishing my diatribe, and I think Sasha could see that too. I wasn't myself. I felt like crying. She stood up and gave me one of her looks, a look that says *don't bother saying shit until you apologize and chill.*

I took a deep breath and started my next sentence slowly.

"I'm sorry, Sash. I didn't mean to talk to you like that. I just...what the fuck, man. What is going on?"

"I don't know, babe. It's all pretty damn scary, obviously, but I mean...If this is too much for us, we can just sell this place and move. But Dan and Lucy told us how to stay safe, and I think it's at least worth getting through the summer to see if this is all real. If this whole 'bear chase' summertime spirit thing they mention in their notes actually happens, then we'll certainly know for sure."

I couldn't even believe what I was hearing, but I felt the same way, so I checked my smartass response.

"Yeah, yeah...I suppose you're right."

* * *

It started to get warmer by the day and stayed above freezing at night. The gardens were planted, Sasha had gotten into a good routine with working remotely, and we'd planted a dozen or so little yearling fruit trees. We weren't entirely sure whether it was the right time of year to do so, but we figured, hey, why would they be selling the little things at the nursery if it weren't? We'd had a big load of stones delivered so I could build up the small stone wall that ran through our yard in front of the house, which had been eaten by the earth a bit over the years and had become hard to appreciate. Sasha was happy. I could see it, feel it, hear it in her easy laughter, and there was nothing more gratifying in the world to me.

I'd also started dedicating around four hours a day to the fifteen acres of ponderosa forest above the house, which hadn't enjoyed much active management in what appeared to be half a century. There were huge snags of limbs and entire dead trees making the woods a premade bonfire and thus a real-deal fire-mitigation project. So, for about a week straight I'd been heading into the woods with Dash and my chain saw, bucking logs and dragging everything into burn piles we'd take care of this coming winter. It was hard work, but incredibly satisfying seeing literal piles representative of the day's work. Dash was in heaven as well, chasing squirrels and even flushing a couple grouse. May had rolled around in full springtime glory.

I was in the kitchen cooking dinner. Sasha was in the office putting together some IKEA-type bookshelf we'd ordered. I was about to cut into a pepper when I thought I heard her gasp. As I opened my mouth to ask if she was all right, I heard her yell.

"Babe, *babe, Harry, the light, the light is in the pond, right now. It's there right now.*"

Ice shot through my veins, goose bumps ripping down the skin of my arms. I hadn't even put the kitchen knife down when I busted into the office. Sasha was standing at the window with her hand over her mouth.

I looked over her shoulder and saw it, same as before, a small ball of yellow light a few feet below the surface of the pond. Sasha locked wide eyes onto mine.

I glanced back at the pond and the light had moved just a few feet to the left. I was angry. That's the emotion this stupid-ass little light brought out of me—anger. I knew what to do, but I was already trying to think of some other way we could test this bullshit, some way we could probe it. Sasha's voice cut through the malaise of my thoughts.

"I'm getting the wood. Come with me and get Dash inside."

Before I could even say anything, she was bolting through the living room. She ripped open the front door and took a hard left to go to the wood pile, and I yelled for Dash as I reached for the spotlight we keep inside.

Sasha was already coming back in with an armful of wood and the hatchet by the time I stepped off the porch and was shining the light around the yard, looking for the dog. I yelled his name a few more times before I found him.

He was at the edge of the yard, in the corner of the fence, facing the same spot in the tree line that had gotten him so worked up last time. His tail was down and his hackles were up. For some reason, seeing Dash like that was what gave me the first real blast of fear.

I screamed his name and he whipped around and sprinted through the yard for me as I went back up toward the porch.

I felt it then. The pressure in the air changed, my ears popped, and my mouth started watering. I could taste metal, felt almost nauseated.

I closed the door behind the dog, grabbed the shotgun from the closet, racked a shell into the chamber, checked the safety, and looked over to see Sasha already in the process of making the fire.

I leaned the shotgun on a chair and bent down to help, but Sasha gently slapped my hand away and smiled up at me.

"It's a one-person job, love. I've got this."

I'll be damned if she didn't look excited. I sat down behind her and thought about how lucky I was to find such an absolute rock star.

Dash was in the kitchen and started barking at the porch door, which faced the tree line that seemed to have him so transfixed whenever the light showed up. Sasha looked back at him but kept working. I could feel fear creeping into me. I wanted to fight something, but panic was competing with the anger. Sasha had the fire going on its own within a minute and scooted back to sit next to me, taking my hand. I called Dash over, and he came and joined us, whimpering as he paced around the fireplace.

Sasha and I sat there in silence for a minute or two, watching the fire. I felt enthralled by the fire, *willing* it to grow, almost devoted to the flames. Sasha turned to look at me.

"I...feel it. I feel something. Is that just me?"

"No, no, I can feel it too."

Sasha nodded and stared down at our hands locked together. She looked frightened but determined. After another minute she glanced back up at me.

"We should see if the light's there."

I nodded, stood, and helped her up. I grabbed the shotgun and started slowly making my way toward the door to the office, holding the barrel in front of me, muzzle at forty-five degrees like I was some upland hunter following a gun dog, briefly amused at myself, as I was entirely unsure what I'd even shoot at.

We slowly walked into the office, looked out at the pond, and the light was gone.

That same feeling of emotional and physical relief washed over me. During my real party phase in college, I'd smoked black tar heroin foilies a couple times, and while that was a long time ago, I can certainly remember the feeling after taking a hit, and *that* was the most comparable sensation I could think to associate this with. I let out a shaky exhale as I shivered.

Sasha grabbed my arm.

"Oh my God, Harry, do you feel that?"

"I mean, what?" I asked, reflexively avoiding an affirmative answer as though it would help stymie the reality of the absolutely insane fuckery surrounding me.

"That...that feeling of just, it's like a release; it's amazing!"

She was staring down at her extended arms and started smiling as she looked up at me and went on.

"It's like...it's like my whole body itched, then all got scratched at the same second, then wrapped in a warm towel!" She laughed at herself, then grabbed my arm and took a step toward me.

"Harry, you felt that, right?"

I couldn't help but laugh anxiously and nod. "Yeah, I definitely felt something." Even saying that out loud shot a bolt of anger into me.

Sasha *insisted* on calling Dan and Lucy and inviting them over to talk about what had happened, raising the suggestion in a way that made it clear she anticipated my resistance, almost pitching the idea.

"Sure, give 'em a ring."

Sasha looked startled, but quickly called them. The call was virtually the same as the last one, except this time, Sasha accepted their offer to swing by to check on us.

Sasha tidied up the house a bit in the minutes after the call, while I just sat on the porch as my anger continued to rise. Whatever the fuck they were doing, whatever the fuck was *actually* going on, I was going to find out tonight.

I stood when I saw their truck's headlights coming down the county road and didn't move until I heard the humming diesel engine go quiet and the sound of their boots crunching into the gravel of the driveway. They hadn't even shut the gate behind them before I was pacing down the walkway toward them, hands clenched into fists. It looked like they were both about to speak at the same time when I cut them off.

"I want to know what the *fuck* this is, and I want to know *right fucking now.*"

Dan grabbed Lucy's forearm and stepped in front of her protectively.

"*No more fucking bullshit*, all right? No more bullshit about spirits and rituals and hauntings or whatever the fuck you're trying to package this as."

I didn't realize I was still advancing on the old couple until I saw the fear in Lucy's eyes as they began pacing backward away from me. I didn't realize the rage in my voice until I heard Sasha's and felt her grab my wrist to pull my hand back from its rigid position, pointing into Dan's face.

"*Harry*, stop it. *Harry, stop it right now, calm down.*"

I realized I was almost about to rip my arm out of Sasha's grasp. I turned away from the frightened couple and stalked back toward the house, hearing Dan, Lucy, and Sasha all calling for me as I went but not actually hearing what they were saying. I just knew that if I was near them for another second, I was going to get violent. I was humiliated and furious. I needed to breathe.

Sasha convinced them to come inside while I paced around the backyard feeling helpless, embarrassed, and enraged. I eventually walked out to the garage in a daze with Dash at my heels. I sifted around one of the big Rubbermaid bins where I keep hunting and fishing gear until I found an old, *very* stale pack of cigarettes I remembered having stashed in there the year before. I grabbed the pack, lit one up, and walked back to sit on the steps up to the front porch.

I was trying to clear my mind, running through verses of apologies in my head, when I heard the front door open, and Dan came out, shutting it behind him.

I glanced up at him over my shoulder. Unsure of what to say, I held up the pack of old smokes. He waved a hand and shook his head once. I watched him as he slowly walked over to my left, hooked his thumb in his belt loop, let out a long breath through his nose. He stared up into the woods to the north as he leaned his shoulder on the pillar on the other side of the steps.

I had exactly nothing to say to this man. But it didn't seem he was taking my silence as rudeness, so I finished my cigarette, without either of us saying anything. I wanted to be enraged at Dan, I wanted *him* to be the threat here, but my instincts were fighting that desire— my instincts were telling me that he was honest, and sane. Sasha's instincts said the same, and I trusted hers even more than mine.

I stood and walked across the cement pathway that led from the porch to the front gate, knelt down, and crushed the butt of the cigarette into the grass of the lawn. When I turned back toward Dan, I stared at him for a moment, almost willing him to speak, and he finally broke the silence.

"I'm sorry you're dealing with this, Harry. It's a pain in the ass to have this on your mind, in addition to everything else. I know it ain't my fault, but...I'm just sorry. It ain't easy, Lord knows."

For a fraction of a second, I thought I was going to attack him. The muscles in my right hand tensed, but the urge fled as quickly as it came and was replaced by a feeling of helplessness. I was still reluctant to say anything that would suggest I believed any of this was real. I shook my head slowly as I lit another cigarette.

I took a few drags, then let out a tense breath and looked up at him, then up into the sky, and shrugged. "Yeah, this is quite...quite uncomfortable."

Dan nodded and replied without looking down at me. "Sure is." I walked back up onto the porch, leaned on the pillar opposite from Dan, and looked over toward him to find him staring back at me.

"Look, I just want you two to be safe here. I know I sound crazy, I know you think I'm crazy, but this spirit is real, and it's only going to get more dangerous, so can you do me a favor and just suspend your disbelief for a minute? You need to hear about what you're going to encounter this summer and fall, and if you never want to talk to me again, fine, that's *just fine*, but at least I'll be able to sleep knowing I tried to prepare you two. So, while Lucy and Sasha are finishing their tea inside, can I finish giving you the rundown I started when I first came over here?"

I just shrugged and shook my head, then planted my ass back on the porch steps where I'd been sitting. "Sure, Dan."

Dan cleared his throat as though he was about to spit, but the loogie never came. "You need to understand that there is a *spirit* in this valley, in these mountains. The Shoshone and Bannock Indians' round these parts gave a name to it I never could remember, so I just call it *the spirit*. Strange things happen around here. Strange and dangerous, but only to the people who live in the valley. As I mentioned last time, it presents itself in a different way depending on the season. This spirit ain't one *thing*, so to speak, but it's what's behind or motivating the strange occurrences which you will, unfortunately, come to know."

Dan directed his gaze from where I sat back up into the dark forest. "You kicked us outta here right as I got to tellin' you about summertime, what we call the *bear chase* season. Seems as though y'all have got this springtime spirit waltz down well enough, so I guess we'll pick back up there."

Dan stepped down from the porch onto the top step, then slowly began the process of shifting his weight to sit down—a process that catalyzed a symphony of dull cracks and pops in his knees and lower back, sounds of a man who's lived a life working with his hands on his feet.

"The bear chase is how the spirit manifests in the summer. It only starts when you're outside; might be that you've gotta be outside for it to happen at all. You'll know it's starting because you'll hear a man hollering in a panicked voice. If you follow the noise of his yelling, you'll see him eventually, a butt-naked man, naked as the day he was born, come running toward you at a slow jogging pace. Whole scene is the same every time. He'll be coming at you out of the trees, naked, pecker dangling, and he'll be being chased by a big ol' black bear. He'll be screaming for you to help him, begging you to save his life, and listen carefully: Whatever you do, *do not let that man get close to you*. First thing you've gotta do is get behind something that you can keep between you and him. This fence around the house is more than enough. Based on what I've seen over the years, he can't open gates or doors, or even climb over things more than three feet high, but no matter where he manifests, he'll be coming *straight at you*, so if you can get inside this fence around the house, or behind one of the cattle fences in the pasture, or even behind a big log, you should be fine as long as you keep that distance; the bear will get him."

I'd already heard Sasha read portions of this description of the summertime spirit event in the notes they'd left for us, so it didn't come as a total surprise, but I still wasn't sure how to respond. I just kept working on the cigarette and nodded.

"Do you have a rifle?"

Dan's question surprised me. I looked over at him. "Several."

"What caliber?"

"Well, I mean... I've got a couple .22's, a .22 mag, couple 5.56s, a .308, got a 30-06, a 7mm mag, I've also got—"

Dan put his hands up, nodded, and cut me off. "That's plenty; any of those will do fine—just make sure to have one near the front door at all times, and maybe another in the garage, and *always* bring one with you when you're working on the land. But as a marine, living out here in grizzly and wolf country, I trust you'd do that anyway."

I forced out the only thing I could think to say. "Yessir."

Dan went on. "I strongly recommend shooting the naked man, Harry."

This surprised me, and I almost started laughing as I looked over at him. I shook my head in disbelief, entirely unsure of how to even respond to such nonsense. At the same time, it was so bizarre and Dan seemed so serious. "Shoot the naked man?"

Dan nodded slowly once. "If you don't, the bear will get him anyway, and watching a man get eaten alive as he's weeping, begging you to save him, and shitting all over himself, well, it's unpleasant, no matter how many times you see it. Don't worry about the bear, it ain't a threat; the naked man is the dangerous one. Pretty simple shit here we're talkin' about, though, Harry. Don't let the man get near you or Sasha, all right? He'll tear you apart. But it ain't that difficult, as he's not *that* fast a runner, and neither is the bear; it's like a light jogging speed. Just make sure that when you hear the yelling, locate the bear chase, get some structure between you and him, and shoot him; the bear will drag him off. That's really all there is to it. This whole spectacle usually only happens three or four times a summer, just like the light in the springtime."

I raised my eyebrows and kept my gaze locked onto the lawn in front of us at the bottom of the porch steps, using all my effort to force a nod of acknowledgment instead of starting to scream at Dan again. I finished the cigarette but didn't bother getting up to crush the butt in the grass, just dropped it onto the walkway and stomped it out. I was at my wits' end.

"Boy." The edge in Dan's voice pulled my eyes back up to his. "You've seen the light twice now, so that means you've felt it leave when you get the fire going—you've felt that sensation in your soul and your bones, like a wave crashin' over ya. I know that ain't a feelin' you've ever felt before, so don't bother denyin' it. If you've got any sense, you'd know that ain't somethin' a fairy tale can do to a man. This is real, and for the sake of your wife, you'd better do what we're tellin' you."

He had me there. Dead in my tracks. He was right. That sensation wasn't just psychological. It was as physical and real as any I'd ever felt before.

I watched Dan's face as he looked away from me, up at the night sky. He took in a long, deep breath through his nose. He considered the scent of the air as one would a glass of wine, then he nodded to himself slowly, as though he was confirming some hunch he'd had. He spoke without looking down from the stars.

"Summertime's just around the corner, son. You can really feel it on nights like this, smell it in the air, and it's important for you to remember..."

Dan slowly lowered his gaze and looked across the porch steps at me. "Springtime's the easy one."

PART III

SUMMERTIME

12

SASHA

⟨❦⟩

THE LIGHT CAME two more times before the spring rolled over into summer. Both instances happened under similar circumstances to the first two. Harry and I were cooking dinner or watching a show, and one of us would walk by the window in the bedroom or office that looked to the south, over the meadow and pond, and see the light. The same process would follow, and for me, at least, it seemed to get easier each time. Dash even seemed to gather that it was just a new routine.

Harry went through the motions as well but wouldn't talk about it much. It was frustrating for me, as we were both experiencing the same *insane* circumstance, yet in his reticence I could read his struggle, see him holding on to the notion this was a hoax. Like disbelief was a lifeline. He'd checked his game cameras at the pond after all of the light instances. Each time there was nothing to show for it, the light not being enough to trigger the motion sensor, and each time he grew more frustrated.

As May came to a close, Harry and I started to discuss the next "manifestation" of the spirit more. Dan and Lucy called it "the bear chase," and described it with some pretty frightening language. The night Harry lost his shit and screamed at them as they came through our gate, Dan and Lucy had left us with notes detailing the summer and fall spirit manifestations, and the bizarre little rules we needed to follow for each. They'd also told us that evening how winter was the "off season" around here, and how relieving it is to have a reprieve from the craziness from the end of fall until the beginning of spring.

On a few occasions over morning coffee or after dinner, I'd get out their notes, and I'd read them out loud and try to start a conversation about it. At this point, I felt it was important to take this seriously, but Harry would just nod along or shrug in response to questions. In his defense, *how the hell should I know* was a fair response to virtually any question someone could raise in regard to the notes.

One afternoon in late May, I was working in the little twelve-by-twelve box-kit greenhouse Harry had built next to all the raised beds, Harry was reorganizing a shed, and Dash started going absolutely ballistic over in the corner of the yard. By the time I'd figured out where Dash was and started yelling for Harry, he'd already made it inside and was bounding down the steps from the porch off the kitchen with one of his hunting rifles. I was trying to calm down Dash, while also looking in the direction of his barking, when Harry—who had the barrel of his rifle resting through a loop in the chain-link fence around the yard, looking through the scope—calmly spoke one word that almost made my heart stop.

"Bear."

I started tearing my gaze between the direction he was aiming his rifle and his face. "Where, Harry, *where*?!"

He responded in a steady, quiet voice. "Big dead aspen along the fence line, two hundred fifty yards out. Black bear sow. You'll see it in a second."

I looked back toward the tree line, found the big dead aspen tree I figured he was referring to, and sure enough, within a few seconds, a large black mass came into view in the grassy glade at the base of the tree. My heart was pounding. It was still May, still springtime, but my thoughts immediately went to the summertime spirit ritual Dan and

Lucy had told us about. *The bear chase.* I looked back at Harry's face, not sure what to say.

The anger in Dash's barking had subsided, replaced with a quieter rendition between low growls.

We knew we were in bear country and knew before even meeting Dan and Lucy that seeing black bears, or even grizzlies, was *going to* happen living here. But with everything we'd learned, I couldn't even speak.

"She's got cubs. Two of them. Come look." I felt a surge of relief. I grew up in an area infested with black bears, and a mama with cubs is the *last* kind of black bear you want to bump into, but hearing she had cubs removed my fear that this bear encounter was about to evolve into something more bizarre and presumably traumatizing.

"Here, come look." Harry stepped to the side, holding the rifle in place, and gestured for me to look through the scope. When I did, I could see them much clearer. The mama was standing in the glade, looking in our direction, occasionally glancing quickly over her shoulder in the direction of two adorable little cubs behind her. I watched one of the cubs stand up on its little hind legs to lick at some sap on the white trunk of an aspen tree.

"*Wooow*... our first Idaho bear sighting!" I looked up at Harry, who smiled at me and nodded.

"First bear."

Harry knelt down and gave Dash a double-handed scratch on both of his cheeks. "Good boy, Dash. That's a good boy. Thanks for the heads-up, buddy." Dash looked up at Harry like he was a general from whom he was eagerly awaiting orders. It was precious.

Harry stood up and reached for his rifle. "Take a couple steps back and plug your ears."

I was so confused I shook my head. "*What?* Why? Are you going to shoot it?"

Harry laughed. "Jesus, Sasha, no, but I'm gonna scare the shit out of it. You're supposed to haze them, make them afraid. I don't want a sow with cubs hanging around here, and neither do you."

He was right about that. I remembered the sheriffs telling us to do that in my hometown: scare bears, throw things at them, even shoot paintball guns at them to keep them away. Pretty sure I'd heard the state biologists refer to it *aversive conditioning* at some point. Keeping them wary of people protects them in the long run. Harry gestured with his head for me to move back.

"Wait, Harry, what about Dash? I don't want him to freak out."

Harry gave me a teasing, almost sympathetic smile. "Sash, he's a hunting dog. I've blasted a shotgun directly over his head a thousand times; you've *seen* me do it at least a hundred times. He barely even notices the noise, just gets excited and thinks there's a bird to go retrieve."

Right.

"Cover your ears, babe; this thing's *loud*." I put my fingers in my ears and watched Harry pull the bolt of the rifle back and slam it into place again in a quick motion. He shouldered the rifle, looked out toward the bear, then settled behind the lens of the scope. A second later, the pressure of the blast hit my face as soon as Harry pulled the trigger, the force sending a jolt through his body, the immense boom of the shot startling me regardless.

I pulled my fingers out and was surprised by the still-roaring echo of the rifle blast, surging out and up the mountain through the afternoon air.

I looked back to where the bear and cubs were, to see all three of them quickly turn back toward the national forest, away from our fence line, and bound up into the trees one by one. On cue, Dash had exploded into action, running down the fence around our yard in a full sprint, mouth open in a wide smile, cutting back and forth, looking at Harry for a direction as to where he should go find the pheasant that wasn't actually there.

Harry yelled out to Dash, *"I'm sorry,* buddy, there's no bird this time. Season's coming, though, so I like the enthusiasm!"

Harry pulled back on the bolt of the rifle and sent an empty brass shell spinning into the grass, which he bent to pick up as he walked toward me. I gave him an anxious, uncertain smile.

"What? I shot the dead tree like forty feet away from the bears. They're fine."

I shook my head and laughed. "No, I know you didn't shoot the bear. I'm just…I dunno, I guess I half expected to see a naked man come running down into the meadow."

Harry pursed his lips in response and shrugged. "Not this time, I guess. There are bears here, you know, just like back home. Not all of them are the puppets of some mountain ghost."

I rolled my eyes and took his hand.

The next night, we were playing gin rummy at the dinner table after finishing our meal. At the end of a game, I looked up at Harry. "You stay right there." He gave me a confused look as I went into the office and grabbed a copy of Dan and Lucy's guidelines.

He raised his eyebrows as he saw what I brought back to the table, but I put a finger up toward him.

"Harry, *hush*. I'm reading this and we're going to talk."

He put his hands out in mock surrender. "All right, all right. Let's hear it." I narrowed my eyes at him, then looked down at the page, cleared my throat, and read through the strange playbook. It covered everything from the naked man's appearance to what kind of things you could put between him and yourself, the strangely slow speed of the bear chase itself, how Dan and Lucy thought the bear was *on our team*, all of it.

I put the pages down and looked up at Harry, who had crossed his arms and was nodding along slowly, looking at me without much in the way of discernible emotion.

"So, what are your thoughts? What if this is really about to happen? Entertain the hypothetical for a minute and just talk about it with me. Dan and Lucy said we were gonna see a light in the pond, and we saw it. They said when we light a fire the light goes away, and we saw that. They said we would feel it when the light disappeared, and we felt that. I think we need to at least *have a conversation* about what we do if this, just like the light, is real. Do you have some thoughtful, reasonable disagreement to doing that?"

He raised his eyebrows and cocked his head to the side, giving me a reluctant smile I recognized as his version of an *all right, point taken* face. He took in a deep breath before responding.

"Look, if this shit were to actually happen, we're just going to have to do it live, babe. I mean, seriously, think about it for a minute..."

Harry held his hands out over the table, appearing to emphasize two parallel lines.

"Our property is adjacent to a national forest, with the closest trails only a bit over a mile up the mountain from our property, trail systems used by literally *tens of thousands* of hikers, campers, mountaineers, climbers, back- and cross-country skiers, horseback riders, foragers, photographers, hunters, anglers, state and federal officials, and others throughout the season. Furthermore, as we saw yesterday, there are *actual* fucking bears in this area. Thus, there's a *real-life possibility*, albeit slim, that an *actual, living* person ends up getting *actually* chased by an *actual* fucking bear onto our property. I'm not just going to agree to institute some kill order on strangers getting pursued by predators whether they're naked or not, because that's just...that's just fucking insane, babe."

He made a good point, and I gave him a nod and a moment of silence as an acknowledgment of that, but I wanted to press. He could sense that, and before I could speak, he leaned forward, put his elbows on the table, and continued.

"That being said..." He dropped his smile and looked me in the eye. "The prospect of this crazy bullshit coming to fruition while you are anywhere near it, alone, makes it palatable for me to temporarily engage this ridiculous babble with some legit sincerity. Plus, developing real-life emergency plans for this land is something that makes both of us feel better. I mean, we've talked about general protocols to follow if we have a black bear, grizzly bear, wolves, bull moose, mountain lion, or pack of coyotes come around, so why not this crazy shit as well?"

I crossed my arms and smiled up at him. "Thank you, *sir*."

"So, if everything happens exactly as Dan and Lucy predict it will in their sinister little manifesto, then I will...*shoot the naked man* before he hurts us. Okay?"

I nodded. "Okay." It was clear he'd actually been thinking about this on his own, even rehearsing that little spiel he gave me in his head a bit. "So, you *have* been thinking about this a bit and, dare I say, even taking it a bit seriously?"

He shrugged. "I have a lot of time to think about shit these days."

I smiled back at him but wasn't sure what to say, after a while settling on "This is just fuckin' crazy."

* * *

"What'd Lucy say this 'summer manifestation' is like? I'm sure you asked her about it."

Harry was right about that, but it would be a more accurate description to say that I *interrogated the shit out of her* about it. That night, and over the coming days, I told Harry about every detail of our conversation I could possibly remember.

A couple days after Dan and Lucy had come over after the second light-in-the-pond moment, Lucy called the house one afternoon to ask if I was interested in joining her on a walk the following day. I immediately told her I would love to, and we made plans to meet around 2:00 p.m. on the county road somewhere between our driveway and the gate that opens onto the road from their pasture, and head up toward the national forest trailhead. Harry was a bit suspicious when he came inside that afternoon and I told him about the plan. But, as I pointed out to him, they're our goddamn neighbors, and we'd need to get to know them better if we were going to be living out in the country like this. He did not have a rebuttal but did make a joke about having half a mind to throw on his old "battle rattle" and creep along outside of our view in case she tried to eat me.

The next day, I had a childish excitement to spend time with her. Despite all the weirdness going on, nothing had changed about the immediate and genuine impression she gave off. She just seemed so grounded, so wise. In fact, all the times I'd seen her since first meeting her in her driveway, I'd just become more attracted to her personality, even the way she spoke.

I grabbed the bear spray and my CamelBak, put Dash's collar on him, and headed down the road to meet her. I caught sight of her walking up the road toward me when I got closer to their property.

As I expected, she was nothing but sweet, fascinating, and wise, and I hung on her every word as we walked back toward our place, and then up past our driveway toward the national forest trailhead, as Dash bounded around in front of us, chasing frogs and doing his little dog-in-paradise routine.

She asked all about how we were settling in, asked about Harry, about how he was processing all this strangeness. She told me all about growing up on a sheep ranch a few counties over, about how she met Dan at a dance hosted by the VFW in Rexburg shortly after Dan got out of the navy, what it was like running an active cattle ranch, and interrupted herself every time we walked by a unique flower, fern, or tree to take a moment to point it out and comment on its seasonal timing or some other unique characteristic. Within thirty minutes of our walk, I was enamored with her—the way she spoke, the way she looked at me to listen, the inflections she put on words, the way she looked over the land, the way she carried herself.

She had a very natural, informal sort of country dialect full of *ain't*s and *sure enough*s and goofy old expressions, but it was punctuated with a shockingly robust vocabulary that suggested she must be a prolific reader. I'd never heard anyone speak like her. This woman could be reading from a phone book and I could listen intently for hours. Her sophisticated yet rugged parlance and her physical grace made her like a living artifact. I'd never even been around anyone like her.

When I asked her if she and Dan had any children, she said they didn't, mostly because they both had rough childhoods, but she also made a comment about how "raising children on land like this is, well…it would be awfully difficult, given the strange circumstances."

She looked over at me. "What about you guys, thoughts on having children?"

I shrugged. "Yeah, I mean Harry *really* wants to have kids. I guess I do too, sort of, at least. Life's just been so fast-paced these last years since we got out of college. I don't know, the time hasn't presented itself. Harry isn't piling the pressure on or anything, but it certainly comes up often enough."

She nodded and looked back up the road. "Well, y'all will get it figured out, I'm sure. I certainly wish I'd had kids sometimes, I feel it in my bones some mornings. Then again, every summer I see that naked man, well…I'm awfully happy I never put any little ones through that."

She suddenly yet gently grabbed my arm and gave me a warm smile. "That is not to say I disapprove of it. I hope that didn't come across as some criticism of your and Harry's desire to raise children out here. I think you two could do it and do a fine job of it, I really do. I just…well, I just don't think I'd have had the stomach for it myself, and I certainly have no regrets having made that decision."

I smiled at her in return. "I understand, I think."

We took in the grand view of the whole valley when we reached the top of the hill, where the road leveled out as we approached the national forest parking lot and trailhead. Lucy pointed out the homestead of the Berry Creek Ranch, the home of the mysterious old Joe.

I looked over at her. "So, Joe is the one who taught you and Dan about the spirit, and shared with you the rules and the rituals to follow?"

Lucy nodded. "Joe and his family were the ones who held our hands through the process. Joe's a private man, but a very good man. He keeps people at arm's length, which is natural around this valley. They've just been here so long, they're sort of, well...the *knowledge keepers* of the valley and the spirit. That's quite a burden, puts quite a bit of responsibility on 'em. I think half the reason Joe, his dad, and his grandad started buyin' up the other properties around here is just so they don't have to watch any more newcomers move in and get stuck with this, well...uncomfortable reality. In fact, if you and Harry hadn't snatched up the Seymour place so fast, I reckon Joe would've. He was over in Montana when your place got listed and hadn't bothered to reach out to the real estate company that owned it ever since the Seymours moved, so he never got any early notice of the listing."

I had a thousand questions, but I was trying to be strategic with my interrogation. Luckily, Lucy went on without any prying.

"So, yes. Joe taught us about how to live here, how to navigate the spirit and the seasons, and when the Seymours bought your place in '96, we offered to be the ones to share the knowledge with them—an offer Joe was happy to oblige. So, you're only the second family we've ever had to, well...*bring into the fold*. I think Joe was relieved, to pass that burden on. I think he'd prefer to keep to himself and focus on his ranch, his kids, and his grandkids."

Lucy looked over and gave me an almost apologetic smile. "But trust me, Sasha, it's just as awkward for Dan and me, it really is. It's no easy thing, looking two smart young people in the eye and giving them the lowdown on the spirit. Don't go thinkin' for a second that I fail to grasp what crazy old bats that makes us look like. I grasp that just fine. But it's important."

Lucy's expression got more serious. "If you don't learn about what to do with each season, terrible things can happen, Sasha. Terrible things."

I saw an opening for one of the questions that had been driving me crazy and went for it.

"Lucy, what happens if we don't follow the rules? Like the light, what happens if we don't light the fire? I know you told us about needing to cover the windows if we hear the drums start and not let anything inside, but, like...what *actually* happens if we don't do those things when the drums start?"

Lucy didn't look over at me, just kept her facial expression fixed and held her gaze down the valley. A length of time passed that made me start to feel awkward, and I was about to change the subject when she turned and looked at me.

"It's not good, Sasha. It's why the Seymours left, you see. They followed the rules close enough through the years, did a pretty good job of it, but it was hard with little kids. Eventually, the year they left, in the springtime, they didn't get a fire goin' in time, and well...they paid the price. No one in the family died, or got too hurt, thanks to Dan and Joe intervening, but that's what prompted them to leave. Within a couple days, they had their truck packed with as much as it could carry, called to tell us they were leaving, and they hightailed it out of here."

I wasn't sure how to respond. "But...what happened? What did Dan and Joe intervene in and stop from happening?"

That was the only time on that walk when I saw Lucy look nervous. She bit her lip, looked at the ground for a few seconds, then back up into my eyes. "Sasha, you have to forgive me, but I would like to think about how to answer that question. I promise that I will, but I need to get to know you a little better first. I hope you can understand that."

I was surprised by her answer, but just nodded. "Of course, no problem, Lucy. I don't mean to pry. I just...this is some *crazy* shit. I want to know what I'm up against. I want to understand what's threatening my husband and me...I want to know what kind of danger we're in."

Lucy nodded. She walked up, took my hands in hers, and looked me in the eye.

"I will tell you this: If you do exactly what we told you to do, each season, each time the spirit presents itself, you will not be in danger, and you will be fine. I know this is a lot, I know this is downright terrifying, and I am not going to lie to you, summer and fall are harder than the spring, but I need you to know that Dan and I will do every last dang thing in our power to make sure you and Harry are safe, I promise you that. Okay, Sasha? I make that promise from the bottom of my heart."

I'm not one for this usually, but in that moment, I trusted her immediately. *Entirely*. I felt like I could see her soul, and every inch of my body and mind believed she truly meant what she said. I could feel the pressure in my tear ducts, but I forced it down.

"Thank you, Lucy. Thank you."

I'd wanted to keep asking about the Seymours and what happened to them after they left. I'd wanted to keep asking about Joe and his family, about why it goes away in the winter, about the spirit and the feeling it gave me and every little nuance of all this craziness that had passed through my mind over the last weeks since they had first come over and told us about everything, but I figured there would be more walks, more talks.

We worked our way back toward our property slowly, throwing a stick for Dash, me telling Lucy about how Harry and I met, about his time in the Marine Corps, and about my parents and my strained or minimal relationship with them. Lucy was generally interested to hear it all, asking questions that demonstrated true, sincere interest. But there was one more question I wanted to ask, one that I wouldn't let wait until our next time together.

When we were coming up on our driveway, I turned to look at Lucy and sent the question her way as directly as I could.

"Lucy, is there any way to, I don't know…*beat* the spirit? Maybe not *beat* it, but put it to rest somehow? Permanently?"

Lucy slowly looked up at me with a tight-lipped expression. "No, Sasha. I do not believe there is. Believe me, we've asked Joe that same damn question a hundred different times in a hundred different ways, and he just says something to the effect of what I told you: *'No, but if you follow the rules, you'll be completely fine. The spirit is a part of this land, just like the weather, just like the seasons.'"*

I was not pleased with that answer, but I wasn't going to lean into it. We said our goodbyes, and she asked that I talk with Harry to find a time to come over for dinner, and said she'd like me to come over so she could teach me to ride her horses, so we could ride together. I was *very* excited about that prospect and promised her I would.

That night, and over the coming days, I told Harry about every detail of our conversation I could possibly remember. He was genuinely interested to hear it. I could tell by the questions he'd asked, the requests for more details, and he even suggested a few questions for when I saw her next. However, I think her reticence with respect to certain specific details, like what happened that made the Seymours leave, only served to solidify his suspicion of Dan and Lucy, or at least his belief that we weren't being told the whole truth.

One particular thing that I walked away from that first afternoon with Lucy with—one uniquely nagging subject I wanted to know more about, one I thought about in bed several nights in a row—was what had happened to the Seymours before they left.

Within a few days, I'd made up my mind. I was going to find the Seymours and figure that out for myself.

13

HARRY

THE TRANSITION FROM spring to summer around here is subtle yet decisive. Sunsets feel longer, crickets start to sing, wildflowers start to pop, dust just seems to hang in the air a bit longer. Then, all of a sudden, you walk outside one morning, and you don't see your breath and you can just smell it—summer. Sasha's favorite time of the year, sun child that she is.

I was happy that Sasha was enjoying her time with Lucy. She sure looked up to that woman and fell in with her pretty quick. I couldn't deny it, I liked Lucy as well. And Dan, for that matter, but I wasn't ready to get all buddy-buddy just yet and was resistant toward his efforts to get to know me.

By early June, Dan and Lucy were coming by unannounced at least once a week to drop off fresh-baked bread or an extra tool they had lying around. As much stress, confusion, and frustration as they and their little narrative of hauntings had brought into my life, it was undeniable that they were, otherwise, absolutely amazing fuckin' neighbors.

Dan was pretty busy running an active livestock operation with only seasonal help. The irrigation by itself would be a full-time job, let alone all the other shit they had to do, and I was impressed with how well he was able to do it, from what I learned about his day-to-day while maintaining my place on the periphery of this relationship between our two households.

Sasha started regularly joining Lucy on her afternoon walks up our road into the national forest. They'd bring Dash along as they'd look for mushrooms, birds, and flowers and just talk about life. I was hesitant at first and voiced my concerns about her trusting them too much, but Sasha has always been the best judge of character I've ever known. She's a thousand times more socially aware and tuned in than I am when it comes to reading other people, and up until we moved out here, I'd trusted Sasha's instincts on people's character pretty much entirely and without question. So, I figured I had to let it go and let her make those calls. I did, however, insist that she bring Dash with her every time she spent even a second with those two.

Dash might be a happy-go-lucky golden retriever, but that little fucker was *fiercely* protective of Sasha. Hunting with him over the last five years, I'd seen him take on a number of coyotes and run them off, and I'd seen how quick he was to snarl and snap at a drunk dude or a panhandler who got too close to Sasha in Denver. I knew he had her back.

Part of Sasha's deal with work—in exchange for them allowing her to basically create this remote position for herself—was that she would fly back to Denver once a quarter for a week or so, at least for the first year, so they could schedule some of the bigger, more important in-person meetings with executives from the client companies she worked with as account manager.

They'd scheduled the first one of these trips for the third week of June and bought her tickets a while back, pretty much the week we moved out here. Even just a month ago, she was *very* excited for these trips, and I was excited for her too. She's such a social butterfly, and I knew she'd miss her friends like crazy, so I figured these trips would be important little reprieves from the isolated ranch life so she could get a change of scenery, go eat a nice meal, and spend some time with her friends.

Over the last few weeks, however, her optimism for the trip had waned, and she'd started getting apprehensive, seeing if she could change it or move it back. I knew she was worried about me being here alone for a week with all this crazy spirit stuff afoot, but I convinced her she couldn't just swear off ever leaving the property again. The night before she was set to leave, she was really wigging out about me being here by myself, so I turned her own reasoning against her a bit.

"Sash, come on. You're the one who's so committed to learning to *actively live in this land* and becoming one with this seasonal spirit bullshit and not letting it dominate our lives. You can't tell me that process includes never taking a trip again, can you? Besides, you wanted to keep this job and make this work; these meetings are a big part of that."

She knew I was right but was just anxious. "Harry, I know that. I just...it's summer now. I don't want you here alone with this *bear chase* insanity."

She looked at me to gauge my reaction, and I met her expectations with an eye roll. "When the naked dude runs up, I'm just gonna offer him a beer and load a bowl for him. I think we need to get him high, maybe throw on some Toots, *get him to chill out a bit, man, you dig?*"

She tried to give a stern look but couldn't help but laugh. "Harry, you can't joke about this while I'm not here, seriously."

"I'm gonna joke about this ridiculous nonsense under any circumstances I damn well please, woman." She tackled me onto the bed for that one.

I would miss her, though, and while I still wasn't convinced any of this shit was real, I was definitely going to be on my toes. Truth be told, I'd thought that if this bear chase craziness was true, I'd pay money and blood for Sasha to not be anywhere near it. The way Dan and Lucy described it sounded fucking terrifying, so if this shit *was* real, I'd be supportive if she wanted to spend every damn summer away from this place. Although, I'd also started to think that if all this craziness ended up coming to fruition, I'm not sure we'd actually be sticking around for more time than it took to pack the 4Runner after the first encounter.

I drove Sasha to Idaho Falls that next morning. It was actually pretty nice, having an airport only about an hour and fifteen minutes from our house where there were three flights to Salt Lake a day, where you could then connect to anywhere. Driving up to that terminal was the first time since we'd moved that I felt like I wasn't actually all that far away from society after all.

I gave her a big hug and a kiss before she went in. She held my face in her hands and looked at me.

"Harry, I mean this. You can't forget."

"Forget what?"

"You cannot forget the *plan* we agreed on." We'd agreed that whenever either one of us was outside our fenced yard through the summer, we'd bring a rifle with us, and no listening to music or podcasts on headphones.

"You can't forget, Harry, that little plan doesn't just apply to me, okay? Promise you'll have a rifle while you're working and that you won't listen to music, all right?"

"I promise, love. I'd bring one with me anyway; remember, the *real* bears of the world are all woken up now and looking for chow."

I watched her walk into the terminal and look back to blow me a kiss. I was going to miss her, but I was actually pretty psyched to have some solo time.

The next morning, I was planning on clearing out the decade's worth of debris buildup along the creek bed and culverts where it ran under the driveway.

I called Sasha to check in when I woke up, and she reiterated the music prohibition and the rifle requirement. I promised I'd abide. I gave Dash some food, crushed some coffee and breakfast, and packed up a sandwich for lunch. I was realizing how badly I needed a bit of alone time as well. I'd been building up subconscious stress with the knowledge that Sasha was within the immediate proximity of all this unexplainable and purportedly dangerous shit I had no control over; with her gone, I could feel it start to drain.

I went out to the shed and started loading up the wheelbarrow with a shovel, rake, pickax, and rock bar, then went inside to my gun safe.

I opened up the safe, reached for my 30-06 hunting rifle, but stopped as my hand passed by the barrel of one of the 5.56 carbines I'd built over the years.

They don't let you keep your service weapon when you "retire" from the infantry, but at the time when I got out, if it were an option, I'd have gladly opted to keep my rifle in exchange for the *"honorable discharge"* written in fancy letters at the top of my DD 256 certificate. I felt naked without it. I felt *alone* without it. I made it a week into civilian life before I started building a rifle that was as close as possible to the M4 I rucked around Afghanistan and have built several more since.

Besides lacking an automatic rate-of-fire option, one of these rifles was as similar to my actual service rifle as possible. Same grip, sights, stock, rail, barrel, sling, even dropped most of my paycheck on a Triji-con ACOG scope; all that shit. Only real cosmetic difference between this rifle and the one I had in Afghanistan was *how goddamn clean* this rifle was. It's crazy how pristine a rifle stays when you're not living outside with it in the dusty mountains and using it as a third arm.

I pulled it out and turned it over in my hands, feeling the old familiar weight. For me, just holding the rifle and feeling its contours is like smelling your grandparents' house or something, just a *deep*, nostalgic familiarity. I guess it's my security blanket.

Why not? I grabbed one of its mags, walked out to the wheelbarrow, and dropped the rifle on top of the tools, forcing myself to *actually* drop it several inches, knowing it needed a few scratches, a bit of character.

Dash and I spent the next five hours dredging the stream channel of logs, branches, leaves, roots, and rocks that had clogged it up over the last decade. The early-summer runoff made the stream heavy and ice cold, but it was a pretty hot day, so it was satisfying work, and the dog was happier than a pig in the mud, playing in the water, napping on the bank, and chasing grasshoppers.

Later that afternoon, I walked up the slope a bit from the stream to a rock outcropping in the sun, where I sat and chugged water and wolfed down my sandwich. Dash lay at my feet, and I was plucking small clumps of dried mud from his paws when all of a sudden he shot up to a full standing position, startling the hell out of me. He looked to the southeast, toward the tree line and boundary with the national forest.

I looked as well but didn't see anything. I cannot deny it, my first thought was: *Naked bear dude?* Nope, no naked bear dude to be seen, or heard. I sat there awhile, staring at the tree line, straining my senses, but all I could hear was the stream trying to compete with the symphonic cadence of crickets.

I stood and Dash looked up at me. *"Hey, buddy."* I grabbed a stick from the grass, held it down to where it almost touched his nose, smiled at him, then threw it down the slope in the meadow toward where I'd left the wheelbarrow on the bank of the stream.

He didn't move. He didn't even follow the stick through the air with his eyes. He just held his gaze locked on my face, then looked back to the tree line.

Adrenaline surged through me.

Now, I've had this dog at my side for going on six years. He is a full-on, incurable, *pathological* fetch junkie. Never, and I mean *not one solitary time*, has he ever been in the vicinity of an object that has been thrown by a human and *not* chased after it. He can be fast asleep in a yard, someone throws something quietly, and some primal instinct shoots a signal to his brain that there is something to fetch. So him *not* fetching means either he's extremely sick, or something else of profound significance to his little dog brain has firmly gripped his attention.

I looked back at the tree line. "What is it, buddy?" Dash looked to me briefly, then back at the forest, and began to lower his head while keeping his eyes level. That's his cue that there's something sketchy to pay attention to, and this time, *I fuckin' did.*

I broke into a full run down the hill from where we'd been sitting in the sun, in the direction of the wheelbarrow I'd left on the bank of the stream loaded with my rifle and tools, hollering at Dash to follow me.

He easily beat me to the stream and fell back into his *somethin' sketchy's over there* posture with an unbreaking gaze on the forest to the southeast.

Muscle memory took over the second my fingers made contact with the grip of my rifle. In one familiar motion, I threw the sling over my shoulder, slammed the magazine into the magwell as I began to turn around, yanked the charging handle back, thumbed the safety off, and took a knee as I brought the stock of the rifle to my shoulder and the scope to my eye. I scanned the entire tree line, listening as closely as I could. In that exact moment, the crickets went silent.

I'm not sure I'd ever heard that happen before, anywhere in my life. *Frogs,* when you walk too close to a pond at night, sure, they'll shut up quick, but crickets? In the heat of the day? Never.

Then I heard the last thing I wanted to hear—a man yelling. It was coming generally from the east-southeast. No discernible words, but there was a very discernible tone, and it was *panic.*

My heart rate spiked immediately; my face went numb with adrenaline. I was walking backward with my rifle shouldered, yelling at Dash to follow.

The stream ran another thirty-five yards or so in the direction I was moving before it ran into a big culvert that passed under my driveway, dumping the creek into the natural stream channel that cut through our pasture on the other side of the driveway.

I'd just significantly strengthened all the cattle fencing along the driveway. Getting on the other side of that fence was my objective.

Congrats, Dan, you've got me dancing through more of your spirit-warding pageantry ran through my mind for a split second, but that reverie was interrupted by the first distinctive word that punched its way out of the panicked yelling: *"Help!"*

I was in a slight depression along the stream, so the meadow to the southeast was obscured by the rise, but I knew that's where it was coming from. I was maybe twenty yards from the fence line now, but Dash still hadn't moved from the wheelbarrow, where he was barking in the direction of the yelling—legs splayed out, head low, and teeth bared like a damn coyote.

I added a lot of volume and some snarl into one more "Dash, COME," which did the trick, as he finally wheeled around and sprinted after me.

As I saw Dash start to move, I turned and fell into a full sprint toward the fence line. As we reached the little rise leading up to the driveway, I looked over my shoulder and saw, for a split second, what looked like a naked man waving his hands above his head. It felt like my gut hit the back of my throat.

I slung my rifle across my side, picked up Dash, and half-threw, half-dropped him over the fence onto the driveway. I planted my foot near the middle strand along a T-post and hoisted myself over.

I stumbled as I landed, but caught myself with a palm in the gravel, pulled my rifle around, spun, and brought the scope to my eye. I took in breath sharply in an audible gasp as I beheld what was filling the lens of my scope.

It was a naked man running through the field and down the slope of the meadow toward the opposite bank of the stream where I'd left the wheelbarrow. He looked a bit older than me, early forties, with a splotchy short beard and short, unkempt hair of the same sandy brown. His bare feet were bleeding, and his tallywhacker—as Dan had promised—was flappin' around for the world to see. He was looking straight at me, through the scope and directly into my eye. He looked terrified, desperate, exhausted, *almost* defeated.

I could hear him more clearly now as well: *"Help! Please wait! Help! Help me, please, please, it's going to kill me, sir, please, PLEASE!"*

Holy shit. I couldn't fuckin' believe it. This was it. Dash was going absolutely ballistic, snarling and barking like a possessed fiend. Then I saw what was behind the man for the first time. A black bear. I glassed it in my scope, and it looked, all things considered, like any of the many black bears I'd seen before. It was certainly a big one, around 450 pounds, male, but nothing nightmarish or unnatural, other than it charging considerably *slower* than the speeds I know black bears are capable of.

I refocused on the man, who was now about to splash through the creek, switching his gaze from me, over his shoulder to the bear, then back again. I could see he was crying. Weeping, pathetically. *"Please, sir, ple-he-ease don't leave me to die, please help! Help me! Please!"*

My internal dialogue had devolved into a manic frenzy. *I should shoot the bear, shoot the bear, just shoot the fuckin' bear, man, Dan never said not to, what if this is real, what if this is a fuckin' coincidence and I'm gonna let someone get mauled?*

The man was about to emerge from the creek bed between me and the wheelbarrow, and the bear was going to drop into a nice, clear opening where I could get a clean shot at its vitals. That's when I thought of something.

There's a wheelbarrow full of sharp, long steel tools directly in front and in full view of this naked man. If I was being chased *by a bear,* any one *of those tools would've been at the front of my mind, and I'd make a fucking* beeline *for them, no question at all. There's a shovel, a pickax, and a goddamn spear of a rock bar directly ahead of him.*

I started screaming right back to the man: "Grab the shovel! Grab the rock bar! Dude, grab the rock bar or the pickax and defend yourself! Dude, get one! It's a black bear—you're *supposed* to fight back! If you hit it with a shovel, it'll back off! Hit it, *fight back!*"

He was close enough to hear every word I said, but he didn't break his pleading. He didn't stop to listen to me. He was almost at the wheelbarrow.

My voiced had reached a full scream pitch at that point. *"DUDE, GRAB THAT SHOVEL AND FIGHT. PROTECT YOURSELF, DUDE, FIGHT!"*

He ran right past it. Didn't even spare a passing glance at the wheelbarrow, didn't break eye contact with me for a second.

"Du...dude...what the fuck, man." I felt tears welling in my eyes. Dash was snarling. The man was maybe twenty-five yards off now, still pleading and crying.

"Sir, please save me, p-please, sir, please just help me, h-help me, sir, please!"

I couldn't talk; I could barely breathe. An abridged version of my old combat-panic mantra kicked in. *Deep breath, you need to move, deep breath, you need to move.*

I grabbed Dash by his collar and started hauling him up the driveway. I kept yelling at the man as I went. "Dude...Why not fight it? Why did you not fight it?!"

I wanted a *human* answer out of him. Any phrase or sentence that was even remotely responsive to what I was saying. It's like my entire sanity, my entire grasp on reality depended on him just saying one thing that would prove to me he was a real, thinking person. Everything he was babbling was just so repetitive, and at this point, it was actually strange for him not to respond at all, even if he was truly terrified and in shock.

I thought of trying something else and yelled out to him over his pleading as he was about ten yards away now, slowing as he approached the slope up to the driveway.

"Sir, tell me your name and I'll pull you over the fence. Sir, *tell me your fucking name* and I'll kill the bear. *Tell me your fucking name!*"

He didn't stop his pleading and weeping. He didn't even register that I was talking. It was unnatural, almost robotic. It's like he had a script. I expected him to at least shut up for a second when I spoke, but he didn't.

He began coming up the rise toward the fence line, only a few feet from me now. I frantically switched between training my rifle on the man's sternum and the bear behind him. Dash was barking less but was growling and keeping his eyes on the man. The man adjusted the course of his flight diagonally up the slope to follow us as I continued working my way slowly up the driveway.

We were all so close now I could tell what the dog was looking at, and he didn't even register that the bear was there, only the man. As the man got to the fence, I roared at Dash to come to heel, pointing at the gravel behind me, a command that worked at least enough to get Dash to back up a few steps so that he was standing at my side, still snarling and snapping his jaws toward the man.

The man stopped when he reached the fence, grasping the top strand with both hands between the barbs, looking at me while openly weeping like a child, barely getting coherent words out. I was, for whatever reason, still talking to him.

"Dude, I'll kill that bear if you say your name. *Just say your fucking name, dude!*"

I made a flamboyant display of moving to his right and aiming at the bear while maintaining eye contact with him. "Tell me your fucking name and I'll kill it. Say *ANY PERSON'S NAME AND I'LL KILL THAT FUCKING BEAR.*"

It's like he couldn't even hear me. "*Please, sir, p-p-please help me over the fence, please don't let me die like this, please!*"

I was still screaming at him over his babbling when the bear reached him. For a fraction of a second, as the bear lifted its front paws, I was about to shoot it. I had added probably a pound of pressure to the trigger when something yanked on my elbow, forcing the muzzle of my rifle into the sky. I looked down, and Dash had part of my rifle sling in his teeth and was hauling it away from me almost as if we were playing tug-of-war with one of his toys.

I released the grip and trigger and grabbed Dash's collar. "*Dash, NO, Dash, what the fuck?!*"

Right as I looked back toward the man—standing there holding the top strand of barbed wire, weeping, snot rolling over his lips and down his chin, looking me right in the eye—the bear rose up on its hind legs behind him and sank its claws into his right shoulder, immediately cutting into him like razors, opening deep white gashes in his skin and muscle that I watched quickly fill with blood.

At the same moment, the bear clamped its jaws down on the space between the neck and collarbone on the man's left side. I saw the man's eyes go wide with pure, childlike horror before the bear pulled him back. The man fell onto his butt in a sitting position and began grabbing up at the bear's face, trying to wrench its jaws free.

A bright crimson braid of blood was streaming from the bite between his neck and collarbone, pouring down his chest and stomach into his pubic hair. His screaming took on a new and much higher pitch. I'd heard it before, that sound. It was the jittery, panicked screaming of absolute, life-changing *pain*.

The bear tried dragging him backward at that awkward angle for a moment, then released its bite. The man took the opportunity to desperately roll forward onto his hands and knees, his mouth wide, drool running down his chin into the grass as he wept in slow, defeated sobs.

As he started to crawl toward me, the bear ripped its claw through the man's shoulder blade, turning the man's right side toward the sky, then bit down into the exposed, pale flesh right at the base of the man's rib cage.

The bear shook its head, and I could hear ribs cracking as I watched the man's eyes squeeze shut, his fists clench, and pain wince through his entire body like an electric shock. With its jaws still clamped on the man's lower rib cage and stomach, the bear put its dinner-plate-size claws on each side of its head as though to brace itself—one paw on the man's breast, and one on his hip—then pulled upward with ferocious strength.

I could see the lower portion of the rib cage splinter like wood as it began flipping outward, and below the cap of pale stomach skin in the bear's mouth followed glistening strands of intestines that coiled from the man's trunk, making it look like some grotesque, dying jellyfish.

The man's eyes rolled back in his head momentarily as he let out a guttural moan, then he looked down at his new wound. His eyes widened in shock as he began gasping as though he'd just jumped into a cold lake. The bear released the mouthful of skin, rib splinters, and guts, and with its claws yanked the man onto his back.

The bear looked down at the man in what can only be described as curiosity. The man looked up into the bear's feral eyes and let out a scream louder than any he'd managed thus far, just as the bear clamped its jaws down on his face, each side of the bear's maw seeming to reach all the way to the man's ears, abruptly muffling his scream like a pillow. The man frantically kicked his legs, pounding and clawing at the jet-black fur on the beast's massive shoulders, then the bear started shaking the man's head violently from side to side. I heard it then—a deep, wet crack of the man's neck.

The man's right leg shot out straight away from him, toes pointed like a ballerina's as his nerves fired their last salvo, then every muscle in his body went limp. I felt something in that moment, like a warm, welcome relief. It made me shudder.

The bear let the man's head drop from its jaws and licked a couple times at the blood that had begun leaking out of the man's ears, then looked up at me.

The bear sauntered three or four slow steps toward the fence, snapping me out of the trance I'd fallen into as I watched the man's brutal death. I shuffled backward, so shocked I tripped over myself, landing hard on my ass. I wrenched at the rifle sling to swing the rifle up and level it straight at the bear's head. I was putting pressure on the trigger and about to scream just as Dash pranced by me, putting himself between the muzzle of my rifle and the bear, and took a few steps toward the fence. I figured he was going to try to challenge the bear, trying to protect me, so I started screaming his name and scrambling to my feet, then hesitated.

Dash's tail was up and wagging. It was up in salute over his back, waving back and forth, which it only ever did when he was happy. I looked past Dash to the bear, and realized the bear wasn't looking at me at all. It was looking at Dash.

Then, on my life and soul, I watched the bear nod at my dog. Fucking *nod*.

It was subtle, but it was a nod, unmistakable, the likes of which you'd give someone passing on a sidewalk. Dash just stared back at the bear, seeming to respond with a flourish of increased tail-wagging speed and a quick little jump, lifting his front paws off the ground a few inches, like he does when I'm playing with him. I was speechless.

The bear looked up at me for a half second, giving me only a passing glance, then slowly turned around and walked back to the man. It clamped its jaws down on his upper arm and began dragging the ravaged corpse away. The thick strand of the man's innards trailed behind him; I couldn't take my eyes off it as it snagged on clumps of grass, picking up flecks of gravel and dirt. I was entranced by it.

I broke my gaze away when I realized Dash was licking my hand. I also realized tears were pouring down my cheeks, and that I'd dropped my rifle to dangle by the shoulder sling under my arm. I took in a deep breath, which immediately became a reflexive and desperate gasp for air, as I—or my brain—realized I hadn't inhaled in far too long. I put my hand on my chest and got my breathing under control. My mouth tasted like vomit. Had I puked? No. Maybe? I don't think so. *What the fuck*.

I pushed myself up to my knees and put my arms around Dash, who just wagged his plume of a golden retriever tail and licked my face, bringing me back down to earth.

I thought back on the whole experience and scooted back to take Dash's head in my hands and look him in the eye. Not sure why, but I just wheezed the question out. "Dash, buddy, did you just fuckin' communicate with a bear?"

Not sure what I expected there. Dash just remained a normal-ass dog, panting in my face. What was shocking was how normal he seemed, though. How...*relieved*. He seemed exactly as he had on the four occasions this spring when we'd start a fire and the light in the pond would disappear.

I walked up to the house and collapsed under one of the hose spigots, where I must have chugged a gallon of water. I spent the next half hour in a haze. A surprisingly familiar haze. Felt just like I had after getting into a gunfight—*after* having been awake for forty hours, just full-on battle fatigue.

I sat on the steps up to the porch trying to make sense of what had just happened. What shocked me more than anything else was how I'd just stood there, dumbstruck, watching a man get viciously disemboweled and killed as he shrieked for my help. *Yes*, it all went down exactly as Dan and Lucy said it would, but that fact only served to ramp up my anxiety and panic. I realized in that moment that by failing to help the man, I'd given in to all of this spirit bullshit. I'd stood there, armed with a weapon capable of killing a bear, a weapon I knew how to use very well, and just let a man get torn apart before my eyes. I felt weak, terrified, humiliated, and ridiculous. I began pacing, feeling like I was on the verge of weeping or slamming my forehead into the side of the house.

Before I knew what I was even doing, I had already bounded into the kitchen, torn my phone off the charger, and was fumbling through a description of having just watched a man get attacked and killed by a black bear on my property.

The 911 operator sounded like a younger, slightly annoyed woman. "Sir, I need you to slow down. I need you to tell me where you live, all right?"

Hearing her ask for my address, for some reason, only served to increase my own panicky internal battle between whether I'd gone insane and just let a man get killed before my eyes, or whether I had indeed just witnessed some impossible spirit-motivated fuckery. Her voice triggered an immediate urge to apologize for wasting her time and hang up the phone, which itself triggered a revolting realization that I'd started to believe all this spirit shit. I wasn't ready for that, so I gave her my address.

I could feel my entire conscience and will pouring into each syllable I spoke, as though reporting this bear attack would formalize my disbelief in this mountain spirit, solidify its fictional nature. She said the Fremont County Sheriff's Office would be there soon, and I hung up on her as she was suggesting I wait for their arrival somewhere safe.

As I waited on the steps that led to the gate through the fence into our yard—giving me a vantage point to see the first responders as they came down the county road—I began frantically trying to rehearse my account of events. I was simultaneously panicking at how I would explain my decision to call 911 to Sasha and, to my surprise, how I could possibly justify my disbelief to Dan and Lucy after having just witnessed an event that they not only foretold down to the last detail, but tried, with great effort, to prepare me for.

After what felt like ten minutes, I saw a white truck emblazoned with the county sheriff's emblem making its way up the county road, kicking out a thin wake of dust in its path. I checked my watch and saw it had actually been almost fifty minutes since I had called 911. I stood up and dusted off my pants, giving the driver of the sheriff's truck an awkward wave as he pulled up the driveway, parked next to my 4Runner, and dropped down from the truck.

He was a middle-aged man in a wide-brimmed white cowboy hat. I could discern from his starched uniform, badge, and nameplate that he carried some rank above a simple patrol deputy. He touched his hat in a greeting as he shut the door to his truck, then looked over at the house and yard as he approached me.

"Been wonderin' if someone was ever gonna move in up here, or if ol' Joe was gonna snatch it up."

He was walking more casually than I'd imagine a first responder would upon reaching the scene of a bear attack. He pulled his sunglasses off and put them into his breast pocket as he approached, then extended his hand toward me, giving me an almost sympathetic look.

"Hi there, yeah, name's Harold Blakemore, wife and I bought the place and moved in a few months back."

He nodded as he shook my hand. "I'm Undersheriff Edward Moss. You, uh..." He released my grip and pointed over toward our pastures without looking away from me. "Dispatch told me you called in a black bear attack on a naked middle-aged male; I guess you told 'em it happened over in your pasture."

I nodded. "That's right. I was workin' down in the ditch. When I heard him, I—"

The undersheriff held his palms out toward me, gesturing for me to slow down.

"Hold up there, Mr. Blakemore, just a sec..."

He pointed toward the steps I'd been sitting on. "Can we sit for a minute?"

I was taken aback. "Uh...yeah, sure."

I sat down, and he sat a few feet to my left. He took his hat off, ran his fingers through his hair, then looked over at me. He held my gaze for a long moment and studied my face before speaking.

"Mr. Blakemore, there ain't no reason for you to be calling this kinda thing in. I have it on good authority that you and your wife have been, well...*briefed*, I suppose, by the Steiners on the unique circumstances of this little valley. I can understand you calling this in, but I think you already know there ain't anything I can do about this, and I think you know why."

My head started spinning. I was so shocked I couldn't even think of what to say. I realized I'd started muttering some angry, defensive response about how it's *pretty goddamn normal* to call the authorities when you witness a man get ripped apart by a bear when the undersheriff interrupted me in a tone firm enough to get me to look up at him.

"Mr. Blakemore." He stood up slowly, put his hat back on, and turned to face me. "I don't know if this is the first time you're hearin' someone actually say this out loud, but whatever the Steiners told you about this place, whatever ol' Joe or his family tells you about this place, well...it's true. Might not seem possible, but it is. You need to listen to them, take what they tell you seriously, because if you don't, there ain't a damn thing law enforcement can do for you. You understand?"

I sat there staring up at him like an idiot, at a complete loss for words. He stared back at me with a mixture of pity and sympathy, the way you'd look at an old widower at his wife's funeral.

"Mr. Blakemore, we're here to serve the citizens of this county, and I do not want you to hesitate to utilize emergency services, but when it comes to all *this* business..." He waved his arm out over the pasture, then looked back at me. "You're on your own. In this little valley, only one who can help you is yourself."

I just stared at him, blank-faced, unable to think of a word to say under the weight of the reality that this insanity was real. The undersheriff put his sunglasses back on as he began to speak. "Wild things go on in old country like this, Mr. Blakemore. You've gotta follow the rules. That's really all there is to it."

I was able to force myself to nod in acknowledgment as he turned and walked back toward his truck. I just sat there with the same stupid expression as he drove down the driveway, then down the county road, and I stayed sitting there for a long while after his truck passed out of view.

That evening I spent a long time sitting on the front porch steps. The exhaustion and shock had worn off, and now the reality of everything was settling like concrete setting in the sun. I had spent the last hour in complete silence, going between staring at Dash— who'd not left my side all day—in complete disbelief, and staring at my phone, jostling between thoughts of calling Dan and Lucy, and, more significantly, calling Sasha.

After the undersheriff's visit, the last shred of my doubt and skepticism had drained away, but *calling* Dan and Lucy, having to tell them about what happened, was a step I wasn't ready to take.

When it came to my thoughts about calling Sasha, I knew, first and foremost, that I wouldn't even be able to finish my sentence without her dropping everything and booking a flight home, and if it meant doing so, she would *readily*, without any hesitation or consideration, quit her job on the spot. It was a Sunday, and her biggest meetings—virtually the entire purpose of the trip—were on the following morning and Tuesday. She'd also convinced her parents to drive to Denver to see her on Thursday for dinner, which was no insignificant thing, given what lazy, selfish, stoner fucks they are. That might be a bit harsh, but I was nonetheless quite surprised they'd even agreed to drive to Denver from Pagosa Springs just to see her, and I know Sasha was too, and how excited she was to see them. On top of that, she'd made coffee, lunch, or dinner plans with her best friends virtually every day that week, which I knew was the reason she was most excited and motivated to go on this trip.

On one hand, I felt a sense of duty to be honest with her and tell her everything, which, barring some experiences from Afghanistan, I'd done a pretty good job of since we started dating a decade earlier. On the other hand, if I told her what had happened, she'd drop whatever she was doing and be on the first flight home. Thus, the calculus had been whittled down to weighing (a) how pissed she'd be if I didn't tell her about the bear chase spirit encounter until after her dinner with her parents on Thursday, against (b) how much harm to her career and emotional well-being would come from her virtually *guaranteed* early departure from this work trip and opportunity to spend time with her family and friends.

I decided I'd go with (a). I knew I'd face a shitstorm for it, one I'd deserve, but I figured it was better for her to be pissed at me than miss out on this trip. I did know, however, that if I waited to tell her until later in the week, I'd damn well better have talked to Dan and

Lucy about what happened by then, because her first question would be whether I had done that or not, and her next call would be to Dan and Lucy to tell them for me.

I sat on the porch drinking and thinking until long after dark, Dash and my M4 rifle never more than a reach away. I came to two primary conclusions. First, *this shit was real*. Real as anything else in this life, at least. Second, I could *never*, under any circumstances, let Sasha deal with that bear chase bullshit alone.

* * *

It took me a few days to start feeling half-decent again, most of which were spent milling around the house or going on hikes with Dash up into the national forest. When I'd talk with Sasha, I'd do my best to mask the morass of shock and self-pity in my own head. By Thursday, while certainly still a bit emotionally removed and in shock, I had started to feel all right.

I mean, *shit*, my entire grasp on the order of the natural world had just been fucked by a deceptively murderous naked man and some bear—a bear I'd spent a lot of time thinking about, and had, unbelievably, concluded to be actually *kinda cool*. Thus, despite feeling as though I was starting to take it all in relative stride, I justified a protracted state of emotional confusion.

I called Dan that Friday morning, the day before going to pick up Sasha. I told him I'd been through the whole bear ordeal for the first time and was just checking in as he'd requested. He did not seem that surprised by my call, or the reason therefor, and just asked whether he and Lucy could swing by later that afternoon. They pulled up the driveway *maybe* twenty minutes later.

I offered them coffee, which they accepted. We sat out on the back porch and I walked them through the sequence of events.

Dan let silence hang in the air for a while after I finished my story before responding. "Well, Harry, I sure am sorry you had to deal with that, and as unpleasant as it is, and as crazy as this might sound, it does actually get easier with time. After a few summers here, and a few dozen bear chase encounters, a new coat of lacquer gets slapped on the way you see things. You really will start to recognize how robotic the routine is, how *inhuman* that man really is. I certainly know how unpleasant it is watching him get mauled, and I would strongly recommend just shootin' the weepy bastard next go-round."

Lucy chimed in. "That's not to say, Harry, that it's not traumatizing shooting a man for the first time, regardless of whether it's part of some crazy old spirit's little ritual. That is hard in its own way as well, especially when you aren't used to it yet. Even if he is some manifestation of the spirit, shooting a crying man isn't an easy thing to do, trust me, but again, it gets easier with time, despite how hard that may be to believe."

I looked up at Lucy.

"I've killed men before, Lucy. *Real* men. I'm far more disturbed by the simple existence of this fuckin'…*spirit* than I am by the act of shooting a man who poses a threat to my wife and my home."

They were both quiet, unsure how to respond. A question came to mind, one that would pivot the subject, perhaps to their relief. "So, I mentioned the bear and the dog, their little…*moment*. Can you tell me what on *earth* that shit is about?"

Dan shrugged and grinned as he looked over to Lucy, inviting her to answer.

"We've had several encounters with the bear chase near the pasture where we keep the horses, and in those moments the horses were terribly spooked by the man, but when the bear arrived, it sort of acknowledged them as well. It's hard to describe, but the bear certainly had an immediate calming effect on the animals. The Seymours got a dog a few years after they moved in here, and they told us the same thing, that the bear would acknowledge the dog instead of them. After we'd seen that moment with our horses a few times, shortly after the Seymours told us about their dog, it was noticeable enough for me to bring it up with Joe and his sons one night we were over at their place for dinner. They didn't say much, but they feel as though, well, the bear represents a balance of some kind. Like starting a fire to balance the light in the pond. I dunno . . . I suppose maybe it's some kinda yin and yang sorta thing."

I didn't know what to say to that, but my mind was already moving on. "I want to meet Joe. I want to talk with him about all this shit. Can I just drive over there and introduce myself?"

This time Lucy looked to Dan, inviting *him* to answer.

"Harry, Joe's a busy man, and a private man. He will come by and introduce himself soon, I'm sure, but I can tell you he'd prefer to do that when he's ready."

I bristled at this a bit. "These are pretty fucking extreme circumstances, Dan. If Joe's halfway sane, I figure he'll understand why it's important that Sasha and I learn as much as we can about all this shit."

Dan nodded and put his hands up as though to calm me, making me realize that perhaps a bit of unnecessary edge had crept into my voice.

"I hear you, Harry, but you've gotta remember, this is how it's always been around here. If Joe had his way, y'all never woulda moved into the valley. Not because he has anything against you, but his family spent over a century trying to buy up the parcels around here so that no one else moves in and has to go through this. Joe's a unique man, difficult to understand, but he's a *good* man, Harry, finest man I've ever known, saved my ass more'n a few times. But lemme tell ya, he sure ain't gonna be warm to the notion that he *owes you* something, and, well . . ."

Dan looked up and forced as warm a smile as I think he was able.

"You're fired up, Har. You're pissed, angry at the fact this is all real, but Joe ain't got a shit to give about that. If he'd not been off at auction in Montana with his boys when this place got listed, he'd have snatched it up as fast as he could've and you wouldn't be here at all.

He ain't gonna treat you without respect just because he didn't get to buy this place—he's a fair man—but I think you're gonna wanna *ease into all this* a bit before you go pullin' up to his place uninvited. I'm meeting with him next week to go over some grazing permit work we're doing together for allotment leases from the Forest Service, and I'll make sure to put a bug in his ear about coming and introducing himself, all right?"

I shrugged. "Fair enough."

After we finished our coffee, I walked them out to the gate, Dash prancing along next to Lucy, looking up at her with adoration. Lucy bent down to give him a head scratch, then stood up and looked at me with a mischievous grin.

"I'd wager a buffalo nickel you haven't told Sasha yet about the bear chase encounter."

Dan turned around and looked at me with feigned surprise. "Ohhh, Harry, *you stupid bastard*. She's gon' have your hide, boy."

I couldn't help but let out an anxious chuckle, unsure of what to say.

Lucy wagged a finger at me. "I know that woman well enough at this point to figure two things. One, if you *had* already told her, she'd have boot-scootin'-boogied back here by now, and *two*, she's gonna be awful pissed you didn't."

"Right on both counts, Luce. I'll see you guys soon."

The next morning, on my drive to the airport to pick up Sasha, I started rehearsing my explanation. I was more excited to see her than I ever had been. Not only did I miss her, but I'd realized what a strain my reluctance to buy into all this spirit insanity had put on our entire relationship. From the beginning, we've been on the same page about pretty much everything in our lives. I mean the big shit *and* the insignificant shit; we're just always dialed into the same frequency. Whether it's where we want to live, people we like, people we *don't* like, our favorite restaurants, our expectations from each other, how we spend our free time, favorite foods, favorite places to ski, fuckin' everything.

More important, I think, is our dedication to making every day and every activity into a date with each other. Every night when we cooked dinner and set the table, every night we watched a movie, every time we took the dog for a walk through our old neighborhood in Denver, every weekend hike, every minute working in the garden, even when we'd have fifteen minutes before work to wolf down a bagel, we did everything *deliberately together*, as though it were planned a year in advance.

I don't know how many people have experienced a relationship like that, but I figured it made me the luckiest guy on the planet.

It all hit me on that drive down Highway 20 toward Idaho Falls, the weight of my love for Sasha. I couldn't wait to see my wife, be near her, join her in taking all aspects of our new life seriously.

But I was having flashbacks to a particular morning long ago. A feeling I'd felt that morning. It was freshman year of college, morning after I'd gotten a DUI and been thrown in the drunk tank. I remember sitting in the back of the courtroom in handcuffs, waiting for my arraignment to start as a vicious hangover coursed through my guts and nervous system like an electrical fire. I remember desperately trying to recall whether the deputy had found the little JanSport backpack with my Glock 17 and a bunch of blow inside, which I'd panic-hucked out the passenger window into a snowbank as I got pulled over.

He *didn't* find it, I'd learn a couple days later. Still have that pistol.

Not sure why that memory was coming to mind so vividly, but in that moment, like this one, I certainly knew I was in some deep shit.

14

SASHA

I WANTED TO REACH across the center console and punch him in the jaw, but I knew silence fucked with Harry more than anger.

We weren't even out of the terminal yet when he made some comment like "*So*, I've got something to tell you," but I already knew, I could read it on him. I made him walk me through everything, from the second he first heard the man until the last moment the bear was visible dragging the corpse back into the forest, and then made him recount the entire story again, with even more detail, answering my questions along the way. He told me about having sat down with Dan and Lucy to talk about it, almost as though *I was supposed to fucking thank him* for doing so, which only frustrated me more.

Harry and I had decided not to tell any of our friends or family about the most bizarre feature of our new home, so even after just a week away I'd been dying to talk with him about it all. This anticipation made his confession aggravating.

I got about sixty seconds into a rant about what a piece of shit he was and how important to me it is for us to be completely straight-forward and open with each other, *especially* when it came to this spirit shit, but I forced myself to breathe and change tack.

Harry's the type who can talk his way out of most trouble, or even spin the dynamics of a disagreement so you start to see things his way. Fucker should've gone to law school. He had a decent point, I had to admit that, but not out loud. I wasn't about to give him an inch on this, so I went with the next best strategy, the best way to frustrate him.

Silence. Continuing an argument like this only gives someone like Harry the upper hand, and thus more time to justify his choices. Silence precludes his ability to wiggle his ass out of an argument and makes him marinate in his own bullshit.

I did miss him, though. I missed him like *crazy*. Even after being together for over a decade, being away from him for a week made me feel like a teenager, looking at pictures of him and counting the minutes until I could see him. Maybe it's normal to get sick of someone eventually, and I'd wondered if getting married when I was twenty-three would result in that happening, but I swear...I just want to kiss, hold, fuck, love, and laugh with that man until I'm too old to kiss, hold, fuck, or laugh.

Even so, he sure can be infuriating.

When we pulled into the driveway, I could feel Harry watching my face. It was a *beautiful* afternoon, the sun was beaming, everything was so green, there was a breeze in the leaves. I couldn't help but smile. I looked at the area where he'd told me about the bear chase happening, and it sent a shiver up my spine, but I was still, surprisingly, *so* happy to be home.

I let Dash out of the back seat and grabbed my bags out of the trunk, intentionally depriving Harry of the opportunity to do so, and went through the gate into the yard.

"Sash..."

I'd already decided I was going to pretend I couldn't hear him until I got inside and took a shower. I could hear Harry fall into a jog to catch up to my power-walk pace.

"Sasha, babe. *Sash, come on.*" He gently grabbed my elbow, and I whipped around to face him, staying silent. He looked at me and took a deep breath.

"Sasha, I'm sorry I didn't tell you about the bear chase. I've already explained why I made that decision, and maybe that was a stupid fucking decision. I'm going to let you be the judge of that. I just need you to know that I'm sorry."

I raised my eyebrows.

"I'm also sorry I didn't take any of this...*hoopla* seriously. I'm sorry I mocked everything Dan and Lucy told us, and I'm sorry I ridiculed Lucy's comments on this spirit thing that you shared with me after your hikes. I can't believe I'm about to actually say this out loud, but I'm now *fully* aware that supernatural shit...*exists*, and it exists here, and it exists in a way that can hurt me, and more importantly, can hurt you. There were about forty-eight hours this last week after seeing that bear chase shit go down when I was planning the best way to convince you to move, if not just insist we move and kidnap you if you tried to stay."

Harry put his hands on my cheeks and kissed me.

"We're a team, we'll always be a team, and I should've told you about that...*encounter* as soon as it happened, and I'm really sorry I didn't, okay?"

I nodded and grabbed his hands. "You can't close me out like that. It's not your place to decide what information I can handle and what information I can't. It doesn't matter what you think I'll do, doesn't matter if you think I'd have left Denver and lost my job and missed out on a chance to see my friends and parents. What I do with information, how I decide to act on it, is *my choice*, okay? You decided to fuckin' marry me, so you're stuck with two things. First, you're stuck with the duty and vow to share everything with me, *especially* big, life-changing shit that happens to you. Second, you're stuck with my reactions to information, whatever they may be. *I decide what I do with information*, just like you do, but you *do not* get to decide what information I get or when I get it."

Harry nodded. "I know. I'm sorry."

"Harry...if we're going to live here with this, with...whatever is

going on here, the only way we're going to do that is by communicat-
ing and keeping each other *constantly* updated on everything we learn,
see, and feel. That is *absolutely critical* to making it out here. You've seen
some terrible things, you've had to go through some terrible things,
I know that, and I want to know every single detail, but most of that
terrible stuff happened before we knew each other, so I'm not going
to dig or pry, and you know I never have. But this stuff, the stuff that
happens out here, no matter what it is or how fucked-up, you don't
get to bury that away to protect me, or to protect yourself either."

I knew I was wading into some deeper stuff we'd had to deal with
over the years, but I figured it was warranted.

"Harry...this is a new struggle, a new battle, for you and for me,
for us, and I know I haven't seen this bear chase yet but *I am not afraid
of it*, okay? *I am not afraid of this place*, not with you here, not with
Dash here. I know that now because I just got the first time away from
here, back in our old home with our friends, a normal town where
all of this spirit shit is still fake and fictional, and the entire time I was
there I *could not wait* to get back here to you and to our home. Part of
my acceptance of this place and all of its strange...stuff is based on
the fact that I know we're doing this as a team. Don't you ever again
give me any reason to think that we're not."

"I won't. I promise."

As I spoke those words to Harry, I was surprised to find that I
meant every damn one. Having just spent a week in a place I'd lived
for so long, with friends I loved—a place we could go back to and
be rid of all the craziness in this valley—really made me realize how
much I loved it here. Maybe—just maybe—this spirit exists to make
me love our home's idiosyncrasies even more. Standing in the front
yard looking up at the mountains, feeling the warmth of the sun,
hearing the trees from the forest above the house, *my forest above my
house*, it just made me feel like I was ready to do this, *really* ready to
do this, just completely drink the spirit-ritual Kool-Aid and live here
intentionally, learn every little nuance of this place.

That afternoon, Harry and I walked around the property from where he first saw the man to where the bear killed him. When we were standing near where he told me the brutal ordeal took place, I looked over and he was frozen, staring at something on the ground.

"Har, what is it?" I walked up to his side, my voice yanking him back from some kind of trance. He looked at me quickly, then back at the ground, and knelt down.

He pulled the grass to the side and I could see it then—a big, well-defined bear print, claws and all.

"Holy shit..." He looked up at me, and with just a look, we were able to share the same thought. *This shit really happened.*

That next week was, perhaps, my favorite so far since we'd moved here. On Tuesday evening, we went over to Dan and Lucy's for dinner. They showed us around all their barns and greenhouses and grilled up some steaks. The beef was "from a steer that was born just under those trees last year," Dan said as he stood at the grill and gestured toward the trees with a rusty old spatula.

A few days later, Lucy gave me my first riding lesson. She'd brought out one of her older mares, Lemons, whom Lucy described as "sweet and slow, a perfect horse to learn on." She showed me how to saddle the horse and put on the bridle. The basics seemed straightforward enough: lean forward and she'll walk, lean back and she'll slow, easy on the reins, heels down, and within a few minutes I was trotting around the corral. Lucy wanted me to spend a few more days in the corral getting to know Lemons, and then she'd start taking me on rides through their pastures, then eventually on trail rides up into the national forest. I was hooked. After dinner that night, as we were watching TV, I even showed Harry several horses for sale in the area.

The next afternoon, Dan and Lucy introduced us to their friend Joanne, who was looking for some pasture to lease for a couple dozen sheep, and we jumped on the opportunity as soon as we met her when she stopped by. We had both grown up around forest fires, and we really wanted some animals to eat down the grass—which had already gotten several feet tall throughout our pastures. That afternoon, we hauled the prefab trusses up to the spot where Harry had started the shed, in the trees where Dan and Lucy said sheep end up spending most of the day anyway.

Around 5:00 p.m., I went down to the house with Dash to pee and fill up some water. I'd just come through the gate and was walking past the big cottonwood trees toward the back porch when Dash—who'd been trotting along ahead of me, still carrying a stick in his mouth that I'd been tossing for him—spun around so fast it made me jump in surprise.

"Jesus, buddy, what's up?"

Dash looked right past me, dropped the stick, lowered his head, and let out a deep, low growl.

I whipped my head around just as fast as Dash had, trying to follow his line of sight. Goose bumps shot down my arms and my mouth went dry. Then I heard it.

A man, shouting in a panicked voice.

I was sprinting through the yard toward the back gate, screaming at Harry before I even knew what words to shout. I got around the large canopy of the cottonwood so that I could see up to where Harry was. He was already off the ladder he'd been on when I'd left, working his way down through the meadow in fast strides toward the back gate into the yard.

I looked to the back gate just when Dash went *tearing* out into the meadow, yowling and barking like a much larger dog.

"Dash! Dash, *come!*" I went sprinting after him out the back gate.

Harry was close now, off to my left, and joined me in chasing after Dash. The dog had gotten to where the meadow dropped off toward the pond, and stopped, planting himself and lowering his head, letting out furious barks and snarls I'd never heard him make before.

Harry came sprinting out of my periphery, getting to Dash before I did. I saw that he had his rifle in his left hand as he grabbed Dash by the collar and started hauling him back toward me.

Right in that moment, I saw it, and froze.

A naked man came bursting out of the forest, his pale skin an alarming contrast to the dark green of the young stand of spruce trees he charged through, waving his arms above his head, and, just as foretold, he was screaming for help.

I looked at Harry in disbelief, and he gestured toward the house with his head. He spoke calmly, deliberately.

"Inside the fence, now."

Despite the supernatural insanity unfolding in front of me, I was almost equally surprised by Dash, how *angry* he was, fighting against Harry's grip on his collar, snarling and barking toward the naked man across the pasture. We got to the gate, and I went in, stepped aside to let Harry and Dash through, then shut it behind them. I dropped the clasp over the fence post, dumped the tools out of the wheelbarrow, and flipped it up to lean against the gate.

I heard Harry from behind me. "Sasha, please help me get Dash up on the back porch."

"What're you going to do?"

He ripped back on the little lever thing on his rifle, which I knew meant it was now loaded, then he threw the sling over his shoulder and looked at me. "I'm gonna shoot the bastard. There's no reason to watch him get eaten alive."

I nodded. "All right, okay, but I'm coming with you. I want to see this."

He looked me in the eye and held my gaze.

"Harry, I'm coming with you, period."

He nodded, and we walked over to the fence line on the south side of the yard, closer to where the naked man was running across the meadow. I could see him then. He looked like a normal, naked middle-aged man. Crying, begging, waving his hands in the air, dick flapping around.

I looked over at Harry. "Is it the same guy, like...does he look the same?"

He nodded slowly. "Same dude. Same everything."

I could get a good look at the bear now. It looked, I guess, like any black bear. What was surprising was its speed. It was moving at almost a slow jog.

I looked back at Harry. He stared up at the sky, closed his eyes, took in a deep breath and held it for a second, then slowly let it out as he raised his eyes back down toward the man. In that moment, Harry had an expression on his face that I don't think I'd ever seen. He looked enraged. He looked dangerous.

"Harry..." I struggled to keep a grip on Dash's collar. The man was getting closer as he came frantically loping toward the fence line, which was about thirty feet in front of us.

"*Harry.*" It looked like Harry snapped out of a trance. He looked over at me. "When are you going to shoot?"

"I'm going to let him get to the fence. If it's like last time, he'll stop, so, easier shot."

I nodded and watched his face as he looked back at the scene heading toward us, then looked back at the man myself. He was weeping, drool and snot pouring down his chin.

"Please help me, please, p-please you have got to help me, I'm going to die, *PLEASE.*"

It was revolting. I felt nauseated watching him. There was not a shred of sympathy or concern for this man, this...*thing*. I could *feel* its ruse, its farce; I could feel this was designed to be a trap. I was disgusted by the entire scene. I looked back at Harry. He looked as though he was about to explode into violence, like his entire body was made of twisted chains ready to burst under tension. I actually had to check a surprising urge to take a step away from him.

The man was starting to slow down to a walk as he approached the fence, with the bear, now clearly in view, doing the same. The bear's fur was obsidian black, putting off a sheen in the late-afternoon sun, with eyes almost as dark. The bear was, I guess, actually quite striking—beautiful, even.

Harry started walking toward the fence and looked back at me. "Keep some distance, all right? Just in case something happens." I followed him anyway, stopping about ten feet behind him once he got a couple feet from the chain-link wall that was, I guess, supposed to be enough to stop this man's course. To my surprise, it did.

His fingers laced around the chain links in the fence as he pressed his face between his hands, weeping and begging. What did this thing want? Why engage in all this craziness only for the people who live here?

What happened next surprised me just as much as the bizarre spectacle of this whole bear chase.

Harry lowered the barrel of his rifle and stepped toward the guy, leaning in only a couple inches away from his face. The bear was still coming. I was about to yell at Harry to get back when I heard him speak.

"This land is mine now. I *took it* from you, and you will never, *ever* get it back."

With shocking abruptness, the man's entire demeanor changed. The desperation, sadness, and misery fell from his face entirely. All the terror and dread that had twisted his features just washed away as though it was a mask getting yanked off his face. His expression was that of pure, emotional agnosticism. Just blankness, like an empty whiteboard.

The man then looked off to our left, to the west. The bear was *maybe* thirty feet behind him, starting to slow. A scream at Harry to shoot the man was already loaded in my lungs, but I was transfixed by the man's face as it began to change.

I watched the man's forehead wrinkle slightly. Then, it appeared as though something had registered to him, like he *realized* something, like the view down the valley to the west had just helped him recognize where he was.

He turned back and looked directly into Harry's eyes with an urgent expression on his face. The bear was directly behind the man and had just begun to shift its weight to its back legs when I saw it. A hauntingly subtle, almost imperceptible flicker of anger came across the man's face.

And Harry shot him.

The sudden, deep crack of the rifle made me gasp in the same moment I saw the bullet strike the man directly in his left tear duct. The man's head snapped back from the force of the bullet, and at that same moment, I felt a release of pressure from my head, a release of anxiety.

The man's fingers slackened around the chain links, and a cloud of pink mist, skull fragments, and brain matter haloed his entire upper body as the cloud caught the dark yellow afternoon light. The bear dropped back down to all fours, staring up at the man as his head lolled back toward us. His left eye and the bridge of his nose were just a ragged, bloody crater. His right eye looked like it had been on its way to pop entirely out of his head but had found just a bit of purchase before completely freeing itself from the socket.

The man's jaw worked up and down slowly as the last electricity in his synapses sputtered out, blood now pouring out of his mouth and nose, and he crumpled down into a heap in the tall green grass at the base of the fence. I let go of Dash and took a few steps to stand next to Harry, joining him in gazing down at the man's corpse.

The bear looked from the naked corpse up into my face. The man's blood and gray matter were flecked into the fur around its wild, dark eyes.

Then the bear looked at Dash, who was standing at the fence line now, opposite the bear, all of the dog's rage and angst gone entirely. Dash's light panting made him look almost as though he was intentionally smiling. My jaw dropped in disbelief as I saw the bear *nod* at my dog. Dash wagged his tail and gently pawed at the fence. Harry looked over at me, anger completely gone, replaced by wide-eyed wonder as he pointed at Dash. I couldn't do anything but match his look of disbelief.

The bear looked up from Dash to give Harry and me a passing glance, then looked down at the corpse, nudging the man's bent knee once with its snout. It dug its jaws into the corpse's shin and calf, audibly crunching bones. I winced but couldn't look away. The bear turned about and began dragging the naked corpse into the meadow. Harry and I reached for each other's hands at the same second and watched the grisly procession in silence until Dash broke our trance, doing figure-eights between our legs as he wagged his tail.

Then, somehow having forgotten about it in the violence of the last few seconds, I remembered Harry's little interlude and decision to *talk* to the man.

I turned to face him. "Harry, what the hell was *that*?!"

He looked a bit like a guilty ten-year-old as he released his rifle, letting the sling over his shoulder take its weight. For a long moment he just stared at the ground, scratching the back of his head.

"Honestly, Sash, I have no idea. I just...I wanted to see if I could cut through its little facade."

I wasn't sure how to respond, but I knew that the prospect of messing with this spirit thing by intentionally trying to piss it off seemed *outstandingly fucking stupid* and dangerous.

"I...I don't think that we should do stuff like that, Harry. I have a really bad feeling about *intentionally* trying to fuck with this thing."

We started walking back toward the porch together in the same moment, both instinctively wanting to sit down.

"You're not wrong, Sash, I just...Have Dan and Lucy ever said anything about that? Has Lucy ever mentioned talking to the man, or seeing something like *that* happen, seeing him get, like...confused and frustrated?"

"Not that I can recall. But either way, I still don't like it, Harry. Why did you do that? What made you even *think* to do that?"

For a moment, that unsettling, dull rage I'd seen in Harry's eyes as the man charged toward the fence spilled back into his face, then it faded just as quickly. Harry unslung his rifle and leaned it against the railing, sitting down on the steps up to the porch. "It just hit me, seeing that scene again, seeing you run after Dash through the meadow, seeing you look afraid, hearing fear in your voice. I guess the allure of his whole act kind of washed off, and it was just…cruel, and wicked. I don't know, babe, I was just pissed."

Harry looked down at the grass below the porch but kept talking. "I wanted to see its *real* self." He looked back up into my eyes.

Hearing him say that sent chills up my spine. Still, though, I understood some of what he was saying. The way Harry had just described it—the manipulative, cruel nature of the whole ordeal—I'd been disgusted by it as well as I watched the chase come toward us. I sat down next to him.

"Still, Harry, we need to understand this better. We can't just go provoking it and trying to bully it into showing itself. I think we need to just…follow the rules, as Lucy and Dan heard from Joe. *Follow the rules, and we can live a safe life here.* That's what Dan and Lucy have been telling us. I really think that's what we need to do."

Harry nodded. "You're right." He looked over at me. "I should just put him down when he shows up. No fuckin' around. I won't do that again."

I lay in bed that night staring up at the dark ceiling for *hours* thinking about the whole ordeal. Seeing the man's *reaction* to Harry's challenge, it certainly made me think, for the first time, about an actual solution to it all. I suppose watching the man drop its little act, seeing it change emotions like that, seeing it *respond* to emotions, made me feel like there was more to this than just a rigid model of *encounter seasonal manifestation of spirit, follow rule, banish, repeat*. It seemed too simple, too shallow.

Each season had its own little rule or ritual, so was it really that crazy to think there was some rule or ritual that *made it all* go away, or one that applied to the whole year, or one that put it to rest for longer? *Something* that could interrupt this cycle?

* * *

I had a busy work week following that whole ordeal, but it was difficult to concentrate. I had started to write down questions I had for Lucy. The bear, the bear and the dog, the reaction Harry forced out of the man—it was all congesting my thoughts.

Adding to my distractions was that I'd finally stumbled upon some records regarding the Seymour family, who had lived here before us. For some reason, I had been reluctant to tell Harry about my efforts to track down the Seymours. I wasn't entirely sure why I wasn't sharing what I was finding as I found it, but I told myself I'd fill Harry in once I actually discovered something of meaning.

I had run into a wall trying to find any information about the family through the Fremont County clerk's office, where I stopped by after doing a grocery run into St. Anthony one afternoon. There were some records, but I was basically just turning up old duplicates of documents we already had in our title report. Easements and deeds with their names on them, that kind of thing.

However, a random business search on the secretary of state database turned up a now-defunct LLC that had been formed in 2008 and owned by both Richard and Molly Seymour. *It was them*, the couple that lived in our home.

The LLC had been administratively dissolved years earlier, with *Failed to submit* entered in the 2012 row of the annual report column, and a document titled *Administrative Dissolution* dated for 2013, showing that the LLC had been dissolved due to inactivity. However, there was an agent named Jack Freeman listed in the formation documents, who'd been the one to submit the annual reports from 2009 to 2011. I looked him up and found he was an attorney with a private practice in Idaho Falls, with an address that matched his annual reports. The website for his practice was relatively up to date, with a press release on one page from just a year earlier, so I was optimistic I might actually be able to find this guy.

One early afternoon later that week, Harry had taken Dash on a hike up into the national forest. After I finished a conference call for work, I had a half-hour window before my next meeting, so I called the number that came up for the private law office of Jack Freeman, which was answered after a few rings by an older-sounding woman.

I asked to speak with Mr. Freeman, and she told me to hold for a moment to check if he was available.

As that awkward hold-line music clicked on, it hit me how unprepared I was to *actually* talk to this person, or what I'd even say. I was starting to anxiously click through the collage of PDFs I had open on my desktop, trying to find the old incorporation information, when I heard the gruff voice of an older man over the phone.

"This is Jack Freeman."

"Uh, hi, hi, Mr. Freeman. My name is Sasha Blakemore, and I'm reaching out today about a couple I believe to be former clients of yours, Richard and Molly Seymour. You're listed as the agent of an LLC they formed in 2008, and on the annual reports through 2011." I wasn't sure where to go from there, so left it at that.

He responded right away, with surprise in his voice. "Well, *man alive*, I haven't thought about them in ages! Gosh, yeah, Rich and Molly, I worked with them on their LLC formation over a decade ago now. Did you say your name was Sarah?"

"My name's actually Sasha."

"Oh, Sasha, forgive me. Well, Sasha, how can I help you? Did you personally know the Seymours?"

Did he just say "did" intentionally?

"Actually, I do not know them, but my husband and I just bought the little ranch they used to own, and they were the last ones who lived here. All we know is that a real estate investment firm bought our property from the Richard Seymour Family Trust in 2012 and was going to use it as a part of some big land exchange or something with the Forest Service, but that deal dragged on for a long time and either fell through or, honestly, I don't really know what happened, but we bought it from the real estate investment group earlier this year."

"Okay…" was all he said in response. *Shit.* I needed something more if this guy was going to give me any information, and I was actually pleased with the fiction I had ginned up on the spot, so I went with it.

"We moved in earlier this last spring and have actually found quite a few things that belong to the Seymours. Some of it appears to be of some significant personal and family value, so I'm trying to get a hold of them to let them know we have it. We just want to try to get in touch with them so that we can return their things."

That came out better than I'd thought.

"Well, Sasha, unfortunately Richard and Molly died in, well, I *think* it was all the way back in 2011. Can you hold for one second? I'm going to go grab their file."

"Yeah, not a problem." My heart rate elevated. *Just chill. It's just a coincidence, gotta be.*

I was only on hold for about a minute before the attorney clicked back onto the line, and I could hear he now had me on speaker as he was turning through pages.

"Hi, Sasha, so yes, I was correct in that they died in May 2011. The Seymours had three children, and I'm just remembering now, actually, unfortunately, two of their children *also* died in 2011. They were Rich and Molly's twins, Mark and Courtney, who died. It was a real sad deal. The twins were only seventeen. I know that because I had a *different* attorney, fella out of Boise, reach out to me that following year and tell me what had happened. He had power of attorney over the trust Rich had set up some years earlier, and he was figuring out the extent of their assets and was in the process of selling the ranch up in Fremont County, which I'd assume is now your place."

"Please excuse my typing, Mr. Freeman; I'm taking some notes on my computer."

"Not a problem. So . . . well, actually, that about sums it up. I agreed with the Boise attorney to just let their LLC lapse into dissolution because it's the cheapest way to do that, no filing fees or whatnot. And, well, that's the last I ever heard from them. Tragic stuff. I remember they were nice folks."

"That's very sad to hear. Mr. Freeman, you said they had three children, but only mentioned two, the twins, as having died as well. Do you have any idea who their third child was?"

He cleared his throat before responding. "Well, that's correct. Bethany was the third; she was Rich's daughter from a previous marriage, and the only beneficiary of the Richard Seymour Family Trust, which that attorney from Boise was dealing with. I've got it written down right here. He was pursuing a sale of their, well, *your* ranch on behalf of Bethany during that spring of 2012. Her name is Bethany Rueckert. All I know about her is what the attorney from Boise told me, which is just her name and a phone number. Looks like a landline. I've never actually spoken to her, but I suppose I could give you her information so you can get her family's belongings to her."

I took down the information he provided, thanked him profusely, and as soon as we hung up the phone, I called the number for Bethany. I was starting to panic as I heard the ringing start, unsure what I'd say, and was relieved when it went to voice mail. I left a message asking that she call me back, making only a vague reference to it being about her estate, then hung up the phone.

All of that went down in the span of about ten minutes, so I leaned back in my chair and took some deep breaths. My first thoughts went to Lucy's explanation of the Seymours having left after messing up the springtime ritual, and her reluctance to tell me what happened to them, and Dan and Joe having something to do with helping save them. My anxiety and heart rate were increasing in lockstep as I put the pieces together in my head. I forced myself to actually write down the main facts about the Seymour family that I'd assembled so far.

Seymour family—parents Rich & Molly, twins Mark & Courtney, Bethany previous marriage.
Bought ranch in 1996.
Fucked up starting fire after light shows up in pond, spring 2011.
Leave valley immediately afterward, spring 2011.
Rich and Molly and twins die, May 2011.
Other daughter alive at least until trust's sale of property in spring 2012.

I reread my list, and what felt like a million anxious thoughts and questions flooded through my mind. I took a deep breath and forced myself to write down next steps, something I've always done when I'm overwhelmed.

Talk to Lucy about what made Seymours leave.
Ask if she knew Rich, Molly, Mark, Courtney died within weeks of leaving.
FIND BETHANY.

15

HARRY

THE BRUTALITY OF the experience with this bear chase fiasco was exacerbated by its stark contrast with the beauty of the land around us. The summers here were *absolutely amazing*, and I could actually see myself starting to view these spirit encounters as more of a nuisance than a source of trauma, like mosquitoes or sand flies. Summer living out here was just *too good*. Besides, I had developed a new hobby: toying with the spirit.

After our last encounter with the bear chase, Sasha had asked me to explain my motivations for taunting the man as he stood on the fence. She wanted to know why I was fucking with him. I lied, and told her I wasn't sure, and that I wouldn't do it again.

I knew *exactly* why I did that; I'd been thinking about it since the first encounter with the naked man, and it worked far more effectively than I imagined it would.

I'd run through a hundred different ways to experiment with this whole "summer manifestation": trapping the man in a cage, shooting the bear, shooting the bear *then* trapping the man, trapping *both* of them separately, using bear spray on them, rigging up an electric fence I could spring up between them, you name it. For some reason, one of the more feasible options in my mind was trying to get through to the man somehow.

Seeing Sasha as terrified as she was when the naked man came trundling through our meadow, seeing the fear in her eyes as she chased after Dash, made me enraged in a way I'd never felt before. I wanted to bully the spirit. I wanted to *torture* it. I wanted to see it for what it was, and I knew one of the best ways to get a rise out of a *man* is to taunt him, bully him, fuck with him. I figured it might work with the spirit, and goddamn, *I was spot-on.*

As soon as I'd said "I *took*" the land from the man, his whole act fell apart. The whole terrified demeanor washed away. It was so profoundly satisfying to see, though I'm not sure why. In any case, I intended to explore that avenue, to continue fucking with it if possible. Way I see it, if we could establish this thing had emotions, or was in any way like people—responsive to being *offended*—then there might be a way to actually hurt it. Sasha couldn't know about that little plan of mine, but I figured it was best that way. She had a good point, about the danger in provoking something like this that we don't even understand, but *goddamn* it felt good to discover it could actually be upset by something. It made it feel human, mammalian. Men and beasts acting in anger make mistakes. I've seen it, done it myself. I intended to exploit that, or at least test the waters a bit.

Despite all that craziness, life was good. *Great*, even. Our gardens were popping off, the evenings were warm, bees and birds were everywhere. I'd finally gotten caught up enough to start doing a little fishing. The rivers had started to drop a bit after their spring snowmelt surge, and I'd begun clocking a couple evenings a week exploring stretches of the Henrys Fork and the Fall River, both amazing trout streams just a few minutes' drive from the house. There's not much that I enjoy more than chasing trout with my five-weight fly rod on warm summer evenings. It's about as much fun as I'm capable of having with pants on.

About a week after our second bear chase encounter, I went over to Dan's place one afternoon to have a beer with him. Sasha had been prodding me to get to know him better, and so I finally called him up and asked if I could bring over a six-pack and shoot the shit. He was ecstatic. Sasha teased me on my way out, hoping I'd enjoy my "first date" with Dan.

I brought Dash along and we kicked down the county road, and then worked our way up the Steiners' long driveway through their pastures. It was a solid twenty-minute walk, over a mile, but their property was breathtaking. Being set back from the national forest a bit farther than us, they had an *unreal* view of the Tetons that's obscured at our place, as we were snugged up closer to where the elevation started getting steep.

I could see a tractor driving between two of the big hay barns set away from the main house, kicking up a wake of dust that appeared to fade when it was obscured by the shimmering heat waves rising off the baking pasture.

When we got closer to the house, we walked up on an irrigation ditch with a channel about two feet deep, carrying a fast-moving flow of gin-clear water out into the pastures toward a stand of huge ponderosas where about eighty cows were sprawled out in the shade. It was *hot*, and seeing the water reminded me to take a sip from my water bottle. Dash promptly jumped in, lying down in the water and scooping in huge mouthfuls. When he got out, he shook himself dry right next to me as I was putting my bottle back in my pack. Stinky dog water isn't something I usually enjoy getting showered in, but it was so cool it felt great.

I saw Dan jump down from the tractor and wave me over. Dash ran up to him and started wheeling around and between his legs, Dan clapping his big hands on his back.

"Sorry, Dan, he's a bit wet, couldn't help himself when we got to your irrigation ditch."

He extended his hand to me. "Ohhh, it ain't a bother, Harry."

I pointed up toward the tractor. "Can I help you with anything?"

Dan smiled at me. "I'm gonna call you Blister."

I wasn't sure what he meant, and my facial expression suggested as much, so Dan went on. "I'm gonna call you Blister because you like to show up *right when the work's done*, don't ya?"

He got me to laugh with that. This guy really was a trove of goofy old one-liners. "Well, I'd have come earlier if I'd known you needed an extra hand."

Dan waved my comment away. "I'm just bullshittin', Har. I'm done for the day, ready to call it. Wanna have a beer?"

I rolled my shoulders and gestured with my head at my backpack. "Sure thing, I brought some with me, but I fear they might be kinda warm at this point."

Dan waved for me to follow him toward one of his barns. "Ah well, shit, warm beer's my second-favorite kind."

I followed him into the huge barn, and we went up a staircase along the side wall to what looked like an old hayloft, where there were some Adirondack chairs and a coffee table next to the large opening that looked out to the east toward the Tetons. I walked up to the opening in the wall and gazed over the view.

"*Goddamn.*" I couldn't help but say it out loud.

"Quite the view, eh?" Dan walked over and sat in one of the chairs, reaching out to hand me an ice-cold can of Modelo.

I raised my eyebrows and he threw his thumb over his shoulder toward a dirty little minifridge against the wall. "Figured I might as well keep a few cold cans a' suds up here, with the view and all."

I put my warm beers in the fridge then sat in the chair next to him, and Dash plopped himself down in front of us, giving himself a backdrop of green pastures stretching out to rolling pine forests, all set under the dramatic, jagged granite spine of the Tetons that went up so high a couple of their peaks almost matched the top of the opening in the wall of the hayloft we gazed through.

"Well I'll be, Dash." Dash looked at Dan and acknowledged his own name with some tail wags. "You could be a model with a set like that, bud."

Dan glanced over at me. "So how y'all settlin' in over there? Couple bear chase episodes out of the way, eh? Never a pleasant experience, but I hope y'all are feelin' like you're getting used to it, at least."

I nodded. Even though Sasha and I'd just accepted the reality of this place and started taking all this insane bullshit in stride, it still felt totally insane talking about it with anyone but her.

"Yeah, I suppose it gets a bit less strange each time. What about you guys? I've just assumed we kinda deal with the same shit, same *manifestations* of the spirit each season. Do you guys see the light in that pond near the barn?

Dan pursed his lips and nodded. "That's the pond where the light comes, indeed. We have other ponds, but it's the only one we can see from the house. Figure that's why it's where the light shows up— wouldn't exactly be fair if it popped up somewhere we couldn't see it, right?"

I was unsure how to respond to Dan's suggestion that there was anything "fair" about how this fucked-up place worked, and instead just pressed on with the next question on my mind. "Y'all had any bear chase episodes this summer so far?"

Dan began to nod before he finished a sip of beer. "Sure, two so far. Middle-aged fella with dark hair, pecker flappin' in the wind, hootin' n' hollerin', beggin' for help, ol' Bruno—that's what I call the bear, not sure why, just stuck—chasin' him down. Same shit every summer."

Dan went on to tell me that they'd actually partially designed the layout of their homestead in a way that made it so they always had a healthy lead on the bear chase. With the way their pastures and fencing were set up, they'd usually have a few hundred yards to work with before the man even got close. Both times so far that summer, Dan had popped the naked man with a bolt-action rifle he carried around with him.

The most recent one was just a few days earlier. "Yeah, he actually managed to get to within about a hundred thirty-five, maybe a hundred forty yards. I was embarrassed—son of a bitch showed up right when I started takin' a leak!"

We shot the shit for the next hour. As was the case since the day I met Dan, I begrudgingly liked the old bastard more and more every time I saw him. He had a genuineness to him, a kind of simplicity and poise that suggested deeper intelligence. His entire adult life had been spent studying, working, and living with the quirks of this land.

We'd strayed into talking about his rotation model for his pastures, how much time the cows stayed on one before being moved to another, making sure to time that right with the seasons and grass growth, how much work went into irrigating the pastures and when to start watering each one, the nuances of using groundwater rights and surface water rights throughout the irrigation season, when and why he moved cows to and from his grazing allotment leases on the national forest. It was a big job. He was explaining how he and Joe had a few grazing leases together, and I used the reference to that man to dig a bit more.

"Dan, what's the deal with Joe? I'm really jonesin' to meet the guy. Did you talk to him about getting us together at that meeting you mentioned a few weeks back? I've got about ten thousand questions for him, about the history of the land, about how his dad, grandad, and great-great-great-grandads experienced and dealt with the spirit. I feel like it's gotten kinda strange, at this point, still never having met the man."

Dan nodded along as I spoke. "I told him you were lookin' to introduce yourself, and he said he'd stop by when it was convenient. That doesn't mean much in the way of specific timing, for Joe. But, Harry, there's no reason to force the introduction. Like I told ya before, he'll come on by and introduce himself. He's a private man, and a busy son of a bitch. Both his boys and their families live on his ranch with him, with a whole mess a' grandkids. Between managing a sixty-five-hundred-acre ranching operation and making sure his sons get the gist of the gig so they can take over one day, he doesn't have a whole lot of time for social calls. On top of that, any free time he does scrape together he likes to use with his grandkids, teachin' 'em the old language, and how to track, trap, and hunt, teachin' 'em to ride, and how to pray in their old ways."

Dan took a sip of beer and went on. "Joe considers himself Shoshone and Bannock and is damn proud of his tribal heritage. His people have been living in the upper Snake River Valley for *thousands* of years. Joe's great-great-grandad used to run with a fella named Pocatello, a chief, but when a treaty was in the works in the late 1860s, Joe's great-great-grandaddy said to hell with moving off to the Fort Hall Reservation and worked out a trade for the original land grant, where their homestead still is today. Way Joe tells it, his great-great-grandad figured all you had to do was get a silly piece a paper sayin' you owned a place, and that's all it took for the soldiers to leave ya be. To a certain extent, that proved to be the case. Joe's great-great-grandad and some other Shoshone-Bannock who weren't fixin' to leave the valley set up on their land. Joe's family certainly had to deal with the rustlers, lynch mobs, and scalp hunters over the years, but the government, as Joe says, just wanted *assimilation* in those times, and they figured an Indian who could read and write, who ran cattle and held deeds for land was damn well assimilated, and they left the little band of Shoshone-Bannock alone for the most part, given the fact that they'd set up under the color a' law."

I'd read about the Shoshone and Bannock quite a bit since we'd gotten here, as well as Fort Hall and the treaty Dan was referring to from the 1860s. Knowing Joe's family was a part of all that history just made me want to meet him even more and added another clutch of questions to my list.

"Point I'm tryin' to make here is that Joe's family isn't just the oldest *landowner* in this valley, as Americans would understand it, but they were here for thousands of years before the first white man laid eyes on this continent. Joe's family heritage is limited to what he teaches his kids and grandkids, just like he was taught by his parents and grandparents. He doesn't want his kids and grandkids to have the burden of holding gringos' hands through dealin' with this old spirit. It's a burden, and something he's worked long and hard to rid himself of, understandably so. Between the 1870s and the 1940s, this valley got busy too, lots of settlers moving out here with land grants from the feds."

I nodded. "Yeah, I'd seen on the old property records that there were as many as thirteen or fourteen families living up here at one point."

Dan nodded. "That's right, and Joe's family is the only one still around. Joe's about my age, but you see...*he is the knowledge* of this land. He is the *steward* of these rules and rituals we're all stuck with now. And while he might only be in his seventies, he's got the full weight of hundreds, *thousands* of years of that knowledge in his heart and soul. You and I..." Dan waved his hand out over the land toward the mountains. "We're just passin' through in the grand scheme a' things. Joe's family's been here since before folks like us got here, and they'll be here as long as the air's still breathable. You gotta recognize the significance of that. He ain't interested in regalin' anybody with old tales or stories, least of all a young buck like yourself who just got here. You've got a *lotta years* in this valley ahead of you, son. There ain't no reason to rush a damn thing."

I nodded, feeling a bit defensive. "I'm doing my best to tread lightly here. I had no idea Joe wanted to buy my place when I made an offer, and I had no idea it would be haunted as shit either. I'm just, well...when you moved here, Joe taught you about the spirit and what it all meant. I just wish I could get some of that knowledge as well, from the *real* locals...no offense."

Dan smiled. "Harry, I was younger'n you when I bought this ranch. Joe and I grew up together, in a way, from young, headstrong whippersnappers into the crotchety old bastards we are today. Runnin' steers, huntin', scrappin' with the Forest Service, goat-ropin' all the other neighbors through the seasons and rituals; you name it, we been through it together. Just be patient; he'll come around."

I felt I'd pressed that issue enough. Dan had put it in a new perspective for me as well. All I knew was that there was some ancient fuckin' *earth spirit* threatening my wife and me. I'd seek any information I could about it, from anyone in the damn world who could give it. Hadn't really put much thought into the impact of my being here until now.

Dash and I walked home later that evening, reaching our driveway right when it was getting a bit too dark to see. Sasha was eager for a full briefing on Dan's and my conversation, which I gave as best I could.

The next week rolled around and it ended up being a busy one. The lady Joanne who'd leased our pasture came by and dropped off over two dozen sheep. We'd worked out a deal where, in lieu of payment for water and pasture space, we'd get a percentage of the sheep's sale at auction, and an option to keep some lambs. It was fun having animals around, made it feel like it was a real ranch.

We'd also reached a point in the summer when we were eating salads every night that came entirely from the garden. We had lettuce, chard, tomatoes, onions, peppers, radishes, brussels sprouts, a shitload of herbs, and what was about to be *way* more potatoes than we could eat. We had been worried about the growing season here being too short to have a productive garden, but Sasha was right in calling for the greenhouse to get set up; it really made the timing all work out perfectly.

"Well, honey, how's it feel?"

I was standing on the back porch, looking out over the pasture, watching sheep graze around the pond. An afternoon thunderstorm had just passed through, so the early evening light on the wet grass made the entire property look like it was bedazzled. I turned back to look at Sasha. "How's what feel?"

She pointed out into the pasture. "Being a real-life rancher now?"

I sat down next to her. "Let's wait and see if they don't all get eaten by coyotes, wolves, cougars, and bears before we start calling ourselves ranchers, eh?"

Dash was lying on the edge of the porch, fast asleep. I was about to stand up to go inside and fill my wineglass when I saw the dog perk his ears and look over his shoulder, up toward the rain shed we'd built on the edge of the woods.

Within one second, he'd rolled over so he could get onto all fours, which he did so fast Sasha and I both looked at each other, then back to him.

Slowly, he lowered his head, and his ears went back. I didn't have to wait for this one. I'd grown to trust that dog's instincts more than I ever had before, and I was bounding through the kitchen to the gun safe in the closet, where I yanked out my M4, a magazine, and even had the thought to grab a pair of shooting headphones for Sasha. As I was running through the kitchen toward the back porch, I saw Sasha was standing over Dash now, looking over her shoulder at me with wide eyes.

"He's here..."

"Can you hear him?"

As soon as Sasha looked up at me and nodded, I could hear it: the first frantic cry of the man, his first distinct shout for help, echoing out over the house from somewhere up in the trees to the northeast.

Sasha started to jog across the porch, her sudden movement startling me. She grabbed a dog leash we had on the outdoor dinner table, quickly looped it around a railing, and attached it to Dash's collar, right as he started barking. He gave her a look of betrayal and pleading. Sasha smiled at him and knelt down to scratch his ears.

"Don't worry, buddy, we've got this."

Fuck me. She caught me staring at her with what must've been a stupid look on my face.

"*What?*" she asked, with a look of almost mocking indignation.

"Nothin', babe, you're just... on it. You're a fuckin' rock star."

She smiled at me, then looked back up to the trees, where the frantic cries for help were becoming more distinct.

She stared back at me with a serious expression, turning her entire body to address me directly. "Harry, I'm going to shoot him."

I wasn't able to get out my first word of protest before she continued. "Harry, *stop*. I need to do this. I can't depend on you to be here every time this happens."

She held out her hand for my rifle. I had no rebuttal. She was right. I'd shown her how to use my carbine rifles over the years, once just a couple months back when we shot some targets down in the meadow.

"All right, but come with me. We need to pick a spot on the eastern fence where we can set up where we'll have a good shot as he's coming through the meadow." I started heading toward the base of the cottonwood trees and kept talking as I went. "We'll want to set up *on the fence* so that you don't accidentally shoot the chain link or fence braces."

When we were getting near the fence, I saw the man for the first time. His pale skin made him easy to spot, so long as he was still near the dark trunks and lower boughs of the trees. I gestured up to him with the barrel of the rifle.

"You see him, Sash?"

She nodded.

I picked a chain link around the height of Sasha's shoulders and slipped the barrel of the rifle through. I bent down to look through the scope, making sure it had a good field of view, then stood back, chambered a round in, and thumbed the safety off. With my other hand, I flipped the dial on the shooting headphones and passed them back to Sasha.

"Remember how these work? You'll be able to hear me, but it'll cancel out the noise of the gunshot."

Sasha looked nervous, but she nodded, then whipped her hair into a ponytail, which she tied off with a hair tie around her wrist. She put the headphones over her ears.

"Can you hear me?"

She nodded.

"Okay, the safety is *off*, all right? Remember, snug the stock into your shoulder, and don't put your finger inside the trigger guard until you're ready to shoot. Put the reticle, the tip of the red arrow, right on the target. Try to aim for his chest, somewhere about seven to eight inches above his belly button, all right? Not too high, not too low."

She nodded again. As soon as the words escaped my mouth—my instructions on where to shoot a man, hearing myself tell my wife how to kill a human—I came within a second of just whipping around and shooting him right then. As though she could sense my internal debate, she put her hand on my arm and looked up at me.

"Harry, I want to do this. I need to do this. *I can do this.*" I just nodded and gestured for her to take the grip of the rifle.

She did, and she took a deep breath as she brought the stock to her shoulder and put her eye up to the scope. I wasn't sure whether to watch the man or the equally jarring scene before me: my beautiful wife, wearing a sundress, aiming my rifle at some weeping, naked demon man.

The man was about a hundred yards and change up the hill, coming directly for us. He was completely clear of the last tree, and running through the meadow, crying, yelling, dick flapping; same dude, same vibe, same shit. I couldn't help but shake my head openly. *What the fuck is this nonsense?*

Sasha was switching between looking over the top of the scope, then back through the scope, trying to get the man on-target, which it looked like she finally did when she settled in, pulling the stock into her shoulder and tightening her grip on the hand-stop on the front rail of the rifle.

"Okay, I've...I've got him in the scope. I've got the arrow on his chest." I could see her shoulders start shaking a bit.

"Just take a deep breath, and fire whenever you're ready. There are thirty rounds in that magazine, so if you miss, all you have to do is shoot again. If I need you to stop, or if the rifle jams, I'll put my hand on your back, okay?"

She nodded without taking her eye from the scope. I stood a step behind and a step to the left of Sasha. Watching my wife go through this moment was, to my surprise, *significantly* more fascinating and disturbing than watching this ancient spirit-driven bear chase. Dash was losing it from the porch behind us, his barks echoing off the hillside. I glanced up, saw that the man was about sixty-five yards away now, then looked back at Sasha's face.

She took a deep breath in and let it out slowly. As she started to take another breath in, she fired the rifle.

I looked up and saw the man's body jerk as he clutched a hand down on the left side of his stomach. He stumbled slightly, reached out to brace himself with his other hand, but didn't fall. He got his footing and fell back into the strange jogging pace. He was about thirty yards from the fence now, his face clearly visible. I could see blood pouring down his stomach and onto his hip from under his hand.

"Take another sh—"

My sentence was cut off when Sasha took two shots in fast succession, back-to-back. I looked up and saw the man's arms drop to his sides and his legs lock up. I could make out two dark spots on his chest: one an inch away from his left nipple, and the other a couple inches below the top of his breastplate, directly in the center of his chest.

His limbs went completely slack, and his face lost all emotion, leaving him with a sleepy, confused look. His momentum carried him forward so that he fell straight down, like a little tree, falling flat so that his knees and face hit the ground at the same second, kicking up a neat little halo of dust. His body came to rest in a straight line between us and the bear.

Dash's barking stopped the second his body hit the ground, and a euphoric feeling rippled through my body.

I reached around the rifle and flipped the safety on, then grabbed it by the magwell as I put my other hand on Sasha's back. She stared at the man's body for another few seconds through the scope of the rifle, then released her grip and looked up at me with an expression like a little girl who just saw a magic trick. Just pure wonder.

"Good job, love. Great shooting." She looked back at the bear, which was, I assumed, looking past us toward the dog. We both looked back toward Dash, who was calm now, sitting as though waiting for a treat, tail wagging along the surface of the porch.

We looked back toward the bear just in time to see it scoop up the man's forearm in its jaws and make a wide turn back toward the forest. The man's body flipped over during the turn, exposing wide streams of blood coming from the two new bullet holes in his pale chest, only slightly obscured by a few pieces of grass and dirt that had stuck to the blood.

I slung the rifle over my shoulder and kept my hand on Sasha's back. When the bear had reached the tree line, she turned slowly to look at me, still sporting the look of amazement and shock.

"Are you...glad you did that?"

She didn't appear as though she'd registered my question, but after about five seconds, she closed her eyes and put her hand on her chest and took in a deep breath. When she exhaled, she opened her eyes and looked at me.

"Yes, I am. I needed to do that. I mean, I never, I don't...that was just *insane.*" She was talking fast. "I shot that man, but it doesn't feel like I *shot someone.* Does that make sense? It doesn't even feel like I killed a *bug.* It's like...it felt like I was cleaning something, like I was removing a stain."

We spent the rest of the night drinking wine and debriefing the experience several times over. I felt a mixture of guilt and pride at having allowed her to go through that, but then again, she lived here too and had to deal with this shit as much as I did. There was no protecting her from the need to follow these rules, these steps. She seemed proud and assured, and it was contagious.

* * *

From there, the summer clipped along without any hiccups, with us enjoying every day.

We actually flew back to Colorado for my old college roommate's wedding, which was my first time away from the land. Dan and Lucy were very happy to watch Dash and keep an eye on the place, and while I was pretty anxious about leaving, when we were at the reception, surrounded by friends and familiar faces, I had a moment where I appreciated our new life more than I ever thought I would—crazy spirit bullshit and all. Obviously we didn't bring up any of the spirit craziness in conversation with our friends, but everyone was ecstatic for us, and I'm pretty sure we left that weekend with ten different tentative plans with ten different buddies to come visit that fall. I wasn't sure how that would actually work out—having guests come stay at our place—but we figured we'd cross that bridge when we got there.

As we were driving up the county road toward our house the afternoon we got back, almost within view of the lowest part of our meadow, Sasha reached over and put her hand on my cheek.

"How do you feel? How do you feel coming back here after that, after seeing everyone and being back in the place we used to call home?"

I looked at her. "I feel hungover."

She smiled and gave me a light smack with the back of her hand. "Really, though?"

"I feel happier than I've ever been, I think."

"Me too, Har. Me too."

Dan and Lucy were waiting in the driveway with Dash, who just about jumped into both of our arms when we got out of the car. We promised the Steiners we'd return the favor of watching the dog and keeping an eye on the sheep however we could and managed to convince them to come back over that evening for dinner.

Normally, having dinner with a couple of old neighbors after partying for three days straight, flying hungover, getting off a plane, then driving for an hour and a half would've been a *uniquely* hellish experience for me that I would've avoided at all costs. Alas, despite my stubbornness, Dan and Lucy really had started to feel like family.

It wasn't just this spirit and the seasonal rituals that created the bond; they were genuinely great people. It felt as though we were filling a paternal vacancy for them, given their never having kids. In fact, Lucy said as much to Sasha regularly.

It did get me thinking, though, about how badly I wanted kids. I'd started bringing it up with Sasha more often in the last months. I tried not to be obnoxious about it, and I'd made it clear many years back that I'd let her make that call, but *damn*, I wanted to have children with that woman. In the times we'd talked about it since moving here, it was a fairly easy subject to put on the back burner, given the first couple months of my thinking we had deluded, maniacal neighbors, followed by the next couple months of settling in with the reality that we lived with some freakish, malevolent mountain spirit. However, that uncertainty started to wane as we got the hang of things, so my normal desire to have kids returned. After a few more conversations about it, Sasha suggested we commit to making the decision after the fall, after we'd seen the scarecrow season and had experienced everything this spirit had in store for us. At that point we'd be in the reprieve of the winter, the spirit's "off-season," as Dan called it.

I was ready, though. I wanted kids. I'd wanted them before we even moved, and every day that passed just made me want to start a family here even more.

16

SASHA

N ICE WORK THERE, suga' pie!"

I was walking down through the meadow with Dash. It was a *hot-ass* day. Harry had spent all morning down near our well, clearing the brush and undergrowth away from the pump and meter, as we'd just arranged to have a new pump installed, one with a bit more power, which would allow us to run an irrigation line.

He'd done a pretty good job too, from what I could see so far. There was a ten-foot circle around the existing well pump we were replacing where Harry had run the Weed Eater, then used a shovel to rip up every last root and clear a nice work area.

Harry dropped the shovel and took his gloves off before wiping the sweat from his face with his forearm. He looked up at me and smiled.

"Well, look at you, *cowgirl*—you off to go ride?"

I lifted my new Stetson hat off my head and gave Harry a goofy, overly exaggerated curtsy. Over the last month, I'd gone riding with Lucy at least twice a week, and we'd even taken a few longer trail rides up into the national forest. I'd grown fond of Lemons, Lucy's old mare she taught me to ride on. I'd started to get familiar with her little quirks and tendencies. I loved it, I loved the bond with the horse, getting used to one another, I loved it all, and I'd grown *quite* fond of having a reason to pick up a bit of the attire as well.

"I'm gonna take the Subaru to their place and we're gonna ride from there; I'm a bit late already. We're gonna head up the first trail a ways to the first big meadow, so probably four or five hours. I brought you some water."

I dropped the water bottle near the shovel and gave him a kiss.

"Be safe, Sash, all right?"

I turned and started back toward the driveway, responding over my shoulder. "I will be, don't worry."

"Did you pack the—"

I spun around and cut Harry off. "Bear spray, CamelBak, knife, lighter, snack, and the radio. All packed."

He smiled back at me. "Well, you're all set, then. *Be safe*, love, seriously."

I waved to him and Dash as I drove down the driveway.

This trail ride was special, and I was anxious as hell about it. Not because of the ride itself, but because of what I was going to talk about with Lucy.

A week earlier, I had been working in the office when I'd gotten a call from a number I didn't recognize. I answered, expecting some spam call recording, and was surprised by a woman's pleasant voice.

"Hi, um, this is Bethany. I got a call from this number a couple weeks ago but have been on vacation until a few days ago and am just catching up on voice mails. The person who called left a voice mail that said something about my father's estate or trust or something?"

Holy shit. I straightened in my chair and tried to force the surprise out of my voice.

"Oh my gosh, yes, hi, Bethany. Did I have the right number—is this the Bethany Rueckert who was the daughter of Richard Seymour?"

"Yes, it is. This is Bethany Rueckert. Richard was my dad. May I ask for your name, please?" I could hear a TV playing, and children talking and laughing in the background. The anxiety of what I was about to ask this woman was starting to rocket into my mind.

"Of course, sorry, my name is Sasha Blakemore. I'm calling you because, well, my husband and I actually just bought a little ranch property this last spring out in Fremont County. Please stop me and correct me if I'm wrong about any of this, but we bought it from a real estate investment firm, who'd owned it for several years after buying it from the last people to actually *live* here, who were, if I'm not mistaken, Richard and Molly Seymour."

The other end of the line was quiet for about ten seconds. If I couldn't still hear the children in the background, I'd have assumed she hung up on me.

"Bethany...? Are you still there?"

"Sorry, one second please." I heard some shuffling, and then the sound of a door closing, which promptly muted the sound of the children's voices.

"Excuse me, I needed to go somewhere I could hear you a bit better." Another long pause, but I did not need to prompt a response this time. "Sorry, but when did you say you and your husband moved onto the property?"

"We moved on this last spring, so we've been here for almost six months now."

"So...have you...excuse me, Sasha, but can I ask why you are calling me, please?"

I figured I just had to tell the truth here, so went with it. "Well, I'm not sure how well you got to know this place, but...it's quite *special*, and it's been a very interesting process getting used to living here. I— we, my husband and I—learned that you and your parents had left in the spring of 2011, under what I understand to have been rather abrupt circumstances, and to be completely frank with you, Bethany, given how unique this place is, I thought that it could be *extremely helpful* to my husband and I to learn about what life was like before we got here, and, maybe, if possible, if we could learn more about the circumstances that prompted you and your parents to leave?"

I could hear her let out a shaky breath.

"Can you tell me what your name is again?"

"My name is Sasha, Sasha Blakemore..."

"Sasha, okay, well...First of all, I left that property in March of 1996, and I haven't even set foot in Fremont County since that day. Second, Molly was not my mother; my mother died several years before my dad met Molly. Mark and Courtney were their two children. They were babies when we moved onto that ranch, and I was almost eighteen years old. I was only there for a couple months. So, well...I really don't have much experience out there that could be helpful, and it was so long ago."

"Oh, all right. Sorry to make assumptions; I wasn't sure. I, well...I'm wondering, then, if you know why your parents left? The neighbors here, see, they have led me to believe they left under some pretty unique circumstances, and I just...I'm just trying to learn more about that."

"Sasha, to be honest with you, I didn't speak with my father one single time between the day I left and about a week before he died. Or Molly, or the twins. My dad and I had a bit of a falling-out, and when I left, I...well, frankly, I wanted to get as far away from that property as I could..."

A chill went down my spine. "Oh, okay. I'm sorry to hear that. I guess...well, I guess if you feel comfortable sharing this, could I ask if your father told you anything about why they left this ranch, when you spoke shortly before he died?"

There was another long silence before Bethany responded. "Well, it was a brief conversation. I had received a message at work from a number I didn't know, and my receptionist told me it was someone claiming to be my father. I regret this a little, but I didn't call him back at first. I actually waited a couple days before I decided I even wanted to. I called back the number he'd left, and it was the number to a little motel outside Pendleton, Oregon. They were able to transfer me to the room he was staying in, and it was Courtney who answered. I didn't tell her who I was. I just asked to talk to Rich."

There was a long pause before she went on. "Sasha, our conversation was very brief, and I don't remember it perfectly, but my dad was absolutely frantic. He sounded like he'd lost his mind. He was talking about how *it*, or *something*, had followed them—he, Molly and the twins—and that, ugh..."

I could hear Bethany start to cry.

"Bethany, I'm so, so sorry to bring this up. I feel terrible. I just—"

"No, its all right, it's fine. Um, yeah, he was just talking about how they were stuck, or something. He kept saying, 'It won't let us leave, it won't let us leave.'" Bethany was crying openly now, but a sense of dread was quickly pushing aside my feelings of guilt for making her relive that moment.

"That's kind of it, really. I tried to get him to calm down. I tried to convince him to come to Boise to stay with me and my husband. I tried to convince him to come meet his grandchildren that he didn't even know existed, but he refused. He said he couldn't bring *this*, *it*, or whatever, near us, that he didn't want *it* to find me."

I could barely talk; I was so terrified my hands started shaking. "Bethany, did you know, or have any idea, what he was talking about?"

"Well...I have an idea, though I'm not sure I believe it. A couple weeks after we moved in, the couple who owned the big ranch—I can't remember their names, but they seemed nice at first—they came over and, like...I don't know, gave us this *talk*. I don't remember it very well; it was more than twenty years ago now, but I remember my dad, Molly, and I got in a *huge* fight about it after they left. I wanted to leave that night; I was terrified of that old couple. About five or six weeks later they came by again, and they dropped something off, like firewood or *holy water* or something. They said it was for the 'springtime ritual,' which would be coming up and we'd have to do soon. Something about that conversation just terrified me and set me right off. I got in another huge fight with my dad. We fought all night long, and that next morning, well, I left. I went to live with my mom's sister in Boise, and I, we...we just never talked again. My aunt called my dad too, a whole bunch of times, told him I was there and safe, but he told her he didn't want anything to do with me, that he *wished me well*, and that was it."

I was in complete shock at what I'd just heard, tears welling in my eyes. I had to force myself to respond. "Wow...Bethany, I'm so, *so* sorry about all of that. I just...I'm so sorry."

"Sasha...is that stuff real? Is that stuff they told us about, is that actually...*real*? Wasn't there something about a bear or dolls or something?"

"Well...I mean, kind of, I guess. Yes. I mean, so far as I can tell, yes, it's real. But, hold on, can I ask you one more thing? If you don't want to answer, you don't have to, but can I ask how your parents and siblings died?"

"Well...sure, that's fine. It was in the news, at least local news, a few small papers out in eastern Oregon. About six or seven days after I talked with my dad, he and Molly and the twins were driving on some remote highway in the mountains in Grant County, Oregon, when they crashed their car. The investigators said it looked like they'd hit a bear and then veered off the road, but that's not what killed them. All four of them were in the car at the time, and they left the wrecked car on foot. About three miles from the crash, they found my dad and Molly, their bodies. They had been crushed under a falling tree. They said it was a huge tree, and that it would've killed them instantly. The investigators were confused, though, because the tree was alive. They said it looked like windfall, like a wind gust knocked the tree over, root ball and all, but it was the only one in the area that had gone down. Mark and Courtney kept going. The investigators told me it looked like they tried to get the bodies out from under the tree, but had given up, and had just kept hiking down the valley toward some ranches. They..."

She was crying again and had to take a second to breathe. "I guess a fire started that same day somehow—they think it was lightning—

it burned a few thousand acres. They found Mark and Courtney's bodies together, at the base of a big rock outcropping where it looked as though they'd tried to escape the smoke and flames."

"Bethany, I'm so, so sorry. I, I don't know what to say . . ."

After a while she went on. "And that was, kinda, it. My dad had set up the trust before we all moved out there, and I was the only beneficiary left, so over the next couple years the lawyers and the state just—I don't know how all that works—they sold their things and wrote me a check, and that was it . . ."

I thanked Bethany for everything and told her the truth about how I got a hold of her and apologized for lying to Freeman the lawyer about having some of her family's stuff. She understood and said I should feel free to call her again if I needed to. Her last words had been echoing in my brain for the past week, though, including the moment I pulled into Dan and Lucy's. She'd said, "Sasha, be careful."

I went into the stable with Lucy and we saddled the horses. I gave Lemons an apple I'd brought from home, and we rode up through the Steiners' property to where a cowboy gate led onto Joe's land, where we followed a well-developed path to another gate that opened onto the county road, a short way below the national forest trailhead. The trailhead had gotten significantly busier with hikers and backpackers as summer progressed. It had become normal to see twenty cars up there by afternoon, twice that on the weekends, and the Forest Service rangers drove up and down the road several times a day. It was actually nice, kind of felt like we weren't so isolated. Plus, I got to enjoy seeing people's faces as they stared out their car windows at our property as they'd pass by, looking out at the beauty of our land, eagerly returning a wave from Harry or me.

There was an *amazing* meadow a couple miles up one of the main trails we'd ridden to several times at this point, one with a little stream where we'd water the horses and Lucy and I would take a break, eat a snack, and chat. Last time we even had a couple beers Lucy brought along in her saddlebag. It was heavenly.

This time we reached the meadow quite a bit faster. There are a few rocky, steep spots that were intimidating for me the first couple rides, but it had begun to actually feel natural. Lemons and I were starting to be able to communicate just through touches, a little change in pressure from my thighs, or a slight adjustment in my posture.

Lucy had brought beers again this time, and we sat on a log next to the stream as the horses grazed nearby.

"So, Miss Lucy, I want to ask you something. Something that's been on my mind."

Lucy looked over at me with mock surprise. "Well now, Miss Sasha, please, let's hear it."

I took a deep breath. "So…it's been quite a while now since you said you wanted to get to know me better before you told me what happened to the Seymours. And, well, I got a little curious. Do you remember Bethany Seymour, Richard's older daughter?"

Lucy looked completely shocked. "I…well, yes, I do, vaguely. I remember she left shortly after the family moved in. What about her?"

"Well, I spoke with her last week…" I told Lucy about our entire conversation. I'd rehearsed this, at length, and I had prepared well. I told her about everything, from Bethany remembering when Dan and Lucy had come over, to her and Richard getting into a fight, to them not speaking for almost fifteen years, to the details of that final phone conversation, to how Richard, Molly, and the twins had died.

By the end of it, Lucy had tears rolling down her cheeks and was holding her hand over her mouth.

I took Lucy's hands into mine and looked her in the eye. "Lucy, I need you to tell me what happened to them." I couldn't help it; seeing that sweet woman so upset, I started to cry as well. "I need you to tell me what all of that means."

Lucy put her face in her hands and cried like a child for a solid fifteen seconds. I didn't know what to do. She finally looked up again. She was so beautiful, in that meadow, in that light, even with puffy red eyes.

Lucy took in several shaky, deep breaths before speaking. "Sasha...
honey, we can't leave this place. You, Harry, Dan, myself...we can't
move away from this valley. We can never move away from this valley.
It's part of what the spirit does, sweetie. It's just...part of the whole
craziness we're all stuck with."

I felt like I was going to faint. My vision started blurring. I did not
foresee myself reacting this way, especially with Lucy, but before I
knew it, I'd stood up and was shouting.

"Lucy, *what*?! Are you fuckin' kidding me?! Wh— How...how
could you not *tell us this*?!"

I collapsed onto my ass right there in the meadow and started
crying like a little girl. The pressure and stress of everything finally
just exploded. At some point Lucy had come over to me and put her
arms around me. After a minute or so I caught my breath, and Lucy
moved over to sit down in front of me.

"Sasha, I am *so, so* sorry. I am so sorry I didn't tell you. I just...if
we had told you as soon as we met, there's not a wax cat's chance
in hell you, and especially Harry, would've taken us seriously. I think
you know that, and by the time you were ready to take us seriously, it
was already too late." Lucy took in a deep breath and looked up into
the sky before she continued.

"So far as Joe and his family are aware, and so far as Dan and
I can tell, all it takes is one full season for the spirit to *get its hooks
in you*, as Dan likes to say. Our only experience is with the Henrys,
one of the last families to have a property up here. Bill and Virginia
Henry. When Dan and I bought the ranch, it was Joe, the Jacobsons
at your place, and the Henrys, on their hundred-sixty-acre parcel up
the road from you on the west side of the road. They'd been there
for about thirty years, and a couple years after we'd moved in had
decided they'd had enough. I'll never forget being in their driveway,
with Dan and Joe, pleading with them to stay. Joe was telling them
they knew what it meant if they tried to leave; they knew the spirit
would find them in short order and put them to death. They didn't

care, though; they knew the price and they were willing to pay it. They felt, well…they felt choosing where to die was better than being a prisoner in this valley. I'll never forget watching them drive down the county road. It wasn't even three weeks later, the sheriffs came by on their way up to the Henrys' place to take an appraiser so they could start an estate sale. They told us about how they'd died somewhere on the coast in Northern California; they'd been camping by a river when a flash flood came through, highest flow event they'd ever recorded on that river, and they both drowned. Joe bought their property, tore down the house, but you can still see the foundation poking out of the grass…"

Lucy shook her head and wiped away more tears. "That's the only time we'd seen it happen until the Seymours left. We heard about their car accident, and we heard about the wildfire they died in, and we knew. But Joe knew even before the Henrys left, and the Henrys knew themselves, after seeing some other folks try to leave back in the fifties. Joe'd told us the spirit would kill us if we ever tried to leave. Joe told us we could live here, learn to exist with the seasons, to live with this land, and have a good life, or we could leave and be dead within a month. We begged Joe, *pleaded* with him to tell us some way to break the spirit's hold on us, anything at all, but he said…well, he said there isn't a way to do that anymore. He said there might've been once, but that the spirit figured it out, and it's just the way it is."

Lucy straightened up and took my hands. "Sasha, when we heard someone bought your property, just this last February, we went to Joe to discuss how we'd go about telling you about the spirit. We'd only done it once with newcomers, only with the Seymours, and it went so badly their oldest daughter ran off. We were *petrified* about it, but we knew we had to tell you about it, or you'd see the light in the pond, not light the fire, probably not survive your first spring. It's hard enough trying to get folks you've never met to follow the rules of this valley, let alone trying to convince them to leave straight away or else they'll be cursed forever. You'd have thought we were crazy. We weren't sure y'all would've even taken the fire-lighting ritual seriously. After talkin' with Harry, Dan figured that y'all had a fifty-fifty chance of even making it through springtime. If we'd doubled down and said *you'll be stuck here forever if you stay in this valley another few weeks*, what would you have thought of us? Do you really think you'd have taken us seriously, and just left?"

In that moment, despite every other retching emotion tearing through me, I knew Lucy was right.

I was already rambling before I even knew what to say. "But, Lucy, I've already left twice—I've taken *two different trips* since we've lived here—and nothing has happened."

Lucy just put her hands out and shook her head. "I, well…it just knows the difference between a *trip* and an effort to leave forever. We take trips too, honey, so does Joe, but we always have plans to come home. I don't know what to tell you…the spirit can just tell the difference. It's like the intent to not return is what makes it come after you."

I knew she'd already answered this, but I needed more. "And you've asked Joe about this? You've *begged* him to share anything at all that might allow us to, I dunno, leave again? Break this fucking insanity?"

Lucy just nodded at me slowly. "Sasha, if I had a nickel for every time Dan or I have talked with Joe and his boys about a way to get rid of this kooky shit, I'd be a *very* wealthy woman."

I just sat there shaking my head. "When Bethany told me about how her parents died, I figured it was because they messed up the springtime ritual, which you told me they had right before they left. I didn't think we were stuck here forever under penalty of, well…what sounds like some kind of natural death."

Just saying that out loud brought the whole memory of Lucy's promise to tell me what happened to the Seymours once she got to know me better, and I launched right into it.

I leaned forward, took Lucy's hand, and spoke in as firm a voice as

I was able. "Lucy, you need to tell me *exactly* what happened when they messed up the springtime ritual in 2011. You need to tell me that right now."

And she did.

According to Lucy, Courtney, the Seymours' younger daughter, had seen the light one evening and intentionally didn't tell anyone. She was a teenager, a seventeen-year-old, and just wanted to see what would happen. I guess Richard and Molly only became aware of the light once they heard the drumming start from the mountains. They frantically got a fire going anyway, even though the drumming had already started, but the drumming had only grown louder, and closer. Lucy didn't know much about what happened while the Seymours were in the house, as Richard and Molly had been in a frenzy to get away from the property as soon as Dan and Joe showed up, but they'd spent three days locked in their house. *My* fucking house. All they told Dan and Joe was that the house had been "surrounded," but they didn't know *what* surrounded it.

Joe and Dan had some kind of meeting scheduled with Richard about setting up a new irrigation system, which Richard had completely missed, so the other two men had hopped in the truck to go see if he was home. When they pulled into the driveway, they saw that all thirty cows and sheep the Seymours had on their property had been skinned—their skins were sewn together with sinew and stretched into bloody, grotesque sails between the cottonwood and aspen trees that surrounded the house, with the animals' entrails festooned through the branches, and the skinned carcasses piled up to block the front door to the house. Lucy wasn't sure why or how Dan and Joe's showing up had interrupted the chaos, but somehow their arrival put a stop to the disturbing siege that had befallen the home. *My* home. She said that when Dan and Joe moved all the animal carcasses blocking the front door, when Richard and Molly emerged from the house, they fell into fits of exhausted rage, and sat in the yard ranting about the *things on the roof—the giggling, shrieking things on the roof.*

I sat there in awe as she told me the whole story. It was a stunning feeling—being told a repulsive, terrifying story as I sat in an abrasively beautiful mountain meadow.

Eventually, when the sun started to dip, we started our ride back down the mountain.

We passed a group of five backpackers on our way down. They looked like college students, young and fit, smartly clad in the freshest Patagonia and Arc'teryx gear. They all stepped to the side as we rode down the trail, smiled and waved. One of the girls even took her phone out and asked if she could take a picture of me, commenting on how great my boots and hat were, and what a "badass" I looked like. I couldn't even respond to her. I just stared down at her, almost confused, as Lemons and I trotted by.

Young, happy people, not much younger than I was, who could have been any group of my friends from back in Colorado. A former home to which I could never return.

Lucy apologized and cried some more once we got back to her place. Dan welcomed us and helped us unsaddle and brush the horses. He could tell there was something wrong, and all Lucy had to do was give him a whispered sentence, and a look, and he knew.

Before I left, he came up and gave me a big hug. He held me by the shoulders for a minute before letting me go and looked at me.

"Sasha...if I could go back in time and have a chance at convincing you and Harry to leave, I promise I'd have done it. But we just didn't think there was any chance on this earth y'all would've listened."

I'd had some time to think about that since learning all of this a few hours earlier on the mountain. I recognized and appreciated what a tough position they were in. They really did have a choice...either tell us *everything*, and we wouldn't have taken any of it seriously, or just tell us how to get through the spring.

Either way, we wouldn't have left—we would've stayed through the springtime at least—and by then, it would've been too late anyway. "I understand your decision, Dan." A tear rolled down his cheek.

Before I got in the Subaru to drive home, Dan called after me.

"Sash, if I might ask...how are you planning to break this news to Harry? I'm just wondering if I should take Lucy to go hide up in the woods for a few days. As good a man as he may be, I have a feeling he won't be as understanding as you on this."

I'd thought about that as well. "Dan, I'm gonna give it a few days to think about. I think it'd be best for us all to tell him together. Either way, I'll let Lucy know before I do."

As I pulled into my driveway, I thought back on the drive home from the airport in June when I was so furious at Harry, so angry at him for not telling me about the first bear chase encounter. I knew how hypocritical it was, but I also knew it was for the best to keep this information to myself for a while, until I figured out the best way to tell him. It was my turn to keep a secret for the greater good—at least that was the excuse I'd hold on to for a while.

17

HARRY

"Shit, Dan, just come out and ask it. All this lead-up is an awful strenuous length to go just to pry for morbid answers to morbid questions. I ain't afraid to talk about this stuff. I just ain't bringin' it up on my own, so you gotta just ask."

"All right, shit, Harry, we ain't gone down this road yet so I figured I'd just feel ya out first, kinda like a new rifle, or a woman, you know?"

I chuckled and reached my hand out for another beer.

We were in Dan's little hayloft man cave, looking out at the beautiful view. It was surprising how the greens and emeralds of the valley got replaced by browns and tans as the heat of the summer bore down on the land. Dan and I had turned our little beer-in-the-hayloft sessions into a fairly regular thing. He was a smart fella, and a trove of knowledge. I enjoyed the hell out of talking with him. He had been taking time out of what I knew were busy days to come help me at our place.

He'd brought his Ditch Witch a few weeks earlier to help me dig some new drainage ditches along the driveway, and he'd bring over hay and feed in his tractor for the sheep and kept refusing my offers of cash, saying he'd just give me a total at the end of the year. Dan would say "you want some alfalfa mix in their diet and I've got a barn full. Joanne keeps 'em alive but feeds 'em the cheap shit; you gotta spoil 'em every once and again."

Dan even helped show me the best way to mend leaks in the sprinkler lines through our yard. He took me into town to the hardware store to show me the right size couplings to buy and then helped me make the repair. He was like, well…a *dad*. First dad-like figure I'd ever had, at least.

I opened my beer as Dan finally asked the question I knew he'd been wanting to ask me for a while now. "So…you ever kill anybody over there?"

I finished my first sip and nodded. "Yeah, I killed some guys."

"Well…how many?"

"Four, for sure. Four I shot and watched die, but I don't know the total for certain. There were a handful of others I could've killed. It's not as clear-cut as it is in the movies, or when you're shootin' at the old bear-chase fella, for instance. Sometimes it is, but mostly it's not. Some guy takes a potshot at our patrol from a ridge above us, a dozen of us light up his position, we find him dead, no sayin' who actually killed him. Or you think you hit someone, they fall, get up, and run off; could've just nicked him, could've missed him entirely, or you could've put one through his liver and he runs off to bleed out in a poppy field, can't say for sure. That kinda shit just happens in combat."

Dan stared at me for a long moment in the low evening light. "Well, I'll be damned. Who was the first one?"

As I recounted the story, I had a flashback to six months ago, sitting in the VA clinic in Denver, walking Dr. Peters through the same experience—shooting the two men hiding behind that old dusty sedan. I gave Dan the basic details of that day, and as we sat there in silence I thought about the way the first guy crumpled onto his face, the look of surprise the second gave before he died.

"Well, what about number three, then?"

I chuckled and took a sip of beer. "Well, sure. Number three was actually just a couple days later. Old grizzled fella, kinda like yourself, probably fifty-five, sixty years old, at least. We were in a city called Mar-jah; it was a whole big mess, quite a fight, actually. We were securing this canal crossing, L-shaped ambush-type security formation; my platoon was all hunkered down behind cover. We had two old Toyota SUVs fulla dudes with AKs roll up and stop behind a sedan we'd rolled out into the road to block it off. Someone kicked it off, I don't know who, but all of a sudden our whole platoon was just unloading everything we had into these two trucks. I was on their right side, behind a little stucco wall, aiming at the rear passenger-side door of the second truck, the one in the rear of the pair, and that old Taliban fella tried to get out. Last thing he ever did was try to get out of that truck. He died right there."

I thought back on that moment. The door of the truck was stuck or something, like the child lock was on, so the guy actually reached out the window to open the door from the outside and I shot his forearm. I remembered how shocked I was by how much blood came from that hole I put in him, how it cut bright red channels through the dust caked on the truck's door. He yanked his arm back inside the vehicle, then leaned out with his left hand to try again, reaching across his body and exposing his head, and I shot him right then. Once in the jaw, and then again in the eyebrow...

"Goddamn, Harry. And you're tellin' me there's a fourth?"

"Number four came along a few weeks after most of the heavy fighting in Marjah had calmed down. We were still in Helmand, we were still in the same area, but out in the countryside. Poppy country. *Dope* country."

Dan laughed.

"We were on patrol and got ambushed by what sounded like fifty dudes but ended up just being four... NCO in my platoon got hit and we all dropped to the deck. I crawled over to the side of the poppy field along a ditch and saw a dude running, real low, right toward me with an AK, scared the absolute piss outta me, but... I got the draw on him, and that was that for him; he died in that poppy field."

In reality, that guy scared me so bad I emptied my whole mag into him, or *at him*, barely aiming at all, missed half the shots I took I was shaking so fierce, pretty sure I shot him in the foot, neck, and ten other spots in between. We just scared the shit out of each other. I can remember the look of shock on his face as he died.

Dan nodded slowly. "So, what about the potential others? Any of those clearer than others, any *strong* maybes?"

I scratched my chin. "During the heavy fighting in Marjah, February, car fulla fighters tried to break through our sector and ran into our whole damn company. I wasn't in a good position when we made contact, so by the time I moved past this little wall and started shooting into the guys in the back seat, I'm pretty sure they were dead. I mean *at least* ten to twelve of our guys were already lighting up that rig, so chances are pretty damn slim anyone was still alive. I just don't know for sure... There was one dude, in the back, who I know I shot. Like I said, there were so many of us shooting, I think one of those poor fellas was able to shoot back maybe once or twice, but they were toast the second they ran into us."

Dan and I sat quietly with our beers for a while.

"Well, thanks for sharing that, Harry. I know you're a tough son of a bitch, but reliving those moments can be rough no matter who ya are. I'm fascinated to hear about it because, well... If I tried to count, I've *technically* shot and killed a man, let's think... around two hundred times? But that's our summertime visitor, and while he screams like a man and he dies like a man, he ain't really a man, so, sure is strange hearing stories about *actually* killing someone."

I hadn't thought about that. I nodded, then looked back up at Dan. "Well, for what it's worth, anatomically... it's pretty damn similar, shooting a real man and shooting the naked man. Seems like he's made up of all the same parts."

Dan looked past me, seeming to consider this. I glanced at my watch and realized I needed to start heading back home for dinner, and announced as much by standing and stretching my back a bit.

"One thing, Dan." I hesitated for a moment, considering how to frame this request in a way that didn't make me seem duplicitous. "I haven't…well…some of the things I told you today…I haven't exactly…"

I looked at Dan's expression. He was confused. I sighed, embarrassed to some degree by what I was about to admit.

"I haven't told Sasha about them. There are just certain things I've done that I've tried to keep…keep her away from and, as close as her and Luce have become, I wouldn't want Sash hearing this stuff by—"

"Say no more, bud. I understand. Today's words stay between us."

I studied his face, surprised by his immediate agreement and total lack of judgment or lecture on being more open and transparent with my wife.

He gave a frowning nod as if to say, *You got it*.

On my walk home that evening I could tell that the seasons had begun to change. Not *really*, but you could see it in little things, like the light in the late afternoon, the tips of the aspen leaves starting to turn, the smell of the wind.

We'd started to wonder whether we'd get another bear chase fiasco, or rather *when*, and as the weeks drew on, it started to make me a little anxious, almost just wanting it to happen to get it out of the way. Something heavy seemed to be on Sasha's mind as well, but with all the shit we were going through—having to digest and simply accept this wholesale revision to all we understood about the natural world, everything we thought was *real*—the once-simple inquiries of *What's on your mind?* or *Is there something bothering you?* became almost comically out of place and meaningless.

Even so, she was happy, perhaps as happy as I'd ever seen her. She was inhaling books on gardening, land management, and livestock, cooking amazing meal after amazing meal from our gardens, riding horses several times a week with Lucy, giving video-chat tours of the land to all her friends, smiling and laughing more than I could ever remember. Her happiness was all I needed to feel the same.

18

SASHA

Iɴ ᴛʜᴇ ᴅᴀʏs that passed after my conversation with Lucy, I was living in my head. Harry had noticed that something was up, but I was good at pushing things to the back of my mind. While I did not tell him about how we were trapped here, never allowed to move again under penalty of some fucked-up natural death, I did tell him about what Dan and Joe had found at the ranch after the Seymours had messed up the springtime ritual. About the skinned animals, the carcasses in front of the door, and the Seymours losing it and leaving that very day.

I just wasn't sure how Harry was going to take finding out about being locked into this valley. I wanted to be as certain as I could be that I shared this information at the right time. After all, the big revelation of the news that had been haunting me was just that we were going to have to live here forever, which, I supposed, was our plan anyway, right? I figured *maybe* I'd just wait to tell Harry about how the spirit would kill us if we tried to move once moving was actually on the table.

Harry was getting more and more comfortable here as well. Or perhaps he was getting more and more comfortable with the fact that our land was possessed by an ancient spirit. He had been out bow hunting for elk the weekend before, and he was getting Dash ready for grouse season. He was in heaven. Seeing him get happier and more content helped me justify keeping the news to myself about not being able to ever leave.

Harry and I were in the garden one afternoon, at the end of our "big potato day." I never thought I'd have a *big potato day*. We'd ended up getting more wooden fencing material and *way* more soil delivered than we'd needed, so after building all seven raised garden beds we had planned on, and filling those with all the plants we'd started in the greenhouse, we'd still had a bunch of stuff left over. Harry went ahead and used the leftover materials to build one big raised bed, fifteen feet by six feet, and just filled that thing with potatoes. *Only* potatoes. So, we'd decided that before it got too cold at night, we were going to go pick them all and sell them at the farmers market. Our first actual sale of produce from the land. It had us pretty giddy.

I pulled up a clump of around a dozen of the red-skinned potatoes and held them out toward Harry. "We made these together, love, and we're gonna sell them for people to eat in their own homes; how cool is *that*?"

Harry smiled at me, then walked over and grabbed me around the waist and pulled me into him.

"How about we go make something else together, eh?"

I rolled my eyes and kissed him. Another of Harry's *let's have a baby* jibes. They never bothered me; he never laid on the pressure too thick; it mostly came up in that same way: He'd make a joking comment like that, I'd roll my eyes, and we'd leave it. He told me before we even got married that he'd let me make the final call on having kids, and barring the occasional comment about it, he'd respected it ever since.

That's when it hit me like a truck.

Since Lucy had told me about the whole *we're stuck here forever* element of living here, up in that mountain meadow about a week and a half earlier, a million different implications of that reality had run through my mind. But standing out in our garden in Harry's arms was *somehow* the first moment I'd been hit with the realization that *having children* here would mean *they* would be stuck here as well— for their whole lives. I felt nauseated as the thought catalyzed a spurt of guilt and panic that rose up through my gut.

"What's wrong, babe?"

I shook it off. "Nothing, love. Just a bit thirsty; it's a hot one."

I went inside for a glass of water. I'd always been on the fence about having children. I was never *against* the idea, and I had fantasies about raising a little boy or a little girl, watching Harry be a dad, but I was just never super jazzed about the idea either. Even so, for some reason, the weight of it all, the knowledge that having children here would mean they'd be born with the spirit's hooks in them as well, brought tears to my eyes. A wave of anger at the spirit, at this place, rolled up inside me. All this time I'd perceived this spirit business as being kind of like the weather, or the land itself, just something completely timeless and out of our control. But thinking about what this meant for kids, if we ended up deciding to have them, it was so fucking *personal*.

I looked out through the screen door leading from the kitchen to the porch and watched Harry as he loaded a wheelbarrow with potatoes, and it all boiled over. Tears started pouring from my eyes. I went into the bathroom to sit down and collect myself. I needed to tell him. I couldn't keep this to myself any longer.

I went back out onto the back porch and looked down at Harry as he washed his hands under the hose. I didn't even have to say anything for him to know something was up.

"Sash, what's going on?" He turned the hose off, looking at me with concern in his eyes, then walked up the steps to join me on the porch. Dash trotted through the yard after him.

"Harry, I need to tell you something," I said. He just looked at me, confused, and nodded for me to go on.

I looked down for a moment, then met his eyes as I began to speak. "Week before last, when Luce and I went on that trail ride, up to the big meadow, she told me something. I just...I just haven't been sure when the right time to tell you would be, or how to tell you."

Harry didn't say anything, just held my gaze. I crossed the porch and sat down on the bench under one of the kitchen windows.

"I told you about what Dan and Joe found up here, in the yard, in the trees, when they came up to check on Richard, about what had happened after the Seymours failed to start a fire in the springtime once the light showed up. What I didn't tell you is what happened after that, and what it all means..."

From there, I let it all spill out, without any interruption. It came out a bit scattered and manic, but I didn't want to miss a single detail. The Seymours, talking to their daughter, how her family had died, how the Henrys died, what Lucy told me about being trapped here. I went through it all.

We'd moved over to the outdoor dining table during my monologue. Harry hadn't spoken a single word, just sat there and took it all in. Once I'd finally finished, he leaned forward and looked at me.

"So, let me make sure I got all that..." When you know someone really well, all you need is a few words to know they're about to make you litigate the validity of information you've only just learned yourself.

"When the Henrys left, in the seventies, they died a couple weeks later in a flood in California. Then, when the Seymours left in 2011, they died a couple weeks later in the whole car crash, tree falling, forest fire combo in eastern Oregon. Bethany left *before* her first spring season here started in earnest, and she's alive...so basically, we have two families that died, almost forty years apart, and they were killed by things—flood, car crash, falling tree, forest fire—that kill people in the western United States every year. I'm sorry, but are you telling me this *entire theory* about being cursed to live here forever is *entirely based* on just these two events that happened over a span of four decades? That's our complete evidence file on this theory? *Just those two* instances?"

I had to admit, even though I had no reason to doubt what Lucy had told me after seeing all the other ridiculous, impossible shit they'd promised us would come true, hearing Harry put it like that made me briefly question the reality of it all myself.

"Well, it's not just that those two things happened right after people tried to move away from this valley, Harry, but also the fact that the week Dan and Lucy moved here, they were told that was exactly what would happen, *then it did*. Then, some years later, another family was told they'd get killed if they tried to leave, they left, and *exactly* what they were told would happen, *happened*. Dan and Lucy told us we'd *feel* when the spirit left, and we did. They told us about every single detail of the bear chase, and *it happened*. Even a *goddamn cop* told you to listen to Dan and Lucy and that this was all real."

Harry was about to launch into some rebuttal, but I cut him off. "You can choose not to believe it all you want, all right? Just like you chose not to believe we'd see some unexplainable light in our pond, just like you didn't believe starting a fire would make it go away, just like you didn't believe the bear chase would happen, just like you didn't believe the bear chase was caused by the spirit after seeing it *with your own two eyes*. You can choose not to believe this as well, but what's the common denominator between all those *other* things you chose not to believe? I'll tell you what it is… *They fuckin' happened, and you were wrong*."

That came out harsher than I'd expected it to, but it *felt* good.

I leaned back in my chair and watched Harry's face as he looked at me for what felt like a long time. He stood up and walked over toward the railing of the porch, looking out over the meadow. I stood as well and was walking over to join him when he turned back to face me.

"That's a decent point there, love."

"Harry, I'm sorry I didn't tell you when I found this out. I know what a hypocrite I am for it, I just…"

Harry looked down at nothing for a moment, then up into my eyes. "You just felt like you wanted to wait until the time was right." He gave me a mischievous grin. Seeing him smile flooded me with relief.

"I suppose we're even then, Sash. I suppose you owed me one for keeping the first bear chase encounter to myself."

"No, this is bigger than that; this is more important. I'm really sorry, Harry. I should've told you immediately. I should ha—"

Harry reached out and grabbed my hand. "Sash, I understand. I'm not upset, okay? I'd have probably also simmered on this one for a while."

I kissed him, and we stood there leaning on the railing for a bit until Harry spoke again.

"Guess that kinda puts the kibosh on having kids, though, huh? Bringing kids into the world for them to just be stuck here forever. Maybe a hundred years ago, but…just doesn't seem right, making that choice for others before they're born."

Hearing him say that triggered such a strong, immediate pang of guilt, it made it feel like my stomach flipped into a knot.

It had taken me a week and a half to even *consider* what never being able to leave meant for having kids, and it was clear that was one of the very first things to come to Harry's mind. Tears started welling in my eyes. I couldn't help it.

"I'm so sorry, Harry. I'm so, so sorry. I know how bad you wanted to have kids here. I know how bad you wanted to raise a family here with me."

I just let it go in that moment, floodgates opened, and I was crying like a child. The pressure of it all fell on my shoulders, and I felt trapped, guilty, and just angry at the reality we were facing. Harry pulled me into his chest.

"It's not your fault, Sash. I know you were on board, but at the end of the day I'm the one who talked you into coming here. And besides, we've been saying for months now how we can see ourselves living here forever despite all the craziness, and clearly, we can still take vacations, we can still travel, so long as we don't *up and move* forever. At the end of the day, honestly, that ain't all that bad."

I wiped my eyes on Harry's shoulder. "I know, I know...I just know how badly you wanted kids, and I agree: I think it would be just cruel to have kids out here, knowing they'd be stuck on this land forever. I feel terrible—I'd started to imagine it and the thought of never seeing you as a father, seeing you love our little kids...I know I've always been on the fence about having kids, I just, I dunno...knowing this, I feel like I got robbed, and I'm so sorry."

Harry leaned in and kissed me. "I'm mostly just bummed we don't have the choice anymore. Even if we never had kids, I just wanted us to have ownership of that. I guess that's the biggest downside of this new part of the... *curse*."

That just made me cry more. I kissed him and we sat there in silence for what felt like a long time.

"Are you mad at Dan and Lucy for not telling us?"

Harry pursed his lips and squinted, then after a moment shook his head. "Nah, nah...Makes sense why they wouldn't tell us right away."

His response wasn't very convincing. "Har, are you sure?"

He smiled at me in response. "I'm not mad at them, Sash, and I'm not mad at you."

19

HARRY

The morning after Sasha had filled me in on the fact that we were stuck here forever under threat of death, I told her I was going up to fish for a couple hours. I got my rod, fly bag, and wading boots into the 4Runner, but had absolutely no intention of going fishing. I peeled into Dan and Lucy's driveway.

I could see Dan and Lucy together, driving through one of his pastures in their truck pulling their hay trailer. He waved as he saw me and turned to start heading toward the house.

I parked and got out of the 4Runner, not sure what I was going to say to them, but damn sure that I wasn't going to let them off easy for this one. My face must've betrayed my anger, because before they parked and stepped down from the truck, they exchanged a nervous glance.

"Hey there, Harry, how's it goin'?"

"So...if we try to move, this spirit fucking kills us. If we have children, they're fuckin' stuck here forever. Seems like some pretty critical information to share with two people you claim to care about, doesn't it? *Are you fuckin' kidding me?* You didn't think to fucking tell us that the *minute* we fucking got here?"

That was actually a much gentler version of the monologue I'd stayed up all night in bed thinking about ripping into Dan with. In my head, I'd imagined him fumbling through excuses and apologies. To my surprise, Dan actually gave me an annoyed, frustrated look as he took his gloves off and threw them up onto the hood of his truck.

"Put yourself in my saddle for a second, Harold. Some hotheaded young buck who you've never met in your life, don't know a damn thing about, moves into the valley, and you've gotta convince him to leave immediately, give up on his dream home without a second thought, and move before an ancient mountain spirit gets its hooks into him and his wife. You *want to* tell him that, but you know there ain't a chance in hell he'll believe a word of it. *Or*, you can tell him something equally crazy, about a light about to show up in his pond and the immediate, lifesaving need to start a fire so the light doesn't trigger some unexplainable force that'll kill him. Tell me, Har, which option do you go for?"

I wasn't sure what to say, and knew he had a point, but launched into it anyway. "Dan, we could've left, we could've been free from this place if *you'd just fucking told us about this*—what in the hell were y—"

Dan fired off a response so fast and so loud that it actually startled me. "*My ass, Harry. Give me a damn break.* If I'd told you that the first time we met, you'd have told me I was a crazy old bastard and kicked me off your land, and *you damn well know that*, I know that, Lucy knows that, Sasha knows that. Do not stand there on my goddamn driveway and blow smoke up my ass and act like you'd have done a *goddamn thing* differently if I'd told you that up front."

Fuck me, he was right. The pitiful sympathy that flushed into his face only made me angrier.

"Well, how the fuck do you know this is even true, Dan? You guys have seen two families leave who just *happened* to die in ways that kill people every fuckin' year, and you're saying that's the only basis and evidence for something you treat as an undebatable truth?"

Dan put his hand on his hip as he leaned against his truck. "Well, Harry, when we moved here, I was told th—"

I put my hand toward Dan as I cut him off. "Joe, Joe told you, yeah, Dan, let me guess, *Joe told you that's how it was*, right? It's true because *Joe told you* it was? Joe hasn't even bothered to introduce himself—I don't even know what this bastard looks like—so excuse me for questioning what some asshole I've never even met deems to be irrefutable truth."

Dan gave me another annoyed look, this time with some anger in his eyes. "Why in the hell would Joe bother telling us about the rules for dealing with each season if he was fuckin' with us? *Huh?* He could've just kept his mouth shut, not shared a damn word of it, and we'd all be dead by now, and you damn well know that. I know you don't know Joe or have any reason to trust him, but why would he bother making sure we knew how to navigate all this fuss and hassle when he coulda just kept his mouth shut and watched us all get killed within a couple months?"

I wasn't sure what to say. I felt like an idiot, like a boy, and I just stared at the dirt between Dan's boots.

Dan took his big hat off, wiped his forehead with his arm, and put his hat back on. "Harry…*maybe* you're right, maybe it's just a coincidence that the Henrys and the Seymours all died within weeks of leaving here, thousands of miles away, and maybe it's a coincidence that's *exactly* what the oldest family in the valley told them would happen if they tried to move away." He shrugged. "Could be. Could all just be chance. But I tell ya what, Harry…"

Dan looked out over the land and waved his hefty forearm toward the mountains. "With all the other batshit crazy things that take place in this valley…*it sure as shit doesn't seem like a coincidence to me.*"

I took a deep breath. As I exhaled, I could feel the anger draining, with frustration and embarrassment flooding in to take its place.

"I'm sorry I came over here like this. I just…I don't know. I'm sorry."

Lucy stepped toward me and spoke for the first time since I'd been there.

"Harry, I just hope you can understand why we didn't tell you on the first day. If we thought you'd have taken us seriously, I promise I'd have told you to pack your stuff and hightail outta here as fast as you could. But I think you know you wouldn't have done that. I think *you know* that would've made you think we were crazy, and heck…you thought we were crazy anyway."

I nodded at Lucy. "I suppose you're right about that, Luce."

They tried to convince me to stay and talk more, but I told them I had somewhere to be. I avoided eye contact as I apologized again for the way I'd busted in there all hot and bothered, then took off. I drove around aimlessly, feeling childish. I was furious more than anything. Furious at being trapped here. Before I knew it, I was at one of the spots I liked to fish on the Fall River; guess I'd actually go fishing after all.

I rigged up my rod and put on a small Adams-style fly I'd picked up from the fly shop in Driggs. I began working my way up the bank, and instead of moving slowly with stealth and scanning the water for rising trout and good fishable seams, as a calm, focused angler would, I stomped and splashed my way along the river, kicking and tearing aside river willows in my path, knocking clouds of little caddisflies off their perches to scatter up into the already-hot summer morning sun.

Venting anger on blue ribbon trout water is something I was very familiar with, and I was pissed. I came around a little corner and glanced up from watching my footing just in time to see a big fish rise, slamming a bug off the surface of the water from beneath. I took a breath and tried to calm myself down as I slowly worked my way out of the willows to a spot where I could make a cast up the bank. I had just hauled some line from my reel and gone to make my first cast when I felt a jolt through my rod that I knew all too well. I'd snagged a river willow on my back cast, and I let out several audible *fuck*s. I could hear them echo over the river as I reached up to brutally yank and tear at the flimsy vertical branch my fly's hook had punched clean through.

The big trout rose again, bursting up through the surface like a torpedo to inhale another doomed bug. The time sensitivity and pressure of getting a good cast out to a big, actively feeding trout fused with my anger at being trapped in that godforsaken valley forever. My heart was pounding in my ears. I freed my fly, ignored the kinks and angles in the fly line—something an experienced angler would have the patience to address before attempting another cast—and began taking a few deliberate, careful casts. The fish rose again, launching its entire body into the air this time. On my final cast, I double hauled on the line and bent forward, putting my entire body into it. I felt another sickening jolt through my rod, but this time I heard the distinctive *snap* I knew meant I'd not only snagged my fly again on the back cast but had snapped the line entirely, leaving my fly twitching somewhere in the willows behind me while sending my line and what remained of my leader out over the river, naked and flyless.

I watched, defeated, as my empty line coiled down onto itself on the water, just in time to see the big trout casually roll above the surface to slowly inhale another mayfly, as though it was celebrating how badly I'd fucked up my opportunity to deceive it.

I clenched my eyes shut and all I could see was red. I spiked my rod down into the shallow water in front of me and screamed out over the river. My outburst was enough to flush a group of ducks upstream, quacking as they launched up away from the water and beat their wings into the echo of my scream. I snatched up my rod as it began to get pulled downstream by the current, threw it into the willows behind me, and sat down hard on the bank. I rubbed my temples as I stared blankly out over the beautiful river, seeing nothing as I let the anger flow through me unchecked, the same words pulsing through my mind.

You can't have children here. You can never be a father.

I sat on that bank for over an hour, watching that big, victorious cutthroat gorge itself and other trout join in. Eventually, my anger was replaced with a sort of contrition. I realized that, ultimately, I meant what I'd told Sasha: Before learning we were stuck here, I had begun realistically seeing us spending our lives here together, despite the spirit and all its wicked bullshit. It would be cruel to bring a child into this world only for them to be effectively cursed to a lifetime of abject incarceration, born into a union with something so dangerous, born in and chained to the venue of this fucking *thing*, this spirit.

On my drive home from my embarrassing morning of verbally assaulting my sweet neighbors and botched fishing, and during the days and weeks that followed, that sense of acceptance and contrition took hold of me. I was the one who'd wanted to move here, I was the one who'd found this place, I was the one who'd brought Sasha into this life sentence, and while we might be able to live happily here despite not being able to ever permanently move, there was certainly no way to justify having a kid and thereby binding them to the same fate. I tried to reason through that justification in many ways and at great length over the following days, failing repeatedly. *It is what it is.*

Sasha continued to be happy as I'd ever seen her, and despite the confusion and emotional turmoil associated with accepting all of the insanity of the valley, I was still about as happy as I'd ever been as well. If some god or spirit or fuckin' *genie* had asked Sasha where we wanted to spend the rest of our lives but not be allowed to move away from, we'd have likely designed a place just like this. Recognizing that fact made acceptance come easier.

One afternoon in late August, with big-game seasons around the corner, I'd set up some rifle targets on the far southern end of our property in order to make sure the scopes on my hunting rifles were dialed in. These rifles were quite loud, and it must've been over a hundred degrees, so Sasha was happily working inside for the afternoon.

I used my range finder to pick a few spots for shooting rests in the meadow above the pond so that my shooting lane would be parallel to the eastern property line with the national forest. I set one up at two hundred yards from the targets and the other at three hundred, spreading out a beach towel to lie on and a cluster of sandbags at each of the spots. After sending four rounds through my 30-06 and feeling satisfied with it, I started on my .308, which I knew would be more of an involved effort, as I'd just replaced the scope. After a few shots from a bipod at around seventy yards, and an entire box of shells at two hundred—the last five of which were bullseyes—I felt awfully pleased with myself and grabbed another box to practice a bit at three hundred yards, from the farthest rest.

I lay down on the towel and set up the sandbags to snug in the rifle, chambered a round. Then I looked down from where I was into the yard to make sure Dash was still sleeping on the back porch and hadn't decided to take a stroll out into the range—he'd figured out how to wriggle under one of the gates through the fence around the yard, and I hadn't gone about closing off the little opening yet. Seeing him sprawled out in the shade on the porch, in the same spot I'd found him as I checked his location before the two dozen other shots I'd already taken that afternoon, I focused on the shot I was about to take, elevating the reticle of the scope slightly to account for the extra range. I felt comfortable, slowly squeezed the trigger, felt the rifle kick back into my shoulder, then blinked my eyes clear to assess the shot placement on the target after the rifle kicked back into my shoulder. Fuckin' *bullseye*. This rifle was well tuned and ready to go.

I pulled the ear protection off my head to adjust my hat, allowing the symphony of crickets to flood into my ears. Right as I was about to pull the muffs back over my ears, I heard something that I'd only ever heard once before.

Every *single* cricket within earshot had simultaneously gone silent.

Adrenaline flooded into my face and my ears started pounding. I pushed myself up to my knees, tore the bolt of the rifle back, slammed a fresh round into the chamber, and held my breath in an effort to hear as well as I could as I began scanning the tree lines around me for what I *knew* I was about to see: a naked man being chased by a bear.

As usual, I heard his desperate, pathetic wailing before I saw him. To my relief, this time it sounded like he was coming from across the entire property, opposite from where I was, from the forest *behind* the targets I'd been shooting at all afternoon. When I saw the man's pale skin as he came flailing through the final trees along the meadow, I actually laughed out loud at the poetic justice of the moment—the fact that this ridiculous bear chase was coming toward me as I sat with two freshly tuned hunting rifles I'd been training with all afternoon by shooting *exactly* where he was going to be.

I also felt that same rage seep into me that I'd felt before. I quickly looked toward the house to make sure that Sasha hadn't come outside, then looked back at the man. Like the last time I'd beheld this ridiculous bear chase, the allure of the man's panic and terror was entirely gone; the whole *act* of the pursuit was empty and meaningless. I just saw this repulsive, manipulative spectacle for what it was: a ploy designed to take advantage of people's instinct to protect, a ploy designed to *hurt*. It made me want to hurt it; it made me want to *torture* it.

I lay back down onto my shooting rest and let the reticle of my scope fall onto the man's chest as he passed by the targets I'd been shooting all afternoon. Seeing his face *enraged* me. For a few seconds, I wanted to sprint toward the yard, so that I could have another moment with the man; so that I could taunt him again, prod him, have another opportunity to degrade and punish the man, the spirit; so I could laugh in his face as the bear ripped and clawed the life out of him.

Then another thought came to mind, one I'd considered the first time I witnessed this insanity and had thought about since. *What if I shoot the bear?* Dan and Lucy never said *not* to, and you'd think if it were "against the rules," they'd have made that abundantly clear. All they said was don't let the man touch you; shoot him or let the bear kill him.

I adjusted my scope to rest the reticle on the bear's chest, over the shoulder of the weeping, naked man. They were about 250 yards off now. Something in my mind told me to just shoot him, just go through the motions. Something else, likely rage—my belligerent sidekick—told me to shoot the bear, to fuck with the system, fuck with the spirit. I had the crosshair of the scope on the bear's center of gravity, so that its jet-black fur covered the reticle as it bounded up and down in its unnaturally slow, awkward pursuit. I pulled the trigger.

The bullet struck the bear's chest as its two front legs were still aloft, midstride, and it buckled forward, its weight and speed carrying its large, flailing body into a full somersault down the gentle slope. After flipping over itself it slammed into the ground, kicking up a cloud of dust, then lifted its head to let out a bone-chilling, high-pitched, yet cavernous roar that echoed across the valley. The noise itself seemed visible as the roar came surging from the bear's lungs, punching out into the hot summer air through a cloud of bloody mist and rivulets that erupted from its mouth and snout. As though the shot had partially paralyzed it, the bear dragged itself toward the forest on what appeared to be only one functional front paw. It frantically kicked at the earth with its rear legs as it tried to support its own weight, throwing clumps of golden, dead summer grass and dust behind it as it continued to bellow and wheeze its agonized roars. It had only been a second since I took the shot, but I knew I'd done something wrong; I could *feel* I'd done something wrong, something unnatural.

I slammed another round into the chamber, but wasn't sure whether to shoot the man, or put a fatal shot into the bear to end its mind-numbing suffering. The jittery, woeful roaring of the bear physically hurt my ears, my mind even, as though my thoughts themselves had some nervous system capable of pain. I adjusted my scope toward the man and was shocked to see he was actually checking the pace of his run, slowing to a walk, then stopping entirely to stand there, staring at me, completely emotionless. He looked at me through the shimmering heat distortion coming off the hot meadow, directly into my eyes through the scope of my rifle. I felt paralyzed for a moment as he just stood there staring up at me, blank-faced, completely still, while the bear continued to thrash and drag its way toward the tree line behind him. Goose bumps covered my entire body as dread coursed through me. *What did I just fucking do?*

I had the scope on the center of the man's chest and had already started applying pressure to the trigger when, out of the corner of my eye, I saw a flash of red in the meadow to my right. Without moving the rifle, I glanced over toward the movement and color, and before I could even think about what I saw, I was already screaming and starting to surge up from my prone position into a run.

It was Dash. He was in a full sprint, tearing across the meadow toward the man, faster than I'd ever seen him run. Faster than I'd ever seen *any* dog run. I was in a full sprint as well, screaming his name as loud as I could, now chasing after Dash as he surged forward.

I had a brief moment of clarity and checked my forward progress. *I needed to shoot this guy before my dog got to him*, and I only had five or six seconds to make the shot. He was about ninety yards away. I shouldered the rifle and aimed toward the man over Dash's back. I was shaking like a leaf, trying to stabilize the shot, staring at the jittery image of the man in the lens of my scope, the bear behind him now only a few feet away from the forest, already partially obscured by the closest trees. I let out a deep breath, and in the split second of stability it afforded me, I squeezed the trigger as the reticle passed over the man's chest.

I missed. I racked the bolt back and slammed another round into the chamber, knowing there was only a second before Dash reached the man. I was still screaming at Dash to heel as I looked back through the scope at the man. In an almost imperceptibly brief moment before I pulled the trigger, as Dash was mere feet from where the man stood, he smiled.

A torrent of bile surged into my throat, making me immediately retch forward, gagging like someone had just shoved their fingers past my tonsils. It was just enough time for Dash to get to the man. He leaped at him from a full sprint, hammering his full sixty-five-pound canine body into the man's chest so hard, knocking him over so fast, he slammed into the ground before he could even reach his hands out to brace his fall.

Dash picked himself up and surged forward toward the man as he released a keening snarl I'd never heard him make. The man put his arm out to try to block Dash's assault, and Dash latched onto it and shook his forearm back and forth so violently I could see it snap unnaturally even from where I was, sprinting toward the melee as fast as I could.

The man had maintained his grin and eye contact with me, but now shrieked in pain at his broken arm, yanking it back protectively toward his chest, using his free hand to try to ward off Dash's attack. Dash clamped his jaws over the man's other hand and tore it to the side with such force that three of his fingers were ripped off in my dog's jaws, prompting another pitiful scream.

The man covered his ruined hand with his other visibly broken and now profusely bleeding arm and was trying to kick at Dash to get him away. Dash took a step back, shifted his weight onto his hind legs, and launched himself over the man's helpless kicking to latch his jaws onto the man's face. The man fell onto his back, which sent Dash into a terrifying frenzy. He was biting, ripping, and tearing at the man's face and throat. The man was shrieking and sobbing helplessly now.

I had abandoned my attempt to get a clear shot past Dash into the man's chest and charged toward the fight. The man was desperately trying to ward off Dash's attacks with what were now two mangled and bleeding hands and forearms, when I saw Dash land a fierce and accurate bite directly onto the man's Adam's apple. The man's eyes went wide with horror as Dash ripped upward with all his strength. I could see his skin part below Dash's jaws and what looked like gallons of blood begin spurting and pouring from the wound, and then from the man's mouth, turning his terrified screaming into a gargled mumble.

When I was only a few feet away and starting to slow, the man's muscles relaxed and his eyes rolled back in their sockets, and Dash let the man's throat fall from his jaws as though he could feel the man's death was now assured. The man feebly pressed his mangled hands with their few remaining fingers awkwardly into the wound on his neck, as though *anything* could stop such profuse bleeding. Dash sank his jaws down into the man's ankle, and, to my shock, started turning the man and dragging him backward toward the forest.

I screamed at Dash again and reached forward, aiming to get a grip on his collar. He released his bite on the man's ankle and whipped around to face me so fast it actually made me recoil and yelp in surprise. I had barely been able to check my reach toward Dash's collar when he bit at the air, directly where my hand had been. He let out a ferocious snarl and bark as he did it, and I could hear the snap of his teeth echo out behind me through the meadow. He held my gaze for a moment as he let out a low, haunting growl that I could *feel*, glaring at me through narrowed, predatory eyes—a wolf's eyes. He slowly turned back toward the man, watching me warily as he clamped down again on the man's ankle and began to drag the now entirely lifeless corpse toward the trees to my left.

I was so shocked I could barely move. I had forgotten about the bear and glanced up to see its bloody trail through the yellow summer grass disappear into the forest. I looked back just as Dash was passing under the first tree, and I was about to take a step forward to follow him when he stopped his dragging and, without releasing the man's ankle, let out another deep, warning growl in my direction that was unmistakable in its meaning, almost as though it had included spoken words: *Do not follow.*

He disappeared backward into the trees, dragging the bloody, mangled corpse of the naked man behind him. I felt entirely paralyzed until I heard Sasha shouting my name from up near the house in an increasingly panicked voice, snapping me out of the trance on the spot where I'd watched Dash disappear. I turned and saw her running through the gate, scanning the property trying to find me. I waved at her and saw relief flood through her. She started jogging down toward where I was standing along the tree line.

What in the hell was I going to tell her just happened? For the first time since making what I now knew was a *horrible* decision to shoot the bear instead of the man, the implications and weight of the whole experience started to sink in, triggering an equally heavy dose of panic and confusion. Sasha was close behind me now, shouting toward me.

"*Harry, what happened?* What the hell was that noise?!"

I turned to face her, lost for words. I was pointing back toward the trees, about to start speaking, when I heard something from where I'd just been staring. I whipped around and shouldered my rifle, back-pedaling toward a position between the noise and Sasha. That's when I saw Dash.

He emerged from the exact spot where he'd disappeared into the trees, and just trotted out of the forest, panting, tail up over his back wagging back and forth. He ran directly toward me, like he would on any other day in any other situation, blood covering his mouth and snout, all the way up around his eyes, looking like a wolf after feasting on the guts of a moose. I hesitated as he bounded toward me, looking up at me as though he was smiling, waiting for me to throw a ball for him.

I slowly took a knee as he approached. "Dash, buddy . . . Come here."

I thumbed the safety on my rifle and slowly placed it on the ground as he approached, hopeful that this was the dog I knew instead of the vicious hellhound I'd just seen tear the life out of the naked man. He trotted up to me and pressed himself into my legs, turning to sit down between my knees, looking up at me with his normal goofy expression, licking my face.

Sasha knelt down at my side, looking with disbelief between me and Dash. Dash wagged his tail rapidly, licking up toward Sasha's face in excitement as she stroked the side of his head. I couldn't help but start laughing.

Sasha looked in shock at her hand, now covered in the blood that coated Dash's face. "Harry, is that Dash's blo—"

"No, he's fine, I'm pretty sure. It's not his blood."

She looked at me with fear and disbelief, then back down at Dash. "...*What just happened?*"

I tried to form the words, but could only shake my head in disbelief, unsure where to start. Dash jumped up, put his paws on my shoulders, and started licking my forehead.

"Okay, buddy, all right..." I took his head in my hands and scratched both of his ears for a moment. I was in awe at the fact that his affection and excitement were genuine, in awe of how quickly he'd gone from primally vicious beast back to just his normal golden retriever self. I stood up and looked back toward the place where this entire scene had erupted.

Sasha started to repeat her question just as I began to answer.

"Sash, you're not going to believe this..."

Over the course of the next couple hours, I walked Sasha through the whole ordeal as it played out in the meadow, and then again once we'd moved to the back porch. She gave me a world of shit about shooting the bear and not just following the rules, but her scorn and rebuke were stymied a bit by our overbearing disbelief in Dash and what he'd done. We both couldn't help but stare at him, attention he seemed to relish as he went back and forth between the two of us, giving us licks and affection.

Once the heat of the day had subsided a bit, we laid out a blanket in a spot in the lawn overlooking the meadow and started going to work on a six-pack. I'd apologized a dozen times for my decision to shoot the bear and for putting Dash in danger, and she'd reiterated the importance of strict adherence to the seasonal rules just as many times, and eventually we just sat there quietly, Dash sprawled out between us on the blanket, fast asleep.

"It's like Dash *became* the bear," Sasha said, breaking our long, comfortable silence. "Or at least he knew he had to finish the bear's job."

I shrugged and shook my head. "I mean, yeah, I guess that makes as much sense as anything can out here..."

She stared down at Dash with a bemused look on her face, then reached out and took my hand as concern tightened the corners of her eyes. "Don't do that stuff, Harry. Don't mess with this."

I kissed her hand, then leaned in and kissed her lips. "You're right. I know. I'm sorry."

She squeezed my hand, and then rested her head on my shoulder, and we went back to our quiet survey of this beautiful valley. The dragonflies and gnats stood out like diamonds over the meadow as they got caught in that sideways, golden light of late-summer evenings.

I'd kept one detail of the experience to myself. One little fact that I knew would only make Sasha upset and afraid. I didn't tell her about how the man *smiled*; about how his smile hit me like a fist in the gut, how his smile made me almost vomit.

A light, warm gust of wind came down from the mountains. Sasha and I looked up at the big cottonwood above us, drawn by the pleasant rustle the wind stirred into the trees. We both watched a little cluster of leaves jump from their branches and ride the wind out over our heads into the pasture.

"Well, there they are."

I looked over at Sasha, who was still staring up at the group of leaves as they twisted and danced over our heads.

"There what are?"

She looked over at me and smiled. "The first leaves of fall."

PART IV

AUTUMN

20

SASHA

THE SHIFT FROM summer to fall happened *fast*. It seemed as though it went from dry mountain heat on the first of September to full-on postcard autumn in a matter of weeks. The aspen trees exploded with fiery yellow color, the evenings got crisp, we could hear elk bugling from the ridgelines above the land, the creeks slowed down to a mere trickle, the granite peaks of the Tetons had fresh blankets of snow, and every evening I felt like I could tell the sun was setting just a bit earlier, the crickets getting just a bit quieter than the night before.

In the days that had passed by since my initial conversation with Harry about how we were effectively stuck here, never allowed to move again under penalty of some fucked-up natural death, I had been watching him like a hawk to try to discern how he was really taking it. At first, I figured he was going to explode, mostly at Dan and Lucy, but I'd been surprised by his confrontation with the news and how he'd processed it since. He'd taken it a *lot* better than I expected.

That all changed after his decision to shoot the bear, instead of the man. It's like he was a toddler sometimes, overtaken by impulsiveness or an urge to test boundaries.

I'd seen this from him before.

Shortly after we'd first started dating, I remember we went on a big hike in a canyon west of Boulder, and we were walking along these steep, sheer cliffs looking down at least two hundred feet to the creek flowing below. I watched him test a boulder perched on the edge of the cliff with his boot, find it loose, and then heave the rock off the edge. It made *so* much noise as it pounded a few times along the face of the cliff, and then a *huge* boom that sounded like it echoed for miles when it exploded into the rocks hundreds of feet below. I remember his face as he watched that boulder fall and explode, seeing a pure, childlike wonder, followed by sincere surprise when I asked him what in *the hell* he did that for without giving me a heads-up.

"I, sorry ... I just, I don't know."

I remember pretty much screaming at him about climbers or kayakers who might be down there and seeing the genuine concern and surprise spread across his face as he realized I was right. He scanned the canyon below for any signs of people, and I saw his genuine relief after finding the canyon empty, followed by embarrassment.

There was another moment several years later. We were floating the Deschutes River one fall, camping along the bank. I woke up in our tent, confused by a strange noise, and vaguely remembered Harry getting up a bit earlier and whispering that he was going to start a fire and some coffee. I remember scootching forward, still in my sleeping bag, and unzipping the entrance to the tent to look outside. I had gasped when I saw the source of the noise: a *huge* rattlesnake, coiled up on itself, head back, beaded tail in the air screaming out its steady warning rattle. I began frantically trying to zip the flap again until I noticed Harry, off to my left. He was sitting there on a log, one leg crossed over the other, directly in front of the snake, maybe six feet away, just staring back at it. I was hissing at Harry to make sure he saw it, thinking he must not have noticed it somehow. Then I saw that Harry had a handful of pebbles and was just throwing them, one by one, slowly, directly into the snake's coiled-up form so that they were bouncing off its body, prompting it to snap forward and bite at the air in his direction. Harry looked like he was aimlessly tossing pebbles into a still pond. He must've thrown ten at the snake before he heard me, which seemed to snap him out of some kind of trance, prompting him to stand up and grab some long-dead sage branches from behind him and shoo the snake into the bushes.

I asked him what in *the hell* that was about too, and he said something like "I dunno, I was still waking up and just…I dunno."

Moments like those were never *that* frequent or *that* crazy, and he'd always be genuinely surprised when I'd snap him out of it. He isn't some pathological adrenaline junkie, in the normal sense—it's not like he's always doing dangerous shit or exhibiting a complete disregard for his own safety. He drives safe, skis safe, and never starts fights. They're just these strange moments where it's like he's the only person left on earth, casually testing the world around him as though he's not totally convinced he's really alive.

That's how I felt about the way he was pushing the boundaries of these seasonal spirit rules. He'd apologize when I'd bring up the potential harm from taunting the spirit, provoking the man on the fence, or shooting the bear, and he'd emphatically agree with me on every point and articulate why he'd made a bad decision—basically say *exactly* what I wanted to hear.

Still, when it came to moments like when he saw the last bear chase emerge from the trees, even though I wasn't there, *I would bet a thousand dollars* he'd had that same damn look on his face—the same look he gets when he kicks boulders off cliffs, tosses pebbles at rattlesnakes, or prods a wasp's nest. A toddler's curiosity, dangerously divorced from consequence.

I told him as much, too, over dinner one night shortly after he'd shot the bear. He wasn't defensive, and agreed with me in his own words, and assured me he'd toe the line from here on out. Again, *exactly* what I wanted to hear.

Dan and Lucy came over that next afternoon, hauling the hydraulic wood splitter we'd asked to borrow to start stacking enough firewood for the winter. They showed us how to use it before we all sat on the porch for a bit.

We'd known this moment was coming. Harry and I looked at each other before Dan even began to speak. In that one look, I urged him to listen. I saw contrition in Harry's eyes, and focus. He nodded to me just as Dan started to speak.

"Well, autumn is upon us, officially . . . figured it's worth talkin' over what we put in that little write-up about the fall season. We know y'all have read through it, but we'll just give you the rundown either way. We call this one 'the scarecrows.' It only comes around two or three times a season, unlike the springtime light and the summertime bear chase. It can only show up at night when you're sleeping." Dan spoke with his hands out in front of him, gesturing for emphasis.

"You'll wake up and find what is just a, well . . . a *scarecrow*, within twenty yards or so of the house. It's a person-size burlap-and-canvas doll-type thing, right? You've seen 'em. Straw-stuffed, old worn-out clothing, pretty realistic face stitched onto it, five to six feet tall, weighs thirty to forty pounds. It'll be in a casual position, a *human* position, sitting on a bench or stone wall, sitting on the steps of your porch like we are now, or leaning on a fence post, somethin' like that. It's never hidden either—it's like it wants to be found as soon as you go outside. There's no life in 'em when you walk up to 'em. You can poke it and it'll fall over, like it's just fulla wet straw. But you gotta move 'em. See, that's the point with this one—*they need to get burned*. That's the only way. The material they're made of ain't like anything else—once they're properly lit and burning, they burn fast. You ain't gotta coax the flames; they burn all the way down to dust in seconds, every time. Again, they ain't all that heavy, but *you gotta move 'em* because if you're within twenty yards of your home when you light 'em on fire . . . well, *they wake up*."

Did this motherfucker really just say they wake up? I looked over at Dan, then at Lucy. As though she sensed my question, or disbelief, she just nodded. Harry leaned back against the wall of the porch, staring at Dan without much expression at all.

"They *wake up* and will try to get their burning body into your home. So, *you gotta move 'em*. And that's where it gets, well, unpleasant. They won't really *fight* you, but they kinda spasm out, and start to make noises, *but only while you're moving them* to wherever you're going to burn them, never while they're still. They'll wake up very briefly, and it's quite startling, but they only stay *alive*, or awake, for a few seconds. They'll grab your hand, or try to stand up, or try to undo the rope you've got tied around 'em—I recommend moving 'em with a rope, to avoid direct contact; some of 'em are strong— sometimes they'll even take a swing at ya. But those brief moments of life are only like spasms, then they go limp again."

Dan adjusted his weight, looked between Harry and me, then continued. "In those moments when they wake up, they're *scared*. Scared for their lives, like they know they're going to die. In those moments they wake up, they can talk too. And cry, *weep*, more like. Again, it's a real brief moment, but they'll start beggin' and pleadin' with ya during those spasms as they try to break free."

Dan cut his hand through the air, catching my attention. "*Ignore them*. They absolutely must be burned by sunset on the same day you find 'em. Again, you two, it's pretty simple shit here we're talking about: Ya find one, drag it away from the house, ignore it when it wakes up as it's being moved, then burn it. That's all you gotta do, all right?"

I forced a silent nod of understanding. Disbelief, concern, and frustration were blending in response to Dan's very sincere and admittedly contagious uneasiness about these scarecrow things. Dan was staring at Harry now, who was staring past Dan, out toward the forest above the house.

"Har, did you hear all that?"

Harry let out a deep breath, then began to nod, responding without adjusting his gaze at all. "Yeah, sorry, quite an interesting thing...I, yeah."

Harry rubbed his eyes, then sat up a bit straighter before looking toward Dan. "You're saying these things get a bit jumpy, but ignore it and burn 'em away from the house."

Dan nodded. "That's right, that's all there is to it."

All three looked over at me when I began to speak. "So, you're absolutely sure nothing happens in the winter? I really don't want to have some kind of surprise here. You're sure none of the other families saw anything either, and that this isn't just something unique to you and Joe?"

Dan responded with a quick shrug and a grin. "Nah, Harry. Winter's the best time of the year 'round here. It's the spirit's off-season."

I looked to Lucy, who just smiled and nodded. Dan went on. "Nothin' happens in the winter; seems as though the spirit hibernates after the last scarecrow gets burned, until the first light in the pond shows up. It's a nice little reprieve, I guess."

I raised my eyebrows as I nodded, trying my best to think of some question to ask. Dan looked down with a disappointed expression and slowly began brushing off his knee with a big leathery hand as he started to speak. "I wish I could explain it more, but that's all I know—spirit just stays away in the winter." He just heaved his big shoulders.

* * *

Over the next few days, then weeks, Harry and I woke up every morning and did a scan of the perimeter, looking for some kind of demonic scarecrow. It made waking up a lot more dreadful than it ever had been. I'd gone riding with Lucy one afternoon, and she made a comment about how she hated the autumn the worst. I understood why.

One night after dinner, Harry and I made a fire and looked back over Dan and Lucy's notes regarding the autumn—what Dan and Lucy call "scarecrow season"—just as we had *dozens* of times over the last weeks. After living through this summer, Harry's last shred of doubt in all this mysterious spirit furor was long gone. He actually had started treating the preparation for the autumnal spirit cameos like a work project.

We sat down on the couch, and I read through their notes out loud.

For some reason, the description of this little seasonal ritual disturbed me *deeply*, far more than the spring's or the summer's. The way the scarecrows would come alive while being moved, the way they'd beg and weep and thrash. While the spring's light and the summer's bear chase were certainly, *completely* fucked-up in their own ways, something about this one just made my hair stand on end; even simply reading Dan and Lucy's description of what was to come made my skin crawl.

Harry assured me he'd be the one to deal with these, at least until I was ready to do it myself. Lucy told me she felt the same way I did, that she hated the scarecrows more than anything else and had to have Dan deal with them, saying she couldn't even be near them without starting to panic, even when they were motionless in the positions in which they'd appear outside on autumn mornings.

Harry almost seemed excited.

"I don't get why Dan and Lucy hate it so much. I mean, they said the scarecrows aren't even frightening to look at, just normal old burlap sacks with faces stitched on. We just went through months of repeated bear chase fiascos—either murdering a pleading man or watching him get brutally torn apart. This seems like a piece of cake, comparatively. Throw on some headphones, crank up the James Brown, lasso a doll, drag it to a burn pile, light it up. Bring it on."

"I hope that isn't all just cocksure gusto, *sir*," I teased him.

Harry smiled and looked down at his hands. "Nah...I mean, we'll see, but I think I've got this. Got the burn pile set up, got my gas can, got the lasso. I'm *rigged to flip and set to jet*, babe."

He got a laugh out of me with that one. I was happy it wasn't bothering him, because even thinking about it racked me with anxiety. Although he certainly had been preparing for it.

He had a burn pile all set up outside the back gate in a spot where he'd hauled a load of sand, measuring the distance to the house first. He'd picked out a gas can to keep by the door with a box of waterproof matches, and he'd even bought a pro-grade roping lasso at the farm and ranch store that he'd started practicing with. It was smart, I thought, being able to lasso the scarecrow while keeping a distance, then haul it out to the burn pile without getting too close. Dan and Lucy thought so too.

A few nights later we had Dan and Lucy over and cooked dinner for them, which we'd started doing weekly, either at their place or ours. Harry showed them his scarecrow burning preparations with pride. As we all walked up onto the back porch, Dan made a comment that gave me a quiet jolt of anxiety about what was to come. "That lasso was the right call, Har, because remember, you've got to burn the scarecrow as you find it, no cutting 'em up or trying to pull 'em apart—that can get you into real trouble—you gotta just burn 'em as ya find 'em."

We ate a long, big meal outside on what I figured might be one of the last warm evenings of the year. Afterward, we sat around on some new outdoor chairs we'd just picked up, stretched out and digesting. Dash was milling around between the four of us, panhandling for head scratches.

We'd grown close enough to begin discussing the *lore* of this place, so to speak. Harry and I weren't ready to accept that we knew everything about this spirit that there was to know, and poked and prodded for more details every time we were with them. Lucy and Dan had also maintained a steady, ceaseless stream of apologies for not telling us about the fact that we'd be stuck here forever if we didn't move right away.

Once again, we assured them we understood their decision, and reiterated our lack of hard feelings.

Something came to me that evening, listening to Harry, Dan, and Lucy talk. I wasn't listening to their conversation, but just staring out into the dark, hearing their voices blend with the quiet chirps of the handful of crickets still braving the chilly autumn air.

In that moment I was overcome with a feeling, a passion almost, that I never really expected. Something about Harry's comment from several weeks earlier. When I told him about how we could never move, and we were talking about what that meant for having kids. He said he was upset by that fact, but it wasn't because I'd been robbed of the ability to have kids and give them a safe life of opportunity, but mostly because I'd been robbed of the *choice* to do that. It was so *personal*. It was such a personal attack on me and my autonomy. The feeling of being overwhelmed was being replaced by an angry drive to *beat* this spirit, to figure it out, to overcome it.

Something about hearing the lively, friendly exchange between Harry, Dan, and Lucy. Something about hearing their voices carry out into the dark pasture. Something about knowing that there was a threat out in that darkness, something that wanted to put an end to conversations, dinners, moments like these.

Sitting there in that moment I made a decision, one that came out of nowhere but to which I knew I'd dedicate everything. If we really were stuck here, if we really were never allowed to leave, if this spirit really had taken out a lease on our lives, what did I have to lose?

Thinking back on the arrangement of everything, the cause-and-effect nature of the light in the pond and making a fire, the bear chase and shooting the man, the scarecrow appearance and purging them with fire—there was such a balanced nature to it, such a give-and-take. I just couldn't accept that there was not some *other* ritual, some *additional* rule, something larger and more encompassing we could do to either banish this spirit or put it to rest.

I made the decision then and there. I was going to figure out how to break this spirit's hold on us, on our land and our bodies. Maybe not tomorrow, maybe not this year even, but I was going to figure it out. And whether it was from old age or the spirit itself, I was ready to die trying.

21

HARRY

I felt around my nightstand with my hand in the dark, trying to locate my phone, blaring its obnoxious little alarm tune, until I found it and mashed every button I could until it shut up. Sasha rolled over and groaned at me.

I could hear Dash's little toenails clicking across the wood floors of the living room, heading from his bed to our room, also prompted into action by the alarm. He had figured out the entire system. It was actually pretty damn cute.

I was going to take him grouse hunting that morning up in a spot in the national forest I'd explored the weekend before while archery hunting; didn't find any elk, but I'd flushed a load of ruffed grouse. The night before, I had gotten all our hunting stuff together in the office. My upland hunting vest, my shotgun, Dash's collars, my backpack, all the gear. Dash knows that whenever that hunting vest and the shotgun come out, it's time to hunt, and he gets hilariously giddy, like a kid on Christmas Eve, twirling around with his tail spiraling out of control. Hunting birds is his favorite thing in the world.

I rolled out of bed and my momentum was abruptly checked by a wince that seized my entire body as fire blitzed up my leg, from my knee to my stomach. When I reached down to massage my scar, a dull but electric ache spread down my back. *God damn*, I thought. It hadn't hurt this bad in a few years. I let out a shaky breath as I rolled my shoulders and kept working my leg.

Sasha put her hand on my back. "You okay, babe?" She really did have a sixth sense for my aches and pains, like she could feel them as well.

"Oh, yeah, just a little achey. Go back to sleep. We'll be back in a few hours, all right?" She nodded as I forced myself to get onto my feet, then she disappeared back into the pillows, stretching out to take advantage of my vacant side of the bed.

The very last memory I have of Afghanistan is of sitting in the rear passenger seat of a Humvee, driving down a dusty road when my view of the countryside was interrupted by a bright blue light. My next memory, what I'd learn was actually a few days later, was of being strapped into a gurney in the cargo bay of a big plane, with some navy NCO sitting in a jump seat next to me. She had a kind voice. "Hey there, Lance Corporal, you're headed to Germany." I don't remember ever seeing her again.

I was told in Germany that the blue light was from an IED blast that almost cut our Humvee clean in half. My buddy Scott was in the seat next to me, I remember. He lost his left leg. My buddy Vasquez was in the front passenger seat. He was killed immediately by a piece of the vehicle that went into the back of his head and sheared the top of his skull almost clean off. My buddy Tucker was driving, motherfucker was *completely fine*, mild concussion, probably, but walked away from it without a scratch. Fuckin' *crazy* how that works. I was pretty lucky too, comparatively. I'd taken shrapnel all across my back and my left leg, bunch of glass in my face, but the real damage was just the orthopedic consequence of the blast: shoulder blade shattered, left femur broken clean through, fractures from my left knee down to several in my left foot, both bones in my left arm broken clean, four fingers and a couple bones on my left hand, half a dozen ribs, and a punctured lung. It was shitty, but I got to keep all my limbs, fingers, toes, eyes, and balls. Thus, not all that bad, compared to others.

I got stitched and stapled and worked on by our corpsman, then at triage at our FOB, then by some CASEVAC medics, then by some docs in Kandahar, then by more docs in Germany, and then another couple operations stateside at Walter Reed. After that was a couple months in recovery, doing PT every day, pretty much just living with a facility full of guys who'd also been torn apart by IEDs.

Who'da thunk it, right? A world-class fighting force of the fastest, meanest, strongest, best-equipped warriors who've ever assembled for combat...laid low by a few illiterate teenagers with some sketchy old Soviet-era explosives, duct tape, a shovel, and some remote-control-car controllers. War certainly seemed to have changed.

I stretched for a bit in the office until the aches began to ebb, then got dressed and started some coffee. Dash was *stoked*, knowing exactly what we were going out to do that morning, just trotting back and forth between me and where I'd piled my vest, pack, and shotgun by the door. I filled a thermos and dropped in a dollop of whatever strange cream alternative Sasha had picked up. Cashews or almonds or hemp, who knows—it all just has that same awkward, disappointing taste.

I put Dash's collar on him, slung my side-by-side shotgun over my shoulder, and went outside, turning to use both hands to shut the door as quietly as I could.

I'd made it the first step down from the porch when my heart leaped into my throat.

A man was standing on our porch to my right, about halfway between the front door and the kitchen patio.

I gasped and flailed around, bringing my hands up, causing Dash to start barking. I stepped back up onto the porch, strained my neck around to get a better look, and my skin crawled.

There, in the silvery pre-sunrise wolf light of autumn mornings, was our first scarecrow.

Sasha, awoken by Dash's barking, whipped the front door open with half-awake panic in her eyes, blanket still over her shoulders. She seemed to gather what was going on before she even had to step outside. She slowed down and put her hand on the door frame, looking at me with wide eyes. All I had to do was nod. She slowly came out and looked down the porch toward the source of the dog's ruckus.

It was a large burlap doll, just as Dan and Lucy said. It wore sun-bleached denim overalls over a canvas button-down, with a straw hat on its head. Its feet were vaguely foot-shaped lumps of burlap, and its hands appeared to be straw-stuffed deer hide work gloves. Even just seeing the side of its stitched-on face, I could tell the facial features were present in shocking detail. It looked like a middle-aged man, with a calm smile and blue eyes. It was just standing there, upright, arms bent, with its gloved thumbs hooked into its overall straps.

Dash had calmed down and was standing at the scarecrow, sniffing its strange burlap foot like it was just a new piece of furniture. Sasha took a couple steps toward it.

"How the hell is it standing like that...? It looks like it's gotta have a frame or something to hold it up."

That was, indeed, perhaps the most abnormal characteristic of the scarecrow. Its weird, lumpy feet were barely touching the ground, yet it stood upright, healthy posture and all.

I looked for wires or strings that could be holding it up, running my hands above and around it, then just shook my head. "I dunno. Dan and Lucy said they'd be in humanlike positions when we find them, and that they'd collapse like wet piles of straw as soon as we start to move 'em."

I grabbed the broom we'd kept on the porch since the leaves had started falling. I extended the handle toward the scarecrow's closest leg, then looked at Sasha for approval. She nodded. I poked its knee inward, and sure as hell, it crumpled in on itself like a bag of leaves. It was shocking how fast the human posture and demeanor dissipated from it, *immediately* collapsing just as Dan and Luce had described. Sasha and I stared down at the strange burlap mass. Dash sniffed around the thing's head, the creepy little nub with contorted facial features protruding from the strange pile.

It was jarring to look at. We went inside and I gathered up my little collection of scarecrow gear—the lasso, matches, and a small aluminum can of diesel.

"Sash, I got this, seriously. Just hang here with Dash, turn up some music in case it gets a tad noisy, and I'll be done in ten minutes, max."

I smiled at her reassuringly. She looked concerned, then nodded. "All right, be safe. I mean it. That thing is disturbing as hell."

We didn't need to say anything more. We'd run through this a hundred times already.

I went outside, shut the front door behind me, and turned to face the crumpled scarecrow. It really did have a fucked-up...*ambiance*, I guess. But more than anything else, I was underwhelmed. I looked beyond it, to where I'd cleared the burn pile outside the back gate. I decided it'd be best to go to the other side of it, down the porch a ways, to rope the thing's lumpy head sticking out from its piled-up body, which would allow me to drag it from its current position toward the steps that led to the yard from the kitchen patio.

My lasso game wasn't exactly on point; it took me six tries to get the thing looped around its head. When I finally did, I slowly pulled the line and watched it tighten around its neck. Damn, I thought, it really was just a burlap sack of wet straw. It made absolutely zero sense how it was physically possible for it to have maintained its standing position. *Think about that later*. I began walking backward, slowly cinching the lasso loop tight around the doll. It was heavy enough for me to get it pretty tight without starting to move it, but I knew any more tension and it'd begin to actually move, which...I guess I wasn't quite ready for.

My heart was pounding. The way Lucy and Dan described how these things came to life in terrified spurts and bursts had been filling my mind since the autumn came. I did a little lap around the area where I was standing, shaking out my hands one at a time. I took a deep breath and decided I'd just yank it as hard and as fast as possible until I could drag it down the steps and get it off the porch. I gripped the rope, put it over my shoulder, walked until I could feel tension, and kept my eye on the burn pile. I counted down out loud: *"Three, two, one,"* and I surged, pulling on the rope as hard as I could.

The scarecrow had some girth but wasn't that heavy. Probably thirty-five pounds. Within two or three seconds, I felt it thumping down the porch steps, I looked back briefly as I dragged it into the yard. *So far so good*. I kept charging, digging into the lawn. I ran as fast as I could until I got all the way to the gate. I began to turn and just as I was about to stop, it happened.

I noticed the hands first, shooting up to the neck. It was lying on its back, head toward me, and I could see it frantically pulling on the lasso around its neck. Feeling the jittery little movements this *thing* was sending up the rope into my palms was so startling and disturbing I tossed the rope aside like it was covered in spiders, then stepped away from it. I could hear it *breathing*, like a grown man seething breaths in and out through clenched teeth. I leaned forward slightly, attempting to see its face under the brim of its hat. Right then, the scarecrow put all its weight into its feet and shoulders, arched its back, and forced its pelvis toward the sky as it feverishly tried to loosen the rope around its neck. In that moment it let out the most tragic, anguished, *haunting* scream I had heard since Afghanistan. Then, like it was controlled by a light switch, all traces of life and strength disappeared, and the scarecrow crumpled back down into a lifeless mass. I stared at the scarecrow in disbelief as the echo of its scream faded and was replaced by the thundering of my heartbeat in my ears.

Holy shit. I opened the gate, then slowly picked up the lasso and cautiously walked out into the meadow toward the burn pile, watching the scarecrow closely for any more signs of movement-stimulated panic. I backed up, bringing the lasso rope to full tension, then turned again, put the rope over my shoulder, and charged ahead toward the burn pile. I ran through it, and then about six feet beyond, until I figured my lumpy straw friend was right where I needed him to be.

I was glancing over my shoulder to confirm the scarecrow's location when it happened again.

I could see its face this time because of the way the lasso knot had tightened around its neck, and that alone was enough to make me toss the lasso again, as though breaking contact would somehow insulate me from the disturbing scene. It reached up and tried to get a grip on the rope. The stitchwork of its face was grotesquely human, moving around in impossible ways. It looked more scared than I felt. It craned its neck up so it could look directly at me from where it lay on the ground, and this time, it spoke. *Screamed*, more like. It only said a single word, but the volume, panic, and visceral terror in its voice amplified with each utterance.

"Don't, don't, don't, DON'T!"

Again, just as fast as it had started, it crumpled backward into the sand of the burn pile, entirely lifeless again even before its screams finished echoing across the cold gray pasture.

I felt sick. I felt *guilty*. It felt like this thing really did grasp the reality that it was about to be executed. I remembered Dan and Lucy's warning—*Ignore the empathy you might feel for these things; they must be destroyed*. I was actually pretty good at that. I'd done it for real.

I approached the scarecrow fast but cautiously, bent down, slackened the lasso knot gently, then slowly lifted the rope from around its strangely intricate face and over the straw hat. I went back and grabbed the gas can, removed the cap, and poured a bit on the legs of the scarecrow. I uttered an *"Adios,* buddy" as I lit a match, then dropped it onto the scarecrow's legs.

Dan was right, these things were fucking *incendiary*. Within five seconds, the entire mass was engulfed in flames, and within thirty, it was dust. It's like it was soaked in diesel.

Welp, that was fuckin' gross. Staring down at the smoking ash, I really did recognize that the whole experience, more than anything else, was *disgusting* rather than frightening. It wasn't as bad as I'd thought it would be, however, and I'd take ten of these fuckers over one bear chase, any day.

I went inside and found Sasha at the kitchen table, looking up at me with a mix of fear and inquiry. I smiled at her.

"It's gone, Sash. It's burned and gone. Nothin' to worry about."

She rattled off five questions in what felt like three seconds. "What about the spasms? I didn't hear it screaming or crying—what was that like? What'd it say? Was it strong when it came to life while you were moving it?"

I put my hands up. "Whoa, babe. It's just…a scarecrow, a doll; it stayed that way, other than very briefly wriggling around trying to get free. It grumbled a bit, then fell back into a lifeless heap. I just dragged it over to the burn pile, lit it up, and it burned like oil-soaked rags. That was literally it. Really wasn't all that bad." She had a concerned look, but relief was competing with the concern, and she nodded. She got dressed and I showed her what was now just a dark gray ash stain on a pile of sand.

I didn't feel comfortable leaving *immediately* after that happened, as though banishing a supernatural scarecrow by fire were some casual thing. So I decided I'd wait an hour, have a shit and a shower, then take Dash out for the grouse hunt.

After my shower, I got dressed again and went into the office, where Sasha was sitting on a conference call. I gestured toward the door to let her know I was going to take Dash to go hunt and leaned in to give her a kiss on the cheek. As I turned to leave, she signaled for me to wait with her finger as she muted her phone, took her headset off, and turned to face me.

"Babe, I feel shitty about not going with you this morning to deal with that."

I just shook my head. "Sash, that's silly. I've got this. Lucy doesn't mess with these things either; she makes Dan do it. I'm happy to. It really isn't that bad. If you want to do it next time, or help me do it, then fine, but I'm happy to do it, and you know I'd prefer you go nowhere near those damn things anyway."

She squeezed my hand and looked down. "All right. Next time."

She looked up and smiled, then Dash interrupted the moment by loudly pawing at the front door. We looked over to see him peering at us through the living room over his shoulder, wagging his tail impatiently, eager to get his morning of hunting under way.

I threw Dash in the car and we headed up to the grouse spot I'd found. It was on the slopes to the north of the Fall River, amazing country that looked on fire with the aspen trees in full autumn colors. Dash and I hiked about a mile before he started to get "birdy." It's a bit different for all hunting dogs, I suppose, but when a bird dog picks up the scent of a game bird—whether it's a pheasant, quail, chukar, partridge, or grouse—they get all worked up and their body language changes dramatically. When Dash gets birdy, he starts making fast, sharp ninety-degree turns, ripping back and forth as he works to follow the scent. This is where the hunting training comes in too, because if your dog isn't trained to hunt, isn't trained to stay close, they'll just charge after the scent and flush the bird way outside of shotgun range. So, training them to stay close *while* they know there's a bird nearby, that's really what makes or breaks a hunting dog. Disciplined enthusiasm.

It really is wild watching a flushing dog work, no matter how many times you see it. You can really see how primal it is for the dog. Dash's nose was glued to the forest floor as he sprinted back and forth through a little glade between some big aspen trees.

"*Daaash*, easy, buddy, close. Stay close." He spared me a quick glance with a frustrated look in his eye I'd learned to recognize—basically his version of saying *Dude, there's a game bird close by; don't bother me.*

He started to home in on an area near a big dried-out and gnarled tree trunk, ripping his entire body back and forth, his tail worked into a full propeller.

I thumbed the safety off.

Dash made one more sharp turn, nose to the dirt, and a pair of grouse exploded out of the grass about a dozen steps in front of him. No wonder people call these things "heart attack chickens." One flew low, directly away from me, quickly disappearing into the understory of the forest. The other carved out to my right, flying into the open sky above the glade. I took a shot, and watched the grouse go lifeless in the air amid a puff of feathers that stayed suspended above the falling bird in the morning light.

Dash was *on it* the second it hit the ground.

"Dash, *here*."

He trotted over toward me, softly gripping the grouse in his mouth. I took a knee and held out my hand, but he dropped it on the ground right in front of me instead, then put his paw into my hand as though I'd told him to shake. I laughed at him.

"Well, that'll do, buddy. *Good job, good work, Dash!*" He sat there panting, looking like he was smiling for a holiday photo, a ring of wet feathers around his mouth. I keep a cheese stick in my hunting vest for these moments, so I stripped the plastic wrap off and held the treat out to him so he could take a big bite.

"We're eating well tonight, buddy. Good work—let's go get some more."

We hunted for another couple hours and flushed three more pairs of grouse. I got one of the first pair, and one of the second, and missed both shots I took on the last pair. So, we had three birds for dinner. When I miss a shot on a bird, I have to call Dash back to me, as he'll just continue his charge ahead looking for the downed bird, driven onward by misplaced faith in my shotgun accuracy. I swear, he has learned to give me a disappointed look when I miss birds and have to call him off the retrieve—a look that says, *You've got one job, dude, I'm out here busting my ass, get your shit together.*

Sasha seemed much more relaxed when I got home, having fully briefed Lucy and Dan about our first scarecrow experience. I cooked up the grouse for dinner that night, one of my favorite meals. My uncles taught me how to brine the legs and the breasts, then roast them in a skillet, basting them with butter. I gave some to Dash mixed in with his kibble, and Sasha and I ate the rest with mushroom pilaf and what I figured was probably the last salad from the garden for the year.

Life went on, possibly as well as it ever had. I think that October was the best month of my life up until that point. We used leaves from the trees to cover the garden beds, drained out the sprinkler lines we had in the yard, and went on hikes up the road and through Dan and Lucy's ranch almost every day. I even got Sasha to come grouse hunting with me a few times.

I'd struck out on getting an elk the month before, during archery season, which I figured was a tall order anyway. I'd only ever shot one elk with a bow, back in college, and it wasn't an easy thing to duplicate, especially in a new place. So, when rifle season rolled around for deer, I took it seriously. I wanted to fill the freezer. Sasha and I had started fantasizing about only eating meat, fish, and game we got or reared ourselves, so I went balls to the wall on getting a buck that season. I'd set up game cameras all over the national forest spots where I'd been seeing deer and good sign, and we even had a few bucks on our land we'd see early in the mornings.

Sasha loved cooking and eating game meat I brought home but wasn't that into the watching-animals-die part. She could do it with grouse and pheasant and ducks but had no interest in big game hunting. She just drew her sentience threshold at mammals, I guess. Opening morning of deer season, I got up real early and hiked up into a meadow about a mile and a half above our property where I'd seen lots of deer. I rucked up there in the dark, using my headlamp. It brought me back, a moment like that. Aside from the relationships and bonds I made along the way, I did not look back on my time in the Marine Corps with much fondness. But there were moments like this—rifle in my hands, heavy backpack on, charging up a steep slope so early most of the world is still asleep—that gave me pangs of nostalgia. It was mostly the guys in my company that I missed, though. The slaphappy, exhausted bullshitting. It made me a bit lonely, being out here without them.

Shortly after first light, a group of does trotted out into the forest clearing I'd set up in, only about one hundred yards ahead of me. I'd hunted mule deer enough to know that, even if it wasn't during the rut, when you see a group of does, there's a decent chance a buck is following somewhere nearby. I watched the does and kept the scope of my .308 bolt-action rifle on the area where they'd left the forest. Wouldn't you know it, a big-bodied, three-by-three mulie buck slowly sauntered out into the meadow. He came in slowly, scanning for threats every two steps. As soon as he'd come far enough into the forest clearing to give me a clear broadside view, I took a shot. The buck dropped in his tracks as the group of does bolted off in every direction.

I never was much of a fan of the field dressing aspect of big game hunting. No matter how many times I'd done it, it was always unpleasant. Not to mention the strenuous process of hauling the meat back to the tent, truck, or now, the house. It took me a few hours to get the animal butchered and the first load of meat home. Sasha was excited. She loved *not* buying meat from the store. She and Dash came up with me on the second meat run. We took all four quarters, the backstrap, loins, rib and brisket, liver, heart, even the marrow bones and hide. When we were done, all that was left in that meadow was a pile of deer guts and a rib cage.

That night, we ate venison tenderloin with wild mushrooms from the land and potatoes from the garden. After dinner we bundled up and sat on the back porch, and for the first time since we'd lived there, we heard wolves howling up in the national forest. It sounded like they were right where we'd butchered the deer. The howling was distinct, but occasionally you could hear a faint snarl and yelp echo down from the forest.

I figured they were fighting over the leftovers of my deer. Sasha, Dash, those wolves, and I were all eating the same animal for dinner that night.

We made steaks, sausage, jerky, and burgers with the deer, and with all the jams and chutneys we'd canned from our garden bounty, we enjoyed amazing meal after amazing meal, trying a new recipe every night for the next several weeks. We ate like royalty. We loved and laughed like every day was our last.

I was taking a shit on the morning of the last Saturday in October when I heard Sasha yelling for me urgently from the kitchen. From the tone of her voice, I knew something wasn't right. I knew scarecrow number two had arrived.

I went out into the kitchen and Sasha was standing in her robe, looking out the window, while Dash had his paws up on the window-sill. I walked up and looked over them. It was a jarring sight.

It was a female doll this time. Looked like a teenage girl. It was sitting straight-backed with one little straw-filled, white-gloved hand resting neatly atop the other in its lap. It sat on the small stone wall that ran through our yard, wearing an old-timey dress and a white bonnet. Its face looked kind of sweet, actually. Serene and peaceful. It gave me the chills. Sasha looked up at me, and I put my arm around her.

"I got this, babe." I knew she'd said she wanted us to burn this one together, but at the same time, I didn't want her anywhere near these things. "It's a piece of cake; just keep Dash inside, turn on some music in case this one's a bit louder than last time, and I'll be back in fifteen, all right? You can come help me if you want, but I've got this, seriously."

Sasha stared out at the scarecrow and looked disgusted—less so than last time, but still like she was repulsed. She took in a deep breath before responding. "I'm sorry, I just do not want to go near that thing, Har..."

I assured her it was all right, did my best to convince her there was no reason both of us had to deal with this shit, and went about gathering my eclectic assortment of scarecrow gear from next to the front door.

I went out to assess the extraction strategy and best egress route from the stone wall to the back gate. I stared at it for a while, and again checked it for wires, rods, or some kind of frame that could be holding it up in such a precisely human position. It was not any less shocking to see how these damp, flimsy sacks of straw could maintain such neat little human postures prior to being moved. Did they just appear out of nowhere? Did these fuckers saunter in here from the forest on their own legs? The thought sent a chill down my spine and I scanned the tree line, half expecting to see other scarecrows strolling about or watching me from afar.

Some kinda mountain-curse magic, I suppose. My list of unexplainable shit had grown exponentially as of late, so I just added it into the ever-expanding *it is what it is* category.

I went and opened the gate ahead of time this go-round and walked back to the scarecrow. I nailed the lasso on the second toss, and when it settled around her waist, I began cinching it tight. I increased the tension until she toppled over into the grass, all human posture and ladylike dignity extinguished immediately. Just a lumpy bag of straw.

I braced myself, put the rope over my shoulder, and began charging across the yard toward the gate and the burn pile beyond. This one felt a bit lighter and was probably only around five feet tall. I was almost at the gate when I felt an unnatural tension in the rope, sending a shot of fear up my back so fierce I tossed the rope from my hands and jogged off to the side a bit before turning around. I almost gagged at what I saw.

The scarecrow—or the *girl*, now—was lying on her side, awkwardly fumbling at the rope around her waist with her straw-filled, white-gloved little hands, quietly weeping to herself. She lifted her bonnet-covered head up to look at me. I was frozen with disgust and disbelief as the jarringly vivid stitchwork of the scarecrow's face moved and gyrated to portray the disturbingly realistic face of a terrified young woman.

"You don't have to do this, sir. Please, *you don't have to hurt me. You don—*"

The life ripped out of her so fast and she crumpled back into a lifeless heap so immediately it was almost as shocking as when she'd woken up. *Jesus fuckin' Christ, these things are disgusting.* I jogged a short lap around her, toward the tag end of the lasso, as I shook blood back into my hands. The *fear* in her voice, the sincerity of her plead-ing. It made me *hate* this spirit again, filling me with the familiar rage at the insidious way this thing went about its business—the wicked ways it manifested and tried to fuck with your head.

I angrily snatched up the lasso, almost *hoping* that would wake it up again, and didn't bother turning around as I began to drag it backward toward the gate.

I got all the way through the gate before it happened again. This time the scarecrow girl gasped, then rolled forward onto her knees, wrapping her arms across her chest, holding herself as she wept and rocked back and forth, her forehead almost touching the ground. I just stood there looking down at her.

She slowly looked up toward me, the sight of which was just as revolting as it had been the first time.

"Why are you doing this to me? What did I do? Please just tell me what I did, please, ple—"

This time, as soon as the life fled from her body and she fell back into the crumpled mess of scarecrow, I immediately hauled on the lasso and didn't stop until the *thing* was squarely in the center of the burn pile. Its pleading and begging were so realistic and shocking that I had to force an internal mantra through my head: *It's just the spirit, there's no girl in there. It's just the spirit, there's no girl in there.*

I crept toward the scarecrow and began gently loosening the lasso, just like before. As I was slowly working the rope up over its head, trying to move it as little as possible, life flooded back into its form so abruptly I stumbled backward through the sand of the burn pile.

She *gasped* as though she'd just been pulled from an ice bath, then brought the balls of her hands up to cover her eyes as she began weeping. I walked toward the shuddering scarecrow and stared down at its face as she, *it*, brought its hands down and looked up at me with pleading eyes.

"Why? Why do you have to hurt me?"

I was infuriated by this whole act in that moment; the theatrics of the spectacle of the spirit or the demon or whatever it was just made me enraged as I listened to the pathetic thing's begging.

I casually splashed gas down onto her strange little antique dress and got my response to her question out before the possessed scarecrow fell lifeless again.

"Because this land is mine now. I *took* it from you."

Right before the weeping little creature returned to its lifeless scarecrow form, *right* at the end of my sentence, its face lost all emotion.

I almost wasn't sure I'd seen it and hesitated for a moment. Then, I struck a match, dropped it down onto the scarecrow, and *poof*. The entire thing roasted down to smoky ash in twenty seconds.

Sasha was relieved it was gone and walked with me as I explained how it all happened, where it had its moments of abrupt and pathetic vitality while being moved, and what it said. She seemed apologetic and down on herself for not helping me get rid of it, but I assured her, again, that I was more than happy to handle these myself.

"Also, Sash, Dan and Luce said they usually only find two or three of these things a year, so that one *could be it*. We could be done with the scarecrows, heading into our winter 'off-season.' How fuckin' nice would that be, if we were just done with this shit until springtime pond lights?"

Sasha looked up from the pile of ash that had taken the form of a weeping teenage girl moments earlier. "That would be quite nice...I just, I don't know. Don't you think it's strange that we didn't *feel* the spirit leave, in the same way we've felt it when we light the fire in the spring, or when the naked man dies?"

I hadn't thought about that, and realizing she was right raised my hackles a bit as well. However, I wasn't about to start complaining about a *lack* of unexplainable, terrifying spirit-related shit. I was happy. We'd been living so large, having such a good time the last few months. Laughing a lot. I was very much looking forward to getting a break from this spirit nonsense for a while.

I shrugged and put my arm around Sasha as we turned to walk back toward the house. "Eh, well...I don't know, babe, but I sure feel fine now that the nasty little thing is burned, and so does Dash."

Sasha smiled at Dash, zigzagging ahead of us, hopping around as he anticipated Sasha's throw of the stick she'd just picked up for that purpose. She hucked the stick for the dog and turned back to me, smiling and nodding in agreement.

"Yeah, I'm just overthinking it. Scarecrow's burned. We're safe and sound."

22

SASHA

⚜

I LOOKED DOWN AT the rock I'd been kicking along the road for the last hundred yards or so. "It's just weirding me out how we never *felt* the spirit leave as we burned the scarecrows, I guess. Every time the spirit presents itself—light in the pond, naked dude in the meadow—I can feel it arrive, and as soon as we follow the rules—light the fire, kill the man—I can feel it leave. Don't you think it's strange that hasn't happened with these yet? I mean, that's what makes them unpleasant to begin with, the *feeling* of the spirit when its little manifestation is afoot, so why would *that part* not be present for this season as well?"

I watched Lucy's face, trying to discern any worry or apprehension. I saw none. "I dunno, Sash. I mean … maybe it's a little different for everyone? I'll admit it's strange. I've watched Dan drag hundreds of those things toward the burn pile over the years, and I guess I can feel something when they're burned; even this season, last week I felt it, but I … I don't have any explanation. I'm not necessarily worried about it, though."

Lucy bent over and picked up the tennis ball Dash had brought along with us since we left the house. She threw it down the country road we were strolling along to get the mail. It's over a mile from our driveway to the mailbox at the junction of the county road and the state highway, so we usually grab it when we're driving in or out, but it's also a nice excuse for an afternoon stroll.

Lucy's answer as to why *our* scarecrows weren't giving us that euphoric sensation when they were burned didn't do much for me, but I nodded anyway.

Since I'd decided I was going to investigate this spirit to its core to try to figure out a way to beat it, I'd been thinking more and more about the time Harry talked to the spirit that one day this summer, how he taunted it, told it he'd *taken* its land. Seeing the man's fear and emotion drain away, seeing it almost look confused and frustrated, it just felt wrong, felt *off*.

"I just don't understand the meaning behind it all, Lucy, the purpose. There just has to be some kind of symbolism or...*motif* that's associated with the ways the spirit presents itself."

I watched Lucy incline her head as if she were giving some deeper consideration to the subject we'd been discussing for the last hour.

"Well, Sasha, it's like I've said before. I think there's a nature of balance that underlies it all. A give-and-take, or a yin and yang. The evil of the light in the water is offset by the good of starting a fire; the evil of the man is offset by the chance of the bear getting him; the evil of the scarecrows is, well...I guess offset by burning the creepy sons a bitches."

Lucy looked back at me from her position several paces ahead, perhaps prompted by my lack of response. "What, you don't think my analysis sound, Miss Sasha?"

"I just don't know. Doesn't really hold water with the scarecrows, though. I mean, spooky scarecrow shows up out of thin air only while you're asleep, and you balance that negative with the positive of just destroying it? Seems a little blunt compared to the other two, doesn't it?"

Lucy nodded in acknowledgment. "I've also thought about how, well...the spirit might only be able to understand *human impulse*, rather than understand the deeper nuances of people and all our strange shit, so it could be that *human impulse* is, in a way, the symbolism underlying the way it presents itself."

I cocked my head to the side. "What do you mean?"

Lucy thought for a minute before responding. "Well, think about how if we try to move away, the spirit kills us, but it *does not* kill us if we go on a vacation—it only goes that far if we have the *intent*, in our hearts and minds, never to return. Our *impulse* is to leave, instead of continue living here in this strange coexistence with this strange ol' mountain ghost, but we're forced to avoid that impulse or pay the ultimate price. And think about the springtime, when you have something evil show up, or dangerous, represented by the light that appears in the water. The rules require lighting a fire in your home to protect your family from that evil, but the act of *lighting a fire to warm your home*, to protect your family from the cold, there's something inherently human about it, no?"

"I guess I'm following…what about the bear chase and the scarecrows: How does human impulse play in with those?"

"Well, for the bear chase, the pleading man, the weeping, naked man, the *human impulse* is to protect the man and harm the beast from the hostile wild, but the rule, the ritual, requires precisely the opposite. The *inverse* of human nature keeps you safe. For the scarecrows, the *human impulse* is to recognize your own kind in another and have sympathy and empathy, but you have to destroy that thing with fire. Or, the opposite could be said, it could be that in the autumn, we're *embracing* the human impulse, as most people's first reaction to a creepy scarecrow showing up is to destroy it, to get it away from their home."

"I suppose…seasons, though, the seasonal nature of it is vexing, being different in the spring, summer, and fall, and then nothing in the winter. Maybe that's to symbolize the time of the year, the reprieve from growth, when most things in nature are dead or hibernating. Not sure how that ties into human impulse, though."

Lucy gave it some thought before responding. "I suppose it could be that *humans* are the only ones who recognize the rigid breakup of *four* seasons. I mean, birds and animals have mating seasons, and hibernation seasons, but the *four different seasons* with delineated temporal boundaries, and the different manifestations of the spirit that work in harmony with these seasonal periods that are really only recognized by humans…Maybe the seasonal presentation of the spirit is, well, a reflection of the spirit's understanding of *how we* recognize and categorize the passing of time based on the changes in the natural world around us. Flowers and warming equals spring, heat and life equals summer, falling of leaves and cooling of the air equals autumn, and the winter, it's like…the reset, the natural slate is washed clean for the next cycle."

I shook my head and rolled my head back. "Jesus…that's some pretty heady shit, my friend. I find it hard to believe you've been a rancher for your whole life and never had an LSD phase."

We both laughed. "Well, Sash, I read a lot, and I've been damned to a lifetime in a beautiful valley plagued by impossible, supernatural goings-on. There's a lot to muse over, I suppose."

I hurried my pace to catch up and put my arm through hers. "You are kind of an old mountain witch, in the loveliest way, Lucy. I mean, you are *literally* a spirit guide who shares old spirit-warding rituals to young newcomers, then wanders the hills gathering berries and mushrooms for stews and teas."

We both chuckled a bit in unison, with Lucy giving me a look of feigned offense and a soft slap on the shoulder. "Well, worse things to be, I guess."

We each grabbed our mail, and on the walk back, we stopped to sit on the bench Lucy had made many years earlier. It was a big dead ponderosa trunk lying parallel with the road; Lucy had used a chain saw to carve a little flat indent into its length.

There was a new kind of chill in the November air, one I hadn't felt before. It had still been cold when we'd moved here in March, but there had been something in the air that promised warm days ahead, a smell or a humidity. Now there was a bite in the breeze that almost coaxed you indoors, a smell and feel of the wind that invited hibernation; it's almost like the smell alone and the falling of the last yellow leaves was an *assurance* of longer, colder nights.

Lucy slapped me lightly on the thigh. "What's got you thinkin' so deep into all this stuff, Sash? I think it's natural that anyone living in this valley would, but don't go tying your brain into a knot about it; you've got, well...all the time in the world to ponder it."

I forced a smile and stared past her toward the Tetons, which were appearing to get more and more blanketed with snow by the day, the granite crags, peaks, and ridge lines that made up the range fading under the pronounced layers of deeper and deeper snow.

"Well...I guess, I'm not sure how to put this into words."

Lucy leaned down to brush some grass and dirt off her boots, then shifted her position to face me more directly. "Well, *try.*"

I thought about my words for a while before going on. "I find it very difficult to believe that there isn't some way to break this cycle. That there isn't some way to put the spirit to rest. That I should accept the perpetual nature of it all. There's a rule and ritual for each of the seasons. Why isn't there a rule or ritual for the lifetime of dealing with the spirit itself?"

I turned toward her. "Think about it like this...there's obviously some kind of link between the spirit and the lifetime of the people who live on the land in this valley. It seems it can only hook into someone who's spent a full season living on the land; otherwise Bethany, the Seymours' oldest kid, would've been killed when she tried to leave. So, for her, the spirit didn't get, I dunno...the necessary and requisite, like, latching time, I guess. Also, as soon as people living in the valley die, the spirit goes dormant on those people's land until someone else comes to live there. It's not like the light in the pond, the bear chase, and the scarecrows still happened at our place in the years between the Seymours leaving and us moving in, right? Furthermore, the fact that it can kill you anywhere means it's ultimately tied to the people, not the place."

Lucy nodded at me thoughtfully, urging me to continue.

"The spirit also seems to be bound to someone's possession of their piece of land, their claim over a little chunk of this place. I certainly can't imagine it has some grasp on property law or studies land surveys and title documents at the county clerk's office. So, it seems more connected to a person's feeling of control over land, rather than the land itself."

Lucy chuckled and cocked her head in acknowledgment. "So, that must mean the spirit recognizes a person's perceived boundaries of possession over a property in this valley, or something like that. Like it can sense or identify what we think we own, what we think we're entitled to control. I would point out, however, that the Henrys sold their land to Joe the day they moved. They signed over title and deed to him before they even got in their cars, so it's not *just* tied to someone's perceived ownership."

I nodded enthusiastically. "Well, then...shit." I giggled and let my shoulders slump down in mock defeat. Lucy joined in laughing.

"Lucy, I just *gotta think* there's a way to break this cycle. The spirit is *beholden* to a person's life, and its manifestation is *beholden* to that person's *belief*. So...how can there *not* be a way to tweak that arrangement, to fuck with that formula in a way to preclude the spirit's ability to get its engine started, so to speak?"

Lucy looked me in the eye and nodded slowly for what felt like a long time before looking down at her calloused hands, massaging one with the other. "You bring up a good point, about the spirit's needs, about its whole...*performance* being linked to a person's life and a person's belief. I have to think you're right, at least insofar as that being a formula it needs to, well, *exist*, I guess, in a way that we can see and feel, but I tell you what...I don't know shit from Shinola when it comes to *interrupting* that formula, or what on *earth* we could do to change it, and I'll say this as well: Any way I could think to do that sounds dangerous as hell."

I couldn't disagree with her on that one.

The next week rolled around, and Joanne, the lady who we'd essentially entered into the sheep business with, came by to drop off a ram to breed all the ewes. Harry was out grouse hunting with Dash, and I walked down to say hello.

"Hey, Joanne, how's it going?"

She picked up a bag of feed, threw it into the back of her truck, and responded with strain in her voice. "Well, I'm still alive."

I joined her as she stood, leaning on the gate that led into the pasture from the driveway, watching the new ram plod around the horde of anxious sheep who'd run over to see their new roommate. Joanne was an intense woman, rough around the edges, with sharp eyes and a face that looked like it had seen three lifetimes of sun. I'd actually grown to enjoy her gruff nature, in a way. I'd made a habit of joining her when she'd stop by to check on the sheep, give them vaccinations, or drop off some feed—which she'd been doing more often now with the pastures grazed down. I don't think she liked me very much, *progressive liberal city slicker* that I am. But I'd gotten the sense that she actually *liked not liking me*, in a low-key way. That she enjoyed the semiregular yet brief conversations and this strange relationship with someone so different from her.

I looked over at her big truck and the horse trailer she'd brought the ram over in. It had a large bumper sticker that showed the dark outline of a wolf in the middle of a red set of rifle crosshairs, as though it was about to get shot, with *Smoke a Pack a Day* scrawled underneath the image.

"What's the bumper sticker about?"

She glanced over at it, then briefly at me, then back at the sheep. "I don't much care for wolves. Don't see any reason for the enviros to be fightin' about 'em, forcing wolves back into this country; they're not the ones who gotta deal with 'em. We got rid of 'em for a reason, *damn good* reason too. Those sons a bitches threaten ranchers' livelihoods."

I wasn't sure how to respond at first. I love wolves—might even be one of my favorite animals. "Well...the ranchers who ran sheep and cattle across the western U.S. back in the 1800s seemed to get by all right when there were lots of wolves around. How'd they deal with the wolves?"

Joanne spit over the gate before responding. "They shot the bastards on sight, sweetheart. They did a thorough job of it too."

Damn. I set her right up for that one. To my surprise, Joanne went on without provocation. "The enviros call 'em a *keystone species*, but they're nothing but predators, destructive things, eat anything they can, even each other. You know that? It's in their nature to hide being hurt; they try to conceal it. Domestic dogs still do that too. If a wolf gets injured bad enough to get a limp or somethin', somethin' it can't conceal, its own pack'll turn on it, rip it to shreds, and eat it, *like they never even knew it.* Ain't nothin' about that species that's worth a damn more'n a bullet."

"Kinda like us then, eh? Sounds kinda like how *people* act. Maybe we've got more in common than appearances would suggest?"

Joanne grunted in response and turned toward me. *"Really?"*

She waved her gloved hand up toward the east, over the national forest and mountains. "We've got laws on conserving the elk and deer and animals up there; we've set boundaries for ourselves; we grasp the concept of scarcity and conservative use. That's how *people* manage the landscape. Wolves? They'll just tear through that same forest and rip everything apart till there ain't nothin' left, till they starve their own kind out. People might do terrible things, but we know they're wrong. Wolves? It's just in their nature to be destructive."

I nodded. "But that's kinda the point, right? It's in their nature, it's in their DNA, it's driven by their survival. They live in packs, have hierarchies; they aren't just total chaos-minded blood machines. They look out for their own and do the only thing they know to survive. Doesn't seem fair to condemn something to extinction just for its nature."

I could see Joanne roll her eyes under the brim of her dirty old Stetson. "Sure, it's in their nature. But if that's the case, then it's *sure as shit in a human's nature* to kill a beast that comes out of the forest to devour the animals we care about and depend on, *devour 'em alive,* no less. We've been doing *that* since we were still in the cave, so killin' the yodel mutts must *just be our nature* too, right?"

I looked over at her and tilted my head, then looked back into the meadow. "Well...*thank God* we don't behave the way we did when we were still in the cave, right? Pretty sure we used to kill and devour anything edible and murder outsiders on principle. You and I'd be slaves. *Thank goodness* humans were able to evolve past *that* phase and leave our violent troglodytic tendencies in the cave behind us. Lord only knows what the world would look like today if we hadn't..."

Joanne gave me a subtle, quick side glance and flared her nostrils, but didn't respond, which sent a little twinge of victory through me. After a while she looked back over at me.

"*Trogluh-what?*"

I laughed, and even got a grin out of her. "I'm gonna head back up to the house. I'll see you next time, Joanne."

I was walking up the driveway when she shouted up at me. "I think those trees up there look like they could use some huggin', Sasha."

I looked back and laughed, giving her a wave. She shot back the semblance of a grin and touched a gloved finger to the brim of her hat.

* * *

November pressed on. It was a beautiful time of year, but there was something somber about it, maybe even a little bit depressing. There's something intense about November afternoons in the mountains, once all the leaves have fallen, all the green has faded away. It's in the light or the way the wind takes on a deep howl as it rips through the mountains and trees above the house. It wasn't depressing in a *depressing* way, though. It just brought a sense of foreboding, like the wind had a motherly, cautionary tone. It's as if the breeze, the dropping temperatures, and the sounds themselves were reminding you to make sure you had enough food stored away, enough firewood split, enough warm blankets.

Dan had lent us his hydraulic firewood splitter, and Harry had been putting it to good use. It stopped running one day and Dan came over that afternoon to help get it fired back up. Afterward, he, Harry, and I were sitting on the back porch, and the discussion went to the two scarecrows that we'd had to deal with thus far, and their lack of…*effect*, I guess, upon being burned. Dan was confused about it, and to be honest, there was something in his features that made me think he was a bit worried by it.

We were having a back-and-forth about the meaning of it, with Harry insisting it didn't matter that we didn't *feel* it when they got burned. Dan and I, on the other hand, while not necessarily alleging it had any ominous meaning, were certainly pushing back against Harry's *it's no big deal* attitude. Dan and I were sitting on the bench at the outdoor table, while Harry leaned against the porch railing, adding to the adversarial vibe of the lighthearted exchange.

Dan took his hat off and wiped his forehead with his big tree trunk of a forearm. I'd grown fond of his little mannerisms like that; they were endearing. He looked up at Harry.

"Harry, it's not like I'm some damn expert on all this spirit hoopla, all right? But I'm tellin' ya, I've been draggin' two or three a' those creepy sacks a' shit out to the burn pile every year since before you were even born, and I ain't *never* burned one without that feeling, you know? The release, the *high* of it. I've *always* felt that feeling watching them start to burn, without fail. I'm not saying it's a big deal or anything that you haven't. I'm just, well…perplexed by it, and a bit perturbed."

Harry fired off a response right away. "Perplexed *and* perturbed, not the two *P*'s, Dan!"

Dan and I couldn't help but chuckle and roll our eyes in response.

Harry and Dan had grown close, and certainly enjoyed grinding each other's gears a bit. It was adorable.

I pointed at Harry with my thumb. "He's just a hopeless smartass, isn't he?"

Dan shook his head. "I don't know how you do it, you poor, patient woman."

Harry grinned and crossed his arms. "Look, Dan, I trust you

beyond measure—I always will—but that's just what happened, all right? Dragged 'em to the burn pile, they woke up a few times, cried and begged, then I burned 'em...What's the big deal? *Call up ol' Joe* if you're so worried about it. Tell him to stop by. I've been dying to meet him anyway, and at this point it's become downright strange that we've still never met. Maybe he can shed some light on this whole lack-of-euphoria-upon-scarecrow-burning issue. I just don't see why it's a problem."

Dan stared off into the east toward the mountains, head elevated slightly so he could scratch his chin. "How about this, *smartass*...?" He gave me a little grin, then looked up at Harry. "I'll be meeting with ol' Joe and one of his sons this coming week. I'll tell him what's going on here and ask his thoughts on it. Maybe ask him to stop by if he can. Latest we've ever found a scarecrow was November twenty-ninth, so you've only got a couple weeks or less for number three to show up, should there even be a number three. So, how about this: If you *do* find a third in the coming weeks, do me a favor and just call me? I'll come right over. I'd like to critique your methods."

Harry nodded once. "Of course, I'd love for you to see my lasso game."

I felt good about that as well. I always felt good after "summoning the elders" to hold little spirit-strategy councils. I knew Harry felt better after talking about this stuff with Dan and Lucy too, despite how nonchalant he was making himself out to be.

The next morning, I woke up early to go for a run with Dash down the county road to our mailbox. It was a nice little three-mile route there and back. I got my shoes on and threw on my gloves, hat, and pullover, grabbed the bear spray, and went outside. I was closing the gate behind me, putting an earbud into my ear, when a bolt of nausea came out of nowhere. I had just enough time to pull my hair back before I puked into the gravel of the driveway. Dash pranced up to me, giving me a concerned look, nudging me with his nose.

I took a knee and spit a few times, then sat back onto my ass to take some deep breaths. *What the fuck was that?* I'd felt great the night before, and we'd eaten soup for dinner from a batch I'd made a week earlier and had eaten three nights since. I couldn't be *pregnant*. I'd been on birth control for fuckin' years. I had just had my IUD removed about two months earlier because the side effects were terrible, but I'd been on the pill I switched to for a month now, and Harry and I were careful in the interim. At least I thought we had been…

Fuck. I ran back into the house, grabbed my keys, threw Dash in the car, and drove into town. I impulse-bought *five* pregnancy tests, and sped home. Harry hadn't even woken up yet, and I paced around outside, chugging water, in a full panic at the realization that I already had to pee, and had been pissing *constantly* over the last two weeks. I went into the half bathroom off the living room and used two of the tests. Didn't have to wait long until I saw that both were positive. *Fuck, fuck, fuck.* I convinced myself, for some reason, that I needed to wait to take the rest of the tests that night to be sure. That day dragged on like molasses. When that evening came around, I took two more of the tests into the bathroom, *willing* them to be negative as I unwrapped them.

An hour later I was sitting on the back porch, on the verge of tears, doing everything I could to hold it together. *I'm pregnant. I'm fucking pregnant.* I was so worked up I almost called my mom, which was a *highly* unusual thing for me to consider in a moment of stress. Being pregnant didn't just mean *being pregnant* anymore. On this land, for my child, it would mean being born into a life without the volition, the freedom, to go out into the world and choose a path like I did. What startled me even more was the fact that, up until this point, even if someone would've asked me a month earlier, I would have had *no qualms, no hesitation*, about getting an abortion. Now, however, I was *angry*. Angry at myself, angry at Harry, angry, most of all, at what this meant. I wanted the freedom to choose; I wanted the freedom to decide whether I was going to do this.

Now, with the freedom of that choice gone, the irresponsibility of having a kid here was so clear that the choice was already made for me. I couldn't bring a child into a life stuck with this crazy bullshit. Not a *chance*. The choice had been taken from me. It was infuriating. Unless I could figure out a way to end this spirit insanity, a way to break it, lift it, banish it, or fucking kill it, there was no way I could live with myself.

Unless I could figure out a way to end this.

Over the following couple days, I put on a world-class clinic in stress internalization. I know I'd just put Harry through the ringer with keeping the whole *we're dead if we try to leave* news to myself, but this was different. This was personal. This was *my* body that was now cooking up a life to be born into abject servitude to this spirit. This news was going to come out on my time, on my terms. What I was thinking about more than that, however, was what in the *goddamn world* could be done to have this child *without* the child becoming fodder for the spirit. There had to be a way to beat this thing, break this thing. I was going to figure it out or die trying. I'd felt that before, but never as viscerally as I did now.

When Thanksgiving rolled around, we still hadn't had scarecrow number three show up. Dan and Lucy put together a big dinner for the holiday, attended by a host of the local agrarian gentry. All nice people, some of whom we'd met since moving here. Joanne was there, and I sat next to and bickered with her throughout most of dinner. Everyone got merrily drunk—everyone except for me, which, conveniently, no one seemed to notice. Dash and a few other dogs guests had brought with them trotted around the table looking for scraps. After dinner Lucy played Christmas songs on their old piano as we all sang along. Dan and Lucy really had become family to us. I looked around that room, and the spirit business that'd been clogging my mind melted away. I saw this lovely, *happy* old rancher couple, surrounded by friends, in their beautiful home. Harry and I caught each other's eye from across the room, and we both smiled. I knew he was seeing and appreciating the same thing I was.

Spirit be damned. We really can have a good life here. We do *have a good life here.*

23

HARRY

THE SATURDAY AFTER Thanksgiving, I got up early to take Dash out for some trout fishing and grouse hunting along the Henrys Fork. The old cast and blast. Rivers would be icing over soon enough, so I felt obliged to get out fishing once more before winter really set in strong.

I was still half asleep when I walked into the kitchen to put on some coffee. I saw Dash staring into the door to the patio and mumbled an assurance I'd let him out to pee in a moment. As I leaned down to pull some mugs out of the dishwasher, I caught something out of place in my periphery. It gave me a start, so I snapped my head over to look out onto the back porch, and there it was. *Scarecrow number three.*

It was a boy this time. Looked like a fourteen-year-old boy, dressed up in goofy canvas pants with a rope belt, a stained button-down, and a bowl cut consisting of bright red yarn. Had a little shit-eating grin on his face too, the little fucker. His arms were crossed, gripping each of his biceps with dainty little hands made of straw-filled work gloves. He was leaning his tailbone onto one of the tall, fancy clay planters that Sasha's mom had, to our surprise, taken the time to purchase and send as a housewarming gift. He had one leg straight, holding him up, with the other leg bent at the knee, his foot on the planter.

He was unlike the other two in one notable way. The first two, the middle-aged man and the teenage girl, while *creepy as fuck* on principle, still had something of a peaceful demeanor, and in their original poses, where we'd found them, they had been staring out ahead of them at nothing in particular, with contemplative looks on their strange burlap faces. This little bastard, on the other hand, had his head turned to the right and was staring directly into the kitchen window with that creepy little condescending smile.

When this one woke up, I thought, I'd make sure to call him a prick before the little spasm of life ended.

As I'd promised, I grabbed my phone off the counter and called Dan. He usually woke up around four thirty in the morning, so I figured he'd have been up for almost two hours already. I was right; he answered after one ring and said he'd finish up what he was doing and head right over.

I went into the bedroom, where Sasha had been passed out just five minutes earlier, to find her sitting upright in bed, wide-eyed, as pale as a ghost.

"Harry...It's here, the spirit, I feel it. It's here right now."

Her tone, the panic in her voice, made my heart start pounding immediately. I sat down on the bed and put my hands on her shoulders.

"I know, babe. I just saw it; it's on the back porch. It's just the same as the last two, same as before. I already called Dan. He's on his way over, and I—"

Sasha cut me off and leaned forward just as I was starting to notice a hint of panic in my own voice. "It *is not* the same as before, Harry. I know it. *Can't you feel that?* I know you can feel that too."

She was starting to cry. I put my arms around her and pulled her into me.

"Babe, it's okay. It's all right, Sash. We've done this before, we're doing it now, and we'll do it again."

With each word I spoke, I felt it more. Sasha was absolutely right. It was exactly how I felt when the light was in the pond or the man was charging toward the fence line. It's like a *foreign* sense of dread, like a contagion, a viral, invasive panic that doesn't actually come from your own mind; it forces its way in. My ears started to pop.

Sasha insisted on seeing the scarecrow, despite my suggestion that she stay in bed until Dan and I got it burned. "*No*, Harry, I need to see this."

I followed her into the kitchen. Dash was still standing at the kitchen door with his head down, hackles standing straight up, letting out a low, deep growl directly at the door. That alone gave me an adrenaline shot that felt like sand pumping into my hands and face. He had barely reacted at all to the first two scarecrows, and now he was acting exactly as if the light was in the pond or the obscene spectacle of the bear chase was careening toward us.

We both stood there in silence, staring at the scarecrow boy casually leaning against the planter on the back porch, beaming his menacing little smile right at both of us. The only noise was Dash's low, guttural growl and the gurgling of the coffee machine.

I turned to Sasha. "See, babe, it's pretty much just the same as before."

As soon as I finished my sentence, Sasha bent over and puked right onto the kitchen floor, her stream of vomit smacking into the runner rug we had between the sink and the island in the center of the kitchen, spraying flecks and dollops up onto the cupboard doors. The suddenness of it made me gasp.

I grabbed her shoulders to help steady her and led her to the sink. Dash was starting to bark now.

Sasha spit a few times, wiped her mouth with a dish towel, turned on the faucet, and just stared blankly down into the sink.

I was switching my gaze between the scarecrow, Dash, and Sasha. *Holy shit. I need to keep my cool.* I poured a glass of water for Sasha and rubbed between her shoulders.

"It's all right. We're prepared for this. We know what to do. It's harmless right now."

She slowly shook her head, tears falling down her cheeks, then looked up at me. "Harry, that thing is not right. That thing is not just…a doll, not just a scarecrow like the others. I can *feel it*. There's something evil about this, Harry. There's something wrong." She started shaking, and barely finished her sentence before she began crying harder. I hugged her for a while, walked her into the living room, and sat down with her on the couch. I needed to make this all right.

I rebelled against that growing anger and tried to act calm for Sasha. I put my hands on her face and kissed her, then smiled. "Dan'll be here any minute, and when he gets here, I'm gonna just pop outside *real quick*, banish this devil doll back to the depths, and then we'll make some lattes, maybe some avocado toast, and just have ourselves a *super chill* little morning, all right?"

She smiled as she shook her head and let out a reluctant giggle. I wasn't sure whether it was appropriate to try to be goofy, and figured it wasn't when her smile was quickly replaced by a look of dread. I went to get Dash, who had worked himself into a frenzied rage in the kitchen, snarling and snapping at the door. I hauled him back into the living room and tried to soothe him a bit, but he wriggled out of my grasp and planted himself in front of Sasha, head low, growling at the walkway from the living room to the kitchen.

I heard the crunch and pop of the gravel as Dan's truck was coming up the driveway, so I started to get my scarecrow gear together. I went to open the front door, and Sasha grabbed my wrist. "Harry, *be careful*, okay?"

I kissed her and tucked her hair behind her ear. "I will be. Just stay in here, all right?"

I opened the front door and blocked the opening with my leg as Dash tried to bolt outside. "You're staying inside with your mom, buddy." He gave me his classic *tha fuck, man, thought we were a team* look as I scooted out the door sideways with the lasso, gas can, and coffee, then shut the door behind me.

Dan was coming through the gate as I walked down the steps of the front porch to meet him.

"Mornin', Harry! Number three, eh? Well, first autumn down! Where's it at?"

I sensed that Dan was trying to do with me what I had tried to do with Sasha a minute ago, acting goofy and overly casual. It made me anxious. We walked along the front of the house to where the porch opened up into the patio off the kitchen, and I gestured toward the "boy" with my coffee and watched Dan's face to see if he had any concerning reaction.

Dan sized up the scarecrow. "Little fella, eh? Welp, let's get to it, then. Lemme see how far you've come with that lasso, shit-kicker."

I nailed it on the first try. The lasso loop came to rest around the scarecrow's sternum, over his crossed arms. I cinched the knot until the tension pulled it over, reducing the uppity, youthful posture to a lumpy, lifeless pile of burlap and straw. Dan nodded at me. He looked nervous. I *felt* nervous.

I walked the rope around until I was in a spot in the yard where I could pull the scarecrow straight toward the stairs that led down from the porch, set it down, and went and opened the back gate. My heart was pounding in anticipation of the little episodic tantrums of dread that made these things so unpleasant.

I backpedaled with the rope until there was tension, turned to face the back gate that led out to the burn pile, then surged forward.

I felt the boy's burlap-and-straw body thumping down the stairs. *Damn*, this one was actually the heaviest yet. Must've been at least fifty pounds. I bent down, tightened my grip, and hauled it with everything in me, plowing through the yard toward the back gate.

Forty more feet. *Thirty*. I tried to get into a full sprint. Twenty more feet. *Ten more feet*. I had just reached the back gate, but it felt like the little bastard had gained a hundred more pounds in the distance I'd made. My shoulders and legs were screaming. I dropped the rope and turned to Dan, who was about a dozen paces behind the scarecrow. I pointed down to it, speaking between heavy breaths.

"Ever move one that far without it waking up at all, without it even making a peep?"

Dan looked even more nervous than before. He'd gone pale and didn't take his eyes off the lifeless scarecrow as he responded. "No, Harry. *No, I have not.*"

I put my hands on my knees and looked down at the scarecrow lying on its back, at that little smart-ass smile still on its face, its goofy bowl cut. I glanced up at Dan as he scanned the area around us, as though observing the air itself, then glanced back at me.

"It's here all right, son. The spirit. It's here. Might not've been for your first two scarecrow mornings, but it sure as hellfire is now."

I couldn't deny that. I felt it. The tentacles of panic were leaching into my mind. The wind was picking up fast. In the time we'd been standing there it had gone from a light breeze to a current of jarring gusts, shaking the giant cottonwoods above us. Dan and I both looked up at the trees. A chill set in and seeped into my bones.

Dan looked down from the trees to my face. "Finish this. Finish this *now*."

I snatched up the rope from the leaf-pocked lawn and backpedaled until there was tension, then rushed backward with all my strength like I was in a game of tug-of-war. My feet broke into the frost-crusted sand of the burn pile. The doll's head was just crossing the threshold of the gate. Then it happened.

The doll sat bolt upright away from me, the force of which tore the rope out of my hands so fast I fell backward hard onto my ass. It scared me so bad I yelped like a child. It was facing away from me, directly at Dan, who shuffled backward so suddenly he fell over as well. The second the boy, the *thing*, reached a full sitting position, it *screamed*.

The scream sounded like a young boy's at first, but it grew deeper in pitch, expanding to sound like five different screams at once. A man's, a girl's, a horse's, a pig's. The air pressure changed dramatically, and my ears popped so hard it hurt. I was immediately nauseated. I could barely breathe. I felt like I was in a bowl of thick, heavy mud. I was starting to raise my hands up to cover my ears when all the vitality in the doll extinguished in an instant, and it crumpled backward into the lifeless pile of lumpy straw-filled burlap, staring up into the sky with that creepy smile.

I scrambled to my feet, hurdled the scarecrow, and sprinted over to Dan. He was propped up on his elbows, eyes locked on the demonic mass with a blazing focus.

I took a knee next to him and he looked up at me. "Well, there's a first time for everything, I s'pose."

I appreciated his humor. It grounded me. We both caught our breath for a few seconds, then Dan put his hand on my back. "Now you know why I hate these things like the dickens. But I will say, I ain't never heard that kinda wailing before. Sounded like a chorus from hell."

I didn't know what to say, other than to reiterate his earlier directive. "Let's get this fucking *done*."

Dan nodded and picked up the gas can. We both scooted quickly out the gate past the lifeless scarecrow, giving it a wide berth. I snatched up the rope again, and slowly backed up through the sand of my burn pile, leaving footprints through the ash of the two earlier, far more harmonious scarecrows of the season. I went backward until I had tension on the rope, and looked at Dan. I might've appreciated that man more in that moment than I'd ever appreciated the company of any man in my whole life. He gave me a stern look and nodded.

I tore the rope toward me and seethed backward with all my strength. I'd dragged the scarecrow until its waist was almost outside the gate when it happened.

The scarecrow shot its arms over to one side, flipping itself onto its stomach in one fast movement, then lifted up onto all fours, digging its feet, knees, and buckskin-glove-adorned straw hands into the dirt.

I tried to fight against its resistance, but it was like pulling on a rope tied to Dan's truck. Again, the rope tore from my hands and I fell backward. Dan slowly paced away from the scarecrow, staring down at it in wide-eyed terror.

I watched as the scarecrow slowly began to lift its head up, until I could see its eyes between the locks of its red yarn hair, staring straight into mine. I shot up to my feet and dove for the lasso. Right as my hands almost grasped it, the boy yanked it back, and I watched with dread as the rope coiled into a pile in front of him. Right then, the boy started giggling.

What started as a giggle turned into a devious cackling that shot ice into my veins and covered my entire body in goose bumps. It grew louder, until the boy was in a fit of raucous, *deep* laughter. The kind of deep, sincere laughter that comes from the belly and the bones. Its eyes were squinted narrow, with piercing, glowing blue pupils boring straight into me. My skin was crawling; it felt like I was covered in insects. I started dry heaving.

Then, as fast as it had started, the life ripped out of the devilish child, and its body thunked back into the earth like a bag of chains.

I looked up at Dan, who was staring at me with true terror in his eyes, a look I'd never thought I'd see on his face. I was shaking like a leaf. I had a slick of stomach acid along my teeth. I forced myself to my feet, then felt like I was going to throw up and had to put my hands on my knees and spit into the sand repeatedly. I caught my breath and managed to form a few words.

"Ever heard one laugh?"

Dan did not respond, or take his eyes from mine; he just slowly shook his head from side to side, until he mustered some words himself.

"Son, we need to get this thing outside this gate *right now*."

My emotions were going completely nuclear; it was something I'd never felt before. I was experiencing a hundred different feelings at once, all at their most heightened intensity. It was like a rolling, white-hot spectrum churning through my brain and gut. I felt rage rotate by for a brief moment, and I grasped at it like a lifeline, like it was my last chance.

I dove for the scarecrow, landing with my full weight on its sickly little face. I seized it by its oily, red-yarned scalp, and with every ounce of strength and will in my body and soul, I tore it out through the gate, screaming my lungs dry until I felt my feet hit the sand of the burn pile.

As I dropped it, a storm of dread hit me as its grotesque little hand shot out and grasped my forearm like a vise, like its buckskin gloves were filled with cold steel. I frantically tore and clawed at its grip with my free hand, trying to pry it away. Dan dove out of my periphery to help try to get the thing's grip from my arm. I didn't notice when it started, but Dan and I were both screaming, *roaring* with disgust, horror, and sheer effort.

As it began to slowly raise its head to look up at me, its other hand launched out and locked around Dan's throat with tremendous force. I stopped trying to free its grip on my arm and began hauling on its other hand. Its grip was so tight that its work-gloved fingers were almost completely buried in Dan's muscular neck.

Dan's eyes and veins were bulging as his face turned a darker and darker shade of reddish purple. I watched, helpless, as blood dribbled out of his mouth down his chin and spurted in thick dollops out of his ears. His right eye burst in the socket, a vertical tear ripping through his blue cornea and sending a torrent of fluid that braided with the blood running down and soaking into the arm of the scarecrow.

I looked back down at the scarecrow, who was still slowly raising its head to look into my face. When its eyes met mine, it smiled.

My bladder and bowels released immediately. Blood started pouring out of my nose and ears. My eyeballs started vibrating. My teeth felt like they'd turned into maggots, wiggling and writhing to break free from my gums. I couldn't move. I couldn't hear anything but the unnaturally loud roaring of blood in my head.

The sinister stitchwork of the scarecrow's mouth began to twist and gyrate as it formed words, but there was nothing *being spoken*—there was no noise at all, while also being the loudest thing I'd ever heard. The scarecrow wasn't projecting particular sounds, but it had a voice—a deep, glottal, sucking voice that was ripping and pounding through my head in a fiendish cadence.

"*You TOOK My Land? Neither BEASSST nor MAN can TAKE from me, Tourissst. Tourists have come in groups and bands to lay claim to this land. The Rock Carvers, the Beast Hunters, the Horse Masters, the Shoshone, the Bannock, Fur Trappers, Gold Miners, the Priestsss, the Homesteaders, all have come and made claims. Your Bones, like their bones and ALL BONES, shall be DUSSST long before my essence goes to seed. I AM THISSS LAND.*"

In an instant, it released its grasp, and Dan, the scarecrow, and I all collapsed into the sand. I couldn't control my muscles and vomited as I lay facedown, filling my mouth with bile that sent me into a coughing fit, which seemed to shock a bit of reflexive control back through my body. I rolled away from what was now a flaccid sack of straw, pushed myself up onto my knees, and forced myself to sit, trying to breathe. I looked up into the sky and struggled to catch my breath. The front of my body was coated in sand-caked vomit and blood. I realized I couldn't see—I actually reached up to wipe away the wet sand from my eyes and make sure they were open. When I felt them and realized I still couldn't see, a shock of panic went through me, but it almost helped clear my mind for the first time.

The first thing that ran through my head was Sasha. *Sasha.* I'd put us in danger. I'd put *her* in danger. What had I done? *What had I fucking done?*

I remembered Dan then. I felt around for him frantically, until I felt the stiff denim of his pants. I gripped his ankles and dragged him a few feet away. I worked back to where we'd all collapsed, feeling around for the scarecrow. I found it and recoiled as soon as I had. I fumbled around in my pockets for the matches, pulled the box out, and used my thumb to find the sandpaper. I pulled out a clutch of three or four matches, slowly reached down until my hand found the back of the scarecrow. I made a note of its location in my head as best I could, struck the matches, held them upside down until I could hear the flame hit the resin and start to sizzle, then dropped them toward the lifeless heap of burlap and straw. I wasn't sure it would catch, until I felt a jarring cough of heat on my face as it ignited into flames. I rolled back toward where I'd left Dan until I felt his legs.

Everything was coming back to me now. The details of everything that had happened as the scarecrow gripped my arm and Dan's throat, piercing through the druglike daze. I was weeping, weeping like a child as I felt my way up his body and locked my arms under his armpits. I could only guess as to where the gate was, but knew I needed to drag him away from the flames.

I made it only a few yards before my muscles seized up, and I collapsed backward, bringing Dan with me so that he fell on top of me. His weight made it harder to breathe than it already was.

I realized I was screaming for help. I was screaming for Scott, and for Tucker. I was feeling around my plate carrier for where I kept my tourniquet, clawing at my neck for my helmet's chin strap. Scott was *just sitting right next to me*. Was he fucked-up too? Shit, he probably was. *We need to get off the X.* I started screaming for a corpsman. *Where the fuck is my rifle? I need my rifle, and I need to move. I need to find my fucking rifle and I need to fucking move. Where the fuck is the corpsman? Holy shit, I'm gonna die here. Goddammit I'm gonna fucking die here.*

My last scream forced me into a coughing fit so intense I threw up again, and it was so jarring it helped me remember where I was. Right before I passed out, I felt Dash licking my face and heard Sasha screaming my name.

24

HARRY

꙳

I WAS ALREADY SITTING up and holding something when I came to. I was warm. I could see. *I can fucking see.* I was in bed, leaning against the headboard. I was holding a glass to my lips with both hands, chugging it down. I had no idea how I got where I was, and a burst of panic went through me, but I couldn't stop drinking. I closed my eyes again and chugged until the liquid was gone, gasping for air after I swallowed the last of it.

I opened my eyes again and a big hand extended in front of me, taking the empty glass and giving me another full one in its place. It was a dark green, minerally liquid.

An unfamiliar voice spoke. *"Drink."* I wanted nothing more in the world, and readily obliged. I chugged half the glass, paused to take a breath, burped, then chugged the second half.

Sasha. I planted a hand on the mattress and whipped my legs over, starting to fly out of the bed when a strong pair of large hands gripped me by the shoulders and slammed me back down into the soft bed, pinning me in place.

"Sasha? Sasha!" I looked up into the unfamiliar face of the man holding me down, still unable to see much more than light and shapes as I frantically tried to blink the vision back into my eyes. A rage surged through me from my toes to my scalp. I gripped the man's

thumbs on my shoulders and was about to rip them down into his wrists when the strange man spoke again.

"Whoa, whoa, *whoa, buddy*, Sasha's fine. Sasha's okay. Dash! Dash, come here!" The man took one of his hands off me and started patting the comforter. In that same second, Dash jumped up onto the bed, wagging his tail so hard his entire ass whipped back and forth, climbing up onto me, licking my face.

"Sasha's fine, Harry. She's with Lucy. I told her I'd stay here with you."

I scratched Dash's head with both hands, half because his affection was comforting and familiar and half in an effort to move him because he'd completely smothered me and blocked my view.

The deep voice spoke again. "Give him some air, buddy. Dash, come here."

Dash whipped his body off me and jumped down to the floor. I pushed myself up again to lean back against the headboard and reflexively rubbed my eyes as though it would help me figure out what the fuck was going on.

I looked toward the voice, more light and detail coming into my vision with every blink. The scene before me was startling.

Standing a couple feet from my bed was a giant of a man. He was a striking figure, tall, wearing a flannel shirt under worn and oil-stained Carhartt overalls. He had long obsidian-black hair tied back in a ponytail. He looked to be about Dan's age, early seventies, but with shoulders as broad as my dresser and a posture that betrayed a strength that was immediately humbling. Dash, to my surprise, was sitting at the man's feet, wagging his tail across the floor, staring up at him as though he were the king of the universe.

I looked up into the man's face with stupid shock when he spoke. "Harry, you can call me Joe."

He took a step toward the bed and extended a hand the size of a catcher's mitt. I took it and it was like grabbing hold of an oak limb.

"J-Joe...Hi, Joe. Where's Sash—"

Joe cut me off. "Sasha's with Lucy, over at their place. She left you this." He handed me a small piece of paper with a brief message scrawled across it:

> *I'm safe Har-Bear*
> > *With Lucy*
> > *Back soon*
> > *Talk to Joe*
> > *Then rest, you need to rest*

Knowing I'd be suspicious until I saw her with my own eyes, she'd used her old nickname for me, and the message was in her distinctive cursive handwriting.

I dropped the note and rubbed my eyes, then my temples, then looked back at Joe.

"Joe . . . what happened?"

Without any change in his facial expression, he responded, *"You tell me."*

I put my fingers to my forehead, as though I could massage some function and recall back into my brain. *Scarecrow, little boy, blue eyes, its voice, its fucking voice. It talked. DAN.*

I ripped my gaze up at him with frenzied, renewed panic coursing through me, leaning forward. *"Joe, what happened to Da—"*

He stepped forward again, putting his massive hand on my shoulder. He did so with less force, but in a way that still made me shut the hell up immediately. He looked down at me, and his features changed subtly. There was sympathy in his eyes.

"Harry, Dan Steiner is dead. He was alive when Sasha found you yesterday morning, but he didn't make it. He died this morning."

I felt a tidal wave of emotions—rage, confusion, hate, guilt—boil up in my gut, and as though he sensed the need to cut that off, Joe squeezed my shoulder and gave me a little shake. "Harry, I need you to get dressed and come meet me outside. We need to talk."

I could only nod. I felt like a little boy, like I had when I'd been caught stealing Pogs at the mall in fifth grade and saw my mom walking into the security office. Joe held my gaze for a moment, then slowly turned and strolled out of my bedroom, casting a subtle glance at Dash, who eagerly trotted after him.

I put my face in my hands and wept like a little boy for a full minute, mind racing as I cobbled together the memory of what had happened. I remembered it all, from the moment it grabbed us, what it had said, blindly setting it on fire, trying to drag Dan away from the flames.

Eventually I pushed myself out of bed, put on some pants, pulled a hoodie over my head, and mashed my feet into some old boots in my closet. I slowly walked out of my bedroom, not sure where Joe would be, feeling as though I were creeping through someone else's home I had drunkenly passed out in the night before.

When I peered into the kitchen, I saw he was standing on the back deck, looking up toward the mountains. He turned when I opened the back door. The light was abrasive, and I had to squint to keep my focus.

He gestured toward the meadow. "Let's take a walk." All I could do was nod and obediently fall in behind him.

We strolled into the meadow and down toward the pond without speaking. Dash was trotting along next to me, licking my hands. Joe slowed his stride as we got to a small rise above the pond, then stopped, looped his thumbs into the shoulder straps of his overalls, and stared up into the mountains.

I stood a few feet behind him, looking up at him in awe of his formidable stature and grace, as though me looking at him was the same as him looking up at the mountains. Joe was quiet for what felt like a long time. Long enough for my mind to wander back to my last memories before passing out: weeping and screaming, damp in my own piss, shit, vomit, and blood. When he turned to face me, it snapped me back to reality, and I stared up at him, almost startled, feeling like a dried shit on a forgotten sidewalk.

"Dan and Lucy have spoken very highly of you and your wife. I like Sasha; she is strong, and wise, it seems."

I nodded. "She is." I was struggling to carry on with the pleasantries, my head throbbing and my heart now aching from the news of Dan's death. "We've . . . well, this is a special place, and I understand that if it weren't for your wisdom, which was shared with us, I don't think Sasha and I would've survived very long here."

Joe just stared at me, *into* me. After a while, he turned his whole body back toward the mountains and spoke.

"It seems you have tried to remove the spirit's mask."

"I . . . what? Its what?"

"Provoking the spirit. Trying to get a rise out of it?"

I felt busted. "I . . . I didn't know. I mean . . . I guess I was just trying to get it to stay away, or understand it more, see if . . . Yeah, I did try to get a rise out of it. I just, I thought there might be a way to get it to leave us alone."

Staring at the side of Joe's face, I could see him smirk, and he responded without looking back at me.

"That's not how it works, tough guy."

"Well, *how am I supposed to know what the fuck is going on, Joe?*" I could hear the anger and panic in my voice rising. "I don't know what this is; I don't know how to deal with this shit. *You're the one* who knows what's going on, and you didn't bother coming over here until terrible shit finally happened, while I don't know what the fuck any of this even is. And there's *nothing* we can do to get it to leave us alone? Haven't your people figured it out by now? All this time in this valley, fucking millennia, and you haven't figured out some native fuckin' ritual or *spirit dance* you can do to—"

Joe wheeled on me, stepping within inches of me so fast and with such force that Dash jumped to the side and I stumbled backward, almost tripping over myself. He didn't speak with discernible anger, or irritation—he just spoke with pure, unbridled force.

"You think my people control this? You think this has something to do with *my people*? You think you can just have the Indians come and do a little dance, sing a few songs, and fix this for you, *white man*? You don't know *anything*. This spirit is older than me. It's older than my people. It's *older than those rocks* up there. It's held sway over *everyone* who's lived in this valley, the first people who *ever set foot in this valley*, ten thousand years before *my people* were even here. The only thing *my people* can do for you, *white man*, is remind you not to be stupid."

Joe looked away, spit out into the pasture, ran his massive forearm across his mouth, then looked back at me with fire in his eyes, talking for the first time with an edge in his voice, the throat rust of anger. "Dan was my oldest friend left, and you got him killed because of your stupidity, because of your bullheadedness. If it weren't for Sasha—if it weren't for Lucy and Dan's love of your wife—you'd already be in the dirt, boy. *You understand me?* Dan told me you were a good man more'n once, and you owe him your life, because if he hadn't, you *wouldn't have woken up this morning.*"

I was floored. Completely unable to think of what to say. I just held up my hands as though it could convey some apology. Eventually Joe took a few steps back and crossed his arms again, and after an increasingly tense silence, he spoke.

"Listen to me, and hear this, if you hear nothing else: The last thing you ever want to do is try to force away a spirit's mask. That can put more than just you in danger, *as you've now seen*. If you'd just followed the steps Dan and Lucy gave you, you'd have stayed safe. *That's all you needed to do. That's all I can give you.* You follow those rules, and you can live a full life here, and as long as your heart beats and you are on this land, you will follow those rules. You promise me that now, Harry."

He took a step toward me, pointed at the ground between my feet, and leaned into my face. *"Right now."*

And I did, immediately, without even thinking, knowing to the depth of my soul that I meant it. "I promise, Joe. I promise."

Joe raised his eyebrows and nodded once. "Good." He leaned back from my face and turned toward the mountains.

I had ten thousand questions for Joe, but I knew I could probably only shake him down for one.

"Joe, is what I've done...? Have I started something irreversible? Is Sasha in danger? Can I come back from this and be safe here, or...as safe as I was before all this happened?" I guess I ended up going for three or four questions.

Joe smiled up at the mountains with a mix of amusement and annoyance.

"The spirit does not hold grudges, Harry, if that's what you're asking. *It teaches lessons*, but I think you needed that one, eh?"

He turned to face me. "It takes a lot for the spirit to break its patterns as it did yesterday. It won't be able to do something like that easily for a long time, and it only would again *if you give it a reason to*. No. The patterns will fall back into place. But the spring, summer, fall, these rules, I'm not sure following them closely will matter for a man like you..."

A mixture of shame, guilt, relief, and, more than anything else, confusion hit me so hard I felt like weeping. Joe turned back toward the house and took a few steps in that direction, but stopped. Without looking back at me, he spoke in a loud, firm voice.

"You are a warrior. That can help you and your family lead this kind of life in old country like this, but not in everything. The warrior heart must be tempered. Pride and rage will kill a stupid man like you anywhere, but *especially* in old country like this. Your wife, Sasha, she's wise. She has good instincts. Think and act together, not brashly on your own. And that hound, Dash, that's a strong one. He sees more than you know. That's your family. Trust them, trust the methods my family shares with yours, and you can live with the spirit through the seasons."

I nodded at his back. "I will. We came here to build a home, to build a life."

Joe turned back to face me with what was almost an inquisitive look. He was studying my face and nodded slowly as he began to speak. "You may yet...though whether or not you and your wife will have a life here, or anywhere, will depend on how you handle the days to come."

"Wait...what do you mean? *What does that mean?*"

Joe kept staring at my face, as though he was trying decipher something, almost as though he was literally trying to read something written on my forehead.

I pushed again. "What else do I need to know, man? What aren't you telling me?"

Joe's inquisitive gaze continued, his eyes seeming to flick between different parts of my face. It reminded me of how shrinks at the VA size you up as you plod through an answer to a question seemingly designed for that purpose. He eventually crossed his arms and looked past me into the pasture.

"The winters in this valley can be long, dark, and hard on brutes like you, Harry. Longer, darker, and harder than they are for others."

The cryptic answer made me want to scream, so I rubbed my temples to calm myself down. Joe sensed I was about to rattle off another string of questions and put his hand up.

"Harry, we'll pick this up later. Right now, I need to be with Lucy, you need to be with Sasha, and that is the last thing I will say to you this day."

The combination of his demeanor and tone did more than dissuade any further comment from me; it *forbade* it. He turned sharply and stormed up toward the house. I was about to follow him when I felt something cold gently touch the back of my neck.

I turned around, looked over the pasture, and saw that it had started to snow.

PART V

WINTER

25

SASHA

WE BURIED DAN Steiner on the first Tuesday in December.

I'd spent the last several days at Lucy's side. She alternated between being an absolute wreck with grief and a shockingly well-adjusted realist. My personal emotional state was only slightly more composed than Lucy's—a forced effort to try to provide some semblance of strength and support. I'd more or less completely forgotten I was *pregnant* those first couple days.

A host of Dan and Lucy's friends were constantly in and out of the house, longtime acquaintances bringing by enough food to feed a small army. Several of the ranch hands that worked for Dan full-time in the summer drove in from Montana, Oregon, and Wyoming. These were real cowboys, hard men, loyal men. They had the kinds of lines in their faces and scars on their hands that can only come from a life of cold wind, hot sun, and hard work. They made sure Lucy didn't have to lift a finger to keep the ranch going, didn't even raise the issue of pay, just went straight to work. Though I wasn't surprised to eventually overhear Joe promising them he'd make sure they got their wages.

Joe spent almost as much time at Dan and Lucy's in the days following the "accident" as I did.

They quietly agreed upon the story that was to be told, about how Dan had an accident with the tractor. The sheriff had come out early that afternoon. Joe met him at the door, where I watched them have a brief exchange from where I stood doing dishes in the kitchen. The sheriff hardly asked any questions; he didn't even ask how Dan died. It was clear he knew exactly what had happened and pursued no further explanation. He just nodded, put some flowers for Lucy on the table near the front door, shook Joe's hand, and left. I wasn't actually that surprised at all. I just went back to doing the dishes and making tea.

Strange things happen in old country like this.

The morning everything happened, I'd sat on the couch as Dan and Harry went out to deal with the scarecrow. I'd been sitting there for a couple minutes, trying to remain calm, until I decided I needed to do something to keep my mind off what was going on. I'd almost completely forgotten about puking all over the kitchen, so I went and started to clean it up. Out of nowhere, the power went out in the house, and in that same second a surge of terror and dread smashed into me like the shock wave of an explosion. I couldn't talk—I could barely breathe—but I knew something was very, very wrong. I sat on the kitchen floor, trying to get in a deep breath, Dash panicking, crying and whining, pacing around in front of me. Out of nowhere, Dash whipped his head toward the door, in the direction of Dan and Harry, and let out the most soul-shaking *howl* that I've ever heard come out of *any* animal, let alone my golden retriever. It shocked the life into me, and I ripped open the kitchen door and was terrified to hear Harry. Harry *screaming*.

I broke into a sprint toward the back gate, Dash right beside me, charging up ahead. I got to where I could see around the big, gnarled trunks of the cottonwood trees and gasped as I saw Harry, covered in blood and sand, screaming while Dan was piled on top of him, lifeless.

Harry was screaming for a corpsman; I've only ever heard him utter the word *corpsman* in his sleep while he's having nightmares. Hearing my husband *scream* that word—hearing that word shrieked in terror then echoing across a cold morning—was one of the more haunting memories of that entire day.

I saw Dan's destroyed face and helplessly shook Harry, begging for him to calm down, begging for him to get up. It's like he was hallucinating. He was screaming other guys' names too, guys I knew he was in the marines with. I finally ran back into the house and called Lucy, who was in the driveway within five minutes. When I saw another truck pull in a couple minutes later, somehow I knew it was Joe before the truck was even in park. Joe's son Elk was with him; I learned that day he was a physician assistant who ran a clinic in town.

Joe got Harry into our bed while Elk saw to Dan, then both left to bring Dan home. Elk said it was almost as if Dan was in a sort of coma. He had some of his staff come over to Dan and Lucy's to set up a makeshift hospital room in their home.

Harry slept for almost twenty-six hours. That next morning, Joe knocked on the door and told me Dan had died just before dawn.

We sat for a while at the kitchen table, drinking coffee. I hadn't taken a shower or changed; I'd barely even hydrated since the morning before. I eventually fell apart and began crying as the reality of Dan's death sank in. Joe didn't seem upset by my state; he just petted Dash, who seemed enamored with him.

It was just me and a strange, large man, sitting in my kitchen; a man I'd thought about on a daily basis for the last eight months, spending hours rehearsing the questions I was going to ask him upon our first meeting. But instead, we just sat there quietly, the only sounds being the old clock on the kitchen wall, the window-muffled breeze through the leafless branches of the trees in the yard, and my crying. It was easily the most bizarre moment in my life.

Joe finally looked up at me. "Do you have any idea what happened out there yesterday morning?"

I truly didn't.

He took a sip of his coffee, then held the cup with both hands as though he was trying to warm them. "It's not easy, nor any casual thing, for the spirit to do something like that. Before Dan passed, he was able to write down a bit of what happened. Said the scarecrow...*spoke*. The little of what Dan could write down suggested it might not have actually been the first time Harry and the spirit had exchanged words."

I was shocked, but then I wasn't. Over the next fifteen minutes, I told Joe *everything*. I described our experiences with the light, all four bear chase encounters, all about Harry telling the naked man he'd *taken* the land from him, how that made the man stop pleading and begging, about how he stared off to the west, and about the last two scarecrows. Eventually Joe put his hand up and thanked me for the detailed account. He was quiet for a while, slowly drinking coffee.

"Sasha, was Harry a soldier?"

"No, he was a marine. Sorry, I mean, *yes*, he was a soldier—he was in the infantry—but he was in the Marine Corps, and marines are touchy when they're called 'soldiers.' I guess it's rubbed off on me." *God*, I felt so awkward.

Joe nodded. "That where he got those scars I saw on his body? In the infantry?"

I nodded. "Yeah. He got, well…he got blown up. By an IED. It happened before we met, at the end of his deployment, two weeks before he was set to come home from Afghanistan."

Joe nodded. "Do you know about some of the things he did over there? Do you know about any men he may have killed?"

I was surprised by the question and shifted uncomfortably, feeling an unexpected pang of shame, knowing that I wasn't actually able to give him an answer; I wasn't actually able to describe what my own husband had been through in much detail at all. "I think you should ask him about that."

Joe nodded and looked down into his cup. We lapsed back into extended silence from there, as the questions I'd wanted to ask him started coming back to me. I was going from one to another, trying to think of the best information to seek, knowing I needed to exercise tact. I don't know why I did what I did next—maybe it was the ticking of the clock; maybe it was my husband, who I'd scrubbed free of his own blood, vomit, and shit the day before; maybe it was the lack of sleep;

maybe it was the stress and grief of a father figure just getting brutally killed in my backyard; maybe it was all of it—but it just came out.

"Joe, I'm pregnant."

Joe looked up at me with what must be his stern version of surprise and held my gaze for a full fifteen seconds before responding. "I get the feeling that wasn't something you planned on."

I shook my head as tears fell from my eyes. "No, and Harry doesn't know yet."

Joe tilted his head a few degrees. "So why do I?"

Once again, I wasn't equipped with an adequate answer. I knew what I *felt*, that I didn't have it in me to tell Harry we were going to have a baby until, *unless*, I was able to find some kind of solution. Some way to *beat* this spirit. Some way to create a life for our child not spent enslaved to a parcel of land, forced to perform rituals to ward off supernatural danger. I wanted to beat this thing, but I think I was too embarrassed to say that out loud. The audacity of it. That I, after less than a year here, was going to somehow find a way around all of this.

I looked up at Joe. Tears were streaming down my face now, but I didn't let my voice shake.

"I know there's a way to get rid of this spirit. Get rid of it for good. There's *got* to be. I know you've told Dan and Lucy there isn't, but maybe you just told them that because the answer is too dangerous, too difficult. But if there is an answer, if there is some way to do it, you've gotta tell me now, Joe."

He stared at me for a long time before he finally spoke, his only acknowledgment of my plea being a subtle narrowing of his eyes. I stared back at him. I tried not to blink.

"Sasha, you've done well, learning how to live here. You've done well by keeping your ear to the ground; seems you understand this land. That means a lot to me. But right now, this morning, I need to ask something of you. I need to ask you to go be with Lucy. I need to talk with Harry when he wakes up, and I don't want Lucy to be alone. She loves you like a daughter, and we need to look out for her right now. *Please.*"

And that's what I did. From that morning, until the funeral, standing over Dan's grave, I barely left her side. I knew Harry needed me, I knew I needed him, but I wanted to be there for Lucy. It wasn't that hard to put myself in her shoes, given the circumstances, and I was in awe of her strength every minute I spent with her.

I'd been able to get a few nights with Harry, who seemed like a different person. Or, rather, he seemed like the person I'd met in that college bar all those years ago now. Pulled back. Living in his head. Drowning in his guilt.

I wept as I watched Lucy take Harry's face in her hands that day, tears pouring down both their faces.

"Harold Blakemore, *this is not your fault. I will live every day I have left on this earth knowing that Dan's death was not your fault.* All our lives, every hour, are subject to the whim and caprice of this spirit; we all share that, and in the end, it takes us all. *Dan loved you, Harry.* He wouldn't have gone out any other way."

I'd told Harry the same things when I'd gone home from Lucy's to sleep during that last week. He'd lie there quietly in the dark as I'd rub his back and tell him he couldn't take the burden for this, tell him he couldn't harbor the guilt. He'd lie there quietly, and I knew he would anyway.

I watched Joe stand over Dan's grave that day we buried him. I watched his sons, their wives, their children. I watched a tear roll down Joe's cheek. Before my eyes, Joe changed from the legendary patriarch of this spirit-possessed valley into an old man burying his old buddy. I saw he had good in him. I saw he cared about Dan. Even in the brief exchanges we'd had at Dan and Lucy's in that week between the scarecrow chaos and Dan's funeral, I could tell that he cared about me.

I knew he had a way to break the spirit, too. I don't know *how* I knew it, but I did. I could see it in his eyes. It made me angry, wondering why on earth he'd keep that to himself. But somehow, I knew that whatever it was, whatever old rule or ritual he knew about that would free someone from the spirit, it came with a terrible price. I didn't care, because I was going to find out what it was, and after all this . . . whatever that grave price was, I'd pay it a thousand times over.

26

HARRY

THAT WEEK BETWEEN the scarecrow fiasco and Dan's funeral, and the week after, I mostly just milled around in an insomnia-like daze.

I'd put Sasha in direct danger, and Dan was dead because of my anger, my fuckup. I taunted the spirit, I coaxed it, and it took its pound of flesh. I felt more worthless than I ever had.

I'd started to feel confident on this land. I'd started to feel at home. Now I looked out over the snowy meadow, and it was like looking at the surface of a hostile planet. Under the circumstances that accompany living here, I truly felt I couldn't trust myself anymore. Sasha did her best to try to convince me Dan's death wasn't my fault. Lucy did as well. Shit, even Joe pulled me aside at Dan's funeral and made some comment about how highly Dan had spoken of me over the last eight months. I knew they were all doing so with the best intentions, but I also knew they were all full of shit. It was entirely my fault.

I'd come to gather bits and pieces from Sasha about her conversations with Joe that week, both the one she had in our kitchen and the other exchanges they'd had at Lucy's as they helped her and prepared Dan's funeral together. That conversation, or those exchanges in the aggregate, had given Sasha a new, surprising confidence. Something had happened to her in the days after that scarecrow going apeshit, something that seemed to catalyze a deeper connection to this place, a more meaningful understanding of this land. I was jealous of it, but I certainly didn't do anything to try to pursue that connection myself.

For that first week after Dan died, all I could think to do was split firewood. I had let that chore fall behind, so day after day, I'd buck logs, heft rounds onto the wood splitter, pull on the lever, and watch the hydraulic blade slowly make the split as I chain-smoked cigarettes. It was meditative. Or maybe it was just a distraction. Whatever it was, I spent that time wallowing in self-reflection, and self-pity. Somehow, however, that routine allowed me to look under my own hood for the first *real* time to reflect on how I'd been wired.

After Afghanistan, it took me a while to "get right" while falling back into civilian life. Not physically; healing and doing physical therapy was the easy part. It was the baggage, figuring out how to be normal again. A big part of that process for me was revisiting trauma, digesting it, and shitting it out behind me on the road of life.

On my eighteenth birthday—a clueless dipshit with zero life experience—I ditched high school calculus, hopped on a bus downtown, and sold my soul to an organization unmatched throughout human history in its ability to tear down and comprehensively redesign young men, from the ground up, into gorilla-brained war fighters. For the next six years, the Marine Corps conventional infantry was my life. The majority of that time was spent in fluorescent-lit, sleep-deprived monotony, punctuated by training stints in fenced-off expanses of the American West. The rest was spent in Afghanistan.

Even though everything I did was decided for me, Afghanistan was the first time in my life I ever felt free. I mean *actually free* and independent. It's where I first learned the ways I was unique, the first time I'd ever been valued by people above me, men I admired. It was the first time I ever experienced being a real source of comfort to others. It was the first time I ever had peers, other men, other dipshits, appreciate me for something.

Also, the "experience of combat" between men fascinated me. It's a defining and inveterate type of human interaction and utility, combat. It's as old as feasting, dancing, monogamous romance, music, hunting; shit, it's older than *farming*. And I don't mean *war*, all that macro-level strategy and geopolitical bullshit. I'm talking about *combat*.

There's a simplicity to it. The fundamentals of combat still transcend time and culture today, which creates a connection to something *old*, something that feels deeply, *tragically* human. The grounded, simple circumstances of combat are almost liberating, in a fucked-up way. At its core, combat is a very honest, straightforward enterprise.

I'm here in this cold, dusty valley to tear that man's body apart with fire and steel . . . *while he'll be trying to do the same damn thing to me*.

The abject, terrifying clarity of it is intoxicating.

However, most of my time in Afghanistan was still, well, frustrating. A marine infantry battalion full of fast, strong, competitive, stupid-ass eighteen-to-twenty-two-year-olds programmed to *eat fucking glass* and do *anything* to protect each other is a terrifying thing capable of terrifying shit. A marine infantry battalion is *not* the kind of tool you use for everything.

Between boot camp and ITB, you're turned into a rifleman, an 0311, a *grunt*. You're designed with the expressly articulated purpose of killing the enemy, storming beaches, sieging fortifications, spear-heading invasions, or bleeding to death while trying.

In my opinion, sending marine grunts to LARP around as street cops in an area filled with civilians *and* a hostile insurgency *dressed* as civilians is hilariously, fantastically fucking stupid. Alas, that is precisely what was expected of us. Checkpoints, searching cars, frisking old people, getting harassed by snipers, driving around, slaloming duct-taped bundles of thirty-five-year-old explosives buried under the road. *Fuck* that noise.

After about a year of that, my battalion joined a seven-country coalition force for the invasion of Marjah. *That* was my high point. That was a *battle*. We went from playing beat cop to bangin' it out against hardened Taliban warriors who'd cut their teeth against the

Soviets when I was still shitting myself. These were *bad dudes* who'd come down from the Kush and tribal Pakistan, openly, *proudly* self-branded as a religious inquisition. Guys who, if we killed them, could no longer beat women and kids for wearing colors or singing in their own homes, or kill young men for learning the guitar or just talking back. That battle *meant* something.

When that operation was mostly wrapped up, it felt to me like we went back to just squabbling with normal assholes like myself: young dudes who were just fucking pissed.

I was done. The spark was dead. I didn't wanna be a fucking *cop*. Then I got blown up. Getting blown up sucks, but it gave me an expedited opportunity to get out, and I jumped. But that meant I had to *separate and integrate* back into twenty-first-century America, which, to my surprise, I ended up managing. There was a rough patch, to be sure, but I did it.

Mostly because of meeting Sasha, but some other friends also showed me you needn't be surrounded by screaming, panic, and death to "find yourself."

Since then, I've grown gentler and more caring, and I've come to appreciate the *immense* value of experiences and relationships *outside* the Marine Corps. I no longer feel my purpose on earth is to fight.

That being said, I'm not wired to think *around* a physical threat. I'm wired to spit in its eye, head-butt it, then heel-stomp its knuckles and balls when it's down.

Thus, when it comes to gracefully navigating the bizarre, horrifying, and violent manifestations of some ancient motherfucking *earth spirit*—one that seems to have developed a *uniquely* individualized distaste for my well-being and sanity—it goes against everything in me.

Another thing that had been on my mind during this little week-long cigarette, firewood-splitting, and self-pity bender was what Joe had said to me the morning I woke up and found him in my room. The cryptic little phrases he used were starting to fuck with my head.

The comment he made about how *men like me* might find the winters here harder than the other seasons. His vague reference to how we *may* have a life here, if we can make it through the days to come. For the first couple days, I figured he was referring to me fuckin' killing myself, but I started to doubt that was his meaning.

I talked about it with Sasha as well, what he'd said. She told me he'd asked about what I did in Afghanistan before getting blown up, which prompted her to begin her own search for anecdotes of those experiences. I employed usual conversational tactics to steer us toward another topic, but it was clear the experiences I'd never told her about were of more interest to her than ever before.

In the week after Dan's funeral, Sasha had started reducing her time at Lucy's, going from sleeping on their couch most nights and spending all day there, to just spending the days there, to now just going over to check on Lucy in the mornings and evenings. I went with her on occasion, to make sure Lucy was doing all right, to make sure she knew I was there for her too.

To our surprise, Lucy was actually doing quite well, better every day. She was a realist, and I think she'd long ago digested the reality that the spirit would kill them, either directly or by virtue of keeping them stuck here in a life sentence.

Seeing Lucy was hard. Despite what she and Sasha said, I knew it was my fault Dan had died. I knew it was my provocation of the spirit that resulted in that explosive little scarecrow experience that caused Dan to suffer a terrible maiming that ultimately killed him. Thus, having the widow of the man who died as a direct result of my bullheaded fuckery *giving me support* as I grieved *her husband's* death, instead of the opposite, was hard to stomach.

I was trying to mask my guilt, grief, and rage around Sasha. She'd stepped up in such a huge way since that morning when Dan and I got all fucked-up. She took care of me. She took care of Lucy. She had Dan's headstone made on rush order. She marshaled the throngs of well-wishers coming by to offer Lucy their condolences and plates of meatloaf; she even started helping manage Dan and Lucy's ranch, working with their ranch hands and Joe to make sure everything continued to operate smoothly despite the loss of Dan's oversight. On top of that, while I'd emotionally surrendered to the chaos of the spirit and my inability to do anything about it, Sasha had this new drive, this almost feverish focus on the spirit, on its nuance and complexity, like it was a puzzle. She seemed determined to become the valley's de facto spirit investigator. Seeing her do all of that, and thinking back on her scraping the blood, vomit, and shit off my unconscious body and sponge-bathing me like I was some hospice patient had brought me to angry, pitiful tears on several occasions over the last couple weeks. She's just…a fucking goddess I don't deserve.

The only thing I could think to do to repay her, to be there for her, was to try to get my own head right.

I was outside with Dash, stacking wood in the firewood shed we'd built earlier that summer. Sasha had excitedly rushed over to Lucy's early that morning, as Lucy had wanted to take the horses out for a ride around the ranch for the first time since Dan had died. I know Lucy's a lifelong equestrian, and Sasha had gotten pretty damn good at riding over the past eight months as well, but horses intimidate the hell out of me and I was always relieved to get that call from Sasha checking in after a ride, including that afternoon when I felt my phone vibrate.

When I picked up, I knew immediately from her voice that something was wrong. It sounded as though she was crying or holding back tears.

"Sash, what's going on? Are you all right? Is Lucy all right?"

"Harry, yes, I'm fine, we're fine. I just need you to come over here now. Bring Dash, please."

I threw Dash in the 4Runner and tore down the county road, almost drifting as I turned into Dan and Lucy's ranch. I pulled up to the big gravel area between their house and their barns and could see the large chestnut mare that Sasha rode, Lemons, still saddled and hitched to the fence in front of the house. Then I saw the ladies. Sasha was sitting on the steps up to Dan and Lucy's porch, her hands on her cheeks. She was *crying*. Lucy was sitting on the next step above with her arms around Sasha, stroking her arms gently and resting her chin on Sasha's shoulder.

I was so confused. I slowly got out of the car, while Dash clambered up into the front seat to jump out and bound over to Sasha and Lucy. Sasha wiped her eyes as I approached, and Lucy kissed her on the head, then both opened their arms to welcome Dash, showering him with rubs as he almost leaped into both of their laps. Lucy was crying too, it appeared. They were both still in their riding boots and jeans and caked in mud from head to foot from their trail ride. Both looked up from Dash as I got close, and Lucy, despite having tears in her eyes, gave me a warm, knowing, sincere smile.

Sasha stood up and did her best to offer me a smile as well as she walked over to me, but her effort gave way and she put her hands over her eyes as she walked into my hug, burying her face to my chest as she began to sob.

"Sash, babe, what's going on, love? What is it?"

I looked up at Lucy. She was sitting there with Dash's face in her hands, scratching both of his cheeks and ears as he smiled up at her, licking her nose. She gave him a long kiss on the forehead, then stood and wiped tears from her eyes. She looked back at me with another sincere, calm smile that seemed so out of place given Sasha's state, then walked toward me.

I shook my head at Lucy and searched her face for answers as I stroked Sasha's back.

"Sasha, Lucy . . . *what is happening right now?*"

Sasha pulled her head from my chest and looked up at me with deep grief and sadness in her eyes, and spoke through shaky, quick breathing.

"Harry, Lucy is . . . Lucy is leaving."

"What?"

I looked over at Lucy, who gave me a tight-lipped smile and a nod before gesturing with her head toward their big truck. I looked at the truck and noticed for the first time that the bed was neatly and generously packed with bags, boxes, water jugs, what appeared to be camping gear, and a decent amount of firewood.

"She's leaving, Harry; she's leaving the valley."

I looked back over at Lucy, who was holding my gaze, slowly nodding, and I did not need Sasha to say *forever* to know that Lucy was leaving the valley for good. She had a look of peace on her face, a look of collected determination, a look of strength.

I squeezed Sasha's shoulders and kissed her forehead before letting go of her and walking over toward Lucy.

"Luce, what, where . . . where are you going?"

Lucy took a few strides to meet me. Instead of responding, she reached up and took me by the cheeks and held me there for a moment, a smile expanding across her face, then pulled me in for a big hug. We stood there holding each other in silence for what felt like a long time, until Lucy took my hands in each of hers and took a step away from me.

"I ain't ever asked you for nothin', but I'm gonna ask two things of you now. The first, I'm asking you to shed any grief associated with Dan's death. Please let that go; leave it behind. It ain't rightfully yours anyway, that grief, so I'm askin' you to get rid of it."

She took in a deep breath, looked at Sasha behind me, and then back into my eyes. "Second, I'm asking you to love, celebrate, and support your amazing wife. That means trust her, that means be a *powerful* listener, that means surprise her, share with her, encourage her, and it also means challenge her, debate with her, but above all, just love that woman with everything you got until your last day on this earth."

I had tears running down my cheeks now.

"Can you do both those things for me, Harry?"

"Of course, Lucy," I told her. She let go of my hands, took a step away from me, and looked past me out over the pasture.

She took in a long, deep breath, then strode over to her and Dan's big truck. She slapped it a couple times on the wheel well, then looked back at me with her beautiful smile. "I'm hittin' the road, Harry. I'm hittin' the road and I ain't ever comin' back. I'm an old woman. I've lived a long, happy, full life in this valley, with all its quirks and beauty. I got to love a *fine* man for most my life. I got to live intentionally. I got to connect with the natural world in a way I never thought possible. Now, well...I'm takin' control for a bit."

Lucy saw I was about to interject and pressed on. "I know, Harry, Lord do I know what it means for me if I leave here with the intention of never coming back, but that's why I'm doin' it. I'm takin' charge of my own fate. I know I won't have long out there." Her expression was one of confidence and surety. "I'm fine with that. I'm not much interested in all this trouble without my Dan by my side. This is what I want, Harry. This is what I *need*."

My question came out quite stammered; I wasn't sure what to ask until I did. "What about the ranch? Where will you go?"

"Ol' Joe left shortly before you got here. He hooted and hollered about this, did his darnedest to talk me out of it, but he knew I'd made my mind up. I damn near had to force him to sign it, but I just gave him the deed. Every last inch of this place is his now. That's how it was always supposed to be, though, Harry. We've been out here on borrowed land and time, and while I don't regret a minute of it, this land never really was ours. I left a few things in the barn for you and Sash, some tools, and that old shitcan tractor Dan refused to give up, just things I thought might come in handy over at y'all's place."

I was speechless, my head was spinning, and I just stood there like an idiot until she went on.

"Dan and I used to go down to this beach in southern Oregon every year, spot where you can drive your truck through the woods, through the dunes, then out onto the sand and camp right there. We'd rarely ever see another soul. You can catch surf perch and crab, make big ol' bonfires. There are freshwater streams right above the dunes in the woods. We always joked about how, if the world all went to hell, that's where we'd go and live out our days, so that's what I'm fixin' to do. That's my new home now."

Lucy smiled at me, then hefted herself up onto the bumper of her truck, cupped her hands over her mouth, and shouted out into the sky toward the mountains. *"You hear that—I ain't ever comin' back to this valley. I got a new home now, old friend."*

She dropped back down and smiled at Sasha and me. She had fire in her eyes, a youthful excitement that felt so rare to see in the face of a woman in her seventies. She looked happy. She looked *alive*.

She walked up to Sasha and took her into a full bear hug. They held each other and cried for a long while, Lucy whispering into Sasha's ear, all of which seemed to make Sasha cry harder and squeeze Lucy tighter. She finally took a step back and wiped Sasha's eyes with her thumbs.

"I love you, Sasha Blakemore. I love you like my own daughter. You've got this, sweetie. You've got this. Don't dilly-dally once I'm gone; you've got something to do now, don't you?"

She walked over and gave me another quick, fierce hug and gave Dash another forehead kiss, then climbed into her truck.

Sasha and I put our arms around each other's waists as we stood to the side so Lucy could back up and turn the truck around, and as she drove past us, she stopped and rolled the window down.

"You two were a blessing to Dan and me. Y'all will make it through this. Your love alone can beat anything in the world, this damn spirit included. Now..."

Lucy pulled a pair of sunglasses from somewhere within the cab of the truck and put them on, then looked back to us with a smile.

"It's time I take the reins for a while. Goodbye, you two."

Sasha and I held each other tight as we watched her truck disappear down the county road. Eventually, Sasha took a step away from me, reached up and grabbed me by the collar with both hands, pulled my face down to hers, and gave me a kiss so fierce it surprised me.

She took her lips away from mine and looked into my eyes.

"Harry, I'm pregnant."

It felt like my stomach dropped into my ass. A storm of excitement, joy, dread, and panic started to churn in my stomach as I thought of what to say, but I just pulled her face in and kissed her again.

For the first time that afternoon she smiled at me, and I just smiled back and shook my head. "Sash, when . . . ? How did—"

"Harry, I love you. I love you more than anything in this world, and we'll talk all about this in a bit, but there's something I need to do. Something very important, and I've gotta do it alone, all right? You've gotta trust me. Take Dash home. I'll be back in a few hours."

I was at a complete loss for words. Confusion joined in with the cocktail of emotions already pulsing through me. Sasha briskly walked from where we had been standing over toward Lemons.

She threw the reins over Lemons's back, and in one swift motion— so practiced it looked like she'd done it all her life—she slammed a boot into the stirrup and swung herself up into the saddle, then guided the horse over toward me.

I stood there in complete fucking *awe* of Sasha for a moment. She was covered in mud, her eyes looked like they were on fire, her hair was back in a braid under her now well-worn Stetson hat. She was the most beautiful thing I'd ever seen.

"Sasha . . . where are you going?"

"I'm riding over to Joe's. There's something I need to talk with him about. I'll be safe."

Sasha kicked Lemons into a run across the driveway, through the gate, and charged out into the pasture.

27

SASHA

I HADN'T EVER RIDDEN this far into Berry Creek Ranch before, but it was only about a mile from the property boundary with Dan and Lucy's land to Joe's homestead. I crested a hill pocked with little clusters of cattle who cleared out away from me as I rode, and looked down to a cluster of barns, stables, and a big, sprawling single-story home.

As I got closer, I could see a spire of smoke coming from what looked like some kind of gazebo, set off from the house in the meadow a bit. I slowed the horse to get a better look and could see Joe and his son Elk sitting on a stone bench next to a fire pit under the structure. I turned Lemons toward them and led her in an arc around the homestead so I could ride up through the pasture without having to bother with any gates. Joe saw me eventually and stood to give me a big wave.

I rode closer and could see Elk had one of his little girls in his lap, fast asleep. Both gave me curt nods, and Joe gestured toward the fire for me to come join them. I dropped down from Lemons and threw the reins up over her saddle, leaving her to graze around as I went through a little swing gate where a path led down to the firepit. I knew Joe expected me, but I wasn't sure what to say when I got to the fire, so I went with "Hi, Elk; hi, Joe," and just held my cold, wind-bitten hands out over the fire and felt the needles of feeling returning to my fingers.

No one said anything for a while. Eventually I went over to a sun-bleached chair near the stone bench where Joe and Elk were sitting and plopped down.

At a silent gesture from Joe, Elk stood, hoisting up his little girl, who stirred a bit, then tucked her head into his neck. "I'm gonna head in. It's nice to see you, Sasha. Hey, and . . . thanks again for taking such good care of Lucy over the last weeks. She's lucky to have had someone like you."

"Of course, it was my pleasure."

Joe and I sat there in silence for quite some time until finally he looked over at me. "I'm sorry to see Lucy go. She was like a sister to me, and to my wife. But I figure she wasn't gonna have it any other way." I'd learned in the preceding weeks that Joe's wife had died about twenty years earlier, younger than she should've.

Thinking about Lucy gave me a burst of sadness. I'd never see her again and couldn't help but dwell on the myriad of potential natural deaths that could be in store for her at some point in the coming weeks. Although, thinking of her helped me style my first question.

"Did she have to leave? Does she have to die out there alone? Is there really nothing we can do?"

Joe did not respond for quite some time, but eventually he looked up at me. "There is more you need to know. About this place. About what is to come."

I inclined my head, inviting him to say more, making it as clear as I could that I *expected* him to say more. He stared into the rising ribbons of gray and white smoke and then spoke.

"*D'ommo.*"

I tried to repeat the word, hearing my own awkward pronunciation as Joe cut me off.

"Winter, the season that's upon us."

His eyes rose to meet mine.

"A *reprieve*, is how Dan and Lucy described it to Harry and me. A break from all . . . *this*."

Joe's hardened expression told me there was more to it than that. "A reprieve for *some*, but not all."

I felt the cold, sickly boil of adrenaline in my gut. "For who, Joe? What do you mean? *What are you talking about?*"

He put his hand up to ward off my questioning and leveled his gaze into my eyes. "Has Harry ever killed a man?"

Joe's question made me scratch a spot on my arm that did not actually itch. I shrugged. "Umm…yes. Yeah, he has. He killed a few people, I think; more than one is all I know for sure. Why, Joe? Why are you asking me that?"

Joe leaned back a bit, then looked into the fire. "You see, Sasha, there *is* a winter spirit manifestation, there is a winter cycle, but only those who've taken another person's life fully experience it."

For a few long seconds, I felt nothing. It's as though the news scrubbed out all my emotions. Eventually, shock, dread, and panic started to seep in, and Joe remained silent, as though he could sense my fumbling through the stages of processing what he'd just said.

I felt like crying again. I didn't think I could cry so much in one day, but I swallowed my emotions. "Joe, what is about to happen? What is the winter spirit?"

Joe slowly pulled his hands from his coat pockets, leaned forward, and laced his fingers together as he put his elbows on his knees.

"The way the spirit manifests itself in the winter…is *through the people you've killed*. They'll show up here, on your land. Together, if there's more than one. It's like the spirit finds them somewhere, finds their likeness, at least, and ushers their ghosts to the place where the person who killed them can be reached, can be tormented. You won't be able to see them, Sasha, only Harry will, but you will certainly feel them, even hear them sometimes. Animals can feel them too."

"Why only Harry?"

"The ghost forms reveal themselves only to those who understand the truth of what transpired between the killer and the killed. It may happen in a flash, but taking another's life is the most intimate of connections, creating a permanent link between them. Only those who truly understand and *feel* the weight of the death can see the ghost's form."

Joe leaned back, crossed one leg over another, and went on. "One day soon, maybe tomorrow, maybe next week, or maybe in February, Harry will walk outside and will see the ghosts of the men he has killed. So far as we've been able to tell, they'll look the same as they did right before they died. It doesn't seem as though it's the *actual* souls of the men you've killed, but their *likeness*. They'll stay on the land for around a month. My great-grandfather told my grandfather and my father that the longest they ever stayed was six weeks. From what I've been told, it takes the ghosts a few days to work up the strength to get close to the house. But eventually, *they get the gumption to come closer*; they'll get *real* comfortable around you. They'll be waiting at the front door for you to walk outside. They'll be outside the bathroom window, waiting for you to take a morning piss. You lie down to go to bed, they'll be outside the bedroom, screaming and ranting. They will do anything they can to get Harry's attention. To be seen, to be heard. The unnatural act of killing leaves the spirits of the killed unsettled. Unsatisfied. They demand to be recognized by those responsible."

My head shook from side to side as I tried to process this information, and Joe continued.

"There is one thing you must do to keep yourself safe from the spirits. This is the *rule* of the season: From sundown to sunrise, as long as the ghosts are on your land, you must keep a candle lit inside the home for each of the ghosts, a candle for each person he's killed. As long as the candles burn, they cannot harm you or enter the house. They will grow more aggressive as their time on your land progresses. More vengeful. Eventually, they will try desperately to get into the home. But as long as the candles are lit, they cannot make contact with you, nor you them."

As I took all this in, something was eating at me. The words erupted from me almost before my mind had fully put the thought together. "I don't get it. What does this have to do with...I mean, everything else, the light, the bear, the scarecrows...?"

I heard myself rambling and trailing off. I settled myself down, took a deep breath, and tried again. "What I mean is, why is this season about *us*? About Harry, and who he's killed?"

Joe shook his head, returning his gaze to the fire. "It is about nature, and man's place in it."

He grabbed a small fire iron leaning against the stones of the fire pit and drew a circle in the dirt between himself and the chair in which I was sitting.

"The orb of light, it represents the furnace of all creation. The beginning. Mother to us all. The womb from which all life comes."

He continued, scrawling a crude bear paw next.

"The bear and man, they represent man's conflict with nature, living not above the food chain but within it. Part of it. The endless conflict between man and beasts of the forests and hills."

Then a simple stick-figure scarecrow followed.

"Next, man's marshaling of the natural world around him. His mastery of soil and seed. His controlling and even deceiving nature itself."

Then he drew an X in the dirt.

"And finally, only when mankind has grown beyond its origins, tamed its predators, mastered the lands, only then do the worst of our instincts emerge. Turning on one another. Spilling one another's blood. There is no more severe trespass against nature than to kill your own."

I stared down at the images, my mind wrapping itself around this simple nexus between the seasons and their meanings.

I looked up at him, shaking my head slowly. "How do you know all of this? How do you know the meaning and, well...the message behind it all?"

Joe smirked a bit, something I'd never actually seen him do, then he shrugged. "I don't. These are just stories, oral histories that've been passed down by my people. This spirit's older than us, older than the first of my ancestors who lived in this old country. Over time, any group of people will eventually assign meaning to the unexplainable."

I looked down at my hands as I stretched my fingers, which were getting increasingly stiff after gripping the reins of the horse on the cold ride here. "What stories did your people pass down about beating or lifting this spirit, the stories about how to end it and leave the valley for good?"

I looked up to find Joe staring at me, and watched him slowly lift his gaze to the long, bare grassy ridge above his house. Eventually, he lifted one of his large hands and extended a finger in the direction of his gaze. "Lightning has never struck that ridge line up there above the house, not once in my life." He then moved his hand a bit, pointing farther to the south, toward the higher mountains and ridge lines that sat below the spires and peaks of the Tetons. "Yet lightning strikes the same old burned trees on that mountain, all spring and summer long, year after year."

It was unclear which specific mountain among the faraway peaks he was referring to. I shrugged and shook my head once. "All right…"

Joe leaned toward the fire, holding his palms out toward the flames, then began rubbing them together as he looked over at me. "Lightning, a force of nature like that, it'll exist in the sky, it'll spend its days angrily moving from cloud to cloud. It only comes down to us, to the land of the living, when it has something to bond with, something to pour itself into. It needs a host, of sorts, to come down from its domain into ours, a conduit."

Joe leaned back, stuffing his hands into the pockets of his large coat. "Some of my ancestors' stories compare the spirit to lightning and suggest that there's something inside of us, inside of a person, that invites the strike, that allows it to come into our realm. I couldn't tell you what that something is. That's just how some made sense of it."

Joe and I sat there for another hour. I asked him what felt like stupid questions, and he gave patient answers. He said he hadn't known of anyone in the valley who'd been burdened by the winter spirit— anyone who'd killed another—in a very long time but promised to help us prepare however he could.

But I knew he couldn't do much. I knew this was up to Harry, Dash, and me now. As the sun began to set, I rode back home through Joe's ranch as fast as Lemons would carry me.

28

HARRY

W<small>HEN</small> S<small>ASHA</small> <small>TOLD</small> me what was about to happen—told me about the winter manifestation of the spirit—I think there was a full hour when I couldn't think, see, or hear. I kind of just blacked out for a bit, sitting on our couch in debilitating disbelief. Over the following days, however, we discussed quite a bit the prospect of my imminent reunion with the mountain-spirit-possessed ghosts of the men I'd killed.

Those conversations with Sasha were more difficult than I'd expected, but not because of Joe's description of the impending weeks of being *literally* haunted, as unsettling as it was. Rather, the conversations illuminated how little I really had told her about my time in Afghanistan. I'd always just left out the details and nuance from the occasional accounts of my time over there. We'd effectively made something of an unspoken deal with one another years earlier: She wouldn't press me about "traumatic experiences" so long as I kept my shit together and went through the motions of the therapy process with the VA. So, as we prepared for—according to Joe—a month or two of dealing with my emotional baggage in an *incredibly* fucked-up and ridiculous way, I was quite surprised by how few anecdotes of combat I'd actually shared with Sasha over the years.

One morning, Sasha asked me a simple question that left me completely stunned, staring blankly at her face: "Do you know how many people you've killed?"

I wasn't stunned because of the magnitude of the question, or my reluctance to consider and answer it honestly. What floored me was the realization that I'd never actually told her before, and that she'd never explicitly asked. Befitting my reticence and obscurity on this subject matter, I think I answered with something along the lines of *Four or five, don't know for sure, guess we'll see.* Befitting her standards on this subject matter, she was not concerned with empirical figures so much as she was with me feeling at peace and confident.

Sasha was probably right too in pointing out that there wasn't much we could do to *prepare* for this season's little spirit dance, other than me trying to get as Zen as possible about what I was about to go through. That was about the extent of Joe's guidance on the subject in the brief conversations he and I had about the winter spirit in the weeks since he'd filled Sasha in: "You'll have to take this as it comes; best thing to do is just get right in your own head, keep those candles burning."

So, that's what I tried to do. That process was actually, surprisingly, pretty damn grounding. Dwelling on the deaths I'd caused, in conjunction with processing Dan's death and, presumably, Lucy's as well, resulted in a bizarre but harmonious frame of mind. Continued focus on the strange constructs of *mortality*, I guess, makes me feel small and insignificant in a comfortable way, and certainly puts a nice sheen on the present.

As we awaited the arrival of these ghosts, we'd fallen into a strange but empowering state of acceptance, Sasha even more so than myself. I think it had something to do with watching Lucy leave, watching her strength and dignity, her knowing confrontation with the consequences of this spirit and mortality itself.

It started to feel like both Sasha and I had begun to recognize that, while we lived in this valley, every time we cooked a meal, every time we ate, every time we made and drank a cup of coffee in the kitchen together, every time we kissed, made love, held one another, could be the final time we'd do that. It wasn't morbid so much as it was calming. Fate had brought us here, and we didn't have much we could do about it other than be in our cozy little home in this now snow-blanketed valley. Seeing Sasha fall into that frame of mind, however, was tragic for me. It also added a drive, a fight, a determination to my will. We would survive, just as we had the seasons before. We would make a life here. Looking at Dash play and bound around the snow every day, watching Sasha dance in the kitchen in the mornings, it gave me something to fight for, something to survive for.

That night, Sasha lay with her head on my chest after we'd talked for a while.

"Are you sure you wanna have this baby?" I asked.

She pushed herself up to look down at me and kissed me. "Yeah, I'm sure. I wasn't sure I was *gonna* be sure, but I am now. I want to have this child. I want to be a mama. That's my choice, and I've made it." She kissed me again. "Do you want to have this baby?"

I nodded. "Yeah, I do. More than anything, though, I want you to have that choice. I just want you to have that control again. I want *us* to have that control again."

She laid her head back down on my chest, and, like the last several nights, we lay there in silence for a long time, thinking of what was about to happen.

★ ★ ★

I woke up on the morning of December 21, and—as I had for a week—sat up, turned around, and immediately looked out the window into the pastures. Nothing. It was snowing pretty hard. My wake-up panic eased. Then I realized Sasha wasn't in bed, which cranked it right back up.

I *never* slept through Sasha getting out of bed, *especially* over the past week, when I'd woken up on the verge of pissing myself when the dog farted or the furnace kicked on.

"Sash?" I said loudly, seeing if she was in the bathroom. I got up and almost ran into the living room, toward the kitchen. "*Sasha?*"

"I'm in the kitchen, babe!" she said. I could hear her smile in her voice, and it calmed me down immediately. I walked in and saw her sitting at the kitchen table with coffee and a book. Dash was at her feet and trotted over to greet me.

"Shit, sorry I didn't notice you get up. I, ugh..." I shook my head and leaned down to kiss her, and as I stood back up, she gave me a smile but something subtle in it betrayed...*something*. I couldn't tell what, but I knew this woman well.

"What?" I asked her. The second the word left my mouth, she let the emotion slip through her smile again. "Babe, what is it?" I asked again, my tone serious.

She closed her book and took a deep breath. *What the fuck, is she about to tell me she's* double *pregnant?* She stood up, took my hands, and looked me in the eye. She had so much strength in that gaze; she had so much faith. I was floored. Then she spoke.

"Harry, it woke me up an hour ago, at sunrise, but I wanted you to sleep. I can feel it. It might be the ghosts, or not, but I'll tell you right now, the spirit is here...I know it." Her demeanor of strength didn't change at all, while my entire stomach shot into my throat and adrenaline surged into my hands and legs. I couldn't think of what to say and wasn't sure I could talk if I did. I'd thought I was prepared for this, thought I'd seen and felt all the ambient dread the spirit could cause, but I'd been wrong.

She was right. I felt it. The spirit. Standing there in the kitchen feeling like I was about to vomit, looking at my wife's beautiful, strong face, I felt the spirit in the air pressure, saw it in the light, tasted it at the back of my throat. In that moment, I don't know that I'd ever felt more childlike horror in my life. Felt like I was in a nightmare, stuck in a dark room, unable to move as something I knew *wanted* me came slowly, giggling down a hallway.

I could feel *them*. I could feel *five*. I knew I'd killed five people, five men. I knew without seeing them. More than them, I could feel the spirit. My peripheral vision started to go dark. My ears were rumbling and I could feel my heartbeat in my face. I took a deep breath and closed my eyes. *Chill, man. Breathe. You are not gonna pass out without even seeing the bastards.*

"Harry." I snapped out of it and looked back into Sasha's eyes, still holding her hands. "Harry, you've got this. *We've* got this. Okay?"

I nodded and took another breath. "There are five. I killed five men; they're here. I can feel them. I know the four, not sure who the fifth is."

A brief, thin fear flushed into Sasha's face at my response, but she forced it away and replaced it with strength, taking a deep breath herself. "Well then, there are five."

My reflexive antidote to panic showed up like a deranged sidekick: the white-hot desire to fight, pleading in *shrieks* for me to get angry. It grounded me, but I reasoned it away, talking to myself in my own head. *Nope, tried that, didn't go so hot last time, you fucking idiot.* I went to the sink and chugged some water. I looked down at Dash, looking up at me, our eye contact activating the motion in his plumed tail.

I looked back to Sasha. *Sweet Christ*, how did I get so lucky as to find these two? I felt like weeping in gratitude, terror, shame, and joy all at once.

"Sash...I need to go find them. I need to go find them by myself. I won't do anything, or go more than a few feet from the fence, I swear to you; I just need to see them alone, this first time."

She looked at me with challenge in her eyes, then nodded.

"Only if you bring Dash, and I'm coming out there in ten minutes, okay?"

I nodded. "Yah, of course." I felt like explaining my need to confront them for the first time alone, but it was something I think we could both feel without an explanation.

I got dressed, grabbed my binoculars, and followed Dash out into the yard. I'd stop and look out into the property every ten steps. I got to the gate and still didn't see anything. Dash and I walked a short way into the pasture, to where I could get a view down into one of the corners of the property, and then ice shot into my veins as I could *feel* the blood leaving my face.

I didn't need the binoculars. Even though they were about 250 yards away, I could clearly see five men standing a few feet apart from one another in a row, defined by the snow like shadows. My heart was pounding. The man in the middle stood out, even at this distance. He was the tallest. His perahan tunban, poncho-size scarf, and pakol hat were all jet black. I raised my binoculars. He was staring directly into my eyes. The older man I'd killed in the ambush, scrambling to get out of the dusty truck.

This isn't fuckin' real. I looked up into the white sky, then back to the house, rubbed my eyes, and looked back into the binoculars. He hadn't moved. I looked at the others. None were looking at me, just gazing around, up at the trees, mountains. They looked confused. I then recognized the two men I'd killed first, and the guy I'd shot on the edge of the poppy field, and then the other…

Fuck me. I guess I'd killed one of those guys after all, in the back of the truck as they tried to break through our line. He was young, maybe seventeen or eighteen. He had fierce, wild eyes, even as he stood calmly, gazing up toward the mountain. I looked back to the older warrior.

Right as I focused on his face again, still sporting a look of focus and an almost parental judgment, he took one step in my direction and stopped. It made my mouth run dry, my hands go numb. The other four looked at him, almost with confusion, then all of them— at the same time—looked up at me, straight into my binoculars, and I could see it, recognition in their eyes. Subtle disbelief chased by anger. But the youngest, the "surprise," he looked different. He lowered his head slightly but held my gaze with an expression of calm, collected, *murderous* hatred.

As I took my next breath, those five men's fury, their fear, their grief, pain, confusion, it all seemed to turn into a noxious gas that rushed into my lungs, where it twisted and weaved into a throbbing, *screaming*-hot cyst that ruptured in my gut and washed through my nervous system as I exhaled. It made me shudder and start to cough, then gag.

I realized Dash was pawing my leg. I patted his head and spoke, more to myself than him. "It's all right, buddy, it's all right."

I felt angry. It was initially directed at these men, but then was refocused, almost forcibly, as if a meat hook in the muzzle of my anger hauled it toward the spirit; like it *wanted* my rage and contempt. It hit me then, the realization that this thing *wanted* me to give it a reason. It *wanted* my rage. I'd thought on that earlier, after the scarecrow, but I *felt* it for the first time now. I wasn't going to give it that. I *couldn't* give it that.

Staring down at them, I wondered if there were any of their old selves in there, if there were any of these men's memories or passions woven into their form by the spirit. I felt like a boy again, walking along the junkyard fence, the beast raging along beside me, my muscles coiled and white-hot, ready to explode into a sprint for my life. Then I felt guilt.

It wasn't really guilt for *killing* them, but more because they got killed fighting at home, or at least relatively close to home, by dudes like me from across the goddamn planet.

I'd accepted this reality years before, but it had never been as clear as it was in that moment. There was no amount of strenuously cobbled-together musings about "serving your country" or the "inveterate nature of men in war" or "fighting for freedom" that can rebut these five men's unalienable right to *absolutely fucking hate me*. But now they were here, outside my home.

I turned and walked back into the yard. As I went to shut the gate, Dash glanced back behind him, tilting his head as he does when he smells a grouse, then looked back at me with urgency. "I know, buddy. Let's go inside."

I sat with Sasha and told her about what I'd seen and who the fifth man was, and she called Joe to tell him that the ghosts had officially arrived.

"What are you gonna name the surprise guy?" Sasha had encouraged me to name the four I knew about over the last few days, so I could describe them to Sasha, and to make it easier for me to explain what was going on, what I was seeing. It was a practical albeit fucking grim idea. I'd decided to call the first two guys I'd killed at the outset of the Battle of Marjah *Hank* and *Pete*; I'd call the older fella I shot in the truck *Bridger*, and I'd call the fourth guy who I shot about ten times *Buck*.

"I dunno...I'll think of something." What the *fuck* had my life turned into?

For the rest of the day, Sasha tried to be as upbeat as possible. She had holiday music playing; she read out loud from one of my old history books about winter solstice celebrations from all over the world. I tried to match her level, but it was tough. Quite impish, I thought, yet fitting, for the spirit to make its seasonal debut on the solstice. I was constantly peeking out a window into the pasture to see if the ghosts were starting to move closer.

We'd picked out a little spruce at the bottom of the driveway to cut down and decorate, and Sash asked if I wanted to go get it with her. I didn't need to respond for her to pick up what my vibe was putting down.

"Harry, we can't let them dictate our lives, all right? I don't want to push you, I can't see them, but that's how I feel we should handle this."

She was right. "Yeah, let's do this."

We grabbed the hacksaw and walked down the driveway, cutting fresh tracks into the snow, with Dash bounding ahead, his red-golden coat standing out against the snow like a warm flame.

I could feel Sasha watching my gaze as I looked out into the meadow. "Can you see them?" she asked.

Four of them had moved a bit closer to the pond out in the pasture and were staring at us. Bridger and three others, couldn't tell which.

"Four of 'em, not sure where the fifth is," I told her.

Sasha squeezed my hand affectionately. "I wish I could see them too. I'm sorry I can't..."

I kissed her cheek. "Thank God you can't."

We got to the little spruce tree at the bottom of the driveway. "This the one?"

Sash responded with a bit of added gusto. "It's perfect. Don't you love it, Dash?"

I smiled. She was trying so hard it gave me a wasp sting of guilt and affection.

I took a knee and started to saw at the little trunk. About halfway through, I gripped the tree with my free hand and pulled to open the cut a bit for the blade. The movement shook snow off the limbs that snuck in the back of my jacket, startling me as the ice hit my neck and went down my shirt.

"Ah, shit!" I laughed, and heard Sasha laugh back at me.

I turned around to throw a handful of snow at her, and what I saw scared me so bad an electric burst of terror-wrapped adrenaline tore through my body so fast that I let out a half scream, half grunt.

My shock yanked Sasha's smile away and replaced it with a look of dread, and she immediately shot her hands up to her face. "Babe, what?!"

One of the ghosts, the young one, the *surprise*, was standing right next to Sasha, facing her, hands clenched in fists, leaning forward toward the side of her face. I started to stand up, and Sasha was taking one step toward me, turning her head to follow my gaze, when he screamed.

Mouth as wide as a human's ever should be, putting what looked like every part of his body into it, he blasted out a raspy shriek that was two-toned in pitch. I winced as the noise smashed into my eardrums like a truck hitting a deer without even tapping the brakes.

With ripples of heat distortion pouring from his mouth like a furnace, the scream had such force it knocked off Sasha's wool hat, blowing her hair and the snow falling around her head sideways. She jumped in terror and lost her footing, stumbling to land hard on her side. I surged up and dove toward her. Dash went berserk, teeth bared, snarling and snapping his fangs at the noise, unsure where to direct the savage attack to which I could see he was ready to dedicate every muscle.

"Sash, are you okay?!"

She had tears welling in her eyes and was staring in shock into, for her, the snowflakes and air where the scream had erupted from. She blinked her shock away, then nodded, looking at me with a forced smile. "I'm fine, I'm fine, I just fell over, won't even be a bruise, okay?"

I helped her up and we turned and began heading up the driveway as we both yelled for Dash to follow us. I glanced at the other four ghosts, who hadn't moved.

"Could you see it before it screamed at me?" Sasha asked.

"Yeah, for a split second. He came out of nowhere."

I looked back to call again for Dash, who hadn't let up his feral snarling. The ghost of the young man was smiling at me with provocation and malice in his eyes. But, to my surprise, he did actually seem a bit uneasy about the dog, like he was trying to hold his ground, flinching very subtly when Dash would lunge with a bark, switching his gaze back and forth between us, as if looking away from Dash for too long might give the dog an opening.

"Which one was it, Harry? Is he still there?" Sasha asked.

"Yeah, still there..." His apparent fear of the dog made my rage boil up behind my eyes more than his cocky little smile did—like it was a weakness I needed to exploit, a broken nose I needed to keep landing punches into. As though sensing my ire, Sasha grabbed me by the chin and forced my eyes to hers.

"Harry, it's okay. Babe, it's okay, the guy just scared me. Screw him, right? Let's go start dinner." She still had tears in her eyes; one ran down her frost-reddened cheek, and while she was forcing a smile, there was sincerity in it as well.

The volume of Dash's barking was amplified by the oppressive silence of a snowy afternoon in the mountains.

I took a deep breath and looked back at the ghost. "You're right, but fuck him. Let's get our tree, yeah?"

Sasha smiled and gave me an approving nod. "Let's go get our tree."

I turned back down the driveway, but I froze before taking a step as my heart leaped into my throat and it felt like my stomach flipped upside down.

The other four ghosts were all on our side of the pond now, fifty or sixty yards away, standing, staring at me, spread out in new positions normal men couldn't have possibly reached in such a short time, or without leaving any tracks in the snow as they'd managed.

"What?!" Sasha asked as she grabbed my hand.

I took a breath and looked back to her, forcing a smile. "Nothin', babe."

I stomped over to the hacksaw, and as if sensing our plan to finish what we'd started, Dash calmed down a bit, looked at me, wagged his tail, then bounded up to Sasha and planted himself, head low, between her and the ghost. I picked up the saw and looked at the young man. His smile was fading, being replaced by anger, which made *me* smile.

"More of a cat guy, eh?" I asked him as I bent down and sawed through the last inch of the tree. I gripped the sappy, cold trunk, hoisted the little tree over my shoulder, and turned to the young man.

His face, all condescension gone, was twisted into a rictus of hate. Looking at these ghosts wasn't *quite* the same as looking at a living person, but the difference was small. They weren't translucent; I could see pores and scars in his skin, tears and abrasions in his shirt, but it was still kind of like looking at something when you're having a migraine. The legs, arms, torso, and head were all *there*, but not *really*—I could only clearly see whatever I was looking at directly. The periphery was just elusive, fuzzy, hard to describe.

We stared at each other for a few long moments. He looked to be only a few years younger than I had been when we last met.

I remembered him then: watching a guy in my rifle company drag his teenage body by the ankle to a row of the other guys he'd been killed with, the friction of the road pulling his shirt up over his head, exposing the bullet holes and coagulated blood covering his stomach and sternum. When his body settled and the shirt came down, revealing his face, I realized he was just a kid. Couldn't have been more than fifteen years old. Then the image of him screaming into Sasha's face flooded in.

I pointed at him with the saw and nodded. "Slick move, for real, top-notch spook maneuver. I'll call you Creeps."

Disgust joined the hate in his glower. As I turned back toward Sasha, my heart skipped a beat again as adrenaline shot through me.

The other four ghosts were all clustered now, only fifteen yards away in the meadow, with Bridger in the front. He looked at me in fiery judgment. My ears popped and my hands started shaking.

As we locked eyes, my mind dredged up long-forgotten details: apprehensively searching his body for a suicide vest, smelling smoky pine in his clothes, leaning across him to untangle his rifle sling so I could pull him out of the truck, the soft tinking of the dying engine. I remembered unceremoniously pulling him out of that smoking, blood-riddled wreck down onto the road. I remembered seeing shattered glass under him and *almost* reflexively reaching down to move his head so he wouldn't cut himself. I remember the brief lance of shock at my even having that trace of humanity left in me. I remember actually feeling proud of myself for having such considerate instincts.

"Harry, what is it?"

I snapped out of my strange recall and looked at Sasha, who had a mask of concern. I shook my head. "Nothin', love. Let's go decorate a tree."

That was a very long night, but far easier than those that followed.

29

SASHA

That evening after our first tango with the ghosts, Harry and I decorated our little Christmas tree and made some dinner. We tried to stay upbeat, but that experience really shook us both.

I'd set up a little candle station in preparation for the first night and those to follow and practiced with it quite a bit. We'd gone over how the rule worked at least four or five times with Joe in the last weeks, and even though he'd never experienced the winter spirit himself, his great-grandfather had, and he was confident in the clarity and effectiveness of this "candle ritual." So long as there were candles burning from sunset to sunrise—the entire time these ghosts were here, whether that was a couple weeks or a month—they couldn't touch us or get inside the house.

I'd actually found some hardy-looking "windproof" twenty-hour candles online that I figured would be more reliable, and ordered a huge package of them. I'd superglued candle holders onto a kitchen tray with handles so we could move it around if need be, and I ordered this big glass orb with open ends on both sides to set over and shield the candles from drafts.

That night we lit the candles, ate dinner, and went onto the back porch, looking out over the pasture at the ghosts, which I couldn't see. I watched Harry's eyes as he watched them. It became a normal thing for me to ask about what they were doing and for Harry to paint a little picture of what these five ethereal things were up to. I guess there was a group of three milling around near the pond, Bridger and another one up near the woods on their own, but all five of them were staring directly at us. It gave me the chills.

I'd decided to keep Lemons over at Dan and Lucy's so she had the barn, the other horses, and the season's worth of hay they'd left us, and to keep her away from the ghosts. Nothing we could do about the sheep, but to both Harry's and my surprise, they didn't seem bothered by the ghosts' presence. Harry said it was like the ghosts and sheep couldn't see one another, but they'd naturally avoid one another, "like little Roombas."

Harry actually slept better than I did that first night. I kept sitting up, checking on the candles, then looking out the window above the bed, out into the snowy meadow. There was something intoxicating about it, knowing things were out in the darkness I couldn't see and were staring back at me.

The next morning, we both woke up early and bundled up to take Dash for a walk. It was *cold*. Flash-frozen-snot cold. We walked behind the house and looked into the pasture. Again, according to Harry's summary, the ghosts were scattered around the property, all looking at us through the gray wolf light the sun was igniting in the clouds above the mountains where it rose.

I thought about the relationship between the spirit and these ghosts a lot. I'd concluded they *were* the spirit—they were its hands, its instruments. It disturbed me to think about these being *actual* ghosts of *actual* people, yanked out of whatever afterlife they found themselves in and forced into the rural Idaho mountains, unleashed to exact retribution upon their killer. Like little pawns, beholden to this spirit they didn't understand as it would whisper down sinister proposals and schemes in some language that's never been spoken, guided by this spirit—which was as foreign to them as it was to us—as they went about their macabre routines. Alternatively, the spirit simply had the ability to conjure up a likeness of those whom the people in this valley had killed in their past, to somehow rip into Harry's mind and build them back up.

Later that day we were loading firewood onto the little sled we used to haul loads up to the porch. I asked Harry about this, about the nature of the ghosts, whether there was any soul left, any memory of who they were. He stood up straight after stacking a few pieces onto the pile and stared at the wall of the garage as though he were trying to read something written there in bad cursive.

He turned toward me after a few moments and gestured at the pasture. His answer suggested this was something we'd *both* been mulling over in our minds. "If those are real ghosts of real men, that would seem to necessitate two *crazy* fuckin' things, even for this valley. First, it would mean a dead man *actually has* a soul floating around somewhere after he dies. Second, it would mean this spirit has access to and *control over* the soul of anyone who's ever been killed. So, if these are *real ghosts* of *real men*, this old spirit would have, I dunno…a *divine omnipotence* that's damn near indiscernible from how most monotheists describe God. All that power over the souls of the dead just to play ventriloquist for a few weeks a year? All that power just to put on some spooky theater for a nobody asshole like me in this little mountain valley? Nah. Even applying the bizarre, fucked-up metrics that exist in this strange place, that's just too much of a stretch."

He looked back out toward the pasture, and I walked over and took his hand. He looked at me and I cracked a smile. "I sure hope you're right about that, Har. If you aren't, we're dealing with some crazy shit."

Harry smiled, almost laughed as he looked down toward our feet, then back out into the empty pasture. Empty to me, at least. "I sure hope I'm right about that as well."

Over the next few days, the ghosts spent their time in the pastures, watching Harry from afar, but started to creep closer every evening.

I could feel the spirit too. It wasn't the same as it had been with the other seasons, but it was present, like an ambient smell, sound, or shade of light. We actually managed to get good nights of sleep those first few days, even as Harry's anxiety kept him up in anticipation of their wailing, shrieking, banging, or other roguish mischief.

The fourth night was Christmas Eve. Before dinner, we bundled up to go out right before sunset for what had become our little routine of seeing what the ghosts were up to. Everywhere we went outside I'd watch Harry's eyes, as though they were my way to see what was happening.

He'd catch me watching his eyes, and I'd feel a bit guilty and look away.

"I'm sorry. I just ... not being able to see them, I can't help it. I want to know where they are."

Harry put his arm around my shoulders and kissed my head. "It's okay, Sash, I don't mind."

Harry explained what they were doing as he watched them all walk along the fence line around the yard, all on their own, hands in their pockets or behind their backs, looking at us, the dog, the forest. Like prison guards, I thought.

That night, we called my parents and some other family. I got emotional about it, thinking about the ways things could go wrong, if the worst were to happen to us. If our adherence to these rituals faltered. There was a lot of that these days, recognition of life feeling much more impermanent than before. It manifested in small, unexpected ways. Looking at a corner of the living room and thinking about how I'd redo it or making a mental note to replace a cooking pan or a lamp, needing new lightbulbs, just little things like that, were followed by the sting of realization that I might not ever get the chance to do them. I wasn't sad. It was more just grounding. It made me appreciate the little moments: Harry brushing my hair behind my ear, the way Dash would put his head in my lap, the sentence of a book someone took the time to write, the taste of bread, the smell of the fire. I was more in touch with my surroundings than I'd ever been. I was *living in the moment* in a way that I hoped I'd be able to continue to do if we found a way to last here.

I thought about the little person in my body, this little child. That gave me strength, and optimism. I was thankful we didn't have a child in this home yet, and that I was so early in the pregnancy that I wasn't lugging around all the extra weight. But I felt them, their little heart, their little body coming together.

Harry seemed to find calm in focusing on ways to keep the house safe. He'd cut out plywood fittings for the bigger windows, just in case we needed to cover them for some reason, and he tested parts of the house to see where the breeze would be the strongest if the doors or windows got smashed down, to see where the candles would be in jeopardy of being blown out. He'd also stashed what felt like *so many guns* around the house, leaving them everywhere, as though they could be of some use against these intangible ghosts. I actually teased him about it, asking him what the best bullets were for incorporeal mountain spirits. He laughed at himself too, recognizing the silliness in the precautions, but I could tell it made him feel safer. I watched him one night in the garage, putting on this vest that had all these pouches for magazines and other things, checking all the little pockets and straps. It was strange, seeing my husband do something from muscle memory that he'd done so many times before, but I'd never actually seen him do.

They were his little defense mechanisms, but he openly recognized that and joined me in making fun of himself, even calling his rifle his "security blanket," the one he'd designed to match the one he used in Afghanistan. Sometimes I wonder how on earth it was *this man* I'd fallen head over heels for.

It was all he could do, though, as the winter days went on, as the ghosts worked their way closer and closer to the house. It was endearing, in a grim, macabre way, watching him check if his rifle was loaded before going outside into the land of these ghosts, knowing the rifle wouldn't actually be of any use.

It was also tragic, watching him go about chores in the yard with that "security blanket" rifle slung across his body. Watching him hold it, walk with it, seeing his thoughtless familiarity with it as he strolled through the snowy yard, glancing anxiously at these ghosts only he could see, the demons of his own making, carrying the tool he'd used to make them. Tragic in a way that made me sad for Harry and sad for what felt like our entire species.

It was that rifle, that life, *that young man I never actually knew*, that young man's fear and violence that was the real genesis story for this winter spirit and the ghosts it brought with it—and when the winter spirit came, when those ghosts came back to him, he found peace by preparing for the same violence with the same tool with the same old enemies.

30

HARRY

CHRISTMAS CAME AND went, and the timid, confused nature of the ghosts seemed to go with it. Every day they seemed bolder, more aware of their objective, more committed to *me*. Their "casual phase" was clearly beginning to sunset, and as Joe had relayed to us, he'd learned that they'd get noisier and more aggressive as their little haunting season progressed.

On the first night of January, Sasha was reading in bed, and I went to engage in what had become my pre-bed evening ritual of moving the candles from wherever we'd been hanging out to where we kept them on the dresser in the bedroom, and then going on what I'd started referring to casually as "ghost recon."

I couldn't help but use the most ridiculous tough-guy voice I was capable of. "Going on ghost recon, babe, back in a sec." Sasha rolled her eyes and grinned at me. The exhaustion on her face shot a lance of guilt into my heart, one that faded as quickly as it came. I took some deep breaths as I walked toward the front door.

It was silly, but I did get some satisfaction from going out to locate the spooky bastards in the dark at least once before getting in bed. I assumed that satisfaction would be short-lived, as I figured it wouldn't be long until they'd make it abundantly clear where they were *all night long*.

I got my spotlight and cracked the door. I couldn't see anything, but I heard whispering to the right, down the porch toward where it opens up outside the kitchen. I stepped out and leaned around to the right and froze as a sharp burst of terror hit me in the solar plexus.

The second I leaned far enough to see down the porch, I saw Creeps and Pete. Standing side by side at the end of the porch in the dim yellow glow of light from the kitchen window, heads lowered slightly, glaring up at me from under their brows. It made my muscles convulse with a desire to recoil and slam the door. They were only there for a half second before sprinting out of view, down the porch on the other side of the house. When I heard their steps go quiet, I realized how hard my heart was hammering. *So it fuckin' begins*.

My eyes were glued to the dark spot they'd jetted away from, convinced one would jump out. Dash was standing next to my left leg, and I heard him growl. Without looking away I spoke down to him. "I know, bud; they're assholes."

I leaned back into the door frame. When my gaze reached the steps heading down from the porch, my body reacted faster than my mind did.

The noise blistered into my ear, making me wince and throw my arms up to protect my face as I buckled down away from the man, the *thing* I'd realized was standing *immediately* to the left of the front door, two feet from me. He'd screamed directly into my ear.

Dash shot past me out the door, planting himself on the porch at the top of the steps down to the yard, barking furiously into the night. I brought my hands down and looked up at Buck. He was standing there shaking his hands at his sides, bopping up and down on the balls of his feet, breathing heavily, glaring at me with boiling rage like a bare-knuckle boxer waiting for the first bell.

I could hear Sasha jump out of bed and come bounding into the living room, where she began yelling at me to tell her what was going on. I took a deep breath. "It's fine, love."

I stepped by Buck and leaned down to grab Dash's collar, hauling him back to the front door. Dash was *pissed*. As I pulled him past Buck, Dash snapped toward the ghost so fast and hard I heard the snap of his jaws echo out into the cold darkness. Buck flinched away from the bite, subtly putting his hands out as though to block the dog.

His reaction was so surprising I froze. Dash didn't even know where Buck was; the dog was just barking and raging around everywhere, clearly feeling *something* was close by; it was just a lucky snap in the right direction. *They really are fuckin' scared of dogs . . .*

"Please take Dash, babe." Sasha helped me pull him in, and I leaned on the door frame and looked back at Buck.

He was *seething*, but I swear I could almost discern a hint of embarrassment flush into his enraged glower. My heart was pounding, but I calmed myself. It was freezing out and Sasha was yelling at me to come inside and shut the door.

I held the ghost's strange gaze and nodded to him. "This here's the dog's porch, his rules, pal." The ghost just stared back at me, *deep* anger in his eyes, the look a guy gets when he's angry at *everything*, not just one dude.

I shut the door and leaned back against it. Sasha looked at me, exasperated. I told her what happened, and we went to bed. I could hear the ghosts run down the porch a couple times that night, but we managed to get some sleep, in between the dozen or so panicked moments of waking up to frantically glance toward the candles where we kept them on top of the dresser, although doing that every hour or so through the night had become commonplace.

By the end of the first week of January, things had progressed. During the day, we'd started limiting our time outside. The harassment of the ghosts certainly helped foster our reclusiveness, but it was mostly because of the frigid temps, wind, and snow that'd shown up just in time for our little spirit session. We went into town to shop and grab food a couple times, but the passes north and east of town were closed, and there wasn't anywhere else to go this time of year within four or five hours. Although we had puzzles, shows, movies, books on tape, some domestic tasks, lots of cooking, and Sasha's one or two work meetings a day to keep us occupied.

We'd take Dash up the county road to wear him out every morning, on either snowshoes or cross-country skis, and the exercise definitely helped keep us sane. The ghosts would be at the door, scream when I'd open it, try to scare me, follow us down the driveway to where they'd stop, unable to follow us off our property up the snowy road; the curious curse boundary, I supposed, the limits of my internalized understanding of ownership and claim to this valley that so enraged the spirit. They'd wait for us there, then follow us back up to the house. The whole thing became ritualistic.

When we got to about two and a half weeks since the ghosts had arrived, we'd begun to feel like it was actually fairly manageable, minus the grim, jarring thoughts about what would happen at night if we let one of the candles go out. We'd gotten used to the ritual of fostering this little clutch of candles at night, and the ghosts' patterns and habits had gotten pleasantly predictable.

When I'd go outside for any reason, one or two of them would be waiting for me. They'd scream at me, then stalk me from the flanks anywhere I went, like a pack of wolves on a bleeding, exhausted elk. Bringing Dash with me made them keep their distance a bit. The bad weather almost made it easier too; it was so cold and windy it was almost as abrasive as their presence. Honestly, with most of the daytime spent inside with Sasha, the days weren't all *that* bad.

The nights were the worst part, and I had to admit to myself, they did seem to be getting progressively worse. Our almost obsessive and matronly stewardship of the candles resulted in constant vigilance, making any sustained restful sleep nearly impossible. Between sunset and bedtime, I'd hear the ghosts ranting in manic whispers on the porch when I was in the kitchen, see them sprinting by a window or just standing in the snowy yard, barely outside the arc of glow from the porch lights, staring venomously into the house.

One evening in the second week of January, I went out to get a charger from Sasha's car, with Dash and my spotlight, fully expecting a jarring encounter. It was *dumping* snow. The slow deluge of huge snowflakes amid the windless, ear-ringing silence was haunting on its own. I got to the car without spotting any of the ghosts. I grabbed the charger, turned around, and froze as a flash flood of adrenaline crashed into my face and hands.

Bridger. He was standing on the tailgate of my truck, about twenty feet away, looking down on me with his arms crossed. He was positioned between me and the light outside the door to the shop, haloed by the glow and illuminated snowflakes, looking like some fuckin' demon prince in a volcanic ash storm. I yelled for Dash. I didn't take my eyes off Bridger until I was back inside the fence, pushing the gate through the fresh snow to shut it behind the dog. When I looked back from the front porch, he was gone.

That same night they started hanging out below the bedroom, yelping, whooping, wailing out of nowhere. By the next night, one had started messing around on the roof, randomly sprinting the length of the house, as the others would shriek, jibber, and moan out in the frozen night and pound on the siding of the house. We had a fan in the bedroom that dulled some of the noise, and I'd started sleeping with earplugs, but it was hard to catch more than three hours of sleep a night.

On Friday night, end of the second week of January, we were reading by the fire and drinking some tea when it sounded—to me—like a fucking *linebacker* crashed into the front door, and—to Sasha—like someone slapped a big, open palm into it.

Sasha jumped and put her hand on her chest. Dash went into a frenzy, snapping and snarling at the door. I leaped to my feet. I was exhausted and pissed. I slammed my feet into my boots and looked out the living room window. Creeps and Pete were standing on the porch, fiendishly staring at the door. The other three were visible but obscured out in the dark, snow-blanketed yard.

I threw the door open and made a grand, ridiculous gesture with my arm, waving it across the porch as I let Dash tear outside, raging into the night. *"The dickheads want to play, Dash!"*

Both ghosts took a quick step back. Pete looked down in angry frustration at Dash's untargeted storm of snapping teeth and snarls, backing up to the porch railing as Dash got closer to him. He looked at me with an icy hatred, then jumped over the railing down into the dark yard. Creeps held his ground. I gestured at Dash as I took a step toward him and raised my eyebrows.

He switched his gaze between dog and me, looking disgusted and furious, almost as if he felt I was cheating somehow. But you could see some kind of anxiety or fear start a melee with the malice on his face. Somehow, Dash sensed Creeps then, aiming his snout vaguely toward the knees of the ghost. The dog got quiet and still as he pulled his lips back, baring his teeth as he slowly shifted his weight to his hind legs, betraying an intent to strike. Creeps leaned down toward Dash and screamed at the dog, face shaking, booming out an ear-splitting exultation half rage, half terror.

Dash exploded toward the screaming ghost in a leash-snapping burst, letting out a deep, bearish growl of his own. Creeps launched off the porch and Dash went screaming after him into the yard as all the ghosts scattered.

We got Dash back inside and calmed him down, hoping that'd keep the ghosts at bay for the night.

It didn't.

A few hours later, around 2:00 a.m., I was torn out of a dream I can't remember, sitting straight up in bed as an ear-splitting scream came from outside the window above our bed. It was an inhuman, beastly wail.

I turned around, got on my knees, and pulled the thick drape to the side to look outside. I'd only moved it a few inches, then thrashed away from the window, almost falling off the bed as I let out a scream of my own.

When I pulled back the drape, I'd seen that Creeps and Pete had their foreheads pressed into the frost-sheened glass of the window, smiling at me with teeth bared, malicious, deranged hatred in their eyes. It was so shocking in my exhausted state I'd slammed my hand into the headboard of the bed as I closed the drape and launched away from the window, shouting obscenities in rage and embarrassment.

Sasha woke into a terrified daze. *"What, Harry, what?"*

We just sat there holding each other, curled up at the foot of our bed, *our own fucking bed*. Dash jumped up into the bed eventually, and for hours I listened to the ghosts giggle and shriek outside as Sasha watched my face. She and the dog would occasionally flinch when a ghost's wail was loud enough to pierce through the bizarre boundary of perception. I was unable to discern which ghost was which; it was just a pulsing frenzy of dreadful noise. Some were right outside the window. Some were off in the pasture. One ran along the roof squealing like an animal for hours.

Halfway through the third week in January—almost a month into this winter spirit's showcase—I was more exhausted than I'd been in years, emotionally and physically. Sasha was tired too but trying to be upbeat. The ambient *feeling* of the spirit had been growing as well. All my old injuries would spasm and ache when I'd get near the ghosts. Most of any calm and peace I'd managed to muster during the first few weeks was long gone, and there was no question left in my mind: The spring, the summer, and even the fall were *infinitely* better than this shit.

After breakfast, I went out to load up a sled of firewood to bring inside. I pulled the little sled behind me as I walked down the snowy path from the porch toward the garage and firewood shed, several of the ghosts whooping and screaming off to my right, stalking along my route on the outskirts of my peripheral vision. Their daytime torment seemed to have a compounding effect, almost like an Ambien starting to kick in. I just watched my footing, feeling like some new inmate getting walked down a raucous prison block toward my new cell, the air heavy with ridicule, screamed promises of torment, and spit. The ghosts, or the spirit, did seem stimulated by my reactions, so whenever possible I'd try to deprive them the satisfaction of acknowledgment.

In the beginning, when I saw their traits for the first time, it had briefly felt like the ghosts were unique, personalized tormentors—individuals, like they had arrived here with some of the real, worldly personality and experience I'd snuffed out when I killed the men. But I'd grown to seriously doubt that. I mused over this again as I glanced up at Pete the ghost and opened the gate through the fence around the yard. He looked back at me with a calm aggression, a rage that seemed comforting and empowering for him. I squinted my eyes and examined his face as though it would betray some answer.

"Nah, you ain't really you in there, are you?" I shook my head at Pete, as though he'd been the one trying to convince me of the legitimacy and provenance of his soul. The ghosts were already there in my head, after all.

A shriek blasted into my left ear, so loud it made me see stars as though I'd been punched in the nose. I flinched down away from the noise and stumbled into the yard toward Pete. I looked back and saw Creeps to the left of where I'd been standing, considering Pete's soul. He smiled at me under narrow eyes. I felt rage boil up behind my eyes but forced myself to breathe. I grabbed the sled and left them both behind, continuing down toward the firewood shed.

I'd filled the sled about halfway with firewood and was reaching with both hands for another clutch of logs when Hank suddenly rose up from behind the firewood stack. Something about this abrupt but slow way he rose up and revealed himself actually made it more jarring than if he'd jumped up at full speed. It terrified me more than any of the ghosts' prior daylight efforts to startle me.

He rose with his mouth open as wide as it could go, eyes rolled back, *screaming* through both exhales and inhales like he was hurt—a panicky, desperate shrieking like he was being eaten alive. It shocked me so bad I stumbled backward, tripped over the firewood-laden sled, and landed on my ass in the snow.

As soon as I fell backward, Hank urgently scrambled over the wood pile on all fours like some kind of goblin, then crawled almost *into* my lap as I scooted away from him, putting his face inches from my own, *raving* in incoherent jibbers and screeches. I closed my eyes and took a deep breath. I stood up and tried to go back to loading the sled, but Hank was jumping and skirting around to stay in front of me no matter where I turned. My ears started pounding—I couldn't juke him.

I screamed *"FUCK"* as I slammed a piece of firewood into the snow, feeling tears well up in my eyes. I could see that my outburst brought a maniacal, victorious grin to Hank's face. I left the sled and almost jogged back inside.

Sasha had watched all this from the living room and hugged me as soon as I got back in, giving me an almost motherly *you did your best* empathetic look. I was furious, embarrassed, exhausted, but couldn't even bring myself to express emotion. I just stood there, blank-faced, feeling beaten and paralyzed.

While there were lots of dark moments like that, they didn't hold very long. All I had to do was look at Sasha and a calm would wash over me. There was also some comfort in knowing this was as bad as it was going to get. After the torment of these ethereal house-guests, the prospect of a man being hewn limb from limb by a bear or a spasming, screaming scarecrow became an almost comforting familiarity to look forward to. We were almost through it.

31

SASHA

❧

On one night in the end of January, Harry and I lay in bed and talked, and had what felt like the first *real* moment of happiness and uninterrupted joy we'd had since the ghosts arrived. We reflected on the fact that this whole spirit season was almost over. We'd called Joe a few days before to ask him—for the tenth time, at least—how *sure* he was about the length of this ghost season. He assured us, yet again, that he'd always been told it usually lasted around a month, the longest ever being around six weeks. We sat there that night and could only trust Joe's word, which meant that we were about a week away from being done with this.

It was possible he was wrong, as he'd never been through it himself, but his rules and rituals had checked out thus far, and it didn't do us any good to question the basis of a timeframe that didn't even make sense to begin with. Harry and I had regularly talked about what it would have been like in the valley back in the late 1800s, when it was more normal for people to have killed others, what their ghosts would've been like, who they would've been. But that night, we could both feel how close we were to being through this. I watched Harry's face as he fell asleep. We'd grown used to sleeping in a candlelit room, unwilling to leave the candles out of reach between sunset and sunrise. Those candles felt like some life support system, like our dialysis machine, like a life raft at sea.

I got up the next morning to make coffee and tea. I stepped over Dash, engaged in his morning stretches, and was walking through the living room toward the kitchen when my phone chirped from the bedroom. I could hear Harry's chime at the same moment. I walked back into the bedroom, and Harry was staring at me with an expression of warning on his face. Both our phones were alerting us to a *severe winter storm warning*—bearing down on us tonight. Eighty-mile-per-hour gusts and up to twenty-six inches of snow. Wind, we'd learned to appreciate, was the enemy of the delicate flame of a candle. It was the primary threat to our lifeline.

Harry finished reading the weather alert, then set his phone on the nightstand and looked at the ceiling. He appeared almost emotion-less, but maybe more exhausted than I'd ever seen him. He sat up in bed slowly and stretched his arms forward toward his toes. I could see him wince as the increasingly fierce morning pain from his old injuries shot fire through his leg, ribs, back, and arm. I went over and rubbed his back. He let out a long exhale, then looked up at me.

I kissed him. "We're so close, Harry. We're so close to being done with this."

Harry just stared past me, nodding slowly. After a moment he looked back at me, grinned, and shrugged. "You're right. We're almost done. We're almost through this, so...Fuck it. Let's just go full fortress. With this storm, let's not risk anything. Let's stormproof this house!"

He leaped out of bed and got straight to work. We hammered ply-wood fittings over the biggest windows in the living room, kitchen, bedroom, and office and brought extra wood into the house in case we needed to make repairs. Harry also cut up a long two-by-six beam into shorter boards, leaving a group of them leaned up next to the front door and another by the kitchen door, along with a clutch of long framing nails and a hammer. He was enjoying himself for the first time in what felt like weeks. He had purpose.

I smiled at Harry as he finished stacking the boards next to the kitchen door. He blushed a bit, gave me an embarrassed smile, then gestured with his head toward the boards near the front door. "Just in case the wind gets real bad and we need to keep the doors from blowing in. I don't wanna destroy the trim and have to repaint the whole damn house, but I figure it's best to have this stuff here just in case, right?"

I put my book down, walked over to him, and kissed him. "I know. I think it's smart. If it gets bad, we can board up the doors. Let's be ready to lock this place down. We're almost through this season. Why take any chances?"

We spent the rest of that day in a bit of a bizarre, slaphappy daze. We were *so close*, but it felt like nature itself was conspiring against us, a knot tightening in each of our stomachs every time a gust of wind picked up and whistled and howled through the big, naked branches of the cottonwood trees towering in the yard.

Harry seemed calm as well. Focused, and calm. He said he felt like he used to before going on a patrol in a dangerous area. "It is what it is, babe; all you can do is get through it."

We ate early that night. It was a *feast*. The last of the tenderloin from the deer Harry got that autumn, grilled veggies, a huge salad, homemade pies—it was amazing. After dinner, we had about an hour before sunset, so we took Dash on a walk down the road. It was snowing hard, and the wind had evolved from gusts into a steady sailing breeze ripping down from the small bit of forest we could actually still see above the house. It wailed and keened in a haunting way. Dash seemed on edge the entire walk, never straying too far from us.

Harry did one more run into the garage, then brought in another pile of firewood from the porch. He dropped the new logs onto the already considerable supply he had neatly stacked next to the fireplace in the living room. The cold logs began to kick off steam as soon as the warmth from the fire hit them.

Harry put a log in, then crossed the room as he took his gloves off and dropped them on the windowsill near the front door. He looked down at the boards stacked next to the door, then over into my eyes, and without having to even discuss it, without saying anything at all, we both began boarding up the front and kitchen doors. I held the boards in place as Harry hammered the large framing nails into the door frame. We worked silently and quickly.

We'd lit the candles and, as we had over the past several weeks, kept them with us wherever we went throughout the house, carrying them on our little "battle tray," as Harry called it. We turned on one of our favorite albums in the kitchen at sunset and danced right there for almost a half hour. When a big gust would make the house groan and the power flicker, our grip on each other would tighten.

Once it got completely dark, the anticipation started to make us both a bit nervous. The wind was bending the boughs of the trees at a steady clip now. When we'd shine our spotlight out into the yard through one of the smaller windows we'd left unboarded in the kitchen, we could see snow beginning to whip sideways across the property. Harry asked me put on tennis shoes, thick pants, and a Carhartt coat, and keep gloves and a wool hat in my coat pockets.

Harry put on his "battle belt," the one he'd wear at the range, over his hoodie. The belt had little pouches, a knife, a holstered pistol, and extra magazines for the pistol and his rifle. He had one of his shorter AR-15-looking rifles on the kitchen counter next to him. Over the last weeks I'd silently lifted my usually strict firearm storage requirements in light of the circumstances. Harry just felt better having a rifle nearby, and without being able to see the ghosts that were tormenting him, I felt better when he felt better.

I watched him as he stared out one of the kitchen windows we'd left partially unboarded so we could see outside. "You worried about the cottonwoods, Har?"

Harry nodded slowly and responded without looking over at me. "Lots of limbs up there that could break windows, and they sure are dancing around...Although I'd like to think they've made it through worse blizzards than this."

We played cards at the kitchen island until almost midnight, not tired enough to try to get in bed. Dash lay at our feet, occasionally picking his head up to whine and look toward the roar of a strong gust. The wind outside was screaming, and it was snowing harder than I feel like I'd ever seen it snow in my life, but sideways, whipped into a frantic blizzard.

I made us tea, and as I went to drop the teapot back onto the stove, all hell broke loose.

A loud metallic pop jerked all of our attention toward the kitchen door to the porch, where we saw the boards we'd nailed across it strain with force, bowing inward toward us under the pressure of the door, which was now acting as a wooden sail under the direct force of the wind. Even though we'd boarded the door frame so that the door itself would not be able to blow open into the kitchen, it was still capable of opening inward about half an inch.

Immediately after we heard the pop, the piercing shriek and volume of the blizzard outside surged into the house through the thin strip of open air. Dash jumped to his feet as the noise of the storm abruptly entered the house.

Within half a second of the storm's shocking infiltration into our home, the thin, strong blade of wind screaming through the crack in the door whipped into my face, making me blink, tossing my hair back.

Wind.

Harry and I locked eyes from across the kitchen, my face likely showing as much piercing panic and horror as his did, then we looked down at the island between us and saw the same thing: the flames of the candles being ripped to the side like flags in a hurricane, the glass shield having little protective effect under the hard, focused breeze. It was only a second, but it felt like time stopped, watching those flames strain in a frantic dance under the wind.

Harry was already sprinting toward the door when one of the boards exploded from where we'd nailed it into the frame and went clattering across the floor. Harry managed to catch the inward progress of the door and put all his strength into slamming it closed, then poured his full weight into it with his shoulders. Even though the door was closed, the shrieking wind now shut out of the kitchen, Harry winced as if it had gotten even louder inside.

I could only guess from the look in his eyes that the ghosts were starting to scream.

I was huddled over the candles, feeling like a songbird over a nest. I heard a loud *thud* and looked up to see Harry's body get jarred as something slammed into the door from the outside. Then it was struck again with enough force to push the door open a few inches into the kitchen before being slammed closed again when Harry's full weight fell back against it. I ran over to help Harry, charging into the door with my shoulder and palms.

Every muscle in my body was searing with full effort. Dash was *raging* at the door, eyes narrowed and feral like I'd never seen, making a guttural, keening growl I'd never heard, ready to launch an attack. I realized Harry and I were groaning with effort and terror. The last smash into the door had so much force it knocked us all the way into a standing position from where we'd been leaning our full weight into the door.

I looked back toward the kitchen island where I'd left the candles and, with terror, saw thick braids of smoke searing off an extinguished wick, snaking up to mix and plume into the light fixture above. Harry and I locked eyes, and I was already sprinting through the kitchen as he was screaming at me to get the candle re-lit.

I dove over the kitchen counter in my path and scrambled up to hunch over the glass shield sitting around the candles, sparking the lighter on the tray. My hand was shaking so badly I could barely line the flame up to the wick. Just as I was about to get it lit, another foundation-shattering *slam* into the door sent a blast of the blizzard through the room, dousing the lighter and another candle.

I watched Harry and Dash at the door. It's like everything was moving in slow motion. I saw these two living things, the two living things I loved more than anything on this planet, facing down an ancient, ravenous manifestation of fury and retribution that was trying to smash into our home, to bring death and violence and butchery into our most sacred space. I sparked the lighter over and over until I got a flame, and I held it over one wick at a time as well as I could with my hands shaking so violently, burning my fingers as I went, looking between the candles and Harry.

I could see the tension in Harry's body, muscles coiled and revving with violent anticipation, ready to explode into whatever came through that door with every possible ounce of brutality.

Then, it stopped. The door stopped rattling in its frame and suddenly it was quiet. An unsettling, dangerous quiet.

32

HARRY

~~~~~~

W E'D DECIDED THE bedroom was where we'd go if it got too crazy in the kitchen or living room, either during the storm or during some moment when the candles happened to go out. It was where we'd make the last stand. It was our Alamo.

When the noise and screaming of the ghosts stopped, I looked over at Sasha, who had three of the five candles re-lit. I screamed at her. "Get Dash and the candles into the bedroom and get them all lit, *now!*"

Sasha dropped the lighter among the candles, picked up the tray, and called for Dash as she started to move. She was carefully moving through the kitchen when something slammed into the window over the sink so hard it shot the plywood sheet we'd boarded it over with across the kitchen, where it connected with the microwave, both of which splintered and shattered upon contact. Glass from the window followed the plywood and exploded into the right side of Sasha's body. She flinched away from the blow, the debris, and the snow that was now whipping into the house, but she didn't stop moving.

I heard the windows behind me over the kitchen table explode. I wheeled around to see all five of the ghosts crawling and squeezing over one another through the shattered windows and splintered plywood in the kitchen. Their inhuman screaming overlapped into a violent, piercing frequency.

As I backpedaled away from the ghosts through the kitchen, I grabbed my rifle from the counter, chambered it, thumbed off the safety, and felt my finger fall to rest on the trigger. It felt like riding a bike. I began to fire—the awful, tinny roar of the short-barreled carbine in the enclosed space sent ringing needles into my ears.

I was shocked to see the rounds hitting home. I guess I'd expected bullets to simply pass harmlessly through these ethereal forms, but had also thought, *maybe*, if the candles went out and the ghosts could get inside to hurt us, maybe they could get hurt as well. To my shock, the bullets were making contact. There was no blood, no visible damage, but the rounds rippled through them like stones through slushy ice. It slowed them down; they flinched and winced as the bullets poured into them. As I fired into the mass of strange, writhing bodies clambering through the shattered windows, the ghosts emitted the most haunting, bone-chilling moan I'd ever heard. It was deep, but jittery and panicked. I might not be able to kill these things with lead, but it seemed they could sure as hell *feel* it, and they did *not* like what they felt. This discovery filled me with excitement and rage. Bloodlust, I suppose.

Time slowed to a crawl as I stood in the detritus of our home— floors covered in splintered wood and shattered glass. I realized only then that my own blood was hitting the floor in Pollock-like spatters as I worked with my rifle in familiar motions, despite my arms being flayed from trying to hold the door closed. My perception of time reverted to something I'd experienced before in combat, able to perceive infinitesimal details as time dilated around me. The five ghosts came surging toward me through the kitchen now. It was like a dream—they seemed impossibly large for the space they occupied, and I couldn't tell if they were moving unfathomably slow or lightning fast.

I went through the old motions: squeezing the trigger until the bolt locked back, then releasing the empty magazine to clatter across the floor while reaching for a full one. I slammed another magazine from my belt into the magwell and continued firing. Each round provoked a wail of deafening rage and horror from the ghosts as they came closer.

I worked my way backward into the living room, turning toward the hallway to our bedroom as the ghosts were only feet away now, seemingly a single mass of noise and limbs. I fired until my mag went dry. The spirit closest to me, Bridger, reached out—his hand looked distorted, like heat rising off pavement, and I could feel pressure as he got closer to me, like two opposing magnets. I drew my pistol and put the muzzle *into* his chest and began squeezing off shots. I felt no fleshy resistance as the gun sank into him, more like a vibration, as though he was composed of static electricity that had taken the form of thick, dry mud. Bridger squealed and roared at the same time as he lunged forward to land a palm in the center of my chest.

It sent me soaring back down the hall toward the bedroom, where Sasha was, my back slamming into the closed door so hard it nearly came off its hinges, all the air blasting out of my lungs. I could hear Sasha screaming for me and Dash barking frantically from behind the door. I couldn't hear my own voice as I coughed air back into my lungs and screamed at her to stay put.

Bridger separated from the others and came surging ahead toward me. Blood from my scalp was blurring my vision. I could feel that implacable *wrongness* of multiple broken bones—my ribs, my clavicle.

I was in trouble. This was it. I was on the X and in deep shit. My turn for a dirt nap. At least I was between them and Sasha.

An old, familiar sensation hit me in that moment, one that had taken hold of me before but that I'd long forgotten. It was a type of calm acceptance that can only happen at the very end, a pure integration into the whim and caprice of chaos. It's not a surrender to but a *communion with* the terminal violence around you. It comes in those moments when firefights get really bad, the air is boiling with noise, friends are shrieking at their own blood, you can't move, you *need* to move, you have broken fingers, broken ribs, a concussion, blood in your mouth, dirt in both eyes.

It's the feeling that comes in that final moment when panic gets so extreme it just collapses into itself, cancels itself out. It's not some feeling that comes when you *think* you're going to die. It has nothing to do with *thinking* about death; this feeling can only come long after that phase, long after you've confronted, grappled with, and submitted to the reality of death. It's a feeling that comes only when you *know* you're about to die, when you *know* you're already dead.

I looked up at the ghosts and wondered if these fuckers had felt that same thing before I killed them.

Just as Bridger was right on top of me, he stopped, as if in suspended animation. His expression twisted with rage and frustration as all of them began withdrawing from the house, as if animated by some unseen force yanking, ripping, and tearing at them from outside like puppets on unseen steel wires.

I didn't understand what was going on. Then it hit me.

33

SASHA

I DIDN'T EVEN NOTICE glass and wood splinters stuck in the skin of my face or any of the blood running from my scalp down onto my shoulders, until I made it into the bedroom. My eyes clamped shut and my heart jumped every time the rifle fire sounded from the kitchen, until I stopped wincing altogether when my hearing was replaced by the dog-whistle keening of damaged eardrums. I willed my hands to stop shaking as I got the tray of candles upright.

All of the candles had gone out under the hail of splinters and glass as I raced into the room. I flicked the lighter twice over the dark wicks with no success. *"Come on!"*

I was screaming in rage and panic as I tried again when suddenly something *slammed* into the bedroom door. It was a body. *It was Harry*. The noise and impact forced me to fumble and drop the lighter. It skidded toward the door. I could hear Harry screaming at me through the door.

"Stay where you are! You hear me?! Stay right there."

I could hear it in his voice—he was hurt. Tears raced down my face as I snatched up the lighter. I closed my eyes for a moment, gathering any reserves of focus and calm I had left.

Flick. The room lit with glowing orange. I brought the flame to the first candle's wick and then the next. The wind outside and the sound of the house coming apart escalated; it felt like a storm bearing straight down our hallway. The second candle lit, the glow growing stronger and warmer. I lit each of the candles as fast as I could, ignoring the searing pain in my palm and smell of burning hair as I held my hand in the flames of the others. Just as the fifth candle caught a steady flame, everything changed.

Like the eye of a storm. While the wind still howled outside, the ferocity of the onslaught that had been escalating just moments before seemed to settle. I could feel pressure in my head release, and a tension spill out from my muscles and joints; a stinging burn on my skin I hadn't even noticed began to fade away.

"They're lit—the candles are lit, Harry!"

I saw the handle of the bedroom door turn. It opened a crack and Harry came falling into the room, his body weight pushing the door open.

"Oh my God, *Harry—*"

I dragged him into the room, catching a glimpse of the destruction in the living room before shutting the door again.

He winced as he propped himself up against the wall. He was in bad shape. Like me, he was shredded with cuts and gashes, though I could tell from his movement and the sound of his breathing that his ribs, and likely more, were broken. The candlelight made his fresh blood look almost obsidian black.

He reached up and put a palm against my cheek, exhaling some small measure of relief. "You're okay." My tears began to flow as he moved his hand down, pressing his palm lovingly against my belly. "Both of you."

Dash stood between us, whining slightly and licking both of our bloody faces.

Harry winced suddenly and looked toward the wall, which I'd grown over the last weeks to recognize as a cue that the ghosts had started screaming. The wind was still whipping against the house, the blizzard shrieked through shattered windows in the kitchen, and debris was clattering against the walls and across the roof above us.

Then, in that moment, as Harry's hand rested on my belly, my hand atop his, words flashed into my mind. Joe's words.

The unnatural act of killing leaves the spirits of the killed unsettled. Unsatisfied. They demand to be recognized by those responsible.

My mind raced for a moment as an idea crystallized. It was almost instinctual. It was both the last thing I could imagine doing *and* the only choice left.

"Harry, listen. Listen to me."

I moved directly in front of him, moving my head to force eye contact and holding it. "Do you trust me?"

He nodded wearily. "Of course, of course I do."

I nodded back, staring at him for a long moment. "Blow them out. Let them in."

"What?! What are you talking about? We—"

"The ritual is designed to keep us safe, to keep them at arm's length, but what if we gave them what they *truly* wanted? More than anything, they want to be *seen*, to be *felt*. They want you to recognize what…"

I hesitated, a lump in my throat, the accusatory sting of the words to follow hesitating at the end of my tongue. "To recognize what you've done."

Harry stared at me, silenced by the statement.

"Joe said it himself. They want to be recognized by the one that killed them. For their anger to be felt. So, what if instead of fearing or fighting them, we let them in? We let them show you what they want you to feel. The anger, the sadness, the confusion. We let them have it all."

Harry's eyes watered and threatened tears as he shook his head. I could recognize the unique expression, the same one I had seen in dim light many nights before when Harry would awaken from a nightmare. An expression scrawled with pain, with trauma.

"I can't, I…Sash, that's insane, there's no fuckin' way." He hung his head.

I spoke through my own tears now, staring down at Harry's face. "I'm sorry I can't see them, Harry. I, I'm sorry I can't face them with you."

Looking into Harry's eyes, I recalled more of Joe's words, his threadbare, baritone voice over the fire pit.

Only those who truly understand and feel the weight of the death can see the ghost's form.

Another realization washed over me as Harry winced again at the sounds of spectral wailing that only he could hear.

"Harry. Listen to me."

He lifted his head up to meet my gaze.

"Tell me. Tell me what you did."

"What? What do you—"

"You have to tell me. What happened. These men, the things you did to them, the things you *had to do* . . ."

"Sasha, what are y—"

I hissed back at him with urgency. "*Harry!* Listen to me."

Every second that passed, my certainty fortified. I knew what I had to do, what *we* had to do.

I pressed my hands on both sides of his face, looking him straight in the eye, nodding quickly as I spoke. "There's no one I know better than I know you. But you've never let me into what happened over there. You've never told me. You never wanted to and I understand why, I—"

"Sasha, stop, we—"

"I *understand* why you didn't want to. I know you carry guilt that you can't explain and that you've done things that I can't imagine, things you think I couldn't forgive . . ."

As Harry listened to me, tears began to well in his eyes, the sight of which only triggered more of my own.

"But I *love* you. And whatever the weight of these things is, I can carry it. I can carry it with you."

It was clear in his expression that Harry didn't understand what I was trying to do. In that moment, as the wind continued to roar ominously and the candles flickered in the escalating storm, I wasn't sure I knew entirely either.

"Trust me." I moved in closer to him. "Trust me. We can do this together."

34

HARRY

So...yeah, that was it. That's how I killed Buck. He was the last person I killed. I remember his face, the expression, that...fear. He was more than just an EKIA. You could see it. He was just...he was just a dude, you know? A dude I'm sure had kids and a wife and, and he was scared. He was scared. I was scared. He was scared and didn't want to die. But he did. I killed him."

I could hear the words coming out of my mouth and see Sasha in front of me wiping tears from her face, but part of me couldn't believe what I was saying. I'd spent years subconsciously yet somehow carefully avoiding this disclosure with her, avoiding revealing these things I had done and been a part of to the woman I love.

I looked at the clock, realizing we had spent the last hour just sitting there—barricaded behind our bedroom door, Dash at our feet, protecting this little family of candles we had pressed between our bodies—telling her the things I had done.

Silence fell between us as I finished speaking. I realized in that moment that this silence was exactly what I had spent so long trying to avoid. The silence after revealing to this woman—this sweet, good, kind woman—the truth of what I'd done. That pregnant silence when everything could change. But even in that moment of dread, that moment I'd been terrified to encounter for so long, I felt some kind of release. I felt honesty, maybe for the first time. I'd finally just put everything on the table.

Sasha wiped her face as she scooted across the floor toward me. She leaned in and kissed me on the forehead, pulling my head toward her in an embrace.

We held there for a long moment until Dash whined, just as a gust picked up and howled through the trees above the house. I looked over at Sasha and heard another sudden wail, a raging, deafening scream from outside.

I winced as it tore through my eardrums, but...Sasha did as well. We locked eyes in a moment of mutual shock.

"Did you...?"

She nodded frantically.

"Did you just hear that?"

She continued to nod at me, with wide eyes and almost a bit of wonder in her expression. "Yes."

We went to the small window in our bathroom together. In the pasture outside, I could see the ghosts' figures through the snow, frantically pacing side to side like eager prizefighters on the opposite side of the ring. They stopped intermittently to scream— desperate screams that bent them over at the waist, screams of body-shaking rage.

My gaze drifted from them to Sasha's face, and I watched her as she stared out toward the ghosts.

35

SASHA

I COULD SEE THEM.

"Sash, can you see them?"

I could only muster a slow nod as I watched five distinct figures through the sideways snow, pacing around as they cast glances toward the window where we stood.

It took me a moment to realize what had happened, though somehow it all made sense. It was instinct that had made the connection to what Joe had told me, instinct that told me if I could *feel* what Harry felt, I would be able to see the ghosts, to see his demons.

It was that same instinct that told me what to do next. My heart was pounding, my rational mind telling me what I was about to do was crazy, but some other part of me knew it was the only way. I was being animated by a deep sense of confidence that I had never felt before.

"I see them."

I turned to Harry, who was looking at me in awe, dried blood crusted along one side of his swollen face. "Harry, do you trust me?"

His expression changed to one of determination, and he nodded. "I trust you."

I took his hand. He squeezed mine firmly.

I opened our bedroom door, revealing the chaos and destruction of the house in front of us. We stood in the doorway together, hand in hand, Dash beside us. In other circumstances it might've looked like a family portrait.

"I love you."

Harry turned to me. "I love you too."

With that, I bent down, lifted up the tray of candles, looked up at Harry through their glow, and blew them out.

36

HARRY

THE PANIC OR fear that I should've felt never washed over me. Maybe it was Sasha. Maybe it was catharsis, finally purging and offloading so much of my guilt to the one person I truly cared for. Maybe it was resignation. But as the smoke rose from the doused candles, and the thunderous approach of the ghosts rose to a deafening roar, I felt a sense of peace and acceptance. Sasha set down the tray, took my hand, and with Dash standing between my legs, we stared out across our destroyed living room toward the front of the house.

I could hear them come storming up the porch with renewed fury—the front door flew off its hinges, the plywood and two-by-fours we'd used to board the door smashed around the room, and the large door itself crushed the coffee table where it landed. Window frames cracked as trim, drywall, paint, and glass splintered and scattered across the room toward us as the ghosts came surging inside. I pressed my legs together on Dash's sides to keep him from charging into the intruders as I felt us both flinch in unison.

As they crossed the threshold into our home, they stopped at the other end of the room from us. All of them, enraged, stacked up in their distorted, mirage-like forms.

Sasha could feel my hand twitch as I went to reach for the rifle hanging at my side by the sling, but she squeezed it tight. I looked over at her.

"Don't fight them," Sasha said, staring at the ghosts. "Not anymore."

It could have just been my trust in her, my concession to her confidence in this, but some quiet part of me understood what she was doing. It was time. We were letting them in.

With that, we took a small step forward. We could see the confusion on the ghosts' faces as we slowly approached, as if our lack of fear or aggression completely upended their sense of how to behave.

Slowly, step by step, we came together in the center of our home. I was looking straight at them. A long moment unfolded, a sense of mutual uncertainty like making first contact with some long-hidden tribe—their previous aggression and rage turned to a confused, almost curious uncertainty.

They looked between Sasha and me, their silent expressions changing slowly as rage faded into something that seemed almost inquisitive, or confused. In that moment, I was overcome by the most jarring sensation since we'd moved into this valley. It felt similar to how I'd felt a few minutes earlier, when I'd finally opened up and put everything out on the table for Sasha to digest. It's like the ghosts saw *through* me; they lacked the same focus, the same personal connection of unbridled hatred they'd maintained since they arrived. Their interest in us faded, like predators who'd given up the hunt, and the weight of toxic malice that had hung low over the valley like a fog since they'd arrived seemed to lift. It felt like I'd cut some kind of tether between them and myself. It felt like the ghosts and I had all been hooked up to a diesel generator that, in that moment, had finally sputtered, coughed, and run out of fuel.

Then, it all happened.

The air pressure in the house flipped, sending a ripping pressure into my eyeballs and eardrums. A roaring started, faint at first, but it grew fast; it felt like it was coming from the center of the house, the floors, the walls, the foundation, the fuckin' plumbing. It grew louder, like wind ripping through a cave. My legs were frozen in place, lungs felt filled with concrete. I looked over at Sasha, and the few remaining lights in the lamps and ceiling fixtures dimmed to the faint glow of a small candle. I felt like I was free-falling; my stomach was in my throat. I was about to pass out as the roaring grew, and then an instantaneous eruption of force that felt like heat, electricity, liquid, and wind *exploded* outward from the center of the house as though the structure itself was letting out a deep, cavernous exhale. The lights immediately brightened again in that moment, and the ghosts dissipated as a ring of flickering light surged out into the blizzard.

The feeling of relief was so heavy it was like a force of its own. Sasha and I both collapsed, breathing as though we'd been drowning, each breath like a burst of mainlined opiates. It was the feeling of the spirit leaving, but stronger than ever before—*deeper* and more encompassing than ever before.

We crawled to each other and held Dash between us.

37

SASHA

Harry kicked at the pillars and roof beams of the porch, which had fallen into a heap of wreckage that blocked what was once our front doorway, then heaved at one until it gave way, allowing him to push enough of the debris away to create an egress from the living room.

He looked back at me and cracked a tired smile. I smiled back. "Well, Har, I guess we finally have a reason to redo the trim and maybe even get some new floors, eh?"

Harry let out a shuddering breath that I assume was the best attempt at a laugh he could muster, then gestured toward the opening he'd made. Dash slithered out of the small opening into the yard as Harry reached back for my hand and helped lead me through the narrow access between the splintered remnants of our porch, out toward the deep snow blanketing the landscape—beaming under the morning sun like gem-crusted gold.

When we emerged, Harry collapsed onto all fours at the bottom of the porch steps, bare hands disappearing into the snow.

I dropped next to him and put my hand on his back between his shoulders. He pushed himself up onto his knees. One of his fingers was horribly broken and jutting out at a forty-five-degree angle. He looked over at me, giving me a sideways grin, showcasing a gap of missing and shattered teeth on the right side of his mouth. I was laughing and crying at the same time as I put my hand on his blood-caked cheek.

He rolled off his knees onto his butt and scooted back to sit next to me, reaching up to gently grab my chin and move my head from side to side, examining my face, which, I imagined, did not look much better than his.

I smiled at him, feeling the bite and singe of the splinters and glass embedded in my cheeks and forehead. "How do I look?"

He leaned in and kissed me. "You look fucked-up, and strong, and beautiful."

EPILOGUE

I WATCHED AS TINY disturbances erupted across the surface of the pond like a thousand little meteor strikes: smallmouth bass nipping and slurping at bugs under the orange evening light. It was quiet, in the way it gets quiet in the mountains. Bugs and birds and wind in the trees. A hundred different noises, all of them natural. Yet somehow, it's like you can't hear a thing.

The spell was broken as Joe stood up next to me. We had stopped bothering to actually cast almost a half hour earlier and had been sitting on the bank of a big pond in the pasture to the west of his house.

I looked up at Joe, tilting my head. A several-minutes-old question still hung in the air between us, unanswered.

Joe let out a long sigh. "I don't know."

The *last* answer I wanted to hear. I'd have preferred for him to just tell me I was wrong and to stay vigilant, so I pressed him for it.

"It's getting warmer every day, Joe. Supposed to be eighty to-morrow. Rivers are starting to drop, the vultures are all back. I mean…summer's pretty much here, and no lights. Nothing at all."

When the weather and weeks of spring came and pressed on without the arrival of the lights, we took it as a welcome bit of luck after our harrowing winter. It was also quite convenient, given the contractors we'd had in and out of our house, putting our home back together. That February storm just *ripped* through our valley, we'd told them.

But as more days turned to yet more weeks without the spirit's arrival, without the lights, we had allowed our hopes to elevate. I found myself torn between almost *wanting* to see the light in the pond, to sink into the familiarity of the routine, and the far greater hope that something more significant might have changed. That what we had done might have afforded us some measure of peace or, even further, an even more dispositive resolution with the spirit.

I reeled in my line and bit the fly off the leader, knocking my new fake teeth out of position. I wiped my hand on my shirt, then used a finger to snug them back into place. I stood, clenching my jaw as a lance of pain shot through my thigh under my old scars, and looked up at Joe, reminded again of his imposing size as he loomed above me.

"It is...a change," Joe finally responded, carefully.

"Right, okay, so, a change. Maybe we...I don't know..."

Joe looked at me, uncertain.

"Maybe we got rid of it?"

Joe chuckled quietly, shaking his head.

"*It* is the land itself, Harry. There is no getting rid of the land. It confronts man based on the ways in which man lives in disharmony with nature. If it has decided to leave you alone..." He gazed into the middle distance, thinking deeply. "Then perhaps you have proven something about yourself. What's clear is something has changed. Perhaps it will be better for you here. Perhaps you will be given peace."

I nodded. I liked what I was hearing, but it lacked the assurance I'd need for the ambient anxiety that'd been building over the last weeks of spirit-free life to ebb.

"Or..."

The one syllable put a knot in my stomach. I looked up at Joe, who returned his gaze to meet mine.

"Or…perhaps you've angered it again; perhaps something far worse is to come. Only time will tell."

He picked up his old baitcaster and began the walk back up toward his sprawling homestead, toward the distant sounds of laughing children.

"Joe…" I stepped toward him as he slowly half turned to face me. "I gotta ask you something, and just give it to me straight, all right?"

Joe neither nodded nor blinked, so I proceeded. "Have you *ever*, even just *one time*, heard from your family, or anyone else, of someone who'd lived here, been through the seasons in this valley, who then moved away, and *survived*?"

Joe stared at me for a long while, then looked straight ahead down the valley. "Yes, I have."

My eyes went wide. Joe took a few steps back toward me. "Can't say if it was true or just a legend, but yes…my grandfather told me a story of an old man who lived in the valley, long time back, before my grandfather's time. Story goes that he lived here in the valley for many years, then finally up and left, moved up into the Salmon River breaks, where he trapped, hunted, and lived out his days in a little cabin. My grandfather said our ancestors would go visit with him from time to time up there, trade with him, talk about how he left and whatnot."

I was speechless. Joe could see it in my face and gave me a half grin. "It's just a legend, Harry. I can't say whether it's true or not. Trust me, if it were, and I knew what you tourists needed to do to leave this place, I'da told you months ago so you'd get the hell out of here and quit bothering me. I'm too old for your angst."

I shook my head, trying to think of what to say as it was already coming out. "Joe, what'd he do? I mean what'd your ancestors say he did to be able to leave? You've *gotta* have more than just that."

Joe looked away, nodding. "Yeah, that's part of the legend too. It's not very concrete, pretty vague actually, as can happen with legends that are passed down through generations, taking on new features, new twists and flavors each time."

I walked up toward where he stood. "Well, what is it? What's the trick?"

Joe chuckled at me. "You're not gonna like it, Harry."

I just stood, staring back, waiting for him to go on. He gave me an annoyed look under furrowed brows. After a long moment, he looked up and scratched under his chin, then locked his eyes on mine as he began to speak. "The legend is that the old man was able to leave because, well, to put it into common parlance that would make sense to your young ears, the old man finally just... *dealt with his shit.*"

I blinked hard, unsure of what to say. Joe put his hand on his hip, and went on, looking past me as he spoke, which he did slowly. "He had emotional baggage, and when he dealt with it, he was able to leave." He heaved his large shoulders in a shrug, looking me in the eye again. "That's the only translation that would make sense to you."

I squinted my eyes and stared back at Joe. "What? What the hell's that even mean?"

Joe just shook his head and smiled. "Let's go, Harry. I'm hungry."

I gazed after him awhile and turned back to the pond for a moment before following him, saying my goodbyes to his family, and driving home.

Later that evening I sat on the porch, Dash at my feet. Sasha came out through the kitchen door. The sounds of food searing in a pan and music from the stereo were a welcome complement to the ranch's complicated, intimidating silence.

"How was fishing?"

I nodded with a smile. "Mellow."

She looked at me, then followed my gaze down to the pond. "Still nothing?"

I took in a deep breath. "Still nothing," I returned.

Sasha sat on my knee and ran her hand through my hair. I could feel her relief. I put a hand on her belly, noticeably grown now.

I wanted to go there. Wanted to believe it, believe that something had changed for the better, believe that whatever she'd done had put all this chaos to rest.

She leaned down and kissed me. I held her there, my eyes closed with her lips against mine—our baby between us—and knew that whatever was to come, we would face it together.

"Come help me in the kitchen. What do I look like, your mama?"

"You look like *somebody's* mama."

She laughed as she disappeared back into the house. I hesitated at the door, looking back at Dash. I'd been doing so more than ever, watching Dash, following his eyes, *willing* him to give me some sign. He'd become our canary in the spectral coal mine that was this little valley. Whatever connection he had to this spirit, his perception of it, had become valuable, a lifeline, like a smoke detector. Our sentry.

I watched him as he stared out into the dark mass of trees swaying under the soft but steady wind along the edge of the property. I saw his ears twitch and nostrils flare as a light breeze hit his face. I wondered if he noticed the warmth in the air, if he had a grasp of the changing seasons, if he knew spring was passing and summer was near, if he knew what that meant.

I thought of the junkyard dog from my childhood and could feel the old sensation of coiled tension in my muscles as that beast would rage alongside me. I followed Dash's gaze up toward the cold, massive granite spires of the Tetons that punched into the sky from the aprons of pine-covered ridges that rolled down to our house.

I heard Dash take in a deep breath and looked back down at him to find his noble gaze still fixed, as ever, on the horizon.

Watching, and waiting.

ACKNOWLEDGMENTS

We want to acknowledge our families: our siblings, Elizabeth and Sean, our parents, Dave and Amy, and our stepparents, Dana and Robb. We are better men for having loved and been loved by you all.

Our gratitude for the wisdom and guidance of our representatives, Scott and Liz, is endless.

And lastly, we are so fortunate and grateful to have such engaged and supportive people in our publishing and editorial partners—Wes, Nick, Autumn, Morgan, Tareth, Laura, Ervin, and the rest of the Grand Central and Hachette family. We couldn't have asked for a better team.

ABOUT THE AUTHORS

Matt and Harrison Query are brothers and best friends.

In addition to writing, Matt is an attorney who does litigation related to water, public lands, and other natural resources issues. Matt and his wife, Sonya, live on their small ranch with their cows, chickens, and bees. Matt is an avid reader and history buff who spends his free time traveling, gardening, or exploring the wilderness around the Western United States with his fly rod and his hunting dog, Tib.

Harrison was born and raised in Colorado alongside his brother and sister. As a keen writer from a young age, Harrison studied writing in college, during which time he sold his first screenplay. He has since written for Sony, Lionsgate, Netflix, and Amazon—writing projects for the likes of Ridley Scott, Andrew Dominik, Chris Columbus, and John Hillcoat. His work has also included the adaptation of work from Kristin Hannah, Nick Pileggi, and Jeff Maysh.